# HIGHLAND HARRY

## MONSTER SLAYER

# HIGHLAND HARRY

## MONSTER SLAYER

## R.C. DAVIS

# DEDICATION

This story is dedicated to my sister, Karen for her inspiration. To Betty R. (RIP) for her assistance in making it possible. Most of all, my wife, Anne, who stood by me, unflinching, as I navigated the quagmire of the creative process necessary to bring this story to the creamy velum on which it is printed.

# CHAPTER 1

## Dark, As Was Chaos...

The bed shook something fierce, prompting Harry to pull his nose from the comic book and stare, wide-eyed, through the open bedroom door. The tremor had been strong enough to rattle the windows down in the entry hall. Another followed, stronger than the first, and the shelves leapt in their brackets. Trophies toppled, and plastic models cascaded to the platinum-colored carpet.

*Okay... that was serious*

Stripping the reading lamp from his head, Harry dropped it and the comic book onto the mattress before rolling off to stand in the middle of the room. He braced for what may follow, hoping the house wasn't going to fall down on their heads. Massachusetts didn't normally have earthquakes, but things hadn't been normal for a long time.

The floor shuddered under his feet, and then an earsplitting, *Crack!* came from behind the house. Dashing to the window, Harry eased an eye around the casing.

Something big, dark, and toad-like, sat in front of a hole it had just made in the eight-foot-high board fence. The beast had forced its way through a section at the back, and pieces littered the ground.

He and his father had built the enclosure just a couple years before, attaching it to the back corners of their two-story Colonial. The force of the creature's blows had sent shockwaves up the entire length. They used to call them privacy fences, however, privacy didn't matter much anymore when all your neighbors were dead.

After shaking off the splinters, the thing blinked large, luminous, yellow eyes that appeared to be looking right at him. Harry ducked back with a gasp.

*They found us!*

It wasn't like they hadn't been expected, though. Now, Harry and his father were going to have to pull up stakes and move. That was the rule. Harry didn't like that rule. Noted zoologists had expressed that, once the monsters imprinted any terrain, it would become part of their territory. The beasts would traverse it nightly, and the Lumsdale's wooden framed house hadn't been designed with a siege in mind.

Peeking again, Harry took in the afterglow of the western sky. There was just enough light to show the size of the beast sitting out there, scanning the house.

*That's right, big fella, take your time, savor your last few minutes of life.*

Harry felt secure for the moment because he was on the second floor, but maybe that was just an illusion. He had grown up in that room. It had always been his safe place. Now, circumstances beyond his control might force him to dump that misconception.

The creature emitted a loud, growling croak. The inside of its cavernous mouth glowed with bioluminescence, silhouetting rows of spike-like teeth. Rocking from side to side, the intruder stomped its front feet. The action reminded Harry of a dead friend's bulldog who was known to perform the same action while impatiently waiting for someone to throw its ball.

There came a creak from the bottom of the stairs and Harry heard his father loudly whisper, "You up there?"

"Yeah, you see it?"

"I see it. You just stay where you're at."

"You don't want my help?"

"No, I can handle this one."

Harry heard his father's combat boots move back across the floor. Then, the sound of squeaky hinges floated up to his ears as Harold Sr. had opened the steel plate shutters at the kitchen window. He had fashioned the opening into a gunport. It allowed a 180-degree perspective of the backyard as well as a place to rest a gun barrel.

The creature reacted to the shutters coming open, and the little red dot dancing over its warty, onyx colored skin. Emitting another rumbling croak, the monstrosity rose up on its back legs and pushed its front claws out toward the house in a threatening manner. This exposed its softer underbelly and the red dot went center. The blast from the twelve-gauge ripped the twilight to echo through the trees.

Even though Harry had expected it he still jumped. A shudder rolled up his spine as he watched the creature fly backwards from the impact of fifteen, .32 caliber pellets traveling in a tight pattern at 900 fps. His father preferred three-inch magnums, allowing six extra projectiles and a butt-kicking amount of gunpowder.

At first, the other slayers had laughed at the use of a laser sight on a scattergun, yet, after Harold Sr. closed up the shot pattern with a standard choke tube, it was he who had the last laugh. The idea stopped seeming ridiculous when it was noted that every pellet found its mark—every time.

The beast now appeared to be stuck in the hole, hanging there, unmoving. Harry closed a fist and cranking an elbow backward, he whispered a triumphant, "Yes!"

From the kitchen below, he heard his father's loud and whimsical, "Technicolor!" and Harry snickered. That was his old man's favorite phrase after spraying monster guts all over the place. All Harry knew was that it had something to do with television transcending from the days of black and white to color. He had to admit, though, most of the monsters did have some pretty colorful innards.

Harry heard the shutters close and then the sound of heavy boots bouncing off the cathedral ceiling in the entry hall. Moving to his door, he waited for his father to start bragging about his new trophy. Instead, all he heard was, "Harry, come down and get your chow. It's your favorite… noodles." That would start their usual jocular banter, something his mother often referred to as, 'a pissing contest'.

"Yeah, right! You know damn well if it were my favorite, it would be pizza. And… when are we going to get some meat in this house?"

"Stop your swearing, you know your mom didn't like that."

"Millions upon millions of people are dead and you're worried about me swearing?"

"Get your skinny butt down here—now! Your favorite noodles are waiting."

Stepping out, Harry peeked over the railing of the balcony style passageway that connected all the second-floor rooms. The design gave the entry hall an atrium like effect and allowed excellent communication with anyone, in any room, on the first floor. He wanted to share some sarcastic wit, but his father was already walking away, the Mossberg Autoloader slung from a shoulder.

Harold Sr. was good with that gun, but he'd had a lot of practice since the spring of 2032. That was the year the beasts first made their appearance in Kilbury. It was soon after that, that Harold Sr. turned Harry onto monster hunting; much to his mother's dismay.

They had found the Mossberg in the closet sized office of an abandoned gun shop downtown. Harold Sr. passed up Harry's suggestion of the fearsome looking 12-gauge Street Sweeper for the want of a more tactical weapon. The double-aught shotshell became a priority when scrounging.

Over time, the search for 12-gauge ammo grew longer, with fewer results. Harry believed it was a poor choice of weapons. Like with most long guns, when your ammo ran out, all you had was a club—and a poor one at that. If the monsters were small and came at you in hordes, the odds of you surviving were slim.

Edged weapons were better, razor-sharp blades for some truly serious dissection. Yet, Harold Sr.'s fighting skills were limited to what he had learned in the Marine Corps. He would have to learn how to wield a long sword, or better yet, a couple of good, sharp, battle axes. It was more effective to 'slice and dice' the beasts than shoot them.

Returning to his room, Harry strapped his reading lamp back on and pulled a thick green binder from his dresser top. Sitting on the edge of his mattress, he studied the cover. Somebody had stamped: 'FOR GOVERNMENT USE ONLY' across the front in bold red letters, and behind that, typed on a 4x4 label, *Extrinsic Biological Aberrations-Identification Manual*'. Harry assumed it was some humorous, but long dead soldier, who had loosely penned over the top of that with a black ink marker: *MONSTERS!*

Opening it up, Harry thumbed through the pages until he found the beast that resembled the one now stuck in their fence.

**Anuraloph: A large, toad like carnivore**...

*Yeah, I already know all that! Just wanted a name to go with that ugly face.*

Adjusting his position, he accidently kicked his butterfly swords that lay sheathed in their rig on the floor. The black leather gleamed in the dim light and he still felt a hint of pride in having fashioned the getup himself. The scabbards formed an 'X' and when strapped to his back, the pommel of each sword stuck up past his shoulders allowing quick access for each hand.

Traditionally, a Wing Chun swordsman would holster them together in one sheath at their side. Yet that always made fumbling a big part of the equation. Laying the manual on his bed, Harry picked up the sword rig and buckled it on. The familiar feeling of the harness brought an odd sense of comfort. These days he just didn't feel whole without it. Returning to the monster book, he flipped through a few more pages, scrutinizing the full color images.

Most of the monsters were smooth skin over cartilage. They came apart pretty easily. Any experienced swordsman could make short work of them. It was the minority that one had to worry about. Unfortunately, they seemed to be the evolving group. Along with the usual fangs and claws, they brought scale-like armor, spikey bodies, stingers, pinchers, and poisonous quills. They were a little harder to kill and needed special consideration.

The creatures had first started making an appearance globally about two years before Harry became a slayer. The Gran Aquifer Maya of Mexico, the Xe Bangfai River Cave of Laos, and the St. Leonard underground lake in Switzerland, were a few of the international sources.

It was the area around the Great Lakes and a large underground body of water inside a cave down south that saw the first of the beasts in the USA. There came reports of strange creatures being hit by cars, unwary anglers being dragged from their boats, and the occasional fateful meeting during an evening stroll. Always at night. Always near water. Then the oceans released what they had and nighttime activity for humans became limited to huddling quietly inside fortified structures.

*Welcome to the New Stone Age—complete with dinosaurs.*

Scientists had taken their work seriously. After determining that it was the warming of the waters that had brought the creatures from the subterranean lakes and the deepest parts of the oceans, they began compiling information about each new discovery. This gave birth to the ID manual, which was then mass produced for police and military. The book just got thicker and thicker.

By the time the monsters had established a serious foothold, a mutated H1N1-like virus was introduced to the world in a most impudent manner and went about wiping out nearly two thirds of the earth's population.

As the news story went, Marcus Velnear, a well-known world traveler, hiker, and photographer, staggered into a hospital in Nome, Alaska and collapsed on the floor of the ER. He had been out trekking across older layers of the now-melted permafrost in parts of Siberia that fell within the Arctic Circle. He and his partner, Igor Ospan, had separated at a Nakupan village on the Bearing Sea. Ospan, on his way back to Ukraine, made it only as far as Harbin, China.

The photos they had taken of themselves posing with an ancient, but well-preserved Yupik woman emerging from the melting permafrost had showed Velnear's extraordinary talent with a camera. Yet sadly, appreciation for his latest set of photos was short lived.

It was known as early as 2018 that unknown diseases, locked in the disappearing permafrost, were just waiting for a new host to arrive. All you had to do was venture out into the middle of nowhere and they became, unexpectedly, yours. The monsters and the 'Bug' proved to be a 'double whammy' for civilization. The people who were supposed to care about a structured method of defense soon lost interest.

Thumbing through a few more pages of the monster manual, Harry soon found himself at the section for beasts whose names started with the letter 'T'. He studied the 'Thulu' for the hundredth time, feeling somewhat obsessed with the biggest of the known monsters. It was a bipedal beast, never any smaller than a large man, and that was before they matured. It had the smooth skin of a catfish, a basketball sized head, and then there were the tentacles hanging from around its mouth like a bad mustache. It sported small, flightless wings, velociraptor like claws, and a long tail with a spaded tip.

Located just below that heart shaped finial, the beast possessed a large, retractable barb, much like that of a stingray. Harry had seen a guy get skewered once. The toxin literally melted human flesh. To watch that man slowly liquefy in front of his eyes left Harry with some serious nightmares.

Having had enough of things that could eat him, he returned the manual to the dresser top and after pulling down the blackout blinds, he moved out of his room onto the balcony-like passageway. Stopping just short of the stairs running down on his left, he took up a fighting stance. Whipping the swords from their scabbards, he performed several routine moves. Shuffling forward, he fought an invisible foe, successfully decapitating every imagined creature that stood in his path.

Harry had been a student of Wing Chun kung fu since the day he turned eight. His education at Bik's Academy included the butterfly swords and long staff. The swords intrigued him most. Progressing to the point of being the best student in his school, as well as the state of Massachusetts, he made his folks and Master Bik proud.

His first weapons tournament, sponsored by the American Association of Wushu, had taken place in his thirteenth year; an important one in Harry's evolution.

Getting tired of pretend battle, he sheathed his swords and sat in a chair just outside his parent's bedroom. Waiting for his breathing to return to normal, he reflected on those past events.

He had barfed his guts out into a wastepaper basket just before stepping into the ring that glorious day. Master Bik came to him and rubbed his back, telling him to focus on his inner Chi, assuring him that puking was a good thing. He could hear his mother yelling, "Go, Harry!" from her seat in the bleachers. Then came the clap of the referee's hands.

Stepping onto the mat to face his opponent, the other kid grinned like it was no big deal. Harry soon found out why—the guy was really good. He bested Harry the first two rounds, their hard rubber swords slamming into each other as they parried blow after blow. Harry's frustration was boiling over by that point and his mind raced to find a solution. Then, something unusual happened.

Everything went into slow motion as the referee signaled the third and final round. *Waltz of the Flowers* by Tchaikovsky flowed into his head, and Harry found himself several seconds ahead of his opponents every move. He had won the round but lost the match because his adversary had received more points. Harry never lost another. The musical/slow motion phenomenon occurred at every AAOW sanctioned event after that day and soon followed him from the tournament floor into the street.

At first, Harry wondered why, *Waltz of the Flowers*? Then he recalled that the mood enhancing tune had been his mother's favorite in his early childhood. It seemed she never failed to play it on their stereo at least one time in her day and would then lightheartedly coerce him into waltzing with her around their entry hall. Harry had always protested, even though he secretly yearned for those moments. Now, perceived aggression triggered the waltz. The music in his head calmed him, and time slowed down to give him an edge.

Harry's experience with his mother brought him consolation. His experience with monster slaying brought something else. It is said that repetition makes one good at their craft. It certainly gave Harry an added perk. A butcher's chart of dissection started manifesting in his mind's eye upon contact with any beast. After about five seconds of sizing up his opponent, Harry would know just where to strike to cause the most damage.

He often wondered if there were any other monster slayers who had the same gift. He supposed one would have to be a swordsman to acquire such a thing. His relationship with his father wasn't good enough to talk about it in a reasonable manner. Then there was his friend, Elizabeth 'Bessie' Brown, who shared the same martial arts experience, but she would rather focus on more intimate things when they were together.

After she was born, her family and friends started calling her Betty instead of her given name, Elisabeth. But when she started talking, she couldn't say Betty, it always came out, "Bessie." So—Bessie it would stay.

Harry hadn't seen her for a while and missed her something terrible. Not wanting to think about her now, he reluctantly pushed the thought of her away and seeing that his parent's bedroom door stood ajar, he snuck in.

He wasn't supposed to be in there; another rule his father had made just after his mother succumbed to the Bug. A year had passed since that tragic day, long enough to numb the pain of her loss, but also bringing the fear that his beloved memories of her would wane.

Harold Sr. had not slept in their room since his wife had fallen ill and wanted everything to remain just as it was. Shortly after her passing, Harry's father seemed to stop caring about much of anything; other than killing monsters, anyway. That was the one thing that drove him from day to day. The obsession of the hunt and the thrill of the kill.

Harry stood gazing at the empty bed where Marjory 'Marji' Jones-Lumsdale had lain for what seemed like a long time, coughing up blood and mucus, as her life ebbed away. The well stained mattress was bare now, his father having used the bed clothes as a burial shroud. The elder Lumsdale had taken to sleeping on the large sofa downstairs after placing it in a strategic location where he could keep watch over the most vulnerable points of entry.

The odor of the bedroom was unpleasant and Harry didn't wish to linger. Walking around the footboard, he pulled back the window blind and looked down at the simple plank marker in the backyard.

His father had buried his mom in the very same ground where his swing set had stood. A happier time before disease, climate change, and the warming of the waters. He glared at the monster still stuck in the fence, then letting the blind fall back into place, he headed for the door.

The framed photo of his mother on the nightstand caught his eye and he stopped. Harry often found himself studying the portraits of Marji that adorned the many rooms of the house. Another effort to keep her alive in his mind. Logic told him to just let it go, she would come when he needed her. But the behavior, born of fear, was now conditioned. The thing was, he wasn't so sure he wanted to be rid of it.

Next to the image, sat a stack of get-well cards collecting dust. Some had come from him, a few from close neighbors, but mostly, from his father. Harold Sr. had made sure a flower had accompanied every one of them.

Taking his small, LED flashlight from his pocket, Harry shined it on the picture, cupping his hands around the lens to filter the light. In the photo, Marji wore her reddish blonde hair loose and long. Her heart shaped face held a full-toothed smile and green eyes shone, playful and friendly.

Harry had his father's triangular face. Everything else was Marji's, though. He too had decided to let his hair grow out, much to Harold Sr.'s dismay. The well-used clippers of his younger days now lay idle in a bathroom drawer.

Thumbing through the cards on the stand, he came across the last one his father had written just before she passed. Harry had been there when Harold Sr. presented it, accompanied by a vase full of roses he had picked from a deceased neighbor's yard. Harry had barely been able to hold it together, trying hard not to dash from the room in tears. Opening the card, he shined his light inside.

MARJI,

GET WELL SOON, DON'T KNOW WHAT I'D DO WITHOUT YOU!

LOVE,

HAROLD

*Well, you do now, dad... we both do.*

Turning off his flashlight, Harry left the room, pulling the door shut behind him. He had forgotten about the extra loud click of the latch and stood waiting for the usual scolding to resonate from below. When the words never came, he turned to the stairway and bounced down the treads two at a time. Making his way into the kitchen, his father said, "There you are! Were you in your mother's room? Thought I heard the door."

"Nope. It was open a bit... so I shut it."

His father glared and making a face that said he didn't believe a word of it, he returned to sharpening his knife. The grind of the old Marine Corps Ka-Bar moving across the whetstone set Harry's teeth on edge. His old man would give the blade a few extra draws across the stone for just that reason, smirking wickedly, while Harry awaited orders.

Standing in a semblance of 'parade rest', Harry fidgeted as he studied his father. Neither the new worry wrinkles in his father's face, nor the age spots visible through his short, grey flattop, had escaped the young monster slayer's attention. The now faded 'Semper Fi!' tattoo was just visible below the sleeve of his father's olive drab tee shirt, and Harry suspected the large 'Marji' tat on the other bicep had paled as well. He was surprised that he wasn't feeling the usual irritation that came when they were together. Instead, there was something akin to compassion. He fought the urge to walk over, throw his arms around his father's shoulders, and plant a big, slobbery kiss on his bald spot.

*Going to start some crap are you, Harry?*

Harold Sr. abruptly stood and pointing to Harry's chair with the knife, said, "Go sit, and I'll get you some of those noodles you've been begging for."

Slipping the knife into the sheath strapped to his left thigh, his father briefly checked the blousing of his fatigue pants before grabbing two of the three ceramic bowls stacked on the table. Then moving his six-foot, two-inch frame to the camp stove that sat atop Marji's now defunct oven, he began to dish out their meal.

He had announced upon arriving home from their early morning scrounge that, they would not be going on patrol come evening. The declaration had put Harry in suspicion mode. Harold Sr. had allowed him to laze about all day without the usual, "Do this, Harry," or "Do that, Harry." A change was coming—the younger Lumsdale could just feel it.

The blackout blinds in the kitchen were pulled down tight. That was supposed to be his assigned task. He was surprised he wasn't getting an ear full. There was something going on in his father's mind other than patrol strategy and defense.

Sitting down, his eyes fell on the half full bottle of antibiotics that still sat atop the useless refrigerator—his mother's last bottle of meds, unfinished. Billed as the best medication available, Harold Sr. had pilfered them from the local pharmacy. They had done no good.

His father's favorite rant at the dinner table was blaming big pharmaceutical and the AMA for the loss of Marji. Harry could expect the topic to come up at any point in their nightly conversations. Harold Sr. always grumbled about the million plus doctors who had overprescribed antibiotics for more than a century, thus, inadvertently cultivating an antibiotic resistant pneumonia that piggybacked the mutated H1N1.

The old guy believed that survivors, like he and Harry, had become immune because they had 'toughed out' earlier bacterial infections. Harry didn't know what to believe. He and his father had caught what seemed like a slight cold that had lasted for less than twenty-four hours. They had recovered just as quickly. It was Marji and the other sixty seven percent of the world's population who hadn't.

"Dad, why are you keeping those pills up there?"

Harold Sr. turned and looked at the bottle and then gazing forlornly at Harry, he said, "I don't know. I suppose I should toss them. But it really doesn't matter, we're out of here in the morning. With this monster coming right up to the house, we won't be getting a single nights peace. We've been lucky so far. But we need to find a place that's a little more fortified, and besides… there is nothing for us here."

*So, that was it! And now they were just going to pack up and move on, leaving everything he knew.*

"But… what about mom? We just going to leave her?"

"Well, son, we surely can't take her with us now, can we?"

"We don't have to go."

"Yes, we do."

"I don't want to."

"Well, we are going, whether you like it or not. I'm still running this show and no eighteen-year-old boy is going to tell me what's best."

"I thought we were partners? I remember you telling me, I had a say. What happened to that?"

"Harry… son, I can't stay here any longer. I want to move up north, maybe go into Canada. After the Marauders fell apart and it was only you and me left, well, I've been wanting to move on for a long time. I was thinking we could hook up with Billy Batschick. Once we get to his place, he and I can plan our next move. It will be good to have another, uh… gunslinger along, if you know what I mean?"

Harold Sr. just stood there, looking down his nose at Harry. The old guy was waiting for the usual resistance, but Harry resigned himself to the fact that his father would probably feel better if there was another adult with them. Harold Sr. and Billy had a history. They had served together in that never-ending war in Afghanistan and were bonded in a way that he and his father were not. This was Harry's understanding from a lifetime of living with Staff Sergeant, Harold Lumsdale, United States Marine Corps.

"I was thinking, Harry, maybe we can find a sturdy cabin up in the woods, somewhere, and start a whole new life outside of the city. Hey! Maybe Bessie and her family can come along? The more, the merrier. What do you say? You and she are best buds, right?"

Harry thought about that for a minute. They were actually more than best buds. He and she had been friends for a long time, too long for their relationship to remain platonic. Besides that, he always liked hanging out with Bessie's family. He hadn't seen her for over a week. Time to make that two-mile trek to her house.

He and Bessie had started sleeping together back when a fruitless hunt up at Bond's Pond had brought his father to a point of reckless obsession in his pursuit of monsters. It had kept them out late, so instead of a perilous trek back home, they overnighted at the Brown's. Harold Sr. had taken the couch in the living room. Harry, of course, had slept in Bessie's room. His father had patted him on the back the next morning, giving him a vulgar grin as if Harry had taken a trophy. Harry had scowled and stomped away, hoping to convey how inappropriate his father's behavior was.

Harry's newly found romance became a coping skill. It helped take his mind off their present lifestyle. Something that changed radically from college, marriage, careers, and children—to the repopulation of an entire planet.

His father turned away and dished up the second bowl of pasta. Harry scrutinized the olive-colored tee shirt stretched across a still very muscular back.

*He probably wants me and Bessie to give him a grandkid. That way the old guy can bounce it on his knee at least one time before he meets his demise at the fangs and claws of some beast.*

Bessie's parents, Jonny, and Joanie, were progressives, and acted indifferently to the two of them sharing a bed. Her little brother, Bobby, a rather precocious little boy, found the whole affair amusing and would breakout in fits of giggling whenever he caught Harry's eye. That lasted until he and his father departed late the next morning. Harry and Bessie became regular lovers after that, and he added condoms to his list of things to scrounge for.

Getting the Browns to come along on the Lumsdale's trek north, just might make it bearable. But Jonny had always given his father the cold shoulder and may resist hooking up as extended family. The two men only engaged in 'fair weather conversation' a term Marji liked to use.

Jonny was more of an educated, creative type. He was full of innovative ideas and could design simple mechanisms that could be utilized for everyday use; however, he had no clue about self-defense.

Joanie was loud and funny. She liked to sneak out back for a smoke on occasion; and not always the tobacco kind. Like Marji, she was dedicated to her family, but was not a control freak like, 'Sergeant Harold'.

"Harry? Earth to Harry," his father said, coming to the table and setting down his bowl.

"Sorry, I was thinking."

"Is that what you call that? Thought maybe you'd given yourself a lobotomy while my back was turned. So, anyway, I want you to pack a bag, your bookbag—not the mountain pack."

"What about my swords? Any pack I wear is going to get in the way."

"Just take a couple changes of clothes, some personal items, and your sleeping bag. Extend out the straps and wear it low. That way, you can grab the knives easily enough, or swing it off, if there is time. Wear your good hiking boots and don't forget to bring your fingerless gloves. They will make it easier on your hands. I'll carry the molly pack with the food, my stuff, and a trauma kit. As you know, the molly pack has got the hydration bladder in it, and we can each carry a canteen."

"They're not knives, they're swords. Butterfly knives are a Manila thing, and…"

"Whatever! Just prepare as if we are going on a hike."

"A really long hike! Like… Canada, is a freaking long way. Why there? Why not south, where it's warmer, or maybe, the desert, where everybody else is heading to get away from the monsters?"

"Harry, just do it, okay? I have a plan and I want to stick to it. I would like your support, not a bunch of crap. Got it?"

Harold Sr. sat back down in his chair and turned up the flame of the lantern at the center of the table. The room grew quiet with just their breathing and the clank of silverware on ceramic. Harry had lost his patience and was fuming. Being with his father too long always brought that.

The first time he met Jonny, Harry told himself, *"Now that's the kind of father I want!"* One time he had even lashed out at Harold Sr., saying, *"Why can't you be more like Bessie's dad?"* His mother got involved and a heated discussion ensued. The end result had been a short term 'grounding', followed by a 'talk of reason' with his mother. She had worked toward making him understand how human beings functioned. Her final statement on the matter had been, *"Regardless how your father is as a person, he still loves you."* The subject never came up again.

Harry studied his father's face while he slurped his noodles. One thing he could say about the old guy; he was focused. He had overheard people talking about Harold Sr. behind his back. Their discussions usually included labels like, *'ego oriented, task driven,* and—*control freak'.* Hide the emotion, hide the pain. Just keep on keeping on.

Harry knew the old guy was rubbing off on him, and their lifestyle perpetuated it. But Harry was resisting his evolution into a quasi-martinet, mostly because he still had Bessie. Harold Sr. on the other hand, had no one—just his only son.

After Marji died, the Lumsdale's went from being a family unit to just being a unit. Him and his father together—constantly—eating, sleeping, working out, and hunting monsters. All the upheaval and death had made people like Staff Sergeant Lumsdale an essential element to surviving any twenty-four-hour period.

Harry just wanted to stay alive and have something to do while he was. Perfecting his fighting art (with and without swords), going for that adrenalin rush that came with slaying monsters, reading books, and being with Bessie, were all those things. Mostly, being with Bessie. He was happy when she was with him. She was the constant in his survival equation and that would always equal contentment.

His father looked up and caught Harry staring. The old guys gaze was steady and unblinking. He didn't smile. Harry dropped his eyes and moved faster through his bowl of noodles. There came an overwhelming desire to get out of there and go uptown like he used to. He just wanted to do kid things again.

Harry's eyes strayed to the cover of a road atlas lying on the table. Plastered over the front were scenes of people visiting historic places. The most attractive to him was a Mardi-Gras scene of people celebrating. Smiling faces, bright lights, and lots of social interaction.

Back when things started to fall apart, he had tried to wander about the city as usual, going to his familiar haunts and hanging out with friends. Everybody was trying to practice proper face mask protocol and were failing miserably. But trying to eat, drink, and talk, with a surgical mask strapped across your face was a pain. Harry and his friends stopped taking it seriously and they paid for their indiscretion.

Harry kept trying to convince himself that everything was going to be okay. It was all going to work out, and one day, they'd be back to normal. But then, his friends started to dwindle in number. The word of one's demise was always brought by another, who in turn, would become the next to go, and then—there were none.

Harry stopped believing in the light at the end of the tunnel and just stayed home. It was a place where barriers and books brought a much-needed comfort. He figured this must have been how the cave dwellers felt. Except—they had no books. He assumed their distraction had been the nightly story hour and all the cave drawing sessions. Then there was sex, along with, hunting, and fighting. He got enough of the last two, so, sex had become a serious goal.

The quiet in the kitchen became too difficult to bear. Fuming or not, he needed to break the silence. Looking up at his father, he said, "You know, dad, I sure miss hearing the army's radios outside at night, I..."

"Just finish up there, son. I want to go out back and check on our intruder. I need you to hold the flashlight."

"Are we going to push that thing down the hill into the trees? You know as well as I do, it's just going to attract more."

"Yeah, might have to do just that… maybe barricade the hole with something, at least for tonight, anyway."

"So, what about mom? Are we…"?

"Forget about it. I don't want to talk about it, Harry. That part of our life is over."

His father's face softened and casting his eyes down at the table top, the old guy said quietly, "Hell, son… nobody gets out alive." Rising to his feet, Harold Sr. moved to the sink.

Dropping his bowl into the water bucket there, he said, "Finish up there, kiddo. We have to get out and get back in before it gets too dark. I want to be inside when the worst of them start to prowl. I got a feeling it's going to be a long night."

He came back to the table and picking up the whetstone, he walked past Harry to the food prep island at the other end of the room. Harry watched him set it down on a small pile of items that had accumulated there throughout the day, things that he assumed were going with them on the road.

"Is there still water in the supply barrel on the roof?" Harry asked, "I want to work out and take a shower before I go to bed."

"Uh-huh. From what I saw before the sun went down, it looked like it was about two thirds full, and… being the sun shone on it all day, I suspect it will still be pretty warm. But if you're any kind of a trooper, then… your man-enough for a cold shower, hey?"

Harry hated it when his father said, *"Man enough."* Harry knew some girls and women who were *"Man enough."* Like the one's he had met at Bik's, and those who wore the uniform of the U.S. Army. Women who had camped outside their houses, guarding the neighborhood until they succumbed to the Bug or got killed in a fight. Harry had always sided with his mother when it came to that subject. Harold Sr. couldn't stand that his son just might be a feminist.

Bessie and he had held seemingly endless discussions on the matter. He discovered she too shared the belief. Harry honestly felt if people could just push that aside—with women and men working together as equals—the human race could make a hell of a lot more progress. The old ways were a hindrance. The macho ways. Sadly—his father's way.

"Yeah, I can handle that. I suppose I'm wo…man enough."

"What did you say?"

"Nothing," Harry said flippantly, and rising from his chair, he moved to the dish bucket. Dropping his bowl into the soapy water, he added, "I'll just go get those flashlights from the closet, now."

Harold Sr. was back to glaring as he watched his son hurry from the kitchen. Harry knew the old guy wanted to say something, but sensed he didn't want to get into a pissing contest either. Harry had taken advantage of the moment. Harold Sr. would get over it. He might even recognize the humor a few minutes later, and Harry might catch him trying to hide a grin or suppress a chuckle as he shook his head in disbelief.

They were about due for that big show-down. The one that was supposed to come about this time in Harry's life. Yet Harold Sr. also knew that his son wasn't a little boy anymore, the evidence was there in their shared experience. Harry had risked his life to kill monsters, eagerly following the old Marine into battle. There wasn't too much he was afraid of at eighteen. His father just couldn't let go of the role he used to play, finally accepting his military days were over.

Harry grabbed two flashlights from the coat closet in the living room and returned to the kitchen. His father was now on his feet, shotgun in hand. Avoiding eye contact, Harry set one of the lights on the table and started shaking the other up and down, feeling grateful for the Faraday technology that allowed for use without batteries. It was a brilliant idea to create flashlights with a mini generator inside. All you had to do was shake them six or seven times to build up the DC current and they were good for about half an hour.

Out of the corner of his eye, he watched his father eject the spent shell from the Mossberg and replace it with a fresh one. Then reaching out his free hand for the flashlight that Harry was activating, he waited. Harry delayed pushing it into the large, rough mitt that edged ever closer. When Harold Sr.'s hand was just inches away, he snatched the flashlight from Harry, who then picked up the second light and moved a safer distance away before energizing it. His father grumbled as he walked to the back door. Harry stuck his flashlight in a rear pocket, turned down the lantern on the table, and followed.

His father unbarred the inner door and pulled it open. After peering through the cracks in the thick, plank shutter, he pulled the heavy metal rods that secured it. The door opening, caused Harry to tense up, and he checked his swords one more time to be sure they would come easily into play.

The shutter swung slowly open and his father shone his light around the backyard. Harry took out his light and without thinking, shook it a couple more times. Harold Sr. scowled back over his shoulder and whispered, "Do you suppose there's a chance we could do this with some degree of quiet?"

Harry nodded sheepishly, realizing he needed to get with the program.

"Ready? Or do you need another minute?" his father said with a hint of sarcasm.

Harry just grinned and adjusted the lens on his light without looking up. His father moved out, not waiting for an answer. Harry followed, keeping his beam low. He stopped a short distance out from the house, illuminating his mother's grave with his light, his father continuing on toward the dead monster.

Harry soon caught up and stopped beside him to study the giant, toad-like creature. It most certainly matched the picture in the ID manual. Its back flippers had meat hook like talons. Pencil like quills covered its entire back, making it look like a giant hedgehog. When Harry passed the beam of his light over the multitude of spines, they reminded him of dew-laden grass at the rising of the sun—each quill tipped with a tiny drop of clear poisonous syrup. The apex of the Anuraloph's back had been forced into the hole, the quills locking it into place. Harry thought it comical, the way it hung there, almost as if it had frozen in mid-cheer for its favorite ball team.

Its huge mouth hung open; its crystalline fangs exposed. The thing truly looked like a cross between a garden toad and an Anglerfish. Harry could have easily placed his whole body inside that mouth. The thought brought him a shiver.

The shotgun had done its work, and the daisy-like pattern of holes in its soft underbelly, still oozed monster goo. Harry could even shine his light all the way through at least four of the perforations. He could just imagine what its topside looked like.

"Anuraloph. It's an Anuraloph," he whispered.

"What kind of a loaf?" Harold Sr. whispered back.

"Not loaf, like bread. L-O-P-H," Harry said, trying to impress his father.

"Okay, fine. All I care is that it's dead-a-loaf, and it's not going to give us any more trouble. So, it looks like we won't have to barricade the hole after all. It's stuck in there pretty tight. I don't think anything else is going to mess with those quills on the other side, so… we're good!"

Annoyed by his father's use of humor, Harry sighed and looked away toward the grave. He wished he had asked his mother the crucial question: 'Why did you marry this idiot?'

Harry suddenly felt the overwhelming desire to prank his father somehow. Maybe fool him into thinking the monster was still alive by secretly making one of its claws move. If he screwed up, though, and got stuck by a quill, it would be a good joke gone bad. His last one, for sure.

Instead of pulling a foolish prank, he said, "So…what if others come because of this one? Do you think they might want to come in and pay us a visit like they did ol' Donny?"

"Well, Donny Dudley was an idiot. He should never have been sitting in an upper window taking pot shots at the critters all night long with that AR-15. Too much like saying, 'Here I am, come eat me!' They knew right where to find him when he wasn't looking. So, we'll take our chances. Besides, I think the only way we're going to get that thing out of there is by battering ram. There's nothing big enough on this side of the fence to do that with. Do you want to be the one to go outside the perimeter and find something?"

Harry shook his head no.

"No? I didn't think so. We are just going to have to be a little more vigilant tonight. Can you do that?"

"I'm hardly sleeping as it is. So, what's another night? The way I figure it, I can make my get away while they're eating you."

"Don't be a smartass, Harry. Just try to do as I say, huh?"

"Whatever you say…pop."

"Okay, let's get back inside. We've been out here way too long."

Harry turned and headed back, Harold Sr. following. Once inside, he watched his father linger in the doorway, his light shining on Marji's grave. Then looking around the yard one more time, he stepped in and secured the heavy shutter. Closing the inside metal door, he threw the bars, top, middle, and bottom. Handing his flashlight to Harry, he propped the shotgun against the counter and went to washing dishes.

Harry returned the lights to the closet and then with scenarios running through his head on how he might defeat an Anuraloph in battle, he went to his room. Changing into sweat pants and a white A-shirt, he topped off his ensemble by slipping on his black, canvas kung fu slippers.

Jumping up from his seat on the edge of the bed, he stopped to study Ip Man, the Wing Chun godfather grinning at him from a poster tacked to the wall. Harry grinned back, tapped a finger, one time, on Ip's nose and dashed back downstairs.

Going into the living room, he found his father already performing his isometric routine, dressed only in his military issued skivvies and the olive-colored tee shirt. The lone lantern that hung from the dead chandelier showed Harry that his father hadn't bothered to look up as he worked his way through a series of push-ups.

*"Once a Marine, always a Marine!"* his mother used to say. Harry believed it too, and one didn't dare say, 'ex-marine' in his father's presence. That was always cause for a raucous rant. There was no such thing as an ex-marine.

Harry decided to perform his nightly workout in the entry hall. Lighting the noisy Coleman lantern sitting on an end table, he moved to the middle of the floor. Pulling his swords from their sheaths, he slipped into a traditional stance, and although something he would never use in real life, it was a good place to start when it came to practice.

Moving through the time-honored movements for the Chinese butterfly swords, he twisted and turned, spinning, jumping, and thrusting. He was able to complete the routine in about thirty minutes. Then after removing his shirt, he switched to practicing modified stances and moves; the ones he used in actual combat.

He noticed that Harold Sr. had finished with his calisthenics and was doing his stretching routine on the floor in front of the living room door. His eyes were on Harry now, and his facial expression said it all—he was proud.

The old guy seemed mesmerized as Harry sliced the air in quick fashion, the silver blades glittering. After another thirty minutes, Harry had enough of practice and sat down to do his own bit of stretching.

Harold Sr. soon moved into the kitchen and dipped a coffee cup into the bucket of drinking water. Harry could see the old guy was still well toned for his age, leaving him to wish his father would take up the blade. Anything long and sharp that was not a gun. A Chinese long sword, a military saber, or even a Scottish claymore. A man his age could still handle a fifty-two-inch broadsword, easily. But he was the old dog that couldn't learn new tricks. He was stuck in his ways.

There was a time when his father carried an M16A4 rifle. A weapon he had taken from an Army truck parked down the block. Harry had watched him carefully remove the muzzle from the NCO's mouth who sat decomposing in the front seat. Harold Sr. had once commented, *"Damn Corporals, don't have the brains they were born with."* But from what Harry could see, the owner of that rifle sure did.

After the 5.56 ammo ran out, all Harold Sr. had left was an empty rifle with a bayonet. For a brief time, he used it very effectively as a 'Pu Dao', stabbing and slicing the monsters to death. But they soon found the Mossberg in a daylight scrounge, and the M16A4 was abandoned. So, Harry had no doubt his father could effectively use a blade. But Harold Sr. was a gunslinger to the core, and sadly, Harry knew he would be that until the end.

Sitting down on his mother's settee that had been pushed up against the basement door, he realized he was listening for a particular sound from the other side.

Since climate change, the weather had gone crazy. The electricity went, and so did the sump pumps. The basements filled with water, and a few other things, namely—Sarleps.

They were piranha like eels that came up through the drains and made the spaces under houses their territory. They showed up as small as sardines, and after eating everything in sight, which included rats, fish— and each other. They eventually grew too big to go squeeze through the drain hole.

When a thunderstorm rolled through, they'd go a little crazy. The ID manual told Harry that the atmospheric conditions perpetuated a kind of mating frenzy among the young, who then feasted on the old. Harry wanted to know how the government had figured that one out.

All he knew was that no one got any sleep on those nights. That was one reason why he was happy the sky had been clear the last two days. The basement had been quiet with only the occasional splash, squeak, and bump against the underside of the floor. His father had secured the door with spikes. That way, no one could go down there by accident and be pulled into the murky depths. The idea of the settee was to keep a rolled-up rug in place against the bottom of the door, sealing the crack.

If a tornado came, they'd have to hope for the best. There was a split level with a walkout basement just down the street. The water simply flowed out over the threshold of the sliding glass doors, leaving damp, foul smelling concrete. The Sarleps could only poke their heads out of the drain on occasion and slobber away as they eyed you sitting on the ratty, blue sofa back in the corner. He and his father could always run down there if they needed to, but always at the risk of being something's dinner.

Getting to his feet, he trudged into the kitchen, expressing mock exhaustion in order to make his father think he had pushed himself to the limits. Helping himself to a drink of water, he grinned at the old Marine.

"All done, mister? Finish your water and head upstairs. I'll let you shower first."

"Ah geez, thanks, dad. That's why I always tell people, who put you down, that you're still a great guy, even if you are a Mari…"

"Okay, enough of that," Harold Sr. said, snapping Harry with a damp dishtowel.

"Ouch! Oh! You're such a brute, you… you, big, strong Marine Corps sergeant, you." Harry said this in his best soprano, a tone meant to push all of Harold Sr.'s buttons.

Finishing his water, he pretended to turn away. Harold Sr. drew back the towel for a second shot and Harry made his move. Tangling his father's arms up in the towel, he then swept his opponent off his feet, making sure to not let him fall too hard on the kitchen floor. Then leaving Harold Sr. there, he moved away, dodging and weaving his way toward the stairs, expecting pursuit. Instead, the old guy just lay where he had fallen, laughing loud and hard.

*Finally!*

Harry hadn't heard him do that since before Marji died.

"You are quite the whipper-snapper there, boy!"

"No, I think you're the whipper-snapper, dad. That's what got you into this trouble in the first place."

"See you in the morning, kiddo."

"Night, dad," he called back as he made his way up the stairs, wishing he could have more moments like this one. He resisted the overwhelming desire to rush back downstairs and throw his arms around his father. But he had tried that once, it had not gone well.

Grabbing one of four kerosene lanterns from a table on the balcony, he went into the bathroom. Finding the box of matches that was always to remain on the counter, he put fire to the wick. Then shutting the door, he locked it to be sure there could be no retaliatory intrusion.

Disrobing, he stepped to the mirror and noticed right off that a 'six-pack' was becoming visible at his mid-section.

*What? No beer belly?*

Chuckling, he examined his arms and flexed his muscles. They were no longer the skinny sticks of his childhood. He was seriously toned, and wondered why he was just now noticing. Bending his six-foot frame down, he studied his face in the mirror. Nature had been good to him, and there was no sign of the acne that had sprouted up in his early teens.

He took a moment to make faces at himself, wondering which one of them he expressed during battle. If it was a goofy one, he really didn't want to know. He ceased his clowning and climbed into the bathtub. Turning the makeshift lever that was haphazardly screwed to the wall, he sent the water to the shower head.

Afterwards, he walked naked to his bedroom, carrying the lantern and his sword rig. Cigarette smoke rolled up to meet his nose, and Harry knew his father was having that one cigarette he allowed himself just before bedtime every night. One of his mother's major peeves.

However, it was a habit that went clear back to his Corps days. So, after one fruitless attempt to talk him into quitting, she just let it go, asking that he at least go outside. Harold Sr. didn't argue, and there had been nights Harry had watched from his bedroom window as his father sat in a chair on the back patio, the cigarette's ember glowing in the dark. Harold Sr. had looted a convenience store close to their home the year before, and filling a garbage bag full, he made off with every carton of cigarettes in the place.

Coming through the doorway into his bedroom, Harry briefly caught his reflection in the tall floor mirror standing in the corner. Stopping, he struck a pose. The lantern turned him orange, highlighting the ripples. His legs, butt, and back, showed the same as his arms and torso.

*Good deal!*

Ten years into his chosen lifestyle and he was right where he wanted to be. Harry worked hard to strengthen his muscles and emulate his martial arts hero. He set the lantern on the nightstand and dropping the sword rig, he posed like Bruce Lee in the, 'Enter The Dragon' movie poster tacked to the wall across the room.

Looking back and forth between the mirror's image and Lee, he compared his arms, chest, and stomach.

*Close enough!*

With his tall, slender build, he would never bulk up to look like some bodybuilder. But his muscles were well defined like his hero's. That had always been his goal. He wondered if Bessie got excited whenever she saw him without a shirt on. He raised his eyebrows several times, smirking at himself in the mirror. Then picking up his sword rig, he placed it strategically on his nightstand for a quick grab.

Returning to his dresser, he slipped on a clean pair of boxer shorts, followed by his old, black kung fu outfit that now served as his PJ's. Comfortable, yet sturdy, they still served a purpose. Moving to his bed, he sat down and finding his soft ninja boots just underneath, he pulled them on. They were good for sleeping, but you didn't dare walk any great distance in them. The lack of arch support left a serious ache, and Harry had learned the hard way. Placing his flashlight next to the swords, he blew out the lantern and stretched out on top of the covers. Pillowing his head in his hands, he studied the ceiling, waiting for sleep to overcome him.

*Be vigilant, Harry, your dad's counting on you.*

Smiling to himself, he fell to thinking about how the day had gone. Downstairs, his father cleaned the shotgun and did last-minute checks.

Then, a different sound… the cocking slide of a .45 semi-automatic. He knew it was his father's vintage, World War II, 1911 Colt.

Something that had belonged to Harry's grandfather. Sadly, he knew why Harold Sr. carried that pistol.

Harry had been privy to overhearing his father telling his mother that the old Colt was really for himself. He kept it close just in the case he should ever get into a bind. Then he told her a story about General Custer and how his soldiers had been trained to save that last bullet for themselves. True or not, it gave Harry a chill.

Harold Sr. could have easily made it a two shot Derringer if that's all it was for. Yet, the Colt semi-automatic had significance. So, that was what his father wanted to end his life with should things go to crap for him in a big way. Staff Sergeant Harold Lumsdale was not going to stick around, incapable of fighting, while the monsters gnawed the flesh off his bones.

Harry shuddered and quickly pushed the thought away. He didn't want that to be the last thing going through his head before he fell asleep. Turning his thoughts to Bessie, he closed his eyes.

Harold Sr.'s footsteps soon announced his presence on the stairs, and then came the clank of the guns being set on the granite countertop in the bathroom. The door never closed, and soon the valve for the roof tank squeaked open, followed by a low, "Brrr." The sound of the water falling into the tub was as soothing as a light summer rain on the roof, and Harry fell asleep to the low strains of the Marine Corps hymn.

# CHAPTER 2

## In Gasping Death To Wallow

Harry was up long before his father. He sat, bare chested, on the floor next to his bed, studying his homemade calendar. The first of May was upon them. Still a month and a half to go before his birthday. Not that it mattered much anymore. There was no real reason to keep tract of time. There were no more parties to go to, no school, the eight-hour workday and the weekend were gone. No more blue Mondays, hump day Wednesdays, or TGI Fridays. Minutes and hours were almost non-existent. There was only the rising and falling of the sun—and that's what dictated.

Harry realized how much he missed Bessie. There was a time when got excited about monster patrol; but no longer. Now, the activity was more like work. More like a job, and his father made sure of that. He didn't look forward to killing, but he did look forward to Bessie's warm skin against his. To lay beside her in bed, talking about silly crap, just being goofy, was the highlight of his life now. Shoving the little notebook back into the nightstand drawer, he felt the anticipation of seeing her later in the day. That motivated him.

Turning his attention to the piles of neatly folded clothing that lay before him on the carpet, he tried to focus on his task. Yet Bessie's face kept coming back, the little overbite that showed every time she smiled, her straight Grecian nose and those deep, dark, greenish-gray eyes— almost always questioning.

He could hardly wait to hug and kiss her. She brought him hope, and if she wasn't on his mind, she wasn't far from it. Smiling to himself, he moved to sorting the piles of clothing, tossing aside anything that wasn't going to be of need.

They had passed a quiet night and he had slept all the way through. The sun was just topping the trees across the street as he worked. Its rays penetrated the huge round top window in the entry hall and finding their way into his bedroom, they bathed him in their radiance.

Harry was relieved that the sky was mostly clear and hoped that the day would be as nice as the one before. He wanted white fluffy clouds and a comfortable temperature for their journey north.

Narrowing his choice of pants to his best kickboxer jeans, he separated them from the others. There wouldn't be any high kicking going on because Wing Chun kicks were kept low, targeting the opponent's knees and hips. But stretchy pants were always good pants, plus, they were tough, as well as fashionable. He could move quickly without them impeding his actions.

Already wearing one pair, he pushed the other two pair into the bookbag. They were followed by three pairs of socks, boxer briefs, two long-sleeved tee shirts (both black), and his short sleeved, 'Gao's Academy of Kung Fu' tee. Picking up his favorite sweatshirt, he laid it out to study the huge, amber Miskatonic University emblem on its grey background. The shirt had been bought at the bookstore on a campus tour one day in Arkham. He couldn't walk away from that garment. M.U. had been his first choice of universities after graduating high school and he had yearned for the day he could be seen wearing that shirt on campus.

*Well…so much for that idea!*

After shoving the sweatshirt into the bag on top of the other clothing, he pulled a blue, long-sleeved tee shirt from a pile and slipped it on. Grabbing his fingerless gloves that sat atop of his nightstand, his eye fell on his Marine Corps issued boonie, the hat's brim poking out from beneath his bed. Pulling it out, Harry blew the dust off the camouflage fabric and ran a finger over the tiny swatches of green, black, and brown. His father had given him the hat years back. Harry didn't like hats, but he knew Harold Sr. would want to see the thing on his head when they walked out the door. It was one of a few gifts his father ever gave him. Putting the hat on his head, he got up and moved to the mirror to check it out.

*No way!*

On top of that, it interfered with his swords. Harry threw the boonie on the bed and moving to his highboy dresser, he opened the top drawer. Pulling out his sketchbook and pencil box, he laid them on top of the dresser and began to dig around among his socks for things he had stashed in there that he might need. He found his large, Buck knife keeping company with several tie tacks, assorted custom-made lapel pins with their witty slogans, and other, now useless, things.

Taking the knife, he had the drawer halfway shut before his eye fell on the pocketbook of Robert Frost poems. A slight smile broke his lips and he snatched it up to slide it, and the knife, into a side pouch of his bag. He loved Frost's poetry. When he was feeling blue or having a bad day, he would often find a quiet spot to read the poems.

His unfinished comic book, from the day before, lay on the carpet, and he added it to the bag's contents, pushing it clear to the bottom where his father wouldn't see it. Harold Sr. didn't like comic books. He'd much rather use them to start the cooking fire than to see one in Harry's hands. Then his attention returned to the sketchbook and pencil box. They would have to come along. Harry had been sketching for as long as he had been practicing his fighting art, and he knew he would sorely miss that creative pastime.

Picking them up, he sat down on the edge of his bed and began to render a depiction of the monster his father had killed the night before.

He liked using charcoal, but had only recently graduated to it from graphite. Harry figured he had at least half a year's supply in the box, along with his pencils. Art stores were rarely looted, so finding replacement medium hadn't been too difficult.

Harry got caught up in his task and half an hour passed before he completed his drawing. It always took him away, and next to reading, sketching was a great way to escape the angst brought about by their present situation. He was surprised his father hadn't called him down to the kitchen yet.

Putting the sketchbook and pencil box in his bag, he strapped it shut. Then after donning his sword rig, he tied the boonie to the bookbag using the same cotton cord that secured his sleeping bag to the loops at the bottom. He took one last look around as he hoisted up the bag. The thought to take a heavy coat for winter played through his mind, but that would be too much to carry. He could easily pilfer (his father's favorite word) a parka when he needed one for the winter months.

Moving down to his mother's room, he found the door wide open. His intent was to steal her picture out of its frame; however, the photo was already gone. Harold Sr. had beat him to it.

Glancing one time at the bed, a memory flooded in of him as a child lying there curled up next to his mother as she read him *Green Eggs and Ham* in her best 'Sam-I-Am' voice. The tears welled up and he quickly turned away from the open door. Stopping at the top of the stairs, he composed himself before going down.

Harry walked into the kitchen, clear eyed and ready for breakfast. That was until he saw his father piling rice and powdered eggs on his plate. His desire for food melted away, right along with the mental picture of butter topped pancakes with maple syrup.

His sudden appearance startled Harold Sr., who must have been lost in thought. Nearly dropping the overflowing plate, the old guy said, "Shit! About time! Thought I was going to have to go up there and jump on your skinny butt."

"I was up long before you."

"Whatever! Sit down and eat so we can get the hell out of here. I want to get to marching."

"What's the hurry? We have all day. The sun's out, there's only a few clouds, hell…"

"Eat! The more time we have, the farther we can get. Oh, by the way, good morning!"

"Morning," Harry said indifferently as Harold Sr. inspected him, his eyes stopping at Harry's hands.

"You been drawing? No wonder it took so long," and grinning, Harold Sr. returned to his task.

Defying his father order to sit, Harry walked to the kitchen drawer that held the household miscellaneous. Taking out a fist-sized ball of heavy cord, a box of matches, and several candles, he added them to his bag.

His father was back to glaring. So, he moved as slowly as possible to his chair and dropping his bag next to it, he sat down. Harry knew his father was fighting the urge to lose his cool. The intense staring was something he did in the past with his troops. The look was to spark intimidation. Harry wasn't falling for it. He wasn't a trooper in staff sergeant Lumsdale's squad, and certainly didn't have to follow orders— even though he did sometimes for the sake of peace.

There had been many a long-winded discussion about what was expected from him. He and his mother used to gang up on his father to remind the patriarch that Harry was his son—not his squaddie. Eventually, he or his mother would screw up and say the word, 'soldier', sending Harold Sr. into his rant, reminding them that Marines weren't soldiers, they were warriors.

Yet, the Marines were done. The Army, Navy, and Air Force—all gone. Now the word 'warrior' had a whole new meaning. Master Bik's meaning. The old man relayed to Harry once that the Chinese people had no specific warrior class, unlike the Japanese, and others.

*"Everybody has the capability to be a warrior!"* Bik said one day after he had overheard Harry ranting to Bessie about the senior Lumsdale.

"Quiet night, huh, dad?"

"Quiet enough, I guess. I heard some activity out back sometime after midnight, but I was too lazy to get up and look. You must have slept right through it all, huh?"

"Yeah, I suppose. But if we had been in any real danger… and not the paranoid kind, I would have woken up."

"Yeah, right. So, I've got everything ready to go. As soon as we are done with breakfast, we're gone. Hear me?"

"I hear you," Harry said, looking past his father to the massive MOLLE pack lying on the counter next to the shotgun.

"Damn, dad, that molly pack is huge. You sure you want to haul that all the way to Canada?"

"Not your problem," Harold Sr. said, smirking over his shoulder, his 8-point cap set low at the front. "That's a Marine's pack. A man's pack!"

Harry broke eye contact and shook his head in disbelief as his father turned back to his task. He noticed the high-tech holster for the .45 was strapped on at his father's right thigh, balancing the fighting knife sheathed on his left. The standard olive drab tee shirt was tucked in at the waist of the utility pants that matched the hat, and those in turn, were bloused into his tan colored combat boots.

*Tucked in. Everything had to be, tucked in.*

Harold Sr. was always making sure that people they met on patrol had no problem figuring out who he was (or had been). Even though he lacked his staff sergeant insignia, he looked like he had come straight off the base and was ready for a day of field training.

"So… dad, you have a picture of mom?"

"Yeah, I took it from her room."

"Can I have one?"

"Take that four by six in the living room. The one on the mantle."

"Fair enough," Harry said, giving his father a sharp nod.

They ate their breakfast in silence. Harry knew his father was anxious—but in a good way. He knew his old man was already planning a route and mulling over all the things that could go wrong. Harry should have known better than to even converse with his father when he was in, 'marching mode'.

*Probably already halfway to Canada in his mind!*

Finishing up, Harry moved into the living room and finding the 4x6 photo of his mother posed in front of their house, he pulled the image from the frame and slipped it into his back pocket. He couldn't help but notice the one that sat to the right of the one he took. The one of his father and mother together with a one-year-old Harry sleeping in her arms. He took it, too. His father didn't need to know. Returning to the kitchen, he found Harold Sr. waiting by the door, his pack slung and shotgun in hand.

*That was quick*!

There would be no time to linger and have second thoughts. The dirty dishes remained on the table, confirming they were done with 314 Morel Street.

*Almost nineteen years his home, how sad…*

"Got your mom's picture?"

"Yeah, took the one off the mantle, just like you said."

"Good, that's a good one. Now, strap on this canteen, and grab your bag, we're leaving by the back door."

He did as he was told, his father unbarring the doors while he did. Then stepping out onto the back stoop, Harry followed. A flock of crows lifted off from the fence near the Anuraloph, taking their raucous calls into the trees. Stepping around his father, he moved out onto the grass. Harold Sr. pulled the door shut but didn't secure it.

"Not going to lock it?"

"Nope, don't plan on ever coming back, and… you never know when somebody might need shelter or anything we've left behind."

Harry wasn't sure how he felt about strangers messing with their stuff. Now he wished he could have taken more.

"Let's go," Harold Sr. said, as he moved toward the side gate.

"Yes, Sergeant," Harry said, knowing the comment would aggravate the situation. But he couldn't help it.

"How many times have I told…?"

"Yeah, I know, sorry, feeling kind of crabby."

"Well, you can just holster those claws, mister, or the crabs going to hit the fan, got me?"

"Ha-ha! Good one, pop! Okay… said I was sorry."

"Whatever."

His father's words trailed off as they watched a single crow return to perch on the fence. The large bird sat just above the dead monster and cawed at them. It seemed to be saying, "Mine! Mine! Mine!" Harry's eyes moved to the dead creature, realizing that the carcass now looked displaced. Without a word, they moved out of the backyard, quietly closing the gate as if they feared waking the neighbors. As they moved along the outside of the fence, Harry's mind went on high alert. His father pushed the butt of the shotgun against his shoulder but kept the muzzle down.

Clearing the corner, they were startled by a couple of vultures flapping up into the trees, hissing and squawking at the intrusion. Harold Sr.'s shotgun came up, ready to fire. Harry's hands rested lightly on the grips of his swords, but the blades stayed sheathed.

Two, big grayish-black lumps could be seen in the tall grass. Both were about the size of a large German Shepard. Neither was moving. Harry and his father let out a simultaneous sigh of relief.

"Recognize them, Harry? You're the monster expert here, you studied that book. What are they?"

"Um, well… they look like Cayhond. You know, those long-legged dog, slash, alligator like things, with a blowhole up underneath that short neck frill. Kind of ceratopsian, ummm… the text said they can run like wolves, and they pretty much act like them too. They can dive down deep and stay under for a long time. Someone told me once, I don't remember who, that they don't swim well. They usually just walk around on the bottom, like hippopotami."

"Well… thank you for that, Professor Lumsdale."

"You asked."

"So, I'm supposing that's what I heard last night."

"Suppose?" Harry said with a hint of sarcasm.

"Shut up," his father said good-naturedly and poked the nearest creature with the muzzle of his gun. That Cayhond had a face full of quills, and the other, had a huge chunk of skin and flesh in its jaws. Harry suspected the amphibious fiend's last meal had been the portion of the Anuraloph that had been blown out by the shotgun. Harry suspected that in its haste to satisfy a ravenous hunger, the Cayhond had snatched up the loose hunk of Anuraloph and fell victim to the quick acting toxin.

*Stupid monster!*

There were signs that there had been others. The big hole in the Anuraloph's back had allowed the rest of the pack to help themselves to its innards. The ground was torn up and a well-worn trail ran up from the woods with pieces of flesh and internal organs strewn along its length.

"What a mess! Damn, Harry, I'd swear this was one of your kills if it wasn't for these dead critters lying around."

"Yeah, well, I…"

"The way you go to town with those swords, geez, boy."

"Gets the job done, huh?"

"Sure does," Harold Sr. said, and laughed. "You always were a mess maker."

Harry was happy to hear his father's laughter. That's two times now in less than twenty-four hours. Dead monsters seemed to bring it out of the old guy. At least he'd be in a better mood for a while.

Harold Sr. said, "Good thing we're leaving. I imagine if we stayed, we'd be getting a whole lot more company in the days to come and not the kind you can invite in for coffee."

He finished his verbal speculation by taking off his hat and rubbing his forehead as if his declaration had prompted a whole new set of worries. Then replacing it, Harold Sr. pulled it low, lay the shotgun's barrel back over his shoulder, and gave Harry a grin before turning away. Heading out across the unfenced backyards that ran to the side street, he stopped for a brief second and said, "Oh, by the way, professor—hat on!"

"But it gets in the way of my swords."

"On!"

Now it was Harry's turn to say, "Whatever!" Unhooking the boonie from his bag, he slapped it on and then kicking one of the Cayhonds, he muttered, "Scumbag."

Spinning away to gallop after his father, he nearly tripped over a child's sun faded, red plastic wagon that hadn't felt tiny hands for many years. Catching up with his father, they walked side by side in silence.

Trying to get into a hiking mood, Harry focused on other things. Somewhere a bird sang a melodious trill, its song punctuated by the cawing of crows. The smell of dead things was in the air and he wished for a gentle breeze to move the stench along.

Passing through Tommy Tomberelli's backyard, his eyes fell on the ragged trampoline that they had played on as tweens. He got a weird feeling in his stomach as he thought about the Tomberelli's. They were the first to meet their demise on his block, all taken by the Bug in just two weeks' time. It came as such a shock that he hadn't cried. He just stood with his mouth open as his mother delivered the news to his father in the kitchen. Looking away from Tommy's house, he focused on his father's MOLLE pack and imagined Bessie's smiling face there.

Instead of crossing over the side street to cut through the next block of houses, his father turned right at the sidewalk, and moved up to the corner of Morel. Harry followed, and they strolled down the middle of the street at a good pace before having to stop and crawl over a cluster of cars.

A pickup had hit the stone corner column of the fence in the Robinsons front yard on the right, the driver's putrefied body remained flailed on the steering column. The old Dodge blocked half the street. A Volvo wagon had come along and crashed into its tailgate. Harry presumed it had tried to whip around at high speed, but the driver had lost control. Then a minivan had hit the wagon and fused into its back end. The inertia of the third, appeared to have pushed the second, perpendicular to the roadbed. The rear bumper of the van had come around to take out the front porch of the Blasdell's house on the other side, and the gaping hole offered a view into the dark interior.

The rest of the oncoming vehicles must have crashed into them periodically, as they flew around the corner in the dark. They all formed a messy gridlock of steel and glass all the way up to the corner. There were no more bodies, but there were plenty of blood-soaked articles of clothing, children's toys, and oddly, the occasional shoe.

Once Harry and his father got through the mess, the street remained clear all the way up to Spencer Avenue in the business district. There, the wreckage started all over again. They had to cut through parking lots, the long grass of overgrown median strips, and shoulder high thickets that had once been rose beds. Their occasional detour even took them through the bays of a car wash to avoid having to scramble over the wrecked cars, trucks, and motorcycles, clogging the streets and sidewalks around it.

They looked at each other in wide-eyed disbelief when they stumbled across a human skeleton free of flesh except for the skull. The face and hair told them it had once been a middle-aged man. The weird thing was, he hung from one of the automatic brushes as if he had tried to hide inside of it or climb up to get away from something.

Harold Sr. didn't say anything, and they just shrugged at each other before hurrying out of the glass sided tunnel. That was the kind of thing that Harry knew would come back to haunt his dreams. Something to bring him awake at two in the morning, soaked in sweat and hoping his involuntary shriek hadn't woken his father.

Harry used to come this way to go to the academy, but that was before the Bug. When they went out on monster patrol, they didn't use this route, instead, Harold Sr. would always lead him down the hiking trail that took them through the woods behind their house in a descent to the Merrimac River. They would then circle back north, using the west bank of Shad Creek to take them to Bond's Pond, and turning south, they would move through the long grass of the golf course in the western suburb with its many water hazards. Eventually they would arrive at the overgrown bike path and head back to Morel Street. It kept them in close contact with all the bodies of water in the area and offered the best opportunity to confront any creature emerging for its nightly hunt.

As they worked their way up to the main drag of the town, Harry noticed there were a good many bodies lying about in various stages of decay. The bloated ones disturbed him the most with their bulging eyes in balloon like heads. He found it hard to believe that they had ever been human beings.

*Just add them to the carwash guy! You'll have a years' supply of bad dream material before you even get to Billy's place!*

A couple of weeks back, his father and he had come across their neighbor, ol' lady Taylor, while on a scrounging foray to the shopping mall. She lay stone cold dead, face down on the sidewalk at Birchy Street and Ivy, her nose cemented to the concrete by a dried mass of green snot. Her tattered, stained dress had been hiked up to reveal that she had lost control of her bodily functions. Lying humped over a couple bags of rotting groceries, she appeared to have struggled only briefly before succumbing to her illness. Strangely, no creature had disturbed her.

At first, they thought she had croaked off in her house because when they checked her residence, no one had answered the door. She must have been gravely ill when she went out looking for food. Knowing her as he did, Harry figured the stubborn, old curmudgeon wanted it that way. She had been one tough old bird.

Harry and his father continued north, finally reaching the far side of the business district. Stopping to rest and drink water, he could see the building that housed Bik's Academy. The front of the small, orange brick structure wasn't shrouded in plywood like the others around it. Harry took it as a sign that Gao Bik may not have abandon his beloved school.

"Can we go down and check on Master Bik? It's been a while. I'm wondering how he's doing."

"Shouldn't be a problem, we're making good time. Maybe he'd like to pack up and come along. Probably not much left for him here in Kilbury."

*Great! Then there would be two people ordering me around!*

"What do you think, Harry? Shall we ask him?"

"Sure, why not. He's a nice guy—when he's not giving commands."

"I bet he's a completely different man outside of his school."

"Ummm… I doubt it."

"Let's go and see."

Returning the canteens to their pouches, they headed in that direction. Upon arriving, they found the large front window had been shattered. However, the polymer sheets Gao Bik had secured on the inside, acted as a secondary barrier to keep the intruders out. Harry found it odd that the thick glass door remained unbroken. Checking the latch, they found it locked. Harold Sr. knocked hard on the aluminum frame but got no response.

"Shall we break it down?" Harry asked.

"I suppose, since he's not answering. He's either not here or can't make it down the stairs to the door."

"Yeah, but he used to spend his days back in his office… probably can't hear us."

A bad feeling started in Harry's gut and radiated outward. He sensed he already knew why Master Bik wasn't answering.

"Okay, yeah. So, you're the kicker, give it a boot."

"Are you sure?"

"Yeah, I'm sure. Give it a shot, just be careful. I don't want you slicing yourself and bleeding out here on the sidewalk."

Harry looked around as if there might be somebody who cared if they broke a window, and then giving the glass a well-controlled, low front kick, he shattered the pane. After knocking out the shards with the toe of his hiking boot, he reached in and unlocked it. Harold Sr. went in first and Harry followed. Stopping just inside, they stood listening, the glass crunching underfoot. The familiar smell of death hung in the air, confirming Harry's worst fear.

Harold Sr. said, "Let's go to the back and check the office. I've got a bad feeling about this."

"That makes two of us."

They moved through the waiting room door and onto the training floor. The large windowless space was extremely dark. The only light within its walls, splashed out onto the crimson-colored carpet through the open office door at the back.

Walking in, they both came to an abrupt halt. Gao Chon Bik was in his chair, face down on the desk, dried bloody mucous gluing his face to the large paper doodle pad. His skin had gone the shade of an eggplant's, his head indiscernible from his neck. Adorned in some kind of a white ceremonial outfit, his right hand still held a pencil that rested on a yellow legal pad. He had written a note in Chinese.

*Well, that's one message that will never get read!*

Harold Sr. let out a heavy sigh and moving to the desk, he rummaged through the clutter on its top. He picked up a box that had been wrapped in decorative fabric and tied with a gold ribbon. Harry watched a sticky note flutter to the floor, but didn't bother to pick it up. After close examination, Harold Sr. set the box down and turned, making eye contact with Harry.

Harry's hands went into his pockets. He shrugged, raised his eyebrows, and said, "Looks like we're too late"

"Yeah, like a week too late. Guess we should have checked on him sooner; not that it would have done him any good. Maybe just to say our goodbyes."

Harry's eyes moved from his father's face to his deceased teacher. The urge to weep welled up and he resisted. Master Bik and he had been together for nearly ten years, but there had been no training for the last seven months. Back when things first started to fall apart, he and Bessie had stopped in on occasion for a visit. Master Bik had tried to keep things going, promising his students he would hold it together for as long as he could.

Harry thought to step out of Bik's office and return to the dark of the training floor. If he lost control and did start bawling, he didn't want his father to see. That would get him a lecture—no matter how bad he felt. He continued to fight the urge, and moving his eyes from Gao Bik's body, he brought them to the framed photos on the wall behind. Another bad idea.

They were mostly of Harry and Bessie standing with Master Bik at tournament. Bessie and he had been the best students at the butterfly swords and had brought the school many trophies. There were other students up there too, but only for the traditional Wing Chun style of fighting, and one of Ralphie Rolfson with the long staff.

Master Bik had never been much on smiling, but by looking at those photos, one wouldn't know. He was beaming from ear to ear in each one, his arm around Harry's, Bessie's, or Ralphie's shoulders. Then to make it worse, below those, were pictures of him as a younger man in different fighting stances, sometimes just standing, holding trophies of his own. Then there were the faded black and white portraits of him as a young boy with people Harry assumed were his family back in Zhao Qing, China.

Harry spun and walked out of the office, rubbing at his eyes. Finding his way to the front, he stood in the waiting room, looking out of the window at the abandon boutique across the street. He never thought he would feel this way about Master Bik.

The sound of a door shutting echoed in the training room followed by his father's heavy boots moving across the carpet. Checking his face in a wall mounted mirror, Harry composed himself. When Harold Sr. came in, he didn't turn around.

"I think this was intended for you, son. The note fell off when I picked it up the first time."

"What is it?" Harry said, turning just enough to see his father out of the corner of his eye. The old guy was holding out that wrapped package with the sticky note stuck to the top.

"Well… read the note!"

"To Harry, from Master Bik," he read and glaring at his father, he said, "Happy now? I read your note."

Harold Sr. shoved the box into Harry's hands and took a step back, not saying a word, the look on his face telling Harry that, out of respect for the moment, he was going to keep his mouth shut.

Harry took the large, heavy gift and moved away to the long wooden credenza built into the wall on his left. Setting the package on top, he untied the ribbon and peeled off the fabric to expose the dark green, papier-mâché box inside.

Chinese calligraphy covered its surface along with a multitude of colorful butterflies. Flipping up the lid, he saw Master Bik's own butterfly swords inside. Harold Sr. must have saw it as an opportunity and pulling a rolled-up note from inside the box, he held it up to the light and read, "To My Best Student, Harry. I won't need these where I am going, but I believe you will. Xie-Xie–Your Devoted Master, Gao Bik."

Glancing briefly at his father, he brought his eyes back to the swords. Harry knew their history. They were the real deal. Not factory cast stainless like his, but a clay tempered steel of the old days. The quillon, knuckle guard, and pommel were all made of brass. The grip, a thimble of carved wood. They were hand wrought and would hold an edge much longer than his own. Now, they were his—bequeathed by death.

Harry picked them up and the wooden grips felt good in his hands. Rotating the blades backwards, he made sure the points didn't contact his biceps. They fell just an inch shy and he smiled. It was almost like they were tailor made for him.

Turning, he looked at his father, who just nodded and said it all with his eyes. It was all good. He replaced the old with the new, putting his modern pair inside the papier-mâché box. Then dropping his arms to his sides, he went into a ready stance and whipped them from their scabbards.

"The reflexes of a cat," his father said, looking proud.

Pushing his new swords back into the rig, Harry realized the papier mâché box was too big to fit inside his bookbag. So, taking his modern pair out of the box, he wrapped them tightly in the colorful fabric and pushed them all the way to the bottom of his bookbag.

"We should go," Harold Sr. said. "I want to get to the Brown's before dark."

"What about Master Bik?"

"Nothing we can do. I closed and locked the office door. He'll be in there until someone, or… something, finds him."

"Please, don't say that. I don't want to even think about the monsters chewing up Master Bik."

"Sorry," his father said, and glancing meekly at Harry, he walked over and locked the front door. Turning, he scanned the room before quickly moving to a six-foot-long, dry-erase board on the wall that once conveyed messages to the students. He startled Harry by ripping it down. Taking it to the door, he leaned it up against the hole in the glass.

"Help me with this, will you, kiddo?" his father said as he started pulling a small, but heavy sofa toward it. Harry grabbed an end and they pushed it tight up against the board to keep it in place.

"That should keep the critters out. We can leave by the alley door. Come on, son, let's make like a shepherd and get the flock out of here."

Harry followed without argument. He felt subdued, like he did when he walked away from a battle well fought. He was happy for the new blades, but not so pleased with how he had acquired them. He had mixed feelings, but he knew he would just have to let time take care of that.

They exited the big steel fire door at the back, allowing the spring-loaded night latch to secure it. Then making their way up the alley, they headed for Bessie's.

After a couple of miles, they found themselves among the newer, more modern homes of Bond's Waterfront addition. It was not that much different from his own neighborhood. Rows of empty houses, the streets clogged with cars and the occasional corpse lying in the most unexpected place, and most likely, an unexpected position.

When they had built the addition back in 2025, they had designed it with Bond's Pond as an incentive to buy lots there. Now, the large body of water sat right in the center of the development, surrounded by ninety acres of maple, willow, and oak. Harry thought it ironic that the one thing that attracted the buyers, had also brought death to the neighborhood.

As the story goes, the pond had been there since the Jurassic. It was noted to be deeper than a Scottish loch, and supposedly, hid monsters for a billion years in its cold, dark recesses. True or not, it didn't matter anymore.

Before climate change and the Bug, the city of Kilbury had tried to fancy-up the area around it. They put in walking paths, benches, and stone grottos. Little vine covered arbors were scattered all over the green space along with tiny gazebos placed at strategic overlooks that allowed visitors a view to the massive pond. Victorian looking strombrellas were placed within small landscaped lawns bordered by short hedges and flower beds. It soon became a smaller version of New York City's Central Park, or at least that had been the idea.

Now, it was just a human trap. Overgrown with vegetation, it was the perfect place for an ambush. Harry was sure people would walk by and say to themselves, 'Oh, what a lovely place to have a picnic,' only to find themselves becoming the main course. Harry was glad it wasn't saltwater. So, no Thulu.

Harry and his father soon came across a Caudator. A salamander like monster, nearly ten feet long. It appeared as if it had tried to climb a wrought iron fence, but had been impaled on the spear like tips. It had a Moray Eel like head and the mouth hung open to expose spike like fangs.

The frilly gills that surrounded its upper neck like a lion's mane, had dried out to look like giant, rotten cauliflower florets. The oversized dewclaws were a faded black, and its skin was now dry and brittle.

Its rear quarters had been chewed, leaving Harry to wonder how far the other feasting beasties had gotten before falling down dead from the Caudator's highly toxic skin.

A block from the Brown's place, they watched as a long-haired man ran across the street dragging a large, green duffle bag. They called out, but he picked up his pace. Disappearing into the shrubbery between two houses, they lost track of him. It was rare to see people moving about, even in the day time. Harold Sr. had to be talked out of giving chase, with Harry refusing to go with him if he did. His father mumbled to himself as they walked, something about the audacity of an eighteen-year-old. Harry looked away and smirked.

They soon came in sight of Bessie's house as they moved up the street into the cul-de-sac. All the homes at the far end sat in a semi-circle, with tiny patches of lawn at the front and huge backyards that bordered on an undeveloped forest. In all the years that he had known Bessie, they had never once ventured out into, 'the woods', mostly because Joanie believed that's where the perverts hung out.

The Brown's house was what Jonny called a Saltbox style, something he had wanted all his life. He built it new back in the spring of 2026, and the Browns packed up and moved over from the south side. Harry remembered how excited Jonny became the first time the Lumsdale family came over for a barbecue.

It was the only white house on the cul-de-sac. It had a green roof with green plank shutters that actually functioned. Jonny wasn't going to settle for those plastic, *"One size fits none, pieces of crap!"* And now, everyone was grateful that he hadn't.

Harry saw that they were still closed, even though it was afternoon. A chill suddenly ran up his spine. He felt like they were being watched.

Scanning the area, he saw Bessie's light blue, refurbished '79 VW Beetle was the only car on the street. There was something odd about the way it sat.

Moving closer, Harry realized that the tires were shredded and the windshield was starred. The side windows were a maze of cracks, and the back window was all but bashed in. He took in the rust-colored spots trailing from the car door to the front porch. The adrenalin rushed in.

"There's blood."

Harold Sr. threw him a look and unslinging his shotgun, he advanced toward the house at the ready.

# CHAPTER 3

## Beloved Bessie Brown

They passed through the gate of the white picket fence with Harry walking backwards, staying close to his father, and keeping watch on what Harold Sr. referred to as, 'their six'. That was their standard operating procedure. More than once the beasts had tried to sneak up behind them. When Harry determined there would be no ambush, he turned to see Harold Sr. studying the blood spotting the small concrete square that served as a porch, his shotgun at hip level, the muzzle pointed toward the door.

There was a partial shoe print in rusty brown and Harry recognized the tread as one left by Bessie's favorite sneakers, 'Streetfighters' by Broone. He knew them well; having pulled them off her feet many times.

"I think Bessie's been hurt. That's her shoe print."

"Well, okay, but we got to get in there first if we are going to help her. If no one answers, we are going to have to break down the door, and that's… only a maybe."

Harold Sr. pushed his gun forward, bumping its muzzle several times against the heavy plank shutter. They waited, listening, all the while scanning the yard and street. After a minute or so, his father knocked again, but this time he pounded harder with his fist. More silence, then the distinct scraping of someone lifting a bar and the squeak of the inner door swinging open.

Harry's swords were out in an instant as he turned and prepared for what may come. A nerve-racking minute passed with only the sound of their breathing. Someone was studying them through the cracks between the thick planks of the shutter. A second bar rasped from its stays, and the thick wooden panel swung open several inches as footsteps retreated across the hardwood floor inside.

Harry moved off the stoop to make more room for his father. Harold Sr. squared up to the doorway and bringing the gun to his shoulder, he turned the weapon on its side and hooked the shutter with the blade of the front sight. Taking a step back, he used it to pull the panel open far enough to allow access.

An unpleasant odor rolled out, an acrid mix of smells, and at the base of them all, the old, familiar—death. Harry got a sinking feeling that things had gone really bad for the Browns. But somebody was still alive inside that house, and deep down, he hoped it was Bessie. But that also meant others were dead, and his expectations of a happy reunion disintegrated into a jumbled pile of emotions.

Harry moved to get a better view into the entry hall. Clothing, cardboard boxes, plastic bottles, and other assorted trash littered the floor. Whoever had opened the door, now stood facing them from the base of the stairs, the large, open doorway of the living room to their left.

He stepped past his father into the house. When his eyes adjusted to the dim light, he saw that the person standing before them was Bessie. Not how he remembered her but, Bessie none the less.

"BB?" he said, pushing his swords back into their sheaths as his father came in and moved cautiously toward the living room.

Bessie's right hand came from behind her back, dropping the butterfly sword in the process. Its point penetrated the wooden floor with a *thunk!* and Harold Sr. reacted by backing away from her, the shotgun coming to port-arms.

She reached her hands out to Harry and in a mere two seconds, she was across the floor and in his arms, squeezing him so tightly he could hardly breathe. Breaking down in raucous sobs, Bessie clung to him, shaking so badly it was all he could do to keep them both on their feet.

When her initial emotion subsided, Harry just held her, allowing his eyes to stray into the living room. All the furniture had been pushed to the walls except for a large wingback chair which sat in the middle of the floor. Just a few feet forward of it, there lay what looked like a pile of bed sheets.

Harry barely heard his father say, "Be right back," before disappearing out of the front door. The sound of the shutters being unbarred, on the outside, filled the room. The old guy was soon back inside and whispering in Harry's ear, "Take her into the dining room, I'm going to open the windows and get some air in here."

He did as his father commanded, and guiding Bessie toward an antique church pew on the far wall, next to the kitchen door, he kicked garbage out of their way as they moved. After pushing several stacks of photo albums off the seat, he pulled Bessie's second sword from the sheath at the small of her back and laid it on the large, wooden, dining table.

She wouldn't let go of him and he struggled to get his bookbag off. Finally accomplishing the task, he let it fall to the floor and they sat down. Bessie's tears were just a remnant of what they were earlier, but her grip hadn't waned. If she didn't relax soon, Harry would have to force her.

He sat patiently watching Harold Sr. unlatch and throw up the sash of the two screenless windows. Then pulling the large hooks on the inside that secured the shutters, he hollered, "Coming open!" and giving each one a quick shove, light flooded the room, bringing a cleansing breeze. Bessie's reaction was to gasp and cover her eyes, giving Harry much-needed relief from her tenacious grip.

Harold Sr. moved to the pile of sheets and knelt on the floor at the same time that Bessie pulled her hands from her eyes. A whimper escaped her lips and she pushed her face into the space behind Harry's shoulder, throwing her left arm across his chest.

Harold Sr. hissed, "Aw, damn," and turning his gaze to Harry, he shook his head in dismay. Without having to be told, Harry knew what lay under those sheets. Leaning right to expose Bessie's face, he twisted his upper body around and embraced her. There was another short stint of sobbing and then she just seemed to run out of gas.

Releasing Harry, she rubbed at her eyes and sniffed. Her hair was a bird's nest of disarray and her makeup was a mess, giving her the appearance of a bizarre looking clown. She hadn't talked since their arrival, and he hoped she would say something soon. Removing his boonie, he tossed it on the table and said, "I'm going to get you some water, okay? Okay, BB?"

Bessie whined pitifully, "No, Harry, please stay," and hugged him yet again, pushing her cheek against his chest. All he could do was lay his chin on the top of her head and rub her back until she had her fill. Another five minutes passed before she relaxed and relinquished. She swiveled to face forward but kept a solid grip on his hand. Her head hung down and her tangled hair hid whatever expression might be on her face.

With her free hand, she reached in and pulled from her shirt pocket what he knew to be a 'Cheer Bear' and examined it. The charm was a plastic semblance of a little bear that could be hung to smile sweetly at you from the rearview mirror. The toy was a promotional offer handed out by the hundreds at a local burger joint. It was supposed to be a symbol of optimism, but Harry found its expression rather macabre and somewhat inappropriate for the moment.

Harry checked Bessie out as she studied the toy. The right sleeve of her red & black plaid shirt had been ripped off at the shoulder. A dirty bandage made from a linen napkin, wrapped her right bicep. Its silver dollar sized blood spot told him that the wound was deep.

Her unkempt hair seemed lighter, almost as if she were going prematurely gray. The torn, brown corduroy jeans she wore, were now crusty and stained. Snot leaked from her nose, but she did nothing to stop it. That annoyed Harry and he wanted to wipe at it the way Marji would his when he was a child. He always believed Bessie had the nose of Venus De Milo, and to see her sniffer draining away like that upended his illusion. A stack of cloth napkins, like the one she had used to wrap her wound, sat on the table top. Grabbing one, he tried, in a clumsy manner, to clean her face.

That brought her out of her musings and after shoving the plastic bear back into her shirt pocket, she snatched the napkin from his hand and rasped out in aggravation, "I'll do it!"

Harold Sr. entered the room carrying the sword she had dropped on the floor. He laid it next to the other and said, "You all right, girl?"

With the napkin pressed to her nose and mouth, her eyes glared at him over the top. "I'm okay," she growled through the fabric.

"Maybe time for a little water? Is there any in the kitchen?" Harry asked.

Dropping the soiled napkin to the floor, she said, "No, I've been drinking out of the shower head… when I felt I could go up those stairs, anyway. The water in the roof tank isn't too bad."

Bessie's eyes strayed up to the banister of the open balcony that connected the upper rooms, much like the one at Harry's house. Then turning away, he felt her shiver. Her hand came back to his, and she squeezed his fingers as a single tear spilled out to run down her cheek.

"Here, take this," Harold Sr. said after unstrapping and handing her his canteen. She took it, and after spinning the top off, she drank a few swallows, hesitated, and then started gulping like a mad woman, rivulets running from the corners of her mouth. Upon finishing, she whispered, "Oh… that's so good. Much better than the roof tank." Smiling meekly at Harold Sr., she tried to return the canteen.

"No, you keep it. Take all you want. We have more."

"Thanks," she mumbled, and after taking a couple of sips, she capped it and set the green plastic flask on the bench beside her.

Harold Sr. spun away, and bounding up the stairs two at a time, he stopped at the top to stare down the balcony to where it led into a short, enclosed hallway at the other end. A long sigh escaped his lips and bringing his eyes back to them, an expression of pity crossed his face. Unslinging the shotgun, he moved forward to disappear into the adjoining corridor.

Pushing her right arm behind Harry's back, Bessie threw her left over his stomach and her face returned to his chest. A low, sorrow filled wail broke from her lips and she pressed her mouth against his shirt to suppress it.

Harry heard a door open but not close. Then another, and finally one that he recognized as the bathroom by its squeaky hinges. It grew quiet for a minute, the silence soon broken by the brief squeal of the valve in the feed pipe that ran down from the water tank. There came a brief spattering of water droplets in the shower stall followed by a confident, "Good enough."

Harold Sr.'s combat boots clomped some more, and three other doors were opened before the footfalls returned. Harry waited for his father to appear, but the clomping was replaced with noises of exertion. Grunts and grumbles emanated out of the hallway, along with the flapping sound of bedsheets.

"Pop? Do you need some help up there?" Harry called, trying to get a clue as to what his father might be doing.

He started to stand, but Bessie kept him in his seat. He felt her squeeze, conveying that she wasn't ready to let him go. Harold Sr. finally answered with, "No, I'm fine. Be back down in a minute."

Harry turned his body toward Bessie and his eyes met moist, dark pools. He took in the same look that he saw reflected in his bedroom mirror the day his mother died.

Harold Sr. stomped back down the stairs and looking straight at Bessie, he said, "I want you to go upstairs, now. Take a shower, change your clothes, and then we will have something to eat. I'm sure you will feel much better afterwards. I'll make us up some food from the molly pack, and Harry… you go with her."

Bessie squeezed Harry's fingers again and said, "I'd rather not. I mean… I really don't want to go up there."

"It's okay, sweetie, I've covered them up. You won't have to look at them."

Harry met her eyes again and she whispered, "Stay with me, okay, Harry?"

He nodded and then turning to his father, he asked in a low tone, almost as if Bessie wasn't in the room, "You said, 'them'?"

"You'll see soon enough, just take her up to the bathroom. Let her shower, and then walk her to her bedroom. Now, go!"

His father moved to the table and picking up a lantern with one hand, he pulled a stick match from an open box on the table and lit the wick. Then walking to the pivoting door of the kitchen, he poked his head in. After a few seconds, he slipped inside, the door swinging back and forth, listlessly. That was followed by the sounds of cupboard doors and drawers being opened and shut.

An assertive, "Go on now, kiddos!" filtered through the wall.

Harry stood, pulling Bessie up by the hand that held his. She took a deep breath, released the air slowly, and let him tow her up the stairs. He kept the tension on, not only to keep her moving, but also to satiate the need to determine the mystery of the upstairs hallway.

Upon reaching the top, she shielded the right side of her face with a hand and kept Harry between her and what lay on the floor. As he suspected, there was what looked like another body under a clean white sheet, lying in front of the open door to Jonny and Joanie's bedroom.

There was another sheet covered lump just inside. It was about the size of a large dog, and a big, webbed paw with linoleum-knife-like claws protruded from under the edge of the cover.

Bessie gave Harry a start when she broke into a run, hauling him toward the bathroom. She slung him through the opening and followed him inside. Slamming the door shut, she pushed her back against it, her face a mask of fear. She closed her panic-filled eyes, and her breath came in short, fast bursts.

The large window on the opposite wall, even though frosted for privacy, offered a good deal of light, and Harry could see the room was just as untidy as the rest of the house and smelled faintly of urine.

*Going to need a good cleaning if we stay more than a night!*

Lowering the toilet lid over yellow water, he sat and waited for Bessie to calm herself. After a few minutes, her breathing slowed. She opened her eyes and silent tears rolled from the corners. Stepping away from the door, she moved past him and stopped beside the shower, now facing away.

"Stay in here with me, okay, Harry? Please? Don't leave."

"I can do that, no problem. You want me to keep my eyes closed?" Harry chuckled, raised his eyebrows, and waited for her to turn around. She never did, but a weak giggle emanated from her lips and Harry's smile grew wider.

*Good! A step in the right direction.*

Harry suspected humor was going to be the key to Bessie's recovery. He just had to keep from overdoing it.

"Don't be silly, you've seen my body before—and how many times?" She threw a slight grin over her shoulder and Harry could tell it was forced.

Bessie unwrapped the bandage from her arm and let it fall to the floor. Harry scrutinized the two-inch-long gash on the ridge of her bicep and decided it was one less thing he needed to be worried about. The wound appeared to have been sewn shut with what looked like dental floss. It was scabbing nicely. She must have cleaned and stitched it herself. One more reason for him to admire her.

Harry remembered back to a time when they had discussed whether they could suture their own wounds—or not. He had sewn up Harold Sr.'s wounds many times, and likewise, but never his own. Now, Bessie was one up on him, making him hope that he had the guts, when the time came, to push that needle through his own skin.

Bessie had always been a brave girl, another thing that attracted Harry to her from the very beginning. Even as little kids, she never backed down. She had a sense of what was right, often backing him up even if she knew that it may not end well for her.

He watched as she unbuttoned her shirt and let the tattered flannel float down to spread out on the floor. Harry wondered what had happened to the missing sleeve.

Bessie wasn't a bra-wearing kind of woman and took to binding her chest when her breasts had grown large enough to interfere with battle. Raphael, a transgender man, and assistant to Master Bik, had suggested chest binders. She had accepted the advice, and soon after, she told Harry she would never go back to brassieres.

Peeling off the greying, sweat-stained wrap, she let it follow the shirt. Then toeing off her blood-covered sneakers, she kicked them into a far corner before standing silent and unmoving to stare out a window that didn't offer a view.

Harry could see where the leather sword scabbard had chaffed and gouged the skin at the small of her back. She ran a finger over the sore spot briefly before unsnapping and dropping her grimy corduroys to her feet. This exposed her pink thong underwear and some well-rounded glutes. He suddenly felt the need to look away. It had been a long time since he had seen her like that, and it wasn't a good time to be getting aroused. Rotating on the toilet lid, he faced the door, waiting for her to turn on the water.

When the squeak of the valve didn't come, he peeked over his shoulder and saw she had lost the thong and was now facing him, her arms hugging her chest. She was crying again.

"BB, time to get in the shower."

She didn't say anything and took a long, stuttering breath. Reaching out her hands to him, she tilted her head to the side and gave him a look of longing. He stood and embraced her, trying not to think about her nakedness—or the fact that she hadn't bathed for quite some time.

Harry had been with other girls before Bessie. Brief relationships that ended abruptly after the first session of awkward intercourse. He was thirteen when he snuck in the window of Britta Donnelly's bedroom; at her invitation.

She had been a stick of a girl with a pretty face, and for some reason—a great deal of experience. And then, Sonja Kruger, two months later at summer camp. A tall, muscular girl, she had been a long-distance runner on the Track & Field team with him at Kilbury High. She was a year older and the dominant half in their two-week long relationship at Camp Whip-Poor-Will. Under her tutelage, he had become quite educated.

He and Bessie remained friends throughout all of his sporadic relationships, and when the two of them grew intimate, he stopped searching for 'the girl of his dreams'. With Bessie, there was such an overwhelming feeling of joy and acceptance that he no longer felt compelled to quest.

They stood in the middle of the bathroom in their embrace for a few minutes before he reached into the shower and opened the valve. Pushing his hand into the stream of water, he waited for it to go from cool to lukewarm.

The open barrel on the roof had been another of Jonny's inventions. He had passed the knowledge along to Harold Sr., who felt he had to one-up Jonny's idea by linking two barrels together for twice the amount of water.

Pulling the plastic curtain open, Harry ushered Bessie inside. She didn't resist, but it didn't help matters when his hand accidently brushed her bare bottom. Turning to look at him with a kind of sad yearning, he tossed her a slight grin and shrugged before pulling the curtain shut.

He wondered if sex might bring her some relief. They would have to talk about it when she was ready.

"Brrr… Harry, it's cold," she said as he listened to her soap up.

"Oh, it's not that bad. Felt pretty good on my hand, anyway."

"Uh-huh… I imagine something else felt good on your hand. But that's not going to happen today."

*There it was.*

So, Bessie wasn't yet ready for that kind of intimacy. She was willing to joke about it, though, and that was good. But now, he was aroused. Until she was dressed (and a few hours had passed) that picture of her standing there naked wasn't going away.

"Think I'll step out of the room for a minute, okay?"

"No! Please don't go," she said and poking her head out through the curtain, she scowled at him, her long hair dripping onto the white tile of the floor.

"Well, okay. I guess I'll just sit back down here and play with myself." She chuckled again and pulled back inside.

He brought his attention to a stack of old magazines on the top of the toilet tank. The October 2032 *Science Times* showed a smiling man in a lab coat and thick glasses, standing in front of others. He was holding up a glass vial for the camera. The caption read: 'Good Bye, Bug! A Vaccine For The Superbug Is Found!'

*Yeah, right.*

Harry suspected everyone pictured on that cover was dead now. Nature ruled, there was no doubt. If you tried to get around her, she would just kill you.

The sound of the valve closing and the water no longer hammering the shower basin brought him from his reverie. Quickly pulling a large bath towel off the rack, he walked over and stuck it through the curtain.

"Thanks," she said.

He was hoping she would take it as a cue to remain inside to dry off, and maybe wrap the towel around herself before stepping out. No such luck.

Moving from the shower onto the tile floor, she smiled at him while working the towel over her body. His blood raced and sweat broke out on his upper lip. Returning to the toilet seat, he sat again to face the door. Picking up that magazine, he tried to focus on the pages, looking over the ads containing things that no longer mattered.

"Shall we go to my room, now?"

He looked over his shoulder and saw the towel wrapped around her hair. She wasn't going to give him a break. He found himself studying her abdomen and noticed that she too had a hint of a six pack, and that her bellybutton was now pierced. A tiny butterfly sword in sterling silver hung from her birthstone there.

*When did that happen?*

That was all the nudity he could stand. Grabbing the last of the large bath towels from the rack, he walked over and tried to drape her.

She stepped back and said, "Really, Harry? Come on."

"Sorry, it's best. If that thing you mentioned isn't going to happen today… then it's best." The bulge at his crotch had become quite painful, and even though they had been together in the most intimate of ways, he still felt embarrassment.

"I'm so glad you're here," she said, her tone low but full of gratitude.

She smiled big, and Harry sighed. His fear that she might have 'gone over the edge' dissolved away. Bathing seemed to have brought some sense of normality. Attempting to throw her arms around him, he pushed the towel forward and wrapped her with it.

"Please?" he said.

Looking up into his face, she whispered, "So glad." Their lips met in a soft kiss. It was Harry who was first to break contact.

She put the side of her face to his chest and just held him, whispering, "I truly didn't think I'd ever see you again."

"Never fear, Harry's... still here!"

"Oh, shut up and just hold me," she said, the snot rattling in her nose.

Harry laid the side of his face on the top of her head and without warning, he felt his confident mood begin to dwindle. There came a serious foreboding, followed by an overwhelming sadness, and his own tears started to well up. He resisted.

*Be strong, Harry. She needs you to be strong. There'll be a better time.*

The portent feeling and the sorrow that accompanied it, troubled him. It brought a mental picture of him alone, in an old boat, helplessly adrift on a dark ocean.

Pulling back, he shook his head as if to dislodge the image. Keeping his hold on Bessie's shoulders, he gazed into her face. She stared back, her dark eyes wide and questioning. He had hoped her expression would be telling—but there was nothing.

*Too confusing... just let it go!*

Bessie pulled him in for a quick squeeze, and then moved by, securing the towel as she went.

"Let's get out of here," she said, and finding his hand, she opened the door a crack and peeked out. Then, cocking her head for a moment as if listening for approaching danger, she flung it wide and hurriedly pulled him down the corridor to her bedroom, throwing quick glances over her shoulder as they went.

After passing through the door, she let go of his fingers and moved to her dresser sitting back in the farthest corner. Harry leaned against the doorjamb just watching her as the sound of pots and pans rattled up from the kitchen through the floor.

Bessie dropped the towel and he quickly looked away by spinning on his heels and gazing out into the hallway. Hearing a drawer open, he peeked back to see her stepping into a fresh pair of blue, bikini style panties. He took advantage of the moment and slipped out. His curiosity pulled him to the body in the hallway and he was halfway there before he heard her call, "Harry? Where are you?"

"Just out here in the hall, don't worry, I'm not going anywhere."

"Don't leave, please!"

"It's okay, I'm right here. It's just… I can't see you naked right now."

"Silly boy," he heard her say as if speaking to a child.

He picked up his pace, hoping to get a look under that sheet before she put the pressure on him to return. Pulling up a corner, he got what he came for, suddenly wishing he hadn't. Jonny lay on his side, back muscles shredded, his throat partially torn out. Harry gasped and dropped the cover. He thought he would be okay with it, but when it's someone you know, versus a stranger, emotion seems to get in the way.

The expression on Jonny's face was one of sheer terror. His blue eyes were wide open and fixed. It was almost as if Jonny couldn't believe that death had found him.

Harry shook his head several times trying to clear the image as if it could be shed like water. Taking a couple of deep breaths, he closed his eyes and emptied his mind like Master Bik had taught him. When he felt he achieved his goal, he moved to the other sheet covered lump. Pulling up the bedding, Harry's eyes fell on the nightmarish predator that was the Cayhond.

Jonny's killer was much bigger than the two that lay dead behind his Morel Street abode. The creature could be found on page twelve of the ID manual. The beast resembled a long-legged alligator. Doc Smith said he thought they might be some version of Ambulocetus or Pakicetus, creatures that whales had evolved from. They had what looked like fur with longer plastic-like hair feathering out from the back of their powerful thighs.

They were fast runners and were seldom found without their pack. Harry was surprised that only one had come to pay the Browns a visit.

He noticed the killer's soft under belly had been cut to ribbons. Ripped from rectum to throat. The small, ceratopsian neck frill that hid its blowhole, had chunks hacked out of it. The upper and lower jaw had been cleaved straight back from the nose to the eye sockets and throat.

It was like it had met a sharp, vertical straight-edge while moving at high speed. In all probability, that was the blow that had made the Cayhond change its mind about invading Bessie's home. Sadly, she had been too late to save her father. Harry figured she was probably dealing with a lot of guilt at the moment.

"Harry?" Bessie called.

Dropping the sheet, he poked his head out of her parents' room to see her left eye peeking around the door jam, while brushing her hair. Walking back to her, he hoped she wouldn't ask questions. But, she did.

"What were you doing?"

"Oh, ummm… nothing."

"Come back in here and stay with me, I'm not naked anymore."

Bessie moved over to stand beside the bed where she could see her reflection in the mirror and Harry followed. She now wore her own stretchy blue jeans, and a red, tight fitting, 'Gao's Academy of Kung Fu' tee shirt.

She had it tucked in, and a wide, brown leather belt was buckled in front, resting loosely over the jean's waistband; outside the loops. That was where she would hang her traditional sword scabbard, a method Harry would never go back to. Whipping a black hoody up from the bed, she put it on but left it unzipped.

Harry was just glad that she was dressed now.

"Still have that tee shirt, huh? I loved mine so much, I wore it out."

"Yeah, I still have mine because… I didn't. Not much on being a walking billboard. I bought an extra-large just in case, though, and now that my boobs are bigger, I'm glad I did."

"Yeah, pretty smart. Wouldn't want your boobs to be unhappy."

"Oh, shut up," she said and kicking a colorful, stuffed unicorn at him from the floor, she gave him a, "Take that!" look.

The toy spun toward his head and he snatched it out of the air and threw it back. She broke into a grin, sidestepped, and caught the stuffed animal. It was nice to see her toothy smile. Harry figured he would wait until later to tell her about Master Bik. Maybe in a couple days. It wouldn't hurt for her not to know. So, unless she brought up the subject, he would keep it to himself.

The grin didn't last, and she now stood silent, her eyes focused on the unicorn in her hands. Then she seemed to snap out of her reflection and dropping the toy, she sat down on the bed. Harry watched her drag her Nuu-Tech Tuflon hiking boots out from underneath and pulling them on, she bloused her skin tight jeans with a pair of thick, wooly, grey knee socks. Upon completion of her task, she jumped up and took his hand, towing him down the corridor toward the balcony. Bessie kept her face turned away as they passed her father's body and upon reaching the top of the stairs, she let go of Harry's hand and ran the rest of the way.

Going straight to the table, she grabbed up her swords. Harry watched her sheath them together in the single scabbard before attaching it to her belt. Harold Sr. suddenly popped out of the kitchen and startled her. She took a minute to compose herself as his father stood eyeing them both, a pan of steaming rice in one hand and a large, metal, mixing bowl, full of canned peaches, in the other.

"Sorry," he said.

She gave him a half grin and drew a long breath through clenched teeth.

The old guy turned to Harry and said, "Push that crap off the table, will you?"

"What crap?"

"Clear the table, will you? I need to set this down"

"I've got this," Bessie said, and after picking up the box of matches and placing them on a nearby pie safe, she swiped everything else onto the floor with her good arm.

"Thanks, sweetie," he said, giving Harry the 'stink eye'.

"Well, geez dad, it's not our stuff."

"Just sit down, I'll bring the rest."

"There's more?"

Bessie didn't argue, she sat down and began to stir the rice. Harold Sr. went back into the kitchen as Harry slid out a chair next to Bessie.

"You know, I would have helped, but it's like, well… it's your stuff, and I didn't want to seem like…"

"It's okay, Harry," she said, patting his leg. "It's done. Now, let's eat."

"Fine."

His father returned with paper plates, plastic forks, one big metal spoon, and a bowl of something that looked a lot like granola with raisins.

"I found this in your cupboard, hope you don't mind," he said, while setting the table.

"It's okay, it's all I've been eating. That, and handfuls of breakfast cereal. I couldn't find the can opener or I would have already eaten those peaches."

"Yeah, I saw there wasn't much in there. Good thing we showed up when we did."

"Yeah, good thing…" she said, grinning at Harry and patting his arm.

Harry spooned a little bit of everything onto his plate and then did the same for Bessie. Handing the spoon to his father, he said gruffly, "You can get your own."

Harold Sr. snatched the utensil from his hand and sneering back, coughed out, "Prick." Then looking at Bessie he said, "Just kidding."

"Yeah, right. Kidding—hah!" Harry said with a sneer.

"You two haven't changed a bit, have you?" Bessie said and chuckled.

"Nope!" Harry and Harold Sr. said at the same time. Laughing about it together, they started in on their meal.

They ate in silence, Bessie quickly scarfing down her meal like she hadn't eaten for a week. Then, not even asking if they wanted more, she helped herself to seconds. To Harry, this was also a good sign. She hadn't lost her appetite after all she'd been through. Catching his father's eye, his old man winked back.

They ate by lantern light since the shutters were still closed in that part of the house. Harry looked into the living room and saw that the sun no longer shone directly through the windows. He also noticed that the bodies and sheets had disappeared. He figured his father must have moved them out of sight while Bessie was showering.

Bessie noticed too.

She immediately stopped eating and sat staring into the living room. Then turning back, she cast her eyes down to her plate and slowly put her fork down. Grabbing the edge of the table with both hands, she said in a low, angry voice, "Where's my mom and my little brother?"

"Dad?" Harry questioned.

"I wrapped them in the sheets and moved them to the mudroom. It's not good for us that they stay in there, sweetie."

"So… we are going to bury them, right?" she said, turning her face to Harold Sr., her eyes smoldering.

The old Marine's face hardened, "Yes, isn't that what you'd want?" The tone of his voice was more challenging than inquisitive.

She relaxed then and picking up her fork, said, "I guess so." Gazing at Harry, he saw her eyes had grown moist again.

Harold Sr. must have saw them too and took it as a sign of submission. His face softened and he said, "We will be sleeping in there tonight. So, it's best that they aren't in there with us. We can take care of them after we eat, or wait until morning."

Bessie didn't look his way as he spoke. Harry could see she was fighting the tears, and probably, a desire to tell his father, "*Don't tell me what to do!*" Harold Sr. just kept talking.

"So, sometime before we go to bed, Bessie, I want you to pack your bookbag with some clothes and…"

She whipped her eyes up to meet Harold Sr.'s unwavering gaze. "Why? Where are we going?"

"There is no sense in staying here. Harry and I are heading for Canada by the way of Maine. Going to try to hook up with my Corps buddy, Billy Batschick. We'd like for you to come along. How does that sound?"

Bessie looked at Harry and then back at his father. Without answering the question, her eyes drifted down to the tabletop.

"I'll give you time to think about it. I know you're trying to put it all straight in your head right now. But you're a pretty smart kid. I know you'll figure it out." With that said, Harold Sr. got up and returned to the kitchen.

Bessie took Harry's hand. Looking into his eyes, she whispered loudly, "I don't want to leave them. It's going to be hard to leave." Her eyes were pleading and her bottom lip trembled.

"I know. I didn't want to leave my mom. But I couldn't let my dad see me get upset about it. It's like he said, we can't take them with us, well… not physically anyway, and you know we can't stay in Kilbury. It's best for us to move on and go someplace without the memories. It does make a lot of sense to me."

"I suppose your right… but it hurts."

"Yeah, it hurts. It's almost like getting hit in the stomach with a baseball bat. When my mom…"

The kitchen door swung open and his father shouted, "Hey! Look what I found!"

Carrying a small, clear pitcher of what looked like cherry drink mix, he tried to set down three plastic glasses, all at the same time. Two slipped from his arm and bounced off the tabletop before heading for the floor. Bessie snatched them out of the air and rolled her eyes as she set them next to the glass he had saved.

"So… what was that about your mom?" Harold Sr. asked.

"Oh, nothing. Bessie and I were just talking."

"Well… okay. So, Bessie, pack several changes of clothes, socks, and some underwear. I see you already have your Nuu-Techs on, so you're all set for shoes. We will scavenge a winter coat and gloves for you when we get closer to the season. No sense in loading yourself down with heavy gear. I'll carry everything else. Just bring your knives, uh…swords! And any other weapons you might want."

"That's all I need," she said. "I don't need a big gun like that cannon you're carrying."

Harold Sr. squinted at her and said, "Crap! Now there's going to be two of you."

Bessie sneered, and Harry winked as he threw an arm over her shoulders, saying, "Birds of a feather."

"Shut up," his father said, leering.

Bessie drained her drink and standing up, said, "Shall we get to work?"

"Good. Bessie, are there shovels in your shed?"

"Yeah, a long handled one, and a short spade that dad had just pillaged from the hardware store." Her words trailed off as she was forced to confront memories of a better time. "Ummm… there's a pickaxe out there too," she added quickly.

"Okay, pull that and the shovels out, and we'll get started digging. Bessie, you pick the place. Harry, use the pickaxe, and she can shovel along behind you. I'll be out soon enough to help you finish up—I've got to go back upstairs." He then locked eyes with Harry, confirming that he still had to wrap up Jonny and bring him down.

Harry drank up and then rose to his feet, glaring at his father who was trying to hurry him along by nodding toward the kitchen. Bessie ushered him through the door just to get him away from his father.

It was dark in there, and Harry ran into the garbage can, knocking it over. Bessie laughed.

"Clumsy."

"I am not, it's freaking dark in here and you're pulling me, so… shut up."

"You, shut up," she said and giggled. Harry recognized the nervous mirth and felt glad. It was one of a few things that would help her get through the burial process.

"Do you have another lantern for this room?"

"Yeah, they are on that top shelf above the camp stove, over there," she said, pointing. "But we'll worry about that later."

"Yeah, or you better have some night vision goggles stashed away somewhere."

"Well… actually, we do. Stole them out of an Army truck last month—just before someone stole the truck. The problem is, they are still attached to the helmet and I haven't figured out how to take them off. But I do know how to turn them on. It's just, I have to wear the helmet if I want to use them."

"I bet you look cute."

"I look cute all the time," she said, and in the dim light, Harry could just discern her sticking out her tongue and crossing her eyes at him.

They moved into the mudroom and unbarred the inside door. Pulling it open, they did the same with the heavy shutter on the outside. Standing quietly in the doorway, they scanned the backyard.

The black, six-foot high chain link fence was still intact. Several of the poles were bent slightly inward, a sign bigger monsters had come to visit.

Harry said, "What do you say? Should we dig in the center of the yard?" Stepping out onto the grey paving stones of the patio, he scanned the area again.

"That's fine with me, good a place as any."

"I was just thinking, if we went too far out, we might not make it back inside if we were attacked."

"Let them come," she growled. Then patting his butt, she moved around him and walked toward the shed. He followed, constantly scanning, staring hard into the other yards and the woods beyond.

Looking west through the trees, he saw why the sun had disappeared so soon. A cloudbank was forming and there were thunderheads in the distance with lightning spider-webbing their tops.

"Looks like rain," Bessie said as she pulled the shed door open. Handing him the pickaxe, she grabbed the shovels and they walked through the almost knee-high grass to the center of the backyard. Harry saw his father standing on the patio, vigilant, shotgun at the ready. He too was studying the weather in the distance with a worried look on his face.

"Right here," Bessie said, stopping at the center of a large brown circle where the grass had given up trying to grow. Harry recalled the trampoline that had once stood there and the first time he, Bessie, and Bobbie, had jumped on it together.

*What is it about burying people where play equipment used to stand?*

Harold Sr. disrupted Harry's reflection by shouting, "That's a good place, just dig inside that circle." Then walking over, he added, "That should be big enough, and remember, only three feet down, no sense wearing yourself out."

Righting a wooden lawn chair, he dragged it close, and lay the shotgun across the arms. Taking the long-handled shovel, he motioned for Harry to get to work with the pickaxe. When he had broken enough ground, his father, and Bessie, began to shovel.

They worked steadily with no one taking a break. Harold Sr. constantly checked to see if the rim of the hole had reached hip height. Harry worked feverishly with the pickaxe where the soil was tough, making it easier for the shovels.

"Good workout, huh?" he said. The other two just grunted in agreement as they labored.

When they finished, Harry and his father returned to the house to bring out the dead. Bessie moved away to a neglected flower bed to focus on other things. Getting down on her knees, she began to make her selection of blooms, trying not to look back.

They placed Jonny and Joanie on the outside with Bobbie in the center. Double checking to make sure everyone was covered with sheets; they went to work tossing in the soil and then patting it down with the shovel blades. Harry gave a low whistle and waved for Bessie to return.

Swatting away what must have been a hungry mosquito with one hand, she carried over a large twist of long-stemmed daisies in the other. Dropping them on the mound, she stood gazing, leaving Harry to wonder if she was actually seeing anything. A few minutes passed before she sat down in the chair, and moving the shotgun to her lap, her eyes returned to the grave.

Harry and his father took the tools to the shed and turning back they watched Bessie jump up as if she had a last-minute thought. Leaning the gun against the chair, she ran to a different flower bed; one full of garden charmers partially hidden by assorted weeds.

Bringing them back one at a time, she set a large, green, jovial looking concrete frog at the head of the grave. "That's for you, dad," she whispered.

"Other side, sweetie. That's your mom," Harold Sr. said, obviously trying to be as gentle as he possibly could about her error. She still scowled at him before moving the frog to the other side. The smallest went to her brother, and then a medium sized one for her mother. All three had their names painted on them. Harry looked back toward the flower bed to see that only one remained. There was no question as to whose name was on that one.

Bessie stepped back and looked at her companions before shrugging and smiling meekly, her face glistening with new tears. She left them then and walked back to the house without a word.

"Looks like rain, huh, son?"

"Yeah, going to have to batten down the hatches tonight."

"I'll take care of the shutters; you stay with Bessie. Maybe get some beds made up in the living room, hey?"

"Sure thing, pops. What did you do with the Cayhond, by the way?"

"Tossed it in the basement. There's about six feet of water down there, so we'll just let those little Sarlepian cannibals have at it. They'll eat anything."

"Doc Smith told me once that they'll clean a body down to the bone in less than ten minutes."

"Yep… he told me the same thing. Let's get going, I don't want to be standing around out here in the dark, yakking like it's still 2025."

They stepped off together, moving toward the house. Harold Sr. slipped out of the side gate to close the shutters. Harry went in the way they'd come out, barring the shutter and the door. On his way back through the house, he stopped for a minute to examine the door to the basement and the heavy writer's desk pushed up against it. Remembering his father needed a way back in, he unbarred the front entrance and waited.

When Harold Sr. slammed the first shutter, there came a thump on the floor in the living room. Harry supposed it must have been Bessie jumping up from the wingback. She suddenly appeared in the large open doorway, eyes wide, swords at the ready.

"What's going on?" she said.

"Dad's just closing the shutters for the night. Why?"

Sheathing her swords, she wiped the wetness from her cheeks.

"Scared the crap out of me, that's why!"

"Don't worry, my dear, I'm here to protect you," he said with bravado, and whipping out his swords, he took a fighting stance, letting go with a Bruce Lee-like, "Whaaa!"

She laughed and played along, saying, "Oh Harry, you're my hero." Clasping her hands to her chest, she tilted her head and fluttered her eyelashes at him. Her demeanor had changed rapidly and then changed again when her eyes fell on his swords.

"Hey! Those aren't your swords."

"Ummm… no, they're not."

"Where'd you get them?"

"Uh… they were a gift?"

"From whom?"

"Long story, I'll tell you later," he said as his father stepped in.

"Time to lock up. Bring down a mattress, will you? I'll get this door and then go and grab mine."

Bessie ignored Harold Sr. and giving Harry her full attention, said, "Don't forget, you promised."

"Forget what?" Harold Sr. asked, looking back and forth between them.

"Oh, nothing," Harry drawled out.

As soon as his swords were back in his rig, Bessy threw her arms around him and looked up into his face with mock admiration. His father huffed and turned his attention to barring the entrance.

Harry tilted his face up to the ceiling with exaggerated confidence and said, "That's right, I'm your man."

"Come help me, my man. I want to drag my mattress down."

"That heavy, ol' thing?"

"Oh, it is not. Its only foam. What are you, some kind of a weakling?"

"Ugg… NO! Me, Harry… me big strong man. You BB… my woman."

"You, Harry… get your butt upstairs and help your woman make nice bed, or she beat you raw!"

"Well, you must be feeling better, huh?" Harold Sr. said.

"Ummm… well, yeah, actually. I'm not feeling so hopeless now that you guys are here and… I'm kind of all cried out for the moment. But it's not over, I'm just trying to…"

"It's okay, we understand," Harry said glancing at his father who nodded in agreement.

Bessie led Harry up the stairs, and they pulled her mattress off the frame and dragged it together down the hall.

"Watch the goo, huh, Harry? I don't want to track that all over the house and be smelling it all night."

"What? You don't like the smell of Cayhond in the morning?"

"No, actually… I'd prefer your morning breath to the stink of that thing any day."

"Thanks, grateful to know."

"What's up?" Harold Sr. said, as he hurried past, checking windows on the second floor.

"Just making up my bed," Bessie said.

"Good idea. Harry, when I get back down, I'll get my bedroll, the sleeping bag, and my molly pack from the kitchen. Also, I think I'm going to have you start carrying your own equipment."

"Duh! Things getting kind of heavy for you, Atlas?"

"You know son, there's a place where the sun never shines. I'd like for you to find it, and then stick that there," he said, following it with a sinister laugh.

"Yes, sir, sergeant, sir."

"Here we go again," Bessie said. "Harry, just grab your end and… let's go."

He squalled like an alley cat and clawed in the direction of his father, hissing. Bessie struggled to keep the mattress upright as Harold Sr. playfully shook a fist at his son. Then turning, he brought a knee up and raucously broke wind. Looking back at Bessie, he said, "Oops! Sorry, couldn't help it, my son brings it out of me."

"Yeah, well, he deserved it," she said and giggled.

"What? I deserved it? Whose side are you on?"

"Oh, shut up mister caveman and help me."

"Who's the caveman?" Harry said, followed by, "Oh man, dad! That's rank! You're worse than that Cayhond."

Harold Sr. broke out in a laugh as he exited the hall into Bobby's room.

After bouncing the mattress down the stairs, they dropped it on the floor next to the wingback.

"You know that I probably won't use my sleeping bag tonight, right?" Harry said with a grin.

"Yeah, I figured that. You can always lay it on top of my mattress, though?"

"Yep, I suppose that would make it comfier."

"Your dad won't mind if we sleep together, right?"

"Naw, in fact, I think he's expecting it."

"But he mentioned your sleeping bag and…"

"Just a slip of the tongue, don't worry about it."

After removing their shoes, they lay down and lightly petted, gazing into each other's eyes. Harold Sr.'s heavy boots sounded on the stairs then moved away into the kitchen. Sliding forward on the mattress, Harry poked his head around the door frame. He watched a light spread across the crack at the bottom of the closed kitchen door. His father was lighting lanterns. Harry could now hear the hiss of a noisy Coleman. His father didn't like them; he preferred the old railroad lanterns with their kerosene or liquid paraffin. Harry presumed the noisy lamp would remain in the kitchen.

Years back, they had scrounged for both. Yet like so many other things that were in short supply, he knew there would soon come a time when they could no longer find liquid fuel or the gas canisters that had once been so plentiful. There were always candles.

Harold Sr. finally showed up in the living room, kicking the bedroll and sleeping bag across the floor in front of him as he progressed, his hands full with the bookbag, his MOLLE pack, and a lantern. He dropped Harry's gear beside Bessie's mattress, then continued kicking his roll across the floor until he got it to where he wanted it. Setting the lantern next to the wall on his right, he set up his bed along the baseboard at the back.

"Now that I think about it, Harry, you probably won't need yours tonight."

"That's right, we're going to share," Bessie said. Harry rose, grabbed his sleeping bag and flung it across the room toward his father.

"Here, take this."

"I will. I'll lay it on top of mine for a little more comfort. I have to admit, this wooden floor is kind of hard. If I was outside, I'd pile up some grass or moss…"

"If you were outside, you wouldn't have to worry about it for very long because you'd be cozy inside the stomach of some Thulu."

"Why I had to raise such a smart aleck kid, I'll never know."

His father lay down on his bed with his back against the wall and pulled the lantern closer. Digging a map from a pocket in his pack, he ignored the other two and began tracing their route with an index finger.

Bessie sat up and removed the belt that held her swords. Setting them close at hand, she lay back down on the outside edge of the bed, her feet now toward the doorway. She patted the mattress behind her to get Harry's attention. When he looked her way, she grinned and raised her eyebrows several times.

"In a minute, huh? I want to sharpen my swords."

Taking a honing stone from a side pocket on his bag, he moved to the chair. Pulling a single sword from its sheath, he ran a finger lightly over its edge and then went to work. Bessie groaned and lay back, sticking her tongue out at him in rejection.

"That's going to take forever, and the noise really sets my teeth on edge. You couldn't save that for later? Maybe go into the kitchen?"

Harry just grinned at her and continued.

The wind was picking up outside and as with most stormy nights, they wouldn't sleep too well. The noise would be continuous, making it hard to distinguish between that and some heinous beast trying to breach the house.

Harry rotated the chair to face Bessie. That way he could have his eyes on both her and his father. Harold Sr. was scrutinizing the map with some intensity, a tiny LED flashlight in his lips as he studied. Harold

Sr. turned his map over and over again, as if trying to determine the safest route for them to take in the morning. In the lantern light, his gold, wire-rimmed reading glasses gleamed as they hung precariously on the end of his nose; his eyes darting back and forth.

Bringing his attention back to Bessie, Harry found her staring at him. She smiled, her teeth gleaming in the light. He could tell she wanted attention, but he wanted to finish with his swords. He smiled in a subdued manner and went back to running the stone up and down his blade. The next thing he knew, she was there, standing beside the chair

"May I sit in your lap?" she asked, her hand on his shoulder.

She didn't wait for an answer. Moving to sit down, she forced Harry to swing his sword out of her way to avoid injury. Coming in backwards she plopped down and swung her legs out over the arm of the chair. Leaning back against the inside of his right shoulder and the chair's other arm, she snuggled in.

"Wow! You weigh a ton."

"Oh! Thanks. I'll remember you said that."

"Just kidding. You're as light as a feather, my love."

Harold Sr. chuckled and they both grew quiet, remembering that they had an audience. After slipping the sword back into its sheath, he dropped the whetstone onto his bookbag with a soft plop.

The first drops of rain started to patter on the shutters as flashes of lighting flickered through the cracks. The thunder rolled, and Harry could feel the vibration through the chair. For some reason, it seemed that thunder was scarier than it used to be, louder and more powerful. Even though it was really the lightening doing all the work, its abrupt bark and ensuing snarl was much more terrifying. As the deep rumble faded into the distance, he heard Bessie softly say, "I'm the reason he's dead."

"What?" Harry said.

"Who's that, sweetie?" Harold Sr. asked, his voice echoing through the room.

"It's my fault that the monster… that… that Cayhond, got into the house."

"No, BB, it's not."

She cut him off, saying, "Yes, it is! Just let me talk, okay? I need to say this. I need to share it, so… so it's not just mine, anymore."

"Go on, Bessie," Harold Sr. said with a sympathetic but uncommon tone.

"Sorry, yeah, go on, tell us the whole thing," Harry said, humbly, as he wrapped his arms around her.

"It was around a week ago, late on Friday. My mother was sitting in that chair right over there," Bessie said, pointing to a big overstuffed Club Chair that now sat facing the far wall, the large white towel that was draped over its back, now hanging askew.

"She had Bobbie on her lap trying to stop his coughing, but she was just as sick as he was. He was so weak; he could hardly lift his head. I knew he was dying. What I didn't know was how close my mom was, herself. My dad and I were working together, trying to help them. He was feeling bad for being immune, and I kept telling him that it wasn't his fault. I tried to cheer him up by telling him that he wasn't the only one. It didn't help much, and we started to get on each other's nerves. I was kneeling on the floor in front of the chair, keeping an eye on them, when Bobbie, in this weak little voice, asked for my 'Cheer Bear'. You know those little bear characters that you can hang on your car mirror? You had to buy a kid's meal at the Brawny Burger to get one."

Bessie patted her chest as if to locate the toy inside her shirt pocket. Harry figured she must have forgotten that it was still upstairs in the ruined flannel she had abandoned in the bathroom. "Hmmm…" she said and then continued with her story. "Bobby didn't seem to like his own bear as much as he did mine. But I didn't want to give it up. That was before he got sick. I felt so stupid… so selfish. Do you know what I mean?"

Harry nodded, lightly patting the back of her hand. She took a deep, stuttering breath and continued. "I got a bad feeling when he asked the last time. It was like it took all of the energy he had left. I just came unglued. Without thinking, I got up, unbarred the doors, and without closing them behind me, I ran out to my car. My dad had tried to stop me, but I wouldn't listen. I kept pulling out of his grip every time he grabbed me. The sun was already down, and it was dark inside my car. I was trying to unhook the toy from the mirror, and I couldn't quite get it. My dad was standing on the porch yelling at me, and that's when the Cayhond showed up. I think it came because of all the noise we were making."

Bessie stopped, sighed heavily, and then took another deep breath. Tipping her head back, Harry saw the glow of the lantern reflected in her tear-filled eyes. She gave him a slight smile of embarrassment and then turning her attention to the zipper on her hoodie, she began running the slider up and down in short strokes.

"It came for me first. I was able to get the car door shut with me inside. It attacked it for a while, butting the metal with that shield thing on its head. It must have got tired of that, so it jumped on the trunk lid and started bashing my windshield. Then it just worked its way around the car, breaking the side windows and then the one at the back. I was so busy watching it, waiting for a chance to get out and run, that I didn't see my dad come out on the porch with that silly Colt Python of his. The damn pistol kicked so hard he couldn't aim. He wasn't a very good shot anyway, and when I first heard it go off, I kept yelling for him to just get back inside and shut the door. He got off all six rounds without even coming close to hitting the monster. That's when the Cayhond turned and went after him. Those things are so freaking fast. He couldn't get the door shut in time. I got out of the car and went after them. It chased him upstairs and he was already starting to scream when I came in the door. My mom was trying to scream too, but all she could do was make this croaking noise. I'm never going to forget that sound—never. I grabbed my swords from the umbrella stand by the door and ran upstairs, kicking his gun out of my way as I went. I was too late. He was on his stomach, holding his throat, the blood... the blood pouring out between his fingers. I saw his back was all torn up, but he was still trying to talk to me."

A sob broke from Bessie's lips and she fought to keep from breaking down completely. A few seconds of silence passed before she said, "That bastard was in their room, just strolling around, poking its nose into stuff like it was there for a visit. I wanted to go in but my dad was in the way, and it was hard to get into position without stepping on him. When it saw me standing there, it made that weird, little, shrieking growl that they make? You know? Then it jumped at me. My dad rolled over, screaming like he was in terrible pain, and brought his knee up. The Cayhond bounced off and fell on its side. It got stuck between my dad and the door frame. I gutted it before it even knew what was happening. I was pretty lucky. I'm sure if I hadn't had that shot, I may have gotten hurt a lot worse than just a glass cut from my car. It tried to jump on me, its guts hanging out. I knew right then I had it where I wanted it. So, I hit it right in the end of its snout with a blade. I was so surprised when I saw it split all the way back to its eyes. The thing actually looked shocked. I had trouble getting the sword loose and the bastard was wriggling around, making it even harder. So, I chopped away at its shield thing with my other blade and I finally broke the first one loose. The thing just fell on my dad and it was kind of weird how he wrapped his arms around it like he was hugging it. I think he was trying to keep it from coming after me. It tried to bite his head, but its mouth wasn't working so great. Then, they both just stopped moving, and I knew… I knew, they were dead."

She started to weep openly as she talked, and Harry had a hard time understanding her. Resting his cheek on the top of her head, the tears he had fought so hard to keep in check, began their slow trek down his face and into her hair.

Bessie was able to find some composure and finished her story with, "I pushed the Cayhond off my dad and then rolled him over so I wouldn't have to look at his face. I grabbed the sheets off their bed, so I could cover him up, and the monster too. I was yelling at my mom as I came down the stairs, but she didn't answer. I walked in and saw right off that Bobbie wasn't breathing. I yelled at my mom, but even though her eyes were open… she wasn't either. I think she may have had a seizure or something. They were all dead, all three of them. All in less than an hour. My whole family—gone—and there was nothing I could do about it."

She turned her face into Harry's chest and heavy sobs racked her body. All he could do was hold her tight as she clutched at his shirt. The noise she made was matched by the howling wind outside. Harry put his face in her hair and everything that had built up inside him for so long, just came pouring out.

Then his father was there, standing behind the chair. Leaning down, he wrapped his arms around them both, laying the side of his head on the top of Harry's. Even in his grief, Harry was surprised. It was the first time since his fifth year of life that his father had voluntarily embraced him, and the minutes seemed to stretch into an eternity as Mother Nature raged on outside.

# CHAPTER 4

## Let The Other Heroes Boast Their Scars

When they finally got to bed, they slept only fitfully, the storm shaking the house to no end. Noises came up from the basement, light hissing squeaks that echoed below as the Sarleps became active in their breeding frenzy.

One time there was a heavy thump on the underside of the floor that brought Harry fully awake. He lay with eyes cracked; his ears pricked. Bessie stirred, but never woke.

His father got up to stand in the middle of the room, shotgun in hand, just listening. He then left them to go check windows and doors. When he finally returned to his bed, Harry relaxed and fell back into a nightmare-filled sleep. He lay with his arm over Bessie, who squirmed and squealed in her dreams, sometimes weeping, one time giggling.

Then he dreamed of his mother. They were in the backyard and he must have been a toddler because he was in the sandbox. There were toy trucks in his hands, and Marji sat close by in an adirondack style chair, reading a book. He could see the title from where he sat, '*How To Love Your Little Monster Slayer*'. Marji was wearing a white dress with little red flowers all over it and a wide brown belt at her waist. Her reddish hair was done up like she had a party to go to. Putting the book down, she leaned forward and smiling at him with perfect teeth, she said, *"Laughing and crying serve the same purpose, my little warrior. Never be afraid to do either."*

She gave him a thoughtful smile, looking like some lady in an advertisement that was trying to sell him something.

When he woke up, it was quiet, and he could see the dim light of dawn stealing through the shutter cracks. The storm had passed and he felt the relief that came with knowing, it wasn't going to be one of those three-day long events that they were so used to.

Bessie still slept, emitting a light snore. Tipping his head back, Harry saw his father was gone and so was the sleeping pallet. There was a rummaging noise from the kitchen and a sweet molasses smell soon found his nose. Grabbing his sword rig, he checked the blades to be sure they would come easy into his hands and then slid off the foot of the mattress.

Once on his feet, he watched Bessie sleep as he pulled on his rig and cinched it to a comfortable tightness. A warm sensation filled his chest as he thought about how much he loved her, and how different that love was from what he had for his mother and father. She was the first person to have ever made him feel that way. Also, she was the one person in his life who had helped him understand friendship. Then they became intimate, and the love intensified.

Forcing on his boots without untying them, he walked to the kitchen. Coming through the door, he found his father at the camp stove.

"Good morning, son. Want to eat? I found a can of pork & beans and some of those dried bread sticks. Oh! And there's also at least a couple pounds of that granola stuff from yesterday. But I'm kind of hoping to take that with us."

Harry mumbled, "Morning," and clearing off the booth in the breakfast nook, he sat down to watch his father cook. Bessie soon burst in and stood with one hand holding the door open, the other on the jamb, her eyes wide with fear.

"Oh! There you are. I was so afraid. I thought I had only dreamed you were here. Then I woke up and you weren't!"

"Sorry," Harry said. "You were sleeping so peacefully, I didn't want to disturb you."

"Morning, sweetie, want to eat?" Harold Sr. asked.

She sighed and said, "Yeah, smells great—for once."

Moving to the bench, she slid in beside Harry and leaned her head on his shoulder. Now came the smell of coffee as it bubbled inside an old, blue enameled pot.

"Want coffee? We've got coffee."

"No, thanks. I'd rather have a Coke," Harry said.

His father came to them and set a can of Coke down on the table. "Knew you were going to say that. Lucky for you, there was a six pack under the sink. It's warm, but caffeine is caffeine. That should get you started. Bessie, want a Coke?"

"Sure," she said groggily. "I had some pretty bad dreams last night. How about you?"

"Oh yeah, had one about my mom, but… I really don't want to talk about it."

"I had a dream, too," Harold Sr. said. "It was about how you two finished your breakfast so we could get our asses on the road."

Pulling another can of Coke from the clear, plastic container, he set it on the table. Then putting the tin of breadsticks in front of them, he returned to the stove and brought back the pork & beans along with the coffee.

They ate their beans and bread in silence with Harold Sr. sitting across the table from them, grinning like he had a secret. Harry suspected it had something to do with the beans and what might come after. Wanting to avoid any flatulence induced banter, he tried to head his father off at the pass, by saying, "I'd like to get in some practice this morning."

Harold Sr.'s grin faded. "There's no time. The sun is already up and we need to get going. Save it for tonight."

"I went without last night. I would really like to stay in shape, you know?"

Bessie leaned into Harry and rested a hand on his arm. "Don't worry, Harry. You'll be okay for one more day. Maybe you and I can spar tonight? What do you say?"

"He has no say. I'm the one who says. And I am saying—save the workout for later."

Harold Sr. looked hard at the both of them, his eyes glittering coldly, obviously anticipating more defiance. Harry looked at Bessie and trying to convey indifference, raised his eyebrows and nodded toward his father as if to say, 'Can you believe this guy?' Then looking back to Harold Sr., he said flatly, "Fine, later then."

"Okay, we'll save it," Bessie said, now glaring at his father.

"Let me out, will you?" Harry said.

"Oh, sure," she said and stood. "I was going to go pack my bag now, anyway. So… you want to come?"

Harry pushed past her, and said, "No, I've got to go get mine ready. I'll meet you in the living room." Bessie followed, mumbling, "Okay," her dismay apparent.

Harry held the door for her and after she had passed through into the entry hall, he caught his father's attention and slowly mouthed, "Prick." His father gave him a wicked grin, one that said, 'I don't give a damn what you think'. Harry let the door close slowly and walked away shaking his head.

Within half an hour they met in the living room, bookbags prepped and ready to go. Harry's father unbarred the door and did the usual checking before stepping out. As the last one to leave, Bessie pulled the door shut and walked away as if the whole process was painful. She closed the little gate in the picket fence like she was closing a chapter on her life, and then she just stood there, looking at the house.

Harry could see a haunting kind of sadness in her face. He and his father knew better not to say anything. She was taking that long, last look before letting go of a place that would remain in her heart, forever.

Standing beside his father, Harry waited for the moment to pass. When it went on too long, he turned his gaze to the storm that was now well out over the ocean to the east.

Its multicolored thunderheads rose from a thick layer of stratus. Lightning snaked through the mountainous bluffs of vapor, occasionally reaching down to strike the Atlantic. He could just make out twin waterspouts circling each other in a dance, contrasting white against the green of the horizon. Swirling tails of new funnels showed themselves on occasion, dropping only part way down before retracting as if embarrassed because they didn't possess the power of the twin sisters spinning below them. The smell of the rain rode to Harry on a west bound breeze and filled his nose.

*Looks like a bad day to be out at sea!*

Bessie soon joined them, saying, "I can't remember ever not living here." Dropping her face down with a sniff, she moved past them on her way to the street that would take them out of the neighborhood.

When they caught up, Harold Sr. said, "We'll head out toward the one-a, but we'll walk the beach instead of the highway. We'll go as far north as Portsmouth today. Then we'll have to move farther inland to avoid passing through the city. Maybe we'll stop at Starks Point for the night. That's about twenty miles. I believe, with the shape we are all in, right now, we can make that in one day."

"Do you think walking the beach will be safe? I mean with the Thulu now coming out in the daylight? They might just be waiting for some tasty morsels like Bessie and I to come along."

"Bessie, and you?"

"Yeah? Why would they want to eat anything as crusty as an ol' Marine Corps sergeant?"

"No, I meant, why would they want to eat you? I can see somebody as sweet as your girl, but hell, Harry, you're as bitter as an old lemon. I can just imagine the look on the Thulu's face. I think there would be a whole lot of puckering going on there."

"Ah, hell dad, there is just no way you could tell through all those tentacles."

They both saw a smile come to Bessie's lips and they knew that their usual bantering had done its trick. Harry gave his father a light shove, and the old guy pretended to lose his balance. Righting himself, he dashed away a few steps and squeaked out the phrase that Harry so loved to use, "Oh, Harry, you're such a brute," then picking up his pace, he moved to take up the lead.

They ambled along in a northeasterly direction toward the ocean, making good progress with only a few car wrecks to work their way around. Crossing the 1A, well north of Salisbury, they moved down to the beach. Turning north toward New Hampshire, they broke into an energetic walk on the hard-packed sand, staying as far away as they could from the surf. This would allow them ample time to run or prepare for battle. Thulu were big and slow coming out of the water, especially if they hadn't been on land for a while. They were more effective killers when submerged, which is why boating was always a bad idea.

The three monster slayers would come across the infrequent human carcass lying on the sand, or the occasional pile of bones left behind by whatever stalked the beaches at night. The seabirds also did their share of picking bodies clean. They continually soared through the air, circling, the sky filled with their calls. Harry hoped that the taste of human flesh wouldn't evolve them from scavengers into predators. Mankind didn't need any more to worry about. Having to keep your eye on the sky all the time, as well as on the ground, would be a pain.

They soon came across a white, rusty sign, with black letters, its green, metal post bent inland at the base. It declared they had reached the border of New Hampshire and were welcome to stay and maybe even settle there. Harry chuckled at the irony.

The sun had now worked its way high into the sky. Harold Sr. had exchanged his eight-point cap for his boonie. Harry realized he had left his behind. His father said nothing. Bessie had wrapped a large, red and white paisley bandana over her head and tied it behind, under her ponytail. Harry supposed if he needed to, he could make a 'do-rag', or they could loot any one of the convenience stores up on the 1A for a baseball cap. But he figured unless his father bitched, he would hold out as long as he could.

About a mile up from the border, on the Seabrook Beach, they saw someone in the distance. A dark figure seemed to be moving in the same direction that they were and in the company of what looked like the biggest dog Harry had ever seen. It wasn't a common sight to see people with pets. The dog population had suffered, and all cats appeared to have gone feral. They were both susceptible to the Bug.

Dogs didn't know how to back down from a monster fight until they got hurt and then it was too late. They were good at detecting the beasts, though. A dog could pick up on a monster long before they showed their ugly face. So, dogs were a serious benefit—if you could keep them alive.

Robby Robson, who had been the Lumsdale's thirty-something bachelor neighbor to the south, had a bull terrier named Alertious Guyus Annoyus, or, Guy for short. He would bark and squeal hysterically if a monster came within a mile of him and his 'Alpha'. They both, along with a few others, had been members of the Morel Street Marauders back in the beginning when monster patrol was a group event. But Guy and Robby had been caught out after dark one night and died together at the Bonanza Mart, five blocks down on the corner of Morel and Pendrake. It was rumored; Robby got a hankering for some beer and took the risk of leaving his house, quite inebriated, after finishing off his last twelve pack. He and Guy had holed up in the store's toilet, putting a good, solid, metal door between them and the horde of Capuchipines that happened upon them. It was suspected the two had been doing okay at keeping the little fiends out, but then Robby had to go and open the door a little too soon.

Harold Sr. had formed that gang of monster hunters back in 2033. When Robby didn't show up for muster one evening, the Marauders went searching. It was the twelve pack of 'Daily's Finest Lager' that had obviously been dropped out front on the sidewalk that caught their attention and clued them in. They had found at least a dozen of the monkey sized monsters dead in the toilet with Robby and his faithful companion. The duo had taken out a few of the little fiends before succumbing to their quill borne toxin. Robby had been a gunslinger like his father and carried an automatic twelve gauge like most of the Marauders. Both it, and the MAC-10 he carried as backup, were devoid of ammunition.

Capuchipines (Cercophystrix) had porcupine like quills that covered their hips and tails. They could fling the deadly darts with a scattergun like effect. Many Thulu had been found, in different states of decomposition, blanketed with the quills. So, human beings really didn't stand much of a chance.

The rest of the little creature's body was covered in dime sized scales, and the males possessed a little red dewlap that would swell up, signaling attack. Their back feet and little front paws had talons that resembled heavy fishhooks. So, if they got on you, you couldn't get them off without ripping your own flesh. Their face was more owl-like than amphibian, they sported a short, square muzzle with a wide, hooked beak instead of a nose, and their mouths were full of piranha-like teeth.

Doc Smith, the only other member of the Marauders to carry a sword (military saber), also sported two .410 Taurus pistols worn like a wild west gunfighter. He was first to laughingly refer to the Cercophystrix as 'Capuchipines'. It always got a hell of a laugh when someone used it. The nickname became a 'thing' within the troop because it was much easier to say than Cercophystrix. Harry sometimes wondered if Robby had died cursing Doc's name.

Harold Sr. shouted at the person with the dog, causing Harry to startle. The adrenaline flowed in. The person stopped for a minute to scrutinize the three of them and then hurried away into a row of cottages that lined the seashore. The dog had barked, but instead of coming after them, it followed the person in an obedient manner.

When they got to where the stranger had stood, they found the tracks of lugged combat boots and large paw prints tattling on the direction their makers had gone.

"What do you think, Harry? Should we follow… maybe make a new friend?"

"You're asking me? Hell, dad, I wish you'd make up your mind."

"What if they aren't friendly?" Bessie said, looking like she couldn't walk another mile. "That was a pretty big animal, probably an Irish Wolfhound… or something."

Harold Sr. looked Bessie up and down and said, "I think we need a break, anyway, maybe move up into some shade and rehydrate?"

"Alright, sounds like a plan," Harry said. "Should probably be on guard, though, just in case they don't want to be friends."

Looking over the cottages closest to them, he noticed that many had a considerable amount of damage. Broken windows, front doors bashed in, some minus the whole front wall with their roofs and porches sagging. Thulu damage, he figured. Probably not a good place to spend the night.

Harold Sr. turned and followed the footprints, his shotgun at the ready. The other two followed close behind, preparing for an ambush. Harry felt like someone had their eyes on them, but glancing in windows and open doors, he didn't see a soul.

They moved up between the buildings, passing small boats stacked on blocks and newer jet skis still chained and padlocked to thick metal posts. Arriving at a concrete parking lot sitting at the front of a place called 'Grunt's Groceries', they stopped and studied the building.

It was a small, old-fashioned grocer like you would find in the older parts of the bigger cities. It stood alone, surrounded by sandy flats and patches of long grass, a short hedge bordering its west side. They passed a waist high stack of green milk crates about seventy-five yards off to their right. A single crow perched on top of one, cawed at them. The configuration of the containers reminded Harry of one of the many forts he had built as a kid. He suspected children had been living in the cottages back before the Bug showed up.

The store had a narrow access road leading in from the 1A. There was a lone gas pump at the east side of the lot, and parked next to that, a tanker truck on flattened tires.

"Harry, go check that truck. I'm going to go and see if I can pick up on those tracks again."

"Gotcha, pops! Be careful, huh? I saw a long object in their hand. Could have just been a walking stick, but... maybe not?"

"No problem there, sonny. I've got this."

Sliding the bolt on the Mossberg half way back, he exposed the red plastic cartridge for just a second, confirming he was locked & loaded. Then clicking off the safety, he walked cautiously across the lot.

Harry and Bessie moved to the truck and knocking up and down the sides of the tank, Harry was able to determine that it was about half full of what the placards said was premium gasoline. Moving to the cab, he could smell it long before he saw it. Stepping up on the running board, Harry glanced in to see a mummified corpse, still dressed in her Shelbi-Con Gas Company uniform.

She sat upright in the seat as if she had been preparing to drive away. Her hands were in her lap beneath a pile of flowers that still looked fresh. Her hair, almost black in color, had been going grey. That's when he noticed the matted blood, along with what he figured to be the exit wound of a large caliber weapon at her temple.

*Suicide or robbery?*

Somebody around there must know her story. There was a good chance it was the one who had placed the flowers in her lap. Perhaps, the person they had seen on the beach.

"What do you see, Harry?" Bessie asked.

Jumping down, he ignored her and walked around the old GMC. Bessie huffed at his indifference, but remained close on his heels.

"Well, are you going to answer me or am I going to have to go back and look for myself?"

"Just a dead person, no sense in looking. Unless you want to have nightmares, of course?"

"No, don't need any more of those. How'd they die, could you tell?"

"Well, she has a bullet hole in the side of her head."

"It's a woman? Anything else? Like…ummm… signs of rape?"

"Let's not worry about it, huh?"

"So, she was…"

"BB! Listen, don't worry about it. It's hard to tell what happened. Whatever it was… it happened a long time ago."

Bessie didn't ask anymore, but her silence said she wasn't happy. She followed him around the truck as he ran a finger along the plow-like blade attached to the front. It was seriously dented, and multicolored streaks of paint covered its surface. It was an odd thing and set Harry to pondering.

*She had been pushing car wrecks out of her way! Risky business when you have a load of gasoline on board.*

Harry moved around to the other side, studying the truck. Stopping, he stuck a finger in one of the many bullet holes he found in the engine compartment and passenger door. He could just imagine what the motor looked like under that hood. In all probability, they should have come across a twisted hunk of blackened steel and the foundation of a burnt-out store.

"What do…?" was all Bessie got out before a flock of crows began a raucous clamor behind them. They both turned to see the birds rise up from that stack of green crates. The crows boisterous cawing chilled Harry, and he and Bessie watched them circle several times before flying east toward the ocean.

"As I was going to say, what do you suppose happened here. And what do you suppose that is?"

"What?" he said, still caught up in his thoughts. Turning his gaze to her, he saw she was pointing toward their feet. Following her finger, he saw the grey of the concrete was tinted a rusty red among pieces of a broken beer bottle. The large stain narrowed to a line that led out across the sand toward the crates. There was no question, it was blood. Focusing on the boxes, Harry could just make out what appeared to be a skeleton like hand resting on a short rusty rod protruding up from the inside. He walked toward it and feeling his bookbag move, he knew Bessie had latched on and was now in tow.

Arriving at the crates, he saw there was a narrow opening on the left allowing access to the interior. Peeking over the top, he saw a body. It had once been a large man who now lay propped up at the back, an arrow sticking out of his right eye socket. Harry could see the broadhead point had exited the back of the skull and was now as rusty as the rifle barrel that the dead guy's hand still held. The birds had picked everything clean that wasn't covered by clothing, and that included a foot, minus a boot.

"O-M-G! That must have hurt!" Bessie said and gagged.

"Yeah, there was probably about two seconds worth of, W-T-F, before he signed off."

"Are you making fun of me?" she huffed, slapping at his shoulder in a playful manner.

"Well? O-M-G? How ancient is that?" Before she could reply, he added, "You don't have to answer, it was purely rhetorical." Turning away, he chuckled and stepped inside the square of crates for a closer look.

Bessie gave him a slight shove, this time saying, "Big meany! There's a dead guy lying right there and you want to be funny?"

"Not like I haven't seen 'em before, you know? Okay, could we just focus, please? I'm trying to figure out what happened here."

"Fine," she said, and huffed a second time.

"So… he had an old bolt action deer rifle, probably a Winchester by the looks of it. There are spent casings everywhere that look like thirty-aught-six. No doubt he's the one who shot up the truck—and that woman."

"You know, Harry, I don't care what size his bullets were. But now that you've figured it out, Sherlock, can we go? I'm about ready to puke from the smell."

"Certainly, my dear Watson. Let's go find my dad."

"Watson?" she mumbled, throwing him a sneer. Grabbing a shoulder strap on his bag, she towed him out of the stack of crates.

Moving back toward the truck, he noticed something just behind the flat, front tire. Pulling out of Bessie's grip, he walked over and got down on his knees to peer under. It was the guy's other boot. Harry reached in to pull it out and his eyes caught movement.

His father was peeking around the corner of the building. Their eyes met, and the old guy pointed up toward the roof. Getting to his feet, Harry flattened himself against the truck's fender. Pulling Bessie to him, he forced her to do the same before peeking over the top of the snow blade.

"What's going on?" she said with a hint of irritation.

"My dad was pointing up to the roof. I think someone's up there."

"Where's your dad? I don't see him."

"He's hiding behind the building. Hold on a sec," Harry said, and poking his head out again, he scanned the roof line.

"It's probably the one with the bow and arrows, right?" Bessie said, and ducking down a little more, she checked to make sure no part of her body was exposed.

Harry saw nothing but a large water tank sticking up past the short wall that formed a façade at the eaves. Harold Sr. suddenly reappeared, giving a short whistle to get their attention. Then waving them over, he disappeared a second time. "Let's go," Harry said, and they dashed across the corner of the lot before sliding in beside his father whose back was pressed to the clapboards of the old building.

"They're on the roof," he whispered, pointing toward some marks in the sand. "They must have had a ladder and pulled it up after."

Bessie started to move away toward the back entrance. Harry put his hand on her shoulder to stop her, but she slapped it away and continued.

"Back off," she whispered sternly, and sidling over, she moved along the wall to the heavy, metal door. She rotated the lever for the latch, triggering a round of explosive barking from within. They all startled and jumped in unison. Bessie looked back, shrugged, and gave them her 'Oops!' face.

"So… they must've put the dog inside, huh? Maybe…"

She was interrupted by a loud scraping noise from above, and six sets of eyes strayed up to the soffit.

"Okay, follow me," Harold Sr. said, and hugging the wall under the protection of the overhang, they moved around to the front porch. They stopped short of the first big window, and Harold Sr. peeked around the frame. There came another round of barking, this time with a clatter like the dog was clawing plywood.

Harry moved around his father for a closer look and saw that the windows had been covered on the inside with graying plywood. A square peephole about the size of a small tissue box had been cut into the panel. The ugliest dog in the world now glared at him through the glass, its large teeth bared in a terrifying snarl.

"Got to be the ugliest dog I've ever seen," he said, staring at the potentially harmful fangs.

"Well, if he gets out, don't tell him, or he's liable to eat you first," Bessie said and giggled.

Harold Sr. eyed her and said, "You're in a pretty good mood, considering the situation."

"No, not really… I'm just nervous."

"Well, let's see if we can end this. You two stay here," Harold Sr. backed out into the parking lot with the shotgun at the ready and yelled, "You, on the roof! Show yourself!"

They watched a shadow rise from the shade cast by the building. Harry's father stopped almost immediately, and they heard the click of the shotgun's safety. This was followed by a woman's voice, saying, "Don't do it! I can get you just as fast as you can get me."

With that, Harry unsheathed his swords and moving out at an angle, he fell in line with his father who stood just a short distance away.

"Damn it, Harry! Did I call you out? No! Now she can use you against me."

"I'm not going to use anyone! If you'll just quit pointing that cannon at me and relax, I'll lower the bow."

Harold Sr. did as she asked, and she stuck to her word. Harry studied her with some disbelief. She looked like a character out of one of his comic books. Dressed all in black, she wore a midi shirt exposing a well-toned stomach, and beneath that, leggings with black combat boots.

A cowboy's duster hung over the entire ensemble, and in her hand, a compound bow. The arrow with its razor-sharp tip, remained nocked on the string. She wore a quiver on her back that was big enough to accommodate about two dozen arrows. But what really interested Harry, was what hung from the loosely strapped belt at her waist. Even at that distance, he could see it was a Samurai sword, possibly a Katana.

Harry thought to lighten things up and said, "That a real Samurai sword?"

"What do you think? It's not like I'm going to bluff the monsters with a fake one."

"So… you're a slayer, too?"

"I suppose that means that you take yourself to be one. Hmmm… haven't seen you around here before. Where are you from?"

"Down Kilbury way, heading for Starks Point," his father said.

"What are you thinking? You believe there are no monsters further north? Don't be silly," she said and laughed. "You should be heading west."

"No, I'm not thinking that. What do you think we are? A bunch of fools?"

"Just pulling your leg. I've often thought about getting away from this place, myself."

Bessie stepped out into the open, her swords in hand. The woman tracked her as she moved to Harry's side.

"Another woman! And a slayer as well? What's your name, sweetie?"

"I'm not your sweetie. So, let's just keep it formal, for now," Bessie hollered up.

"Very well, how are you called?"

"You can call me Bessie, and this is Harry, and that's his dad."

"Okay then, and dad's name? Or do I just call him sarge?"

"I wouldn't do that," Harry said as his father cleared his throat. Looking over, he could see that Harold Sr. was doing all he could to muster his diplomacy.

"Well, then what is it, mister army man?"

"Marine Corps! Staff Sergeant, Harold Lumsdale."

"Not anymore, Harold," she said with a husky laugh. "I haven't seen any soldiers for a long time. They're either dead or became monster slayers like you."

"So, let's cut the soldier crap. Who in the hell are you?"

"Who in hell is right, and not just in the biblical sense. Winifred 'Winnie' Winterkill… Doctor."

"Not anymore," Harold Sr. said.

"Like, as in, medical doctor?" Bessie asked.

"No, as in, Professor of Anthropology from down Providence way. Brown to be exact. Indigenous Studies."

"I suppose you're pretty good with that sword, huh?" Harry said.

"Good enough, I'm guessing. Still alive, anyway."

Harold Sr., sounding annoyed, said, "Okay, enough chatter. Could you come down here, please, so we don't have to yell up?"

"Promise me you won't be mean and I will."

"Oh, crap! Aren't we passed that now?"

"It's okay," Bessie said. "You can trust us."

"Yes, I can see that you're no threat. Well… at least until threatened, right?"

"Exactly. Now, if you would, please?" Harold Sr. said.

Winnie moved toward the back of the store and disappeared. Harry heard a squeak of hinges, followed by a loud, *Clunk!* They stayed where they were and sheathed their swords as Harold Sr. slung the Mossberg. Winnie soon came around the corner, smiling, the bow hanging limply in her hand.

"Hey! How'd you get down without a ladder?"

"Hatch on the roof. Don't have a key, you know. If I must go somewhere and lock the back door, I leave by the roof and use my ladder. I just hide it when I'm gone."

"How does the dog get down? Teach him to climb a ladder?" Harry said.

"I let him out first and then lock the door. She will wait for me to come down."

"So… you've had burglars?" Bessie said.

"Well, let's say, I've come home to find an unexpected guest inside."

"Are you, ummm… Bushi?" Harry said. "You know, like the Japanese warriors that practice Bushido?"

"Oh! No, just an Algonquian swordswoman with years of experience. Fifteen to be exact. I took it up at the tender age of sixteen. The Katana is just my weapon of choice. Better to slice and dice then try to shoot them. Swords don't run out of ammunition. You'd be better served with a good battle axe," she said, looking at Harry's father.

"Blah, blah, blah. Heard it all before," he said.

Harry didn't miss the look in his eyes. The old guy was attracted to their new friend. She, in turn, ran her eyes up and down Harold Sr.'s muscular frame before turning her attention back to Harry.

"You sound just like… him," the old guy said.

"Smart kid."

"Smart ass is more like it."

"Yeah, once a gunslinger, always a gunslinger," Harry said, sneering back at his father.

Winnie, her eyes still on Harry, said, "I see you've got yourself some Bat Jum Dao. The butterfly swords, and not the modern ones, either. You are… Wing Chun? You and Bessie."

"Oh, you know them?" Harry asked.

"I know a little about the Chinese arts. But mostly, Japanese."

"So, right. Yeah, Bessie and I grew up together. We studied under Master Gao Bik, in Kilbury."

Winnie walked over and surprised them by shaking each of their hands.

"How do you do?" she said each time with the manner of a diplomat.

When Winnie took a hold of Harry's hand, he held her slender but strong fingers in a firm manner and looked hard into almond shaped, dark brown eyes. Harry saw in them what he always referred to as, 'Wisdom' or using a favorite phrase of his mother's: *An old soul.* " Her hair was course and the darkest brown he had ever seen. It had been cut into a bob at one time, but now showed a little shaggy. Winnie's face was more round than oval, her skin, tanned and a little windburned. She sported high cheekbones and her nose was broad, but small enough to be considered cute.

Winnie kept the eye contact going for some time before pulling her hand away and then used it to push the hair out of her face. Turning her gaze to Harold Sr., she said, "So, this is your son? By blood?"

"I claim him as such, anyway. Why?"

"There is something in his eyes that tells me he's not a typical boy."

"Oh, he's typical all right. Just another smart aleck kid."

"No… he's not," she said, looking back into Harry's eyes. "He has a warrior's soul."

Harold Sr. scoffed and said, "Oh, okay... whatever"

Harry didn't know how to react. He thought to question her, but she took his hand again and sandwiched it between both of hers. Those dark eyes bored into his and he felt himself start to blush, the warmth moving up his neck. Then Bessie stepped over and wrapping her arm in Harry's, she pulled his hand from Winnie's grip.

Turning her face to Bessie with a hint of exasperation for breaking the connection, Winnie said, "You're more than just friends, aren't you?"

"I suppose you could say that. Maybe I can say… just to clarify things—he's mine."

Stepping back, Winnie laughed and said, "I can see that. Don't worry, Bessie, I prefer older men." She then threw Harold Sr. a disarming smile and a look that if anyone weren't paying attention would probably miss. Harry looked at his father, who now shrugged slightly, and cocking his head, raised his eyebrows as if he was guiltless in the situation.

"Okay, let's go meet Kappa."

"Who?" Harry said.

"My dog, Kappa. She probably can't wait to meet you. It's been a long time since we've made new friends."

The four of them walked around to the back of the store. Bessie still clung to Harry's arm and Harold Sr. lagged behind with a weird look on his face. It was like he was trying to figure something out. Winnie swung the door open and it hit the wall with a *thunk*! She held it there as the big black dog got to its feet and walked to the opening. It lowered its head, its eyes darting back and forth. It then came out, stiff legged, moving slowly, and as it walked by Winnie, she grabbed its wide leather collar.

"Sit!" she commanded.

The huge dog did exactly as told. Harry heard a low growl, and he hoped he wouldn't have to kill a dog today. He really liked Winnie, but things could go south on them in a heartbeat if the dog got cranky.

"No!" she said with authority. Kappa dropped its muzzle toward the sand and looked at them out of the tops of her eyes.

"Everybody, meet Kappa. Kappa, meet everybody."

Harry saw the tail give a couple short wags as Winnie rubbed the dog's ears.

"It's okay, girl. They're our friends, now."

Without thinking about it, Harry reached out with a closed fist, allowing the dog to sniff it. Gingerly touching its nose to his knuckles, the dog then stood up. Winnie allowed her to check them out. Bessie first, and then Harold Sr. It walked around them, sniffing. Spending less than a minute with Bessie, it then promptly walked over and goosed Harold Sr. who jumped and emitted a, "Hey! Not so personal, huh!"

The dog ignored him and moving to Harry, she sat down at his side, leaned against his leg, and looked at the others.

*Good, so much for the danger.*

Winnie grinned and said, "Well, that's a good sign. She likes you, Harry. Never seen her do that before. I guess that does it for introductions. Anyone hungry? That's one thing about living in a grocery store..."

She led them inside, and after closing the door, she threw the two heavy bars that secured it. Walking toward the eastern most wall, she motioned for them to follow. Harry saw there was what once must have been a small office at the back that she had converted into a tiny bedroom.

"Dragged a small, but almost new, mattress up from one of those cottages. Figured if I was going to stay here, I might as well sleep in comfort, hey? The room is just big enough with a little space left over so I can shut the door. Of course, I had to make a few changes, but... it works."

"How long have you been here?" Harold Sr. asked.

"Uh... a long time."

"Alone?"

"Well..." was all she said and changed the subject. "You can toss your gear over there," she said and pointed to the baseboard of a wide expanse of empty wall that stood between her bedroom and a door marked 'Toilet'.

She grew quiet for a minute, looking at the floor like she was carefully framing the statement that Harry knew was coming.

"So, no, not always alone. Only since April of last year. Just me and Kappa, now."

Bessie asked, "So, there was a friend, or…?"

"Maybe, but I'll tell you later. When I get to know you a little better, okay?"

There was tension in the air now. Harry could see by Winnie's face that it hurt to think about what it was that she had to tell them. He suspected maybe a husband or a lover. Bessie, as if to cut the tension, said, "So, do you have a working toilet? I really have to go."

"Yeah, it's the original one. You can see it there. Ran a hose down from the barrel on the roof. So, after you flush, just turn the spigot, and refill the toilet tank, will you?"

"All the comforts of home," Harry said.

"Yeah, not sure how long that's going to last, though. Probably until the sewer backs up. Then I'll have to go back to peeing in a five-gallon bucket and tossing it out in the morning." They all laughed as they watched Bessie move to the door of the restroom.

"So, anyway, there's plenty of food to pick from. Mostly in cans, except for the cereal, crackers, and cookies. Grab what you want and then we can cook it on the camp stove. That's it, over there on top of the coffee bar. The breads and rolls are all bad. Even if sealed, they're still a risk. I should probably take the time to toss them all out, but… help yourself."

Harry could see that she had set up her living area just outside her bedroom door, away from the windows. A space had been cleared out about the size of a large pickup truck. A card table sat at its center, accompanied by two folding, metal chairs. The place had the charm of a cowboy saloon, with exception of the coffee bar she had mentioned.

The walls were standard plasterboard over wood studs and the ceiling was the underside of the roof, the decking visible between the massive rafters. The big display windows were limited to the area around the entry. Thick plywood had been screwed-on over them as well as the front door. Winnie had barricaded it with things like an ice maker, a pop machine, an old fashion Space Invaders game, and of all things, an ATM with a colorful logo that declared, '*Your Money Is Always Safe With Bayside Bank!*'

The rest of the windows were long, narrow, transom-like sashes that ran high along the back wall just below the ceiling. They allowed in just enough light so you could see to move around without running into something.

There was the hatch Winnie had mentioned. A narrow ladder had been fixed to the wall just to the right of the back door and ran straight up to the opening. Harry could see that the trapdoor had been secured with a massive barrel bolt.

Moving to stand next to the coffee counter, he found a copy of the monster ID manual laying at the end. It was extremely worn, and the vinyl on the front cover had separated at the seams. Pieces of clear tape had been used to hold it together. Grabbing it, he held the manual up for all to see and said, "Hey, you have one too."

"Yeah," Winnie said. "Found it at the local law enforcement office. Must have read it a thousand times. Kill a monster, come back, read up on it. Kill another monster, come back…"

"Yeah, we know the drill," Harold Sr. said. "Harry, more than I. He's the specialist on the critters. For me… it's more like, just show me where they're at!" Everybody laughed and Harry put the manual back where he had found it.

Kappa walked away to enter Winnie's bedroom and lay down on the mattress. Positioning herself so she could keep an eye on everybody, she let out a heavy sigh and rested her muzzle on the blanket. Harry and his father started walking up and down the aisles until they found something they liked. Winnie went to work setting up two more folding chairs.

The toilet flushed, and Harry grinned to himself. It had been a long time since he had heard that particular noise. He thought it strange how the sound of a flushing toilet could spark such memories. Turning toward the door, he watched Bessie come out, combing her hair. She saw him watching her and gave him a seductive smile. He smiled bigger and raised his eyebrows.

"What? What are you smiling about? It doesn't stink, give me a break, huh?"

"No, it's just… I haven't heard that sound in a while. Never thought I'd enjoy the resonance of flushing toilet."

"Oh, okay, thought maybe you were going to make fun of me for smelling up Winnie's place."

"Naw! Harry wouldn't do that. Would you, Harry?" his father said, placing several cans of Palo's Beans & Franks on the counter.

"Well, you know dad, if you're going to eat that stuff, I suspect it's you who's going to get the razzing."

"Been a long time since I've heard family banter like that. Kind of nice to have company again," Winnie said as she hung her bow.

Taking off the duster, she draped it over a stack of boxes, giving Harry a clear view of the sword. Harry stood eyeing the Katana, a can of spaghetti in each hand. He wanted to ask more questions about Winnie's choice of weapons, but Bessie said, "So, I can have anything? I mean, of the food?" Harry decided to ask later and moved to the counter to open his cans.

"Yes, my dear, whatever you want. I have set nothing aside. So, help yourself."

Moving to a rack of baked goods, she grabbed a package of yellow, crème filled sponge cakes. Studying the package's contents, she said, "Hmmm…" and then beamed at Harry as if they shared a secret.

Winnie said, "I'd recommend something else. I mean… I know those things have enough preservatives to last a millennium, but you'd have to be careful of the fungus."

"Just looking," Bessie said and pushed them back onto the rack next to the boxes of moldy donuts. She moved down an aisle and soon returned with crackers and sardines.

"Mind if I share your spaghetti, Harry?" Winnie asked.

"No problem. Looks like my dad has more than enough stuff. You could probably share with him, too."

"Yeah," she said and chuckled. "Like we need to have two people cutting lose in this confined space."

Winnie gazed at his father and gave him that look again. It was something in her eyes. If a girl at Harry's high school gave him that look, he knew it was time to ask her out. Britta Donnelly had given him that look. That's how he knew. He wondered how he would feel if he saw his father with another woman. It would be strange, for sure. But he wouldn't stand in the way of the old guy 'seeking comfort', as his mother used to say.

Glancing at Bessie, who now sat at the table cranking open the sardine tin, he saw her eyes were on them as well. She, too, must have caught Winnie's look. Nothing much got past that girl. Looking squarely at Harry, she grinned and ripped open the airtight bag that held the soda crackers.

They were soon sitting together at the small table. With little knee room, their lower extremities were making acquaintance as well. They sat in silence, just eating. Harry decided he couldn't wait any longer to ask his mental list of questions.

"So, how long have you been a swordsman? I mean, a swords person? Oh crap! I mean… Oh! You get me, right?"

"It's okay. Seems like a hundred years ago when I think about it. Like I said earlier, my father got me started when I was sixteen. I was kind of the leader of a group of sword toting girls back in Providence. That was long before the Bug… and the monsters."

"And… the sword?"

"Belonged to my father. An indigenous boy learning the ways of the samurai back in nineteen eighty something Rhode Island. Taught me everything he knew."

"So, it's the real deal? Not like the replicas that Bessie carries?"

"What? Replicas?" Bessie snorted.

"Yeah, it is, but don't underestimate modern steel. Those are some wicked looking swords you have there, Bessie. Expensive and well made. Good steel blades. They'll do the trick, right?"

Winnie and Bessie exchanged a grin, then looking at Harry, Bessie said, "Right!" After sticking her tongue out at him, she took a bite of her cracker/sardine sandwich and then laughed, spraying him with crumbs.

"Hey… you slob!"

Reaching down, she unsheathed one of her swords and slammed it hard on the table, causing everyone to jump.

"We'll see who's a slob," she laughingly bellowed, spraying him a second time.

Harry brushed the crumbs from his shirt as he looked down at Bessie's sword. The hybrid's wide, thick blade, rounded out toward the tip, curving inward slightly on the backside. He could even make out the thin, razor-sharp edge picking up the lantern light. They both used the same sharpening method, a simple honing stone, and they would sit for nearly an hour whetting that edge after every battle. The hybrids were better quality than his old ones and he knew it. More expensive, with a 440C Stainless Steel blade. Bessie now had five kills under her belt, plus the Cayhond that killed Jonny.

Bessie's first had been a Cercophystrix. A lone scout that showed up one evening when Harry and his father had stopped to spend the night after a fruitful patrol at Bond's Pond.

He and Bessie had been sitting out back of her house at sundown. The creature sprang over the fence and rocketed across the backyard toward them. They didn't have much time to react. Harry saw it first, but Bessie was in his way. He had been amazed at how fast she came up out of her lawn chair. His swords were out a second later, but she beat him to it, and with blades gleaming in the afterglow, the Cercophystrix's, head came right off. They never sat out back again.

Her second and third had been young Caudators, no more than five feet in length. They were so slow; she had literally punctured them to death. Her forth and most serious battle before the Cayhond, was a creature known as a Struhia. An Emu like beast, except, no feathers.

It had the skin of a trout, a tiny T-Rex head and a mouth full of flesh ripping fangs. Its short little arms, ending in a single claw, were nearly useless, and its stub of a tail had webbed spines instead of feathers projecting backwards. There were three eagle-like claws on each of its large webbed feet positioned at the end of long slender legs.

The beast could run with the speed of a Cheetah and its goal was to hold you down with one foot as it disemboweled you with the other.

Bessie had left the house for a walk at Bond's Pond after her and Harry had an argument. It was still daylight, but the Struhia had come up out of the water and hidden in a dark grotto, waiting. She said the fight had lasted nearly half an hour and at the moment she thought she was losing, she got in a blow that removed a foot. When the beast could no longer stand, it just snaked out its head at her in an attempt to snatch her in its jaws. A head that she soon removed with a single swipe. That was the only thing that seemed to work with most of the creatures.

Jonny wanted her to have the absolute best of everything and that included her swords. But they had no real use before the Bug, other than display, or for Bessie to fondle and maybe practice with in the privacy of her bedroom. Harry, on the other hand, had to pay for his weapons.

They too, had only been for show. Practice at the school and tournament was limited to plastic or wooden swords.

Winnie asked, "What's the story on yours, Harry?"

"Gifted to me by my Sifu, Master Bik. We stopped by for a visit. He… uh, had died from the Bug, but he left these for me in a box with a note."

"So, that's some old steel, presumedly Damascus, supposed to hold a keener edge. What did you carry before?"

Harry grinned, got up and going to his bookbag, he pulled out his other pair, still wrapped in fabric. Laying them on the table next to

Winnie, he pulled open the wrapping before returning to his seat. From there, he watched Winnie take one out and look it over.

"So, uh… no offense, but not as high quality as Bessie's."

"You buy what you can afford," Harold Sr. said, forcing a grin.

"No less effective," Harry added, "Lots of monster blood has been shed by my less than quality swords."

"No doubt," Winnie said, "But that wasn't my point. Lots of blood has been shed over the history of mankind by mediocre weaponry. Isn't it really more about the will of the warrior? To soldier on… no pun intended," she said, bringing her eyes to Harold Sr. He grinned and she continued. "We all are playing a part here, and from the looks of this tribe… doing the best we can. Right?"

Winnie looked around the table at them, receiving a nod from each one. She then, pulled the cloth back over the swords on the table, and leaning back in her chair, she gave her guests a moment to fathom her words.

Harry grasped that Winnie was complimenting them, and he felt flattered. They had gotten a glimpse of 'Professor Winterkill', another version of the woman before the world fell apart. Tired of sword talk, he wanted to know more about her. Catching her eye, she cocked her head, grinned at him, and said, "You have a question?"

"Yeah," he said. "Do you know the story of the tanker outside?"

"Hey, yeah, what about that?" Harold Sr. asked.

"There's a body in it. A woman…" Bessie blurted out, getting a hard look from their host.

"A body?" Harold Sr. asked and then looked at Winnie, who had cast her eyes to the table top.

"I suspected it was going to come to this, but I suppose…" she said, now looking around at everyone. "That's my sister, Winona—and that's her truck."

"So, what happened?" Harry asked. "I mean… if you don't mind?

"Didn't you want to bury her?" Bessie chimed in.

"Give her a minute," Harold Sr. scolded.

Winnie's eyes got moist and placing her elbows on the table, she made a fist with her right hand, and wrapping her left over it, she brought them to her lips. She seemed to be focused on a point behind Harry as she prepared her explanation.

"Winona is the reason I'm here. She drove for Shelby-Con almost all her adult life. I was the intellect; she was the carefree soul with a longing for the open road. I was struggling in Providence. Everybody was dead, and I was alone with a much younger Kappa. I had no idea what had happen to Winona. Wasn't even sure if she was among the immune. Then one day in April, she just showed up, pulling to the curb in front of my place in her truck, which, for some reason, had a snowplow blade attached to the front.

*"Pushes all those junk heaps right out of the way!"* Winona told me when I questioned her about it. She wasn't going to let anything keep her from the highway. She loved that truck. So, I just left her body in it. I thought of laying her down on the seat, but it just didn't seem right. She'd want to be able to see the road."

Bessie asked, "So, ummm… why is she dead?"

Winnie drew a heavy sigh, and after glancing around briefly, answered with, "We didn't get that much time together. Spent the first night drinking wine and talking about the past. Then the next morning we were off for places unknown. I have to say that Winona was always bombastic. A real tomboy. I think that's what they used to call her type, right? I packed a bag and we headed north. We couldn't get off at the ninety-three exit because of a serious pile up. She wanted to check out access to ninety-five and go west. We ended up on the one-ay, and then pulled in here to fuel up. One thing about a gas truck… you always have fuel."

Winnie gave a halfhearted chuckle and removing her hands from her lips, she placed them flat on the table in front of her. A short sob suddenly escaped her mouth and a tear rolled down her cheek. She bravely scanned the surprised faces of her companions, stopping at Harold Sr., who reached out and softly patted the back of one of her hands. It surprised her, but it surprised Harry even more.

His opinion of his father had been challenged a great deal since their departure. He wondered if the old guy was going soft. Harry found himself torn between wanting a more empathetic father versus a staunch leader, who would always at the top of their game.

Winnie took Harold Sr.'s hand and gave him a subdued smile as she composed herself. Taking a deep breath, she continued.

"Winona knew she could drive for a long time before the fuel petered out. So, she vowed she would "*Keep on trucking!*" until she burned the last drop of Shelby-Con Premium in that tank. She told me just hours before we pulled in here, *"Winnie, my dear, if I can't drive, I might as well be dead."*

More tears rolled out of Winnie's eyes, and she sighed heavily, still clinging to Harold Sr.'s hand. Bessie's tears came now, leaking in silence as she watched. Harry just sat blinking, not sure what to do. Even though he felt bad for Winnie, he wasn't really feeling the emotion of the moment.

"So, anyway, we pulled into Grunt's place and she stopped where the truck now sits. She didn't even get a chance to cut the engine before we heard the gun go off. The tires deflated, one by one. I grabbed my bow and quiver and tried to get out my door. That's when the guy jumped up from behind those crates out there and started shooting at the cab. I fell out and slid underneath the truck. When I scrambled out on Winona's side, I threw open the driver's door to pull her out, but she had already been hit and fell into my arms. I think I lost my mind at that moment. After laying her down, I nocked an arrow and came around the front of the truck. He was standing right there. I figure he thought he had gotten us both and came to check. He stumbled backwards and lost a boot. I ducked back behind the truck and brought the bow to full draw. I figured 'do or die' and coming back around, I walked straight toward the guy, who was already back inside the crates, closing the bolt on that rifle. The second before he put his eye to the sights, I put an arrow in it. He dropped and didn't get up. I figured Winona died almost instantly. Luckily for me, Kappa was unharmed back in the sleeper where I had her tied."

Kappa heard her name and came out to nose at Winnie's arm. Letting go of Harold Sr.'s hand, she gave her furry friend a hug around the neck. Kappa then lay down, her long tail thumping the boards of the floor. An awkward silence filled the room with only their breathing and dog noises. Winnie gave them an embarrassed grin and started in again.

"So… I stayed. I moved into Grunt's Groceries. Came across Mr. Grunt, dead behind that front counter over there, two bullet holes in his body. One in the neck, the other in his chest. He's the only one I buried. Sitting my sister up in her seat, I put in some flowers, said an old Algonquian prayer for her, and that was that. As for the son of a bitch that shot her, I left him for the crows. I had just found my sister, then I'd lost her again, just like that. I can't bring myself to leave now. I keep thinking I can't abandon Winona, not like this. So, every twilight, I hunt the beach and cottage neighborhoods. Sometimes I get lucky and I'll take down a monster. I suspect someday they'll get me. I'll go down fighting, and like Winona, I'll be doing what I love. Then we'll be together, forever, chasing the animal spirits."

"Animal spirits?" Bessie said.

"Oh, just an Algonquian thing. Anyway… should we clean up?"

Grabbing some of the paper plates from the table, she pushed then into the big plastic garbage can. Harold Sr. rose to help as Bessie reached out and took Harry's hand. He figured she needed comforting after hearing Winnie's sad story, but he wasn't done asking questions. Remaining in his chair, he said, "So, what about your dog? Is she a monster killer, too?"

"Kappa?" Winnie said, and the dog got up and went to her.

"No, she's strictly for human confrontation. She learned her lesson the hard way."

Bending down, Winnie grabbed Kappa's collar and pushing some of the dog's hair aside on a hip, she revealed a large circular scar. The dog's head dropped into a submissive position like she would only tolerate the manipulation from the one human who mattered most.

"I suppose if I were in a bind, she would join in. But it would probably be her last. I know she would give her life for me in a loyal, but 'ignorant of death' kind of way. You know how dogs are. I certainly wouldn't want to lose her. Life at Grunt's Groceries would get awfully lonely."

Harry's father had been silent, just listening to the talk. Normally, he would have interjected a dozen sarcastic comments by now. So, Harry knew his old man had something on his mind.

"What does she do when you're in the middle of slicing up some Thulu?"

"Oh, she hangs back and barks like crazy, doing her doggy dance. Don't know what I'd do if I ran across any of those little monkey-like beasties. You know of them?"

"Yeah, we know 'em," Harry said. "Cercophystrix, or Hystrix, for short. We had a friend once who called them, Capuchipines. Just trying to be funny, you know?"

"Yeah, that is clever. He must have been a funny guy, or… girl?"

"Yeah, he was."

"Oh, I'm sorry."

"Naw, it's okay. That was a long time ago. He was a professor like you. A really smart, old guy. He was kind of helpful when it came to trying to figure things out. Died of a heart attack."

Harry's words trailed off as he thought about Doc. Winnie just gave him a smile, cleaned up the rest of the table, and moved to wipe down the small stove. Then pulling two lanterns from the cupboard underneath, she struck a match. Subject closed.

"Suppose we should prep for sleep?" Harold Sr. said.

"I have a foam pad stashed away for Kappa. I use it on those restless nights when she's patrolling the room, doing the watchdog thing. That way she can lay down out here and not be in there bugging me when I'm trying to get my beauty sleep. Tonight, it can be yours, Bessie."

"Oh, thanks. I love dog hair."

"I would have given Bessie mine, and slept on the floor, but a thick foam pad is better than an old sleeping bag, any day," Harry said, wanting to make sure that Winnie knew he was looking out for his girl.

"Well, what do you know, chivalry in the twenty first century. Let it go, Harry, I can see this woman can take care of herself."

"Yeah, Harry!" Bessie said, giving him a playful shove.

"But, I…"

"Yeah, son, give it a rest," Harold Sr. added.

"Hey now, old man, who's the one…?"

They all laughed, leaving him to feel the flush coming up his neck. He turned his face away and fiddled with a plastic fork. Group teasing was a rarity as of late. So, Harry was willing to tolerate it—for the moment.

Leaving one of the lanterns on the counter, Winnie passed by with the other, tousling his hair as she went. She smiled with a look of empathy on her face and walked to her room. For a minute, Harry wondered what it would be like to be with an older woman. There was something seductive about a sword wielding, intelligent, yet dangerous, female.

Watching her move away, he noticed how lithe she was in her walk, agile and precise in her movements; like a ballerina. Her bare midriff showed tan and taut. A picture of her sunbathing nude on the roof, formed in his mind. Harry felt the guilt creep in and glanced over at Bessie who now had her back to him as she chatted away with his father at the coffee bar. He felt the flush again, happy no one was looking. He could never be unfaithful, no matter how much he was tempted, but it didn't hurt a thing to fantasize. What he really wanted to see, was Winnie in action with that Katana. Maybe he could convince her to perform a Kata in the morning before they took off—if they took off.

Their host disappeared inside her room and Harry stood, gathered his trash, and dumped it. Moving to his bookbag, he intentionally bumped Bessie who was kneeling at hers. She playfully whined and squeaked out, "Meany." Harry gave her an exaggerated smile in return and crossed his eyes.

Harold Sr. placed Harry's old swords on the coffee bar next to a now defunct microwave and folded up the card table to place it against a wall. The chairs followed, opening up the space for bed making. Grabbing up the sleeping bag, he brought it over and playfully threw it at Harry, who picked it up and started to complain about Harold Sr.'s brutish behavior. His father just patted him on the shoulder and returned to his own bedroll.

Winnie was standing just inside the doorway of her room, stretching, her spine arched backwards, arms wrapped over her head. Tilting her face up, she yawned with her eyes closed. Then she moaned with the pleasure that comes with a good stretch, and it stirred something in Harry. Her silhouette displayed every irresistible curve on her body, and he found it hard to look away.

He threw a quick glance at his dad who was now taking off his boots. Setting them aside, Harold Sr. lay down along the baseboard of the coffee bar and stretched.

Harry knew that his father had picked that spot so he could see the front door and windows.

Taking his cue, Harry rolled out the sleeping bag where he could see the back door, being careful not to block Winnie's line of sight as she lay in her room.

"This your spot?" Bessie asked, startling him out of his moment. Turning, he found her standing right behind him, her bookbag hanging from a hand.

"Uh… ummm…yeah! Uh…where are you sleeping?"

Before she could answer, Winnie came to them in her stocking feet and handed Bessie a roll of blue foam.

Bessie giggled and dropping the foam and bookbag to the floor at Harry's feet, she said, "Right here!" Smiling at Winnie, she gave her a, "Thanks!" The older woman smiled back and returned to her bedroom. Before closing the door, she threw a brief glance toward Harold Sr., who lay watching. Harry caught the slight nod that was intended only for Winnie. She then pulled the heavy panel shut, the latch clicking defiantly.

Harry spread out his sleeping bag, ignoring Bessie for the moment, all the while, wondering if she had noticed him ogling their host. Laying down on his back, he smiled up at her as he toed off his boots. Then remembering the sword rig that was now gouging at his shoulders, he unbuckled and lay it within arm's reach.

He felt tired and knew he could sleep. They had walked over twenty miles, and he detected the growing stiffness in his legs. Bessie rolled the foam out alongside him and toed off her own boots. After she finished, she produced a short travel toothbrush from a back pocket and walked to the toilet. Looking back over her shoulder, she grinned and wiggled her butt at Harry.

Normally, that would have been an invitation for sex, but under the circumstances, he figured she must have been teasing. There was no way that could happen tonight. He looked at Harold Sr., who was now sitting on his bedroll, his back against the cupboard, his stocking feet stretched out in front.

Harry scowled at his father, giving him his best, 'Mind your own beeswax' look. His old man just raised a leg slightly off the floor and broke wind. Harry waited for the triumphant grin that usually followed, but instead, there came a look of embarrassment. Harry realized Winnie's door was open again, and she was now passing him on her way to his father. She was obviously braless in a tight, white muscle shirt, and black, loose legged sleep shorts. She stopped to stand in front of Harold Sr. and said, "Do you two ever stop?" Not waiting for an answer, she added, "Mind if I sit here?"

"Please do," his father said.

"If you don't mind the smell," Harry muttered.

Winnie threw him a playful sneer as she gracefully lowered herself down next to Harold Sr., who had turned his face away from her to take a few short sniffs. Then, making eye contact with Harry, he shrugged.

Looking at them sitting there together, Harry saw something he never thought he'd ever see in his lifetime. There was his father, sitting hip to hip with a beautiful woman, looking like a nervous school boy.

Winnie sat with her knees up, the loose legged shorts leaving nothing to Harry's imagination. To avoid an embarrassing reaction, he rolled over onto his stomach and faced away.

The door to the toilet opened and he listened to Bessie approach. His bookbag slammed onto the floor next to his head and he scowled up at her.

"I just realized we can use our bags for pillows. So… I brought yours."

"Good idea, BB," he said, rising up on his elbows. "Just try to avoid smashing my head, next time, huh?"

"Oh, I didn't even touch you, you big baby."

Laying down next to him, she pulled fingernail clippers from her pocket. He pinched her on the hip in retaliation for the bag. She squealed and slapped his hand. Harry laughed and lay back down on his side, facing her. Bessie finished with her manicure and after pocketing her clippers, she initiated the evening conversation.

Everybody told their story, starting with Harold Sr. and the Lumsdale family history. Then, Harry by himself, telling Winnie everything Harold Sr. had left out. When it was Bessie's turn, the exchange became more humorous and her antics brought a few laughs until she got to the point where her family died. But no one wanted a return to the tears, so she stopped there. Three quarters of the way through Winnie's early years, Harry drifted off to sleep.

He awoke several hours later, laying on his other side with his face to the end of the shelving unit. Harry smelled dog. Without moving his head, his eyes tracked Kappa's legs as she padded by. She walked to the ratty, old carpet runner that ran from door to door along the checkout counter at the west wall. Laying down, she pushed her nose to within a foot of the bottom of the back door and settled in.

Bessie lay tight up against him, facing his back. Her left arm lay over his waist and light, purring snores ruffled his hair. There was a quiet conversation taking place somewhere. Lifting his head, he looked over Bessie to discover why Kappa had chosen to relocate.

Harold Sr. stood in the bedroom doorway, his back against the jamb, his left side toward Harry. Winnie stood facing him with her arms hanging loosely around his waist and looking up into his face. Harry watched his father push her hair out of her eyes, and leaning forward, he whispered something in her ear. Winnie giggled, and it brought a low chuckle to Harry's lips. That surprised them, and they both threw him a look. Retreating inside, Winnie pulled his father with her. Just before the door closed, he saw his father grin and wink at him in the dim light of the lantern that would burn all night.

Bessie stirred, talking in her sleep. "I'll take pizza," she mumbled, followed by a more enthusiastic, "Get off me, you silly goose."

Harry grinned in the dark, thinking back to the days when life was a carefree romp. Memories filled his mind of them hanging out at Digg's Pizzeria, the movies at MaxKino, and then there was Vintage Gamz, where he played all the old arcade machines like Dragon Slayer, Deadshot, and Kung Fu-U. It left him to wonder where all those kids were now, their faces just a blur, the sounds of those places a distant echo in his mind.

The light from the lantern in the closet found its way out through the crack at the bottom of the door. There came the sounds of escalating passion and he thought to wake Bessie to take advantage of the situation. But he was too tired. So, he remained, watching the rays of light stretch out across the floor toward Kappa where they turned her eyes a demon green every time the dog looked his way. Just before drifting off, he saw her ears prick and her nose go into overdrive. She rose to her feet and pushing her snout to the bottom of the door, a low, throaty growl floated to Harry's ears.

# CHAPTER 5

## The Battle Closes...

Harry awoke to Bessie rolling over in her sleep. Glancing across the room, he saw his father had returned to his bedroll. Kappa was no longer lying where he had seen her last and with the closet door being shut, Harry assumed Winnie was still asleep. He got to his feet, and after slipping on his boots, he grabbed his sword rig and bookbag before walking to the front of the store. Coming around the corner of the first shelving unit, he startled Kappa. She jumped up from where she lay by the front entry, and growling at him, she approached, stiff legged, her eyes just slits. When she caught his scent, she stopped, whimpered, and sat down to watch his face. Harry reached out a closed hand to allow her to sniff him. She licked a knuckle and Harry said, "Good puppy."

The sun had just broken the horizon and light streaked in through the windows at the top of the north wall to fill the space where they stood. Moving to an old kitchen chair sitting at the end of the second rack of shelves, Harry dropped his bag, sat down, tied his boots, and then strapped on his sword rig. Kappa moved to the rug at the back entrance and sat down in a pool of sunlight.

"Perfect picture," Harry mumbled. Opening his bag, he took out his sketchbook. Kappa, hearing his voice, rose to her feet.

"Crap! Oh, well, just as good, I guess. Got to be quicker than your subject," he muttered as he went to work, sketching the big dog as she had been. His stomach grumbled, attracting Kappa's attention and she walked to him. Because she was so large, she could almost lay her chin on his shoulder as he sat.

After returning his sketchbook and pencil box to his bag, his hands moved to Kappa and he ran his fingers through her thick fur. Her dog breath bathed his face, and he said, "Damn, dog, you need a mint."

She whimpered and moved back to the door. Circling a couple of times, she sat down and promptly farted, a pleading look apparent on her bushy face.

"What's wrong, girl? Got to go? All right, just give me a minute. This is something you should really be asking Winnie."

Harry knew he should seek permission, but he didn't want to wake their host, especially for something as simple as a piss. He had a dog back when he was eight years old. A Scottish terrier named Frisky. They were together for two years before Frisky took off after a squirrel, but caught a fast-moving Plymouth instead. So, he knew the signs. Kappa had probably been holding it for hours.

Harry decided to wait, hoping Winnie would hear the dog's commotion and get up to attend to her. Turning his attention to the shelf on his right, he studied a large plastic jar labeled, 'Bardot's Vienna Fingers'. A faded label showed a picture of some smiling, long dead, model with a French beret pulled down over blond hair. She was sticking a cookie in her mouth through a set of snow-white teeth, her eyes saying, 'Take the picture, will yah!'

Screwing off the plastic lid, he saw the seal was still intact. Breaking it open, the lovely smell of cookies rose to his nose.

"Better than your breath, hey, fido?"

Kappa whined again, stood up, and went to bouncing from foot to foot. The potty dance his mother had called it. Something all kids do before graduating to standing with their hand clutching at their crotch.

He bit into a cookie, and even though a little stale, he found it edible. Stretching out his hand toward Kappa, he offered her some. She came to him, sniffed it, and refused, giving him a look that said, 'You got to be kidding?' She didn't sit when she got back to her spot, and Harry now feared the dog had reached her bursting point.

"Okay, fine, but if I get in trouble, I'm pointing my finger at you."

Harry moved to the door, and Kappa made a noise that sounded a lot like a sigh of relief. Throwing off the two bars, he turned the knob of the spring-loaded night latch and pushed it open, realizing too late, he had broken Harold Sr.'s #1 rule. *'Never open a door until you know what's on the other side.'*

From that point on, things moved pretty fast.

Somebody—or something, pushed it closed on him, pinching him between it and the jamb. Instead of doing the smart thing and sliding back inside, he pushed his head out, followed by his body. The heavy metal panel closed, and the night latch clicked, locking him out, minus Kappa.

There were two of them out there and his adrenalin dump was right on time. His swords were out in less than a second. He gave the creatures a quick once over and he was sure those large, lidless black eyes were doing the same with him.

The beasts walked upright like a man and stood as tall as he. They were muscular but looked like skinny Kangaroos. They had wide, flat, pentagonal shaped tails, fringed by a narrow strip of membrane that was supported by short, sharp, spines. Their human like arms were heavily webbed from elbow to hip, with amber-colored talons on their front paws and flipper-like feet. Their skin was the sickly yellow color of a catfish's belly with a wide, segmented olive-green stripe running down their backs.

Harry couldn't get over the shape of their heads. They were almost comical and he felt himself grin despite the dire situation. It was as if someone had attached a large Barracuda on the creature's short neck right where the fish's belly would be. Instead of a fishtail at the back there was a crest that curved down and was webbed from the tip to the base of the creature's neck. Harry could tell they were not meant to travel too far from water. When they moved, it reminded him of scuba divers trying to walk in full gear.

One of them stood a short distance out in the sand lot; the other had been behind the door when he opened it. When the heavy metal panel nudged the creature, it nudged back; only harder. They chirped, clicked, and squeaked as if surprised by his arrival. They looked at him, at each other, and then back to him as if trying to decide what to do. Kappa was raising a ruckus just inside, leaving Harry to wonder how long it would be before his support team arrived. He faced off with the one closest to him and its mate started toward them in a clumsy walk.

Harry backed away in a curving line, moving out into the sand, so he could clear the building. His immediate opponent followed. The other beast started too, but the door swung open and slammed into it, nearly knocking the beast off its scuba flipper feet.

It attacked the metal panel, its claws sounding like fingernails on a chalkboard as they scrabbled over the steel. The one closest to him, turned its head to look back, and Harry saw his chance. Back peddling further out into the sandlot, he hoped to draw both monsters away from the door; but the one closest, stubbornly remained.

It's chirping opponent turned back to Harry and chased him. Then crouching to leap, it reached out its claws, a loud hiss escaping its fang-filled maw. The music flowed in and Harry's world slowed to a crawl. The butcher's chart came as expected and at the same time, the creature went airborne.

It sprang more vertical, than forward, as if trying to smash Harry with its weight. He at once spun away to avoid being crushed and swiped a blade at it in the process, missing his mark. The beast turned toward him, crouching for another leap. Its head bobbed sharply as a whitish dewlap bloomed at its throat.

*Ah! The male of the species!*

Its large black eyes rolled around like it was trying to judge distance. Harry was already sidestepping before it even left the ground. It could swing its claws at him but couldn't change direction until after it touched down. Harry's goal was to get in behind it and chop off its head.

The monster was slow in moving forward, but it could turn with great speed. Its short flat tail now projected up at about a thirty-degree angle, and the short, sharp spines stood straight out, reminding Harry of a saw blade. If he didn't clear the tail when it spun, those spines could easily rip out chunks of his flesh.

The beast dipped its jaw down into its dewlap and then sprang again. Harry sidestepped and cleaved its arm. But instead of slicing through cartilage as with the Thulu, the blade's keen edge struck bone.

"Crap!"

The monster let go with a high-pitched squeak as blood leaked from its wound. Unfortunately, the arm remained intact and functional. Changing tactics, it stomped straight at him in a clumsy manner, swiping with its claws. Harry danced away, his sword blades glittering in the rising sun.

He made contact a few more times, but only enough to make it slowly bleed to death. One time he moved too close on a spin, and a claw grazed his lower back. He yelped in pain and more adrenaline coursed in.

*"Got to quit messing around, Harry!"*

He knew what he was supposed to do in order to end this, but he needed to get behind the monster, and it, wasn't letting him.

Looking past the creature for a mere second, he saw Winnie was now free of the building and preparing to battle the other. Her sword was out, and she went into what he knew as the Ko Gasumi stance. Turning her body sideways to the beast, she held the sword just above her head with both hands keeping the blade parallel to the ground, it's tip pointed at the creature.

His father was next out the door, shotgun at the ready. The door remained open and he could see Bessie struggling to hold Kappa back with a two-handed grip on the dog's collar. Winnie forced the other monster to backout into the sand as Harold Sr. moved to flank the beast.

Harry's eyes returned to the creature in front of him as it prepared to launch. He heard his father's voice above Kappa's frenzied barking, "Let me have him, Winnie! Let me have him."

"No, stay back! You might hit me or Harry by accident."

Harry was already moving when his opponent reached the apex of its leap. He spun right, but the monster stayed with him. He realized that if he didn't do some serious damage soon, he was going to run out of energy.

Recalculating his methodology, he didn't wait for it to reach the zenith of its leap. He spun out wide, but instead of continuing in his arc, he came straight back and jumped up to land on the flat of its tail. Bringing both swords into play, he focused on its neck.

The beast's head popped right off and tumbled to the ground as its lifeblood bubbled out. Leaping off, Harry spun around in midair to watch the large body collapse to the sand. It flopped about like a fish out of water, then stopped, quivered, kicked its legs once, and then lay still.

He turned to see the others still struggling with the larger female. He watched his father moving around, trying to get a shot as Winnie slashed and stabbed the creature over and over with no great effect. Harold Sr. must have saw his chance and stepping in, he pushed the shotgun's muzzle against the creature's lower leg and pulled the trigger.

The limb dissolved in a cloud of flesh and blood, the heavy pellets raising a spray of sand as they ploughed into the earth. The beast threw back its head and shrieked at the sky. Harold Sr. back peddled away as Winnie danced in, and not missing a beat, she cut the beast's shriek short with one smooth motion of a double-handed strike to its neck. The Katana's sharp blade met little resistance and Winnie's triumphant kiai filled the air.

"Technicolor," his father sang out and laughed raucously.

Harry's brain finally registered the sting at the small of his back, and putting a finger to the wound, he brought it around to see a crimson smear. If there had been poison, he would have known by now. Letting out a long sigh, he turned his attention to the others.

Winnie was now leaning against the wall, trying to catch her breath, sword still in hand. Harold Sr. stood with one foot on the creature, the butt of the gun on his hip with its muzzle pointing skyward. He was grinning at Harry like it was all about staff sergeant Harold Lumsdale, the brave hunter with his trophy kill.

Bessie released Kappa, who broke from the doorway, and clipping Harold Sr. on the way by, she knocked him from his victory pose. Running out to sniff Harry's kill, she squatted and doused the dead monster's leg with a shot of urine.

Bessie had followed Kappa out. Running to Harry, she threw her arms around his waist. He held his blades high above his head to avoid cutting her by accident. Putting the side of her face to his chest, she huffed out, "I'm sorry. I couldn't get out the door, and the dog was…"

"Don't worry about it," he said, and kissed the top of her head.

Stepping away, she stared in shock at the blood transfer running up the inside of her arm. "You're hurt!" Grabbing his elbow, she spun him around to examine his back.

"Yeah, the bastard got in a lick. How does it look? Okay?"

He winched as she probed. "Just a scratch, but your shirt's ruined."

"Crap, now I'm going to have to schedule a shopping day," he said. "You know how hard it is to find a good shirt these days?"

"You can just stop that now, Harold Tecumseh Lumsdale. You always sound like your dad when you say shit like that."

"Really? Hmmm… I don't know if that's good, bad—or both."

She had called him Harold and used his middle name, the one he never shared. So, he knew he'd better listen because that was her signal that she was serious.

"Give it a rest, huh, Harry?" she said, confirming his thought. "You could have been killed."

Because she couldn't get in the game, he had troubled her to fear for him. She must have been torn between him and the dog. Harry felt she had done the right thing, though. He just wasn't sure how to tell her.

Still trying to catch his breath, his lungs burned slightly from the fight. But the adrenaline had heighted his mood and he felt intoxicated. The fact that he could be killed and eaten, never crossed his mind until hours after a battle. Then the reflection was always brief before his focus returned to the present. Words in his mother's voice rolled through his head, *"So very dauntless."*

*Well, mom… maybe so?*

Moving over to the monster, Bessie gave it a boot, saying, "Piece of crap!" Then turning to the fish like head, she kicked it, causing it to go airborne and spin away. Smacking into a stack of fifty-gallon, steel drums, they rang as if to signal the start of a boxing match.

"Round one!" Harry sang out.

"Whatever," Bessie responded solemnly, followed by a giggle that indicated a mood change. "What are these things, anyway? Never seen anything like them before.

"No idea. Don't remember seeing them in the army's ID manual."

"It almost looks like a boney Pterodactyl without the wings."

"A what?"

"You know, one of those dinosaur birds? Except with a barracuda face. You know what I mean?"

"Sphyrator," Winnie shouted as she sheathed her sword. Then studying the other monster, she added, "Or… just ol' fish head, if you like."

Harry acknowledged with a wave as they both looked her way. Handing Bessie one of his swords, he said, "Hold this, will you?" Pulling a ratty, blue handkerchief from his pocket, he wiped his swords clean and then let the smelly rag fall to the ground.

"Everything okay, out there?" his father hollered.

"Harry's got a scratch, but he'll live.," Bessie shouted back.
Harry wrapped his arm in Bessie's and they walked back to the store.

Upon arriving, Harold Sr. grabbed his son and turned him around in his usual brusque manner. Looking him over, he said, "You're okay, no stitches needed. We should get you cleaned up though. Stay here, I'll be right back." Disappearing into the store, Harry heard the all too familiar rustle of the trauma bag.

Winnie moved over to face Harry. Bessie, still clutching his arm, moved in closer as if to protect him from the older woman. Winnie's dark eyes bored into his, her face deadly serious.

"I saw that move you made. Who would have thought of that? No… you're not the run of the mill monster slayer."

"What do you mean?"

"You know what I mean, Harry. I've seen it before. My friend, Numees, back in Providence, she had it. It's how you move when you fight. Just like you know your way around any monster. All you have to do is study it for a few seconds and then you know just how to kill it. Am I right? I'm right, aren't I?"

Harry stared back, but his mind was blank. He'd always wanted to talk to someone about it. Now, he had an opportunity. Yet he felt reluctant, almost like he didn't want to discuss it in front of Bessie, or his father, for that matter. He had no choice, though. No doubt he would gain something from talking with Winnie. If he denied it, he may not get another chance.

"Yeah, it's true."

"The slow motion? The dissection chart, and…"

"The music?"

"Yes, the music. For my friend, Numees, it was a tango. Ummm… Por Una Cabeza, if I remember correctly. And you?"

"Waltz of the Flowers."

"Ah, Tchaikovsky… yes, of course."

"My mother's favorite."

Bessie had been hanging on Winnie's every word and said, "What in the hell are you talking about? These… charts and music?"

"When Harry goes into slayer mode, he has a special gift for fighting."

"You never told me about that, Harry. What gives?"

"I meant to, was just… waiting for the right time."

"What? When I was old and grey?"

Harold Sr. came out the door with the orange canvas trauma bag, and walking over, asked, "Who's old and grey? You talking about me behind my back?"

The look on Winnie's face told Harry she would respect his decision to talk—or not. Reaching out she lightly gripped his upper arm for a few seconds, still keeping the eye contact. It was like she was trying to read something in his eyes but wasn't having any luck. When Harold Sr. got close enough to check out Harry's wound, Bessie snatched the trauma bag away from him.

"I'll do this," she said, and towing Harry away from the other two, she took him over to an upturned five-gallon bucket and commanded, "Sit your butt down and take off your swords. Oh, and your shirt too."

He did as she told him, knowing it was her way of contributing as well as eliminating any regret. Isolating him would give them the opportunity to converse without interruption from Harold Sr. or Winnie.

"Help me get this thing away from the building, will you, Harold?" Winnie said.

"Sure thing, Winnie."

But Harold Sr.'s eye was one them and suspicion clouded his brow. He would want to know what they were talking about while they were out there, but Harry knew the old guy would wait until later to ask.

Winnie grabbed the dead creature just above its remaining webbed foot, and Harold Sr. grabbed its arms. They drug it together out to a high sand dune and pushed it over the edge. Harry kept an eye on them, watching as they moved to stand side by side and look back toward the store. They were having a conversation, and it appeared to be getting heated. Every once in a while, they would break eye contact to look elsewhere.

Harold Sr. was the first to walk away. Taking off his hat, he rubbed his face and forehead. Bad sign. That was something he did when he'd lost control of the situation. Winnie soon followed him and just above the morning breeze, Harry heard her call out, "Harold, please… I just can't."

"What do you suppose they're talking about?" Bessie said.

"Don't know, but it sounds like an argument. I suspect my dad is trying to talk Winnie into doing something she doesn't want to do. Like… go with us."

Turning back, he saw the two had stopped again and were now standing toe to toe, their voices low. Winnie's hand rested on his father's upper arm.

"They were together last night. I mean, really, really together," Bessie whispered.

"Yeah, I know."

"How do you feel about that?"

"Okay. It's been a while since mom died, and… we all have to move on, right? That's kind of a life rule if I remember correctly."

"Yeah, I suppose. Maybe easier said than done. But I know what you mean. I think your dad needs somebody. Not just us. Somebody closer to his age—and a woman," Bessie said with a subdued giggle.

"You know, BB, I honestly wouldn't mind if it was Winnie. But I don't think she's the one for him. Besides only being about half his age, she's an Academic. My dad's not even close. I think they could be together for a little while, but he's too bossy, and she… well, she's the woman I think every woman wants to be."

"Yeah, like me. I would give anything to be her."

"Really?"

"Yeah, really. To be that smart and to be the warrior that she is. Did you see her fight? Oh, I guess not, you were kind of busy fighting, yourself."

"I caught a bit of it, and I agree. But you're pretty damn good too, somewhat extraordinary, if anyone were to ask me."

"Yeah, I'm the special one. The sage of the Bat Jum Dao!" she jokingly announced to the sky.

Laughing, she patted the tape holding the 4x4 gauze square to his skin, and grabbing his head, she twisted it around and kissed him hard on the lips. They held it for a few seconds, until he heard his father stomp by, going inside. They both turned to watch as Harold Sr. disappeared through the open door. Winnie had stopped several yards away to watch him too. Turning to look at the two of them, she shrugged, and hooking her thumbs in the waistband of her black leggings, she looked down and started toeing lines in the sand with her boot. Turning suddenly, she walked to the other decapitated monster head and punted it just like Bessie had done. She kicked it so hard it spun through the air with a strange whistling noise and almost made it out to the embankment. Then standing with her back to them, she shook her head, sighed, and said with exasperation, "Men!"

Harold Sr. reappeared carrying the bookbags and MOLLE pack. Throwing theirs on the ground by the wall, he said, "Pack it up kids, we're out of here."

"But, dad, I…"

"Don't but dad me, get your other shirt on, and let's get on our way. We've got a good ways to go, and besides, we have to find a place to spend the night."

Winnie turned away, dropped her head, and walked inside; Kappa close on her heels.

"Right here is a good place," Bessie said with a note of irritation.

Harold Sr. glared at her, giving her his staff sergeant look.

"Ummm… okay, I'm going to go get my toothbrush, I'll be right back," she said, obviously trying to avoid eye contact as she moved toward the door.

Harry felt his ire rising. But he knew it was a bad time to get into an argument with his father. Especially after the old guy just finished one with Winnie. It would end the same way as when his mother was alive. Harold Sr. would stomp away and go somewhere to cool off. Yet there was no other place to go. If he stomped off now, it would be irresponsible.

He would just have to calm down on their walk north or in the night after they stopped—wherever that was. Looking through the open door, Harry could just make out Bessie and Winnie in a tight embrace.

When Bessie came out of the door, her cheeks were wet with tears. Harold Sr. was watching her, and she gave him the 'stink eye' as she passed. Walking to her bag, she crouched and stuck the toothbrush inside. Harry grabbed his sword rig and getting to his feet, he walked to his own bag, running a finger across Bessie's shoulders as he passed. Dragging his bag over next to her, he knelt and fished out another shirt.

Harold Sr. had moved to stand behind them. Harry rose, turned around, and pulled on the shirt all in one motion. When his head popped out of the collar, his eyes met his father's in a glare, and for the first time in Harry's young life, it was Harold Sr. who was first to look away.

Bessie picked up her bag and moved toward the corner of the building where she let it fall. Harry watched her inspect her swords. Afterwards, she just stood there, staring out toward the ocean, hands in pockets.

He started toward her, but heard Winnie come out. Looking back, he saw she was fully dressed, duster and all. She leaned her bow and quiver against the wall and came to him. He turned to meet her and for a second, his eyes strayed past her to his father, who had stepped over to lean back against the wall. Pulling off his hat, Harold Sr. rubbed his eyes and forehead a second time.

Bringing his focus back to Winnie, Harry matched her unflinching stare. She was studying him again. It was the look a teacher would give a student—one full of wisdom and knowledge, with some kind of statement soon to follow. After a while she took his hand with her right, and placing her left on his upper arm, she lightly squeezed and said, "Take care of them, Harry."

He didn't know what to say. So, in the words he had so often spoken to his mother, he replied, "I promise."

She smiled and nodded. Releasing him, she started to step away, but he grabbed her in an awkward hug. She didn't embrace him back, she just let him hold her for a moment. When he let her go, she took a step backward and stuck her hand out as if for another shake. But instead of taking his hand, she gripped his forearm. So, he gripped hers back.

"Warriors til the end, hey, Harry?"

"Til the end."

Cocking her head, she smiled big and then walked to his father. Harold Sr. came off the wall and faced her in a kind of parade rest, his face stony in the proper Marine Corps fashion. It didn't matter, Harry could tell she didn't care how tough he thought he was. Grabbing his tee shirt with one hand at the chest, she yanked him in and kissed him, long and hard. Harold Sr. didn't resist, but he never touched her back, his hands simply falling to his sides, the butt of the shotgun swinging slowly back and forth on its sling.

When they finished, she took a step back, and Harry saw something pass between them. Their eyes said it all. Then picking up his pack,

Harold Sr. walked away. Harry turned and followed. As they passed Bessie, she reached out and took his hand.

He lost count of how many times he looked back as Winnie and Kappa shrank away into the distance. Never budging from her spot, her black duster flapped in the morning breeze. She watched them go, Kappa pacing back and forth, seemingly anxious to get on with the day.

When the three of them reached the crest just behind the cottages, Harry turned back for one last look. Winnie had vanished. Like a leaf in the wind, she had wafted out of his life.

# CHAPTER 6

## On My Ever Honored Father

Upon gaining the beach, they continued north with Harry scanning the sky. The sun sat just above the eastern horizon, veiled by a light smattering of red tinted clouds.

*Red Sky at morning, sailor take warning!*

It was a Boy Scout thing if he remembered correctly. Harry felt a slight shudder at the thought of a storm while they were out on the open road. Crossing the fingers of his free hand, he wished for a safe spot to squat for the night. He detested the feeling that came with an 'after dark' arrival to any unfamiliar sleeping place. A traveler just never knew what might be lurking. It made him think about a movie he saw once, where a little boy got lost in the woods and sat down to rest on a log, only to discover it was a sleeping dragon.

*What a surprise!* Harry hated surprises these days.

Bessie finally let go of his hand and started seashell hunting as they made their way in the direction of Portsmouth. Before moving out toward the breakers, she said, as if to herself, "Sure hope we are going to have breakfast soon… just kind of hungry, is all."

Harry suspected she hoped to prompt his father into action, but the old guy seemed to be lost in thought and said nothing. So, she continued with her hunt. After a mile or so, Harold Sr. dropped back to walk beside him, but he didn't want to talk to his father right now. He blamed him for Winnie not wanting to come along. There had been hope that she would join them. Together, they would have made a great team, and he was certain his father had ruined it by saying something that had terminated her interest in the prospect.

Harold Sr. didn't look at Harry when he said, "Just so you know, Winnie didn't want to come. I asked politely, but she just said no."

It was like his father had read his mind. Harry stopped walking and the weary looking sergeant came around to face him. Harold Sr.'s eyes were pleading. The two stood at arm's length, just studying each other's faces. Harry's eyes moved over his father's shoulder to watch Bessie in the distance. She bent down to pick up something from the ground and noticed they had stopped. Collapsing onto the sand, she sat crossed legged, tossing whatever she had found up into the air, and after catching it, she tossed it again.

"So, you didn't say anything that would make her not want to come?"

"No! Why would you think that?" Harold Sr. scowled. "I wanted her to come, just as much as you did." Then looking down, he confessed in a tone just above a whisper, "I needed her to come. But it didn't seem to matter."

Harry felt somewhat overwhelmed by all the changes. One sensual night with a woman and staff sergeant Harold Lumsdale had become human again. He had never confided or confessed anything, ever, to his son. A sign of weakness by Harold Lumsdale standards. Harry wondered if maybe his father had grown tired of a revenge driven life. Maybe even tired of playing staff sergeant. Sex could do that to a person. He recalled how Master Bik had once addressed the class about that very thing. *"No sex before tournament!"* Harry thought it hilarious because many of the students on the training floor that day weren't even twelve years old. He had to force himself not to laugh at his teacher. You didn't laugh at Master Bik.

It had been over two years since Harold Sr. had lain with a woman. Maybe it was his age, or maybe—loneliness. Also, Winnie was a certain kind of woman, like Bessie had said. Harry suspected if Winnie had come-on to him, she would have been difficult to resist. Gazing at Harold Sr. in the growing light, he saw his father's vulnerability.

There came the realization of how dependent he was on the old guy. Despite all the Harold Sr. bashing, and the open resistance to just about every request or command; Harry needed him. He believed if his father lost his edge they would be in trouble. Harry found himself hoping time would cause his father to fall back into his old habits—something he never thought he would want.

Stepping past Harold Sr., Harry took up the lead, his father hesitating to follow—almost as if he didn't want to put any more distance between himself and Winnie.

Bessie, seeing that Harry was moving again, got to her feet and continued with her diversion. There was a good chance she was thinking about the distance they had to cover. She had never been one for walking, probably why she had hung onto her car for so long.

Harry figured he was good for twenty-five, maybe thirty miles a day; if there weren't too many hills. The same for his father. But they might have to push it back for Bessie because of her shorter legs. He felt an urgent need to talk to her, to find out what she was feeling.

Before Harry could pick up his pace to catch her, Bessie slowed and grinned at him over her shoulder. Apparently, she too wanted to reconnect. When he moved up beside her, she turned her attention back to the seashell in her hand and said, "What's up, slowpoke?"

He tickled her under her ribs, and she winced, giggling. Pretending to stumble, she crashed into him. Harry tried to push her away, but Bessie spun around behind him and performed a controlled, double palmed strike to his lower back. Harry almost fell on his face, but she grabbed his shirt and yanked him upright.

When they finished with their horseplay, they walked in silence for a minute before Harry asked, "How are you? I mean… like with Winnie, and all?"

"I'm okay with it. She didn't want to come, she told me so. I kind of begged her too anyway, inside the store when I said my goodbyes. I could tell by the tone of her voice that I shouldn't ask a second time. She told me she had other plans and really wanted to go back to Providence. I heard her and your dad talking in the night. Even though I was still half-asleep, I could tell, without her saying it, that she didn't see the sense in going north. But your dad didn't want to give up his plan."

"I am thinking, he's having second thoughts about that plan, now. But you know how he is. He wants to hook up with his old buddy, band of brothers and all… if you know what I mean?"

"I just hope you don't become that stubborn, Harry. I plan on spending the rest of my life with you and I don't need that."

"Don't worry about me. My old man has that Marine Corps disease. I'm not the military type. You remember in school how they taught us about the indigenous people? The original people in this country before the Europeans came? They called the young men, 'Braves'. Do you remember?"

"That's all fine and dandy for you, but what about the women? I mean… look at Winnie. That's her ancestry—I assume."

"Oh… yeah, well, my point is, I'm not the soldier type, I'm a Brave, or correctly—a warrior. And well… you can be a… bravette!"

Harry's attempt at being funny was met with a slap on his shoulder and a loud raspberry from Bessie. Then she said, "I can be a Brave, just like you! It is the twenty first century, you know. So… screw the old rules."

"No, you screw them."

"You won't get jealous?"

"What…?"

"Forget it. Just don't get too stubborn, and we'll get along just fine, Harry T. Lumsdale."

"Fine, whatever you say, Ms. Elizabeth B. Brown."

Harold Sr. had caught up, and looking back at his father, Harry could see he was deep in thought as he walked, his face down, his hands stuck in his pockets. It was apparent the old guy regretted his decision, and probably, his own pig-headedness. Harry hoped time and distance would help Harold Sr. bury the memory and bring back the man that his father was two days before. At least until they got to where they were going. They needed to stick to the plan and be in the right mindset to do so. Sadly, Harry doubted his father would ever meet another woman like Winnie. He hoped once they arrived at Billy's, his father would feel he had accomplished his mission, find it wasn't worth it, and want to return. Also, that they wouldn't be too late and find that Winnie had left her dead sister's makeshift gravesite to return to Rhode Island.

The beach remained wide and clear all the way to just east of North Hampton. Then it turned rocky and they agreed to move up onto the 1A. They stopped, exhausted, just south of a place called Fox Hill Point.

Holing up in a giant tree house behind a dilapidated mansion, they ate a cold supper of army food that consisted of prepackaged meals that Harold Sr. referred to as, 'M.R.E.'s'.

They took turns standing guard. Sleep came with some difficulty for the three. Harry's ears were pricked all night long, and he suspected the others were too. The fear of a possible storm waned when it never showed up. So, not only did they remain monster free, but they also stayed dry.

Departing their cramped quarters long before the sun came up, they stuck to the dark highway, passing around the occasional pile up. After several miles, Bessie complained that she never got her morning pee, and dropping her bag on the weed strewn asphalt, she stepped out of sight down a narrow concrete walkway between two beachside cottages.

Harold Sr. called out, "Careful, sweetie, still kind of dark back there with these clouds. Maybe use your flashlight, huh?"

"Don't worry, nothing would dare keep a girl from her morning pee. Besides, I… oh crap! Harry!"

Her flashlight came spinning out of the entryway and landed on the far shoulder of the roadway. It continued to gyrate, casting eerie shadows in all directions. Harry's swords were out in an instant as his father's shotgun came to bear. They ran to the mouth of the opening and Harold Sr. shined his light inside. Harry felt a second dose of adrenalin rush in as his father exclaimed, "Oh, shit!"

The walkway between the buildings was no more than three feet wide. Bessie stood at the far end with her back to them, swords out, squared in a stance. The fishy smell reached them long before they saw its source.

An immature Thulu stood a few yards away from Bessie, hooting, and menacing her with its claws. "Get out of here, you freak!" she yelled, threatening the beast with her swords. It stood its ground, making gurgling noises through the whisker-like tentacles.

The monster took a step toward her and cut loose with a weird, screeching cry, nearly drowning out Harold Sr.'s "Bessie, run!"

Harry moved closer but stayed clear of her battle zone. The urge to step in and help was overwhelming, but the space wasn't big enough. Bessie would have to push forward or back up as far as the highway.

Unless she could clear the buildings, she was on her own. Then surprising them both, she let go with her high-pitched battle cry and

went to work.

Her swords glittered in the illumination of Harold Sr.'s flashlight as she moved with the skill and agility of a confident swordsperson. The creature's left forearm soon parted, and bouncing off a wall, it fell to the ground squirting greenish-blue blood. The Thulu screamed like a wildcat, a cry that rose in pitch when Bessie chopped off the other arm. Using just its feet, the armless beast tried to rake her with its hook-like talons. The spaded tail darted in and out at the same time, trying to skewer her with its stinger. The creature had difficulty keeping its balance as it whipped its tail about, and the four-inch-long spike missed its mark every time, occasionally embedding itself in the wooden clapboard siding of the cottages.

It finally stopped moving and just stood as if calculating a different approach. The stumps, where its arms had been, leaked its life's blood. Harry wondered how long it would take before the amphibious brute succumbed to its wounds. Bessie wasn't going to wait.

She spun and putting her back to the creature, she leaned slightly forward at the waist as she drove both swords to the rear with a single, underhanded thrust. The blades entered the Thulu's gut with such force that it rose several inches off the ground before toppling backwards.

Bessie's adversary rolled away down the slope and coming to a stop, it struggled to get to its feet, hissing frantically. "All yours," Bessie rasped out. Falling back against a cottage wall, she gasped for air.

"I hear you," Harold Sr. said, and pushing past, he rushed down to the flailing creature. Stopping about five feet away, he fired two rounds into its head. The second one took the face clean off and sent thick pieces of Thulu whisker flying in all directions. It stopped writhing, and in the beam of Harold Sr.'s light, they watched the bluish-green blood trickle down a well-worn path toward the beach.

"You okay? Did he get you?" Harry said, inspecting Bessie for wounds.

"No. I'm okay. Thought a few times that he was one up on me, especially with that tail whipping about. But then I took his arm at the elbow and I knew right then that I was the one with the upper hand. No pun intended," she said and laughed nervously. It caused her to cough and she fell forward into his chest. Harry caught her and she let her swords fall point first into the sand beside the concrete walkway. Her arms wrapped his waist and she let out a long breath that ended in a slight sob. The odor of urine filled his nose and Harry said, "I'm guessing it didn't give you time to complete your mission?"

Bessie composed herself and said, "Uh, yeah. He, uh… literally scared the piss out of me. Good thing I still had my pants up. I hate fighting with my bare ass hanging out in the wind. I was just about to step around the corner, which would have put me in range of the bastard's claws. But I saw his tail slither into sight for a second, and it stopped me in my tracks. I blinded him with the flashlight just before he smacked it from my hand. That gave me time to back up and pull my swords."

"It was a good fight, and just think, it didn't even last ten minutes."

"Yeah, typical male," she said and chuckled."

"What?"

"Sorry, trying for a little humor, here."

"Oh, yeah. Got you. Ha-ha."

"Anyway, hate to think what would be happening right now if it had gotten me with that tail." She squeezed Harry a little tighter and he had to work harder to breathe.

Harold Sr. came jogging back to them, saying, "Oh man! Girl, you did a helluva job. Did you see that, Harry? This girl's got some moves!"

"Yeah, dad, I know all about Bessie's moves."

"You okay, sweetie? He didn't get you, did he?" Harold Sr. said excitedly, shining his flashlight over her legs, butt, back and head, before blinding Harry as the flashlight beam swept across his face.

"I'm okay, will you go grab my flashlight for me?" Bessie asked, sounding a little annoyed.

"Sure thing," Harold Sr. said, hurrying away.

"That last move was pretty gutsy," Harry said.

"It was spur of the moment, but I figured it'd work as long as I kept moving and was sure to bend forward far enough to keep my head out of its mouth. Good thing their reaction time sucks. I can still imagine the feeling of those tentacles wrapping themselves around my face." Bessie shivered, and Harry briskly rubbed her back.

"Well, you've got one up on me when it comes to Thulu. I've never had the pleasure."

"But you did get one of those fish headed… Pterodactyl… kangaroo things. That counts for something," she said, and pressed the side of her face to his chest. She chuckled and coughed. Harry could feel her starting to relax, and she unclasped her fingers at his back, allowing him to take a deeper breath.

"Hey, you two, could we get on with it?" his father said, and moving back to their side of the highway, he directed the beam of Bessie's flashlight into the shadow filled space.

"Sure thing, Pop's," Harry said, pulling his hands from Bessie's back.

Stringers of Thulu goo went with them, shining like spider web in thc beam of the light.

"Suppose we should end our little moment? I mcan, I've loved smelling you and all, but—daddy says it's time to go."

"All right," she said, and after taking his hand, she quickly jerked it away.

"Oh, yuk, looks like I slimed you."

Harry put his fingers up to his nose, took a whiff and abruptly pulled them away. Making a face of disgust, he wiped them on the side of the cottage.

Bessie bent and pulled her swords from the ground before walking away. Smiling over her shoulder, she said, "You enjoy that, now. My slime is your slime." After sheathing her swords, she pulled off her now repulsive hoodie.

"You might want to clean those swords, Bessie. You get too much gunk inside that scabbard and they're going to be hard to pull out," Harold Sr. said.

"Yeah, maybe later, but right now I want to change my clothes."

"All right, have it your way—I'm just saying."

"I hear you," she said with a hint of aggravation as she walked to her bookbag.

Harry approached his father and stretched out his hand, silently demanding he turn over Bessie's flashlight. Harold Sr. pretended to offer it, but a second before Harry could take it, his father pulled it back and shined it in his son's eyes. Then turning away, the old guy chuckled, and walked to Bessie, where he turned it off and dropped it into her open bag. It disrupted her rummaging, and Harry was pretty sure he heard her growl.

Harold Sr. smirked and moving a short ways up the highway, he stopped to stand on the center line, gazing north. Then glancing back, he gave them a look Harry couldn't decipher. He seemed like he was in a better mood now. Bessie's battle seemed to have cheered him up a bit. He had gotten to fire his gun three times since they left Morel Street.

"I want to change my clothes. Can we hold off moving for a while and… do you think I can use some of our drinking water to wash up a bit?"

"Oh, sure kiddo, no problem," Harold Sr. said, and pulling his canteen from its canvas sheath, he came back and handed it to her. "Thanks," she said. Giving her a brief grin, he turned and walked away without a word. Strolling up the highway, he stopped just past the cottages to stare at the ocean. Harry noticed his father was slouching. The sun broke through the clouds at the horizon and the old guy stood up straight as it bathed him in its rays. Harry thought it odd that the moment felt so final.

It was what people used to call a 'Kodak Moment'. It had something to do with a kind of camera from the early days. But the phrase fit. It was almost like the scene had been posed. It was the kind of picture that would stick in your memory forever. The light fizzled as the clouds closed up, and Harold Sr. moved farther up the road to stop by a large, dead tree. Pulling his knife from its sheath, he started carving in the bark.

The moment left Harry troubled, like it was some kind of foreshadowing. It made him wish he had argued to stay with Winnie for a little while longer and that he had not been so easily swayed to adhere to what seemed like a bad plan from the beginning.

Bessie was making a hell of a racket and Harry turned his attention to her. She was trying to climb over the chest high counter of a roadside booth that sat on the highway's western shoulder. It was the type where the top half was open on three sides when the shutters were up. A low shed roof shaded the interior and a sign at the front told him that they had once sold the best hotdogs in Rockingham County. Its white paint had faded and flaked, every flat surface becoming a canvas for anybody with a spray can.

Bessie dropped in and disappeared. She went to removing her clothing, her face popping up occasionally with a grin. There were grunts and groans punctuated with a few 'damn its'. She soon grew silent and Harry assumed she had gotten through the most difficult part of the process. Water began trickling out of the bottom to run across the asphalt and she broke into a rendition of 'Whistle While You Work'.

Harold Sr. had moved even farther up the road and was now reading an old sign tacked to a post. Harry could tell he was anxious to get moving, but he wanted to be polite for Bessie. He would keep his wisecracks to himself.

Bessie tossed out what must have been an old bandana that she had used as a washrag. It landed with a wet plop on the shoulder. A few minutes later she was dressed and climbing out, now attired in black, skintight cycling pants bloused with some light blue leg warmers above her hiking boots. The red tee shirt had been replaced with a pink one, and the hoodie was swapped for a long sleeved, blue, and white plaid flannel shirt. She could have easily been mistaken for an aerobics instructor had it not been for the swords strapped to her waist.

"All set BB? Can we go now?"

"Yeah, I'm ready. Thanks for being such a good boy," she said, rolling up her sleeves.

"Yeah, whatever. Those look comfortable—those pants. Kind of stretchy, huh?"

Bessie strutted over to him and when she got close, Harry pinched at some of the springy material covering her thigh. Pulling it out, he let it snap back.

"Ow! Oh Harry, you're such a brute," she said seductively and pretended to be aroused by making the appropriate face and moaning her pleasure.

"Are you two ready yet?" Harold Sr. shouted. He was back in the middle of the road now, hands on hips.

"We're coming," Bessie said.

"You look like mom standing there with your hands on your hips," Harry shouted.

His father didn't reply, instead he hiked a leg, and even at that distance, Harry could hear the staccato bark of the old guy breaking wind.

"What's that, Harry? Oh, thought I heard you say something," Harold Sr. said to the sky. He threw them a half grin and trudged away. Harry and Bessie traded looks and he gave her a shrug before stepping off to follow.

They made good time under a partly cloudy sky with his father maintaining the lead most of the day. Harold Sr. seemed distracted, and his mood was brooding. Harry knew he was still thinking about Winnie. He wasn't 'marching' like he typically did, instead, he walked with hands in pockets, just plodding.

Bessie didn't get her breakfast, so she ate whatever she had stashed in her bookbag. Harry just drank water, planning to coerce his father into stopping for a meal soon. Halting to rest at a place called Rye Harbor, Harry began to feel they weren't going to make good time on this day. After a ten-minute breather without conversation, they continued and soon found themselves surrounded by forest. Harry assumed they had entered what once had been a state park.

They came across an abandoned ranger station and finding a window with a broken lock, Harold Sr. crawled in and opened the front door for them. They found water in the form of small plastic bottles inside a mini fridge. They refilled their canteens and the hydration bladder before shoving the remaining water bottles inside the bags and the MOLLE pack. Harold Sr. came across a large wooden box full of M.R.E.'s stashed under a desk. Harry figured the park rangers had pilfered them, just like his father had.

They sat together at a table in the center of the room, studying Harold Sr.'s map and eating a light lunch of poppy seed pound cake, p-nut butter with crackers, and dried cranberries. They even tried the pasta with vegetables by just adding cold water, but not cooking the mess. It didn't work out. They saved the remaining unopened packets for when they could make a fire.

His father stashed as many M.R.E.'s as he could in his already oversized pack, grinning like he had found gold. Harry hoped that was a sign his father was coming out of his funk. The old guy turned away and Harry heard him say, "Let's go troops, got to make Stark's Island by dark."

After about five miles, Harold Sr. disappeared behind a large sign next to the road. Harry assumed it was for a pee break. He called out, telling them to continue and he'd catch up. His father had never done that before. Normally, he would have had them halt and stand waiting. This worried Harry even more. He wanted to pull the old guy aside and ask him what the hell was going on. There would be plenty of time for that once they arrived at Billy's. So, pushing it out of his mind, Harry took point.

The highway soon turned away from the beach to take them into Portsmouth. So, they got off at the 1B in order to keep moving toward their destination. It was when they were halfway across the bridge over the Piscataqua River that Harry noticed the ominous black roll cloud in the west. It was a sure indication that they were in for a hell of a storm. They would have to pick up their pace and maybe even jog for a while.

Harry had run track and field every year in middle and high school. So, he was no stranger to running. He knew that Bessie and his father, who now lagged in the rear, may not be able to maintain that kind of pace. Bessie too had fallen back a little, but when the wind came up, she hurried to him with a look of worry.

"Dad!" Harry called back, and when his father looked up, he pointed west toward the cloud bank moving through the sky like a colossal steamroller. Harold Sr. halted for a few seconds, staring at the stunning cloud formation, and then breaking into a run, he moved past them, yelling, "Let's get off this bridge and get to Billy's before that storm hits. Looks like a big one. I don't want to be out here if it drops a waterspout."

Lt. William 'Billy' Batschick had his cottage on the south side of the island, about a mile from the 1B on the shore of Little Harbor. Once they cleared the bridge, they could move down to the narrow rocky beach and keep up their present pace until they reached Billy's place. Harold Sr. had showed them on the map, back at the ranger's station, that there was a dirt road that ran to the cottage from the north. They supposed Billy would use it if he wanted to drive somewhere, but Harold Sr. told them that Billy preferred to use his boat to get around. It was an old, converted gillnetter of the sternpicker variety that he had bought after returning home from the war. He used it for pole fishing in the harbor, visiting the seaside grocers, and of course, his favorite tavern on the shore of Shapleigh Island.

The roll cloud passed overhead just as the three of them cleared the bridge. Taking a well-worn path down to the shoreline, they trotted east. The sky grew dark and the wind picked up, filling the air with sand and other debris. They were in a bad spot now because they moved along a body of water in near dark conditions. They were basically 'fish in a barrel' if a monster showed up. Harry felt the air grow cold and a spattering of raindrops dotted the narrow band of sand on which they ran. They soon reached a point where they had to climb over tree roots and large stones. Acquiring a few bumps and bruises in the process, they finally arrived on the beach adjacent to Billy's faded blue cottage with its white trim.

Harry saw a long pier and a dock with a semblance of an open lean-to, where the boardwalk ended at the shoreline. The old, red gillnetter, who Billy had christened 'Fidelis', floated at the end of a heavy rope about a hundred or so feet out. Billy obviously knew boating and had rigged the craft to keep it from bashing itself against the dock in foul weather.

From where they stood, they could just make out the cottage roof through the long grass growing up from the white sand of the dunes surrounding it. The pier ran toward it and then turned into a broad apron made of creosoted boards that ended at the bottom of a set of wooden steps.

The rough stairway granted access to the top of a short embankment that bordered Billy's tiny front yard. Jumping up onto the wooden apron, the three climbed the short set of stairs and stopped at the top to study the cottage.

Every pane of glass at the front was broken or missing completely. Harry got that bad feeling again. Something was wrong. It appeared that no one had been around for a while, and his father's face showed his dismay.

Then the rain came all at once, like a planet sized bucket had been dumped on them. Without a word, they dashed for the cottage as lightning fractured the sky. A sudden thunderclap caused them to duck as a gust of wind bent the trees and took Harold Sr.'s cap from his head, only to be caught with a quick snatch of his left hand.

They flew in through the open front door, stopping just inside for a quick scan of the interior as Harold Sr. returned his cap to his head. Harry knew the situation was twice as dangerous because they hadn't a chance to check it thoroughly.

Unsheathing his swords, he held them point down at his sides. Bessie took his cue and did the same. Harold Sr. stepped further into the room, the shotgun pointing forward from his hip.

"Dad?"

"Just keep your eyes peeled, huh?" his father said without looking back.

Harry turned his face to Bessie, and she stared back with fear in her eyes. "No one home, I'm guessing," she said, her words barely audible above the wind.

Her hair, free from its bandana, flew crazily about her head. A few minutes passed and when nothing came roaring out of dark doorways or closets, Harold Sr. nodded his okay to stand down. Sheathing her swords, Bessie worked her hair into a ponytail. In his heightened state of alertness, the act seemed unnecessary and it aggravated Harry.

"What are you doing? Can't that wait?"

"Can you just… shut up and let me move past? I'm still getting rained on, here."

He sneered at her and stepped up beside his father. She came in and moved left to back up against the wall. Brown leaves blew across the floor and then swirled inside the empty living room. The breakfast nook and kitchen, on their right, had its share of yard waste swirling around inside along with food wrappers and a couple of thin, plastic grocery bags.

"Looks like no one's been here for a while," Harry said.

"Yeah, wonder what happened to Billy," Bessie chimed in. "Maybe he just abandoned the place. Kind of a bad spot to have a house, you know? Nothing like having every kind of monster imaginable right in your front yard. I mean, you haven't talked with this guy for how long? And look, all the furniture's gone, only the boat's still here. There's no truck or car that I can see. So, maybe… he just packed up and left?"

"You might be right, sweetie… you just might be right. Well, least we'll have a place to stay for the night," Harold Sr. said and walked over to poke his head into what looked like a bathroom. Turning on his flashlight, he shined it around inside.

Harry gave his father a look of disbelief.

*What the hell are you thinking? We can't stay here!*

Harold Sr.'s statement cemented Harry's belief that his father had lost his edge. He was going to protest, but Harold Sr. had moved out of sight and Harry didn't want to yell.

It grew darker as the storm raged. Harry walked back to the front door and closed it but didn't throw the bar. Billy hadn't bothered reinforcing the entryway with a plank panel, and the windows still had the standard louvered shutters. The thought of spending the night there only made his bad feeling worse. The upper floor still had to be checked. So, the threat remained, as far as he was concerned.

Harry and Bessie pulled out their tiny flashlights and moved farther into the living room. A gust of wind blew the front door open, causing it to slam against the wall, initiating 'on-guard' stances for the two.

"Oh man! Scared the…" Harold Sr. said coming back into the room and glaring at Harry like it was his fault.

Harry ignored him and looked away to take a drink from his canteen. He then passed it to Bessie, who took her share before handing it to Harold Sr., who took a long drink and then set the canteen down against the baseboard of a nearby wall. He then hoisted off the MOLLE pack and dropped it beside the canteen. Making eye contact, he nodded toward the staircase and moved up the creaky steps.

Harry and Bessie, now hopped up on adrenalin, followed him up to the open arcade that connected the two small bedrooms on the second floor. Harold Sr. went right, and they went left.

The two found the room just as devoid of furniture as the first floor. The faded flowered wallpaper had been taped up in some places, and a bare, unbroken bulb in a plastic socket swung at the center of the ceiling from a heavy cord. A single pull string hung from it, and tied to the end was a small, green, plastic army man.

*So, Billy has a sense of humor! Wonder what he's got tied to the pull string in the other room?*

Harry felt Bessie back up to him, her face to the door. He was glad to have her. They made a good team. She was always thinking ahead of the game. She had not slain as many monsters as he, but Jonny had not been obsessed with monster hunting like Sergeant Harold. Her father just wanted to keep his family safe and was satisfied with letting the beasts come to him. Harold Sr. wanted to hunt them down and was grooming his only son to be a death-seeker—either the enemies, or his own. Harry knew that his father was the martyr type and as the old saying goes, *'When seeking revenge—be sure to dig two graves'*. Harry was sure that included monster hunting.

Moving to the window, he turned off his flashlight and looked down on the small, overgrown backyard. The rain pelted the glass and beat relentlessly on the roof. Shrubs, vines, and a multitude of weeds had taken over everything behind the cottage. There was no fence, only a short hedge enclosing a patchy lawn and some old trees whose branches scratched incessantly at the side of Billy's home.

Wiping the condensation from the glass, Harry could just make out a narrow flagstone path running out from the backdoor. It ended at what looked like an old well, its moss covered stone wall rising to about hip height. A crankshaft on square wooden posts, stretched across the opening and a yellow polypropylene rope wrapping the heavy rod, trailed down inside.

Lightning flashed, and Harry looked back to check on Bessie. She now faced him, wide eyed, her swords at the ready. Moving up beside him, she peered out of the window, and when her hip pressed against his leg, he felt her tremble.

*I wonder if she can tell I'm nervous too?*

The lightning flashed again and bringing his focus back to the yard, Harry's eye caught something round and white next to the wall of the well.

*Volleyball?*

The next flash of lightning told him no—human skull.

He focused hard on that spot and when the next flash came, he could just make out what looked like a vine wrapped skeleton projecting from the undergrowth.

*Billy?*

"BB, do you see…" but that's all he got out, because there was some movement on the top of that short wall. It looked like something had climbed out to sit there and study the cottage. Something large and monkey like. Harry's view wasn't clear—but it didn't need to be. He knew what it was, and his father needed to know, like… right now.

Turning quickly, he bumped into Bessie who stood paralyzed, staring out through the glass. She was trying to speak, but the words weren't coming. He hurried to the door and she hollered, "Harry! Hey, don't leave me here alone! This place is freaking me out."

"Dad? Where are you?" he yelled, trying to be heard above the storm as he sprinted toward the other room. The lightning flashed, and he saw his father with his back to them, standing at the side window, looking east toward the Atlantic. As Harry came in the door, a light breeze washed over his face.

*Is there an open window in here?*

Taking out his flashlight, he shined it across the room and yelled, "Dad, you need to see this." Harold Sr. turned, looking like he had just come out of a daydream. The expression on his face was one of surprise as if he had forgotten why he was there.

Bessie pushed in and shined her light on Harold Sr., as well. The old guy's shotgun was now slung on his shoulder as he stood looking at them, confused. In his hand, he held a tiny red, white, and blue object with a short piece of cotton string dangling from it. Harry took a couple steps closer and saw it was a plastic figurine of a Marine in dress blues. Putting two and two together, he figured it had been tied to the ceiling light's pull string and his father had broken it off.

"What you got there?" Bessie said with a hint of panic in her voice.

"Dad?" Harry said. "Hey! Pops! Snap out of it! There's something you got to see."

"What's that, son?"

Harold Sr.'s eyes trailed back down to the plastic toy in his fingers and grinning, he said, "Look what I found. Man! That Billy, he was always coming up with some quirky crap."

"Dad! Listen to me. There's a problem."

Harold Sr. brought his face back to them and his expression changed to something more pleading. It was like he already knew Billy was dead, and in his dying, his buddy had taken Harold Sr.'s dream with him. He never, in all of Harry's lifetime, looked so vulnerable, and at the worst possible moment. Harold Sr.'s eyes dropped back down to the tiny, plastic Marine in his fingers. He said something, but Harry didn't hear it because it was lost in Bessie's scream.

Her flashlight hit the floor, went out, and rolled past Harry's feet. He whipped around to see her terrified expression. Following her eyes to the window, he brought his own flashlight to bear.

The pane of glass in the lower sash was broken out, and on the sill, sat an owl-faced monkey creature. Its mouth was open, showing piranha like teeth as it squeaked and hissed at them. Large dark eyes turned to slits and pointing its scaly, beaked muzzle back over its shoulder, it let go with a loud, whistling howl. Harry didn't have to understand the language of the Hystrix to know what that meant. Others would be coming to join their scout, so he, Bessie, and his father, had less than a minute to get the hell out of there. The creature spread its little arms like it was going to take flight. This exposed the webbing underneath, making it resemble some mutation of an oversized flying squirrel. A large red dewlap swelled at its throat. It bent forward and issued a screaming hiss directly at Harry as two more creatures appeared, their faces peeking over the window sill.

Then there were six, then eight, and soon, ten or more gathered at the window, peering in at the three of them like a curious flock of crows. Then they parted like a wave, and a much larger one moved in to take the place of the scout. It studied them for all of two seconds, then issuing a short bark, a tsunami of Hystrix poured into the room.

"Hystrix! Dad! Let's go!" Harry shouted, as finger long quills thudded into the woodwork next to his head. Turning, he threw an arm around Bessie's waist and carried her with him as he sprinted out into the arcade. Bessie found her feet halfway to the stairs, and twisting out of Harry's hold, she took off at a run. Not wanting to waste time, she jumped from the top of the stairs to touch down on the first floor with a *Thump!*

Looking back over his shoulder, Harry expected to see his father right on their heels. But instead, the old Marine had stood his ground. Everything went into slow motion for Harry as blast after blast racked his ears, the gun spewing its own thunder and lightning. The creatures fell by the tens, but it wasn't enough.

Harry stopped running, turned, and started back. His swords were in his hands, but he couldn't remember pulling them. Before he got to the doorway, his father bellowed, "Get out! RUN! Go now while you can!"

Harry flinched as he watched poison quill-like darts find their mark, his father's grunts punctuating each one. It dawned on Harry that his father was trying to make time for him and Bessie to escape. It was the only way the two of them would get out of that house unscathed.

"Harry! Please!" Bessie yelled from below.
"Get out of here… NOW!" his father ordered through clenched teeth as the amount of time between gunshots grew longer. A creature leapt through the door into the hallway making for Harry's face. He chopped

it down, filleting it like a fish. Back peddling to the stairs, he jumped like he'd seen Bessie do.

Meeting her at the front door, he followed her out, and then passing her up, he continued down the path and jumping from the top step, he landed, stumbled, and then rolled across the apron. He realized he had been cussing up a storm all the way out, threatening every monster in the world with a most agonizing death.

For a few seconds, he remained seated on the rain drenched boards looking back at the cottage. His mind raced as the rain soaked him to the skin. Bessie soon appeared, and she too jumped. Landing on the boardwalk, she surfed past him on the wet wood. Coming to a stop, she turned and grabbing him under the arms, she pulled him to his feet.

"Come on, Harry, we've got to go, or we're next. We got to find some place to hide."

The shotgun was still blasting away, the front window of the upstairs bedroom flashing after every pull of the trigger. Then it went silent. Harry pushed his swords back into their sheaths but stood fast in the pelting rain as Bessie used every ounce of her strength to try to pull him toward the dock.

The lightning continually lit the sky, every flare overlapping the next, and then above the sound of the rolling thunder, Harry heard the single report of the .45.

Raising his face to the ragged clouds, he opened his mouth and a growling howl issued forth. All his anger, rage, and sorrow, poured out in a single primal scream. It seemed to go on forever as his tears mixed with the stinging rain. His anguished wail dwindled to a whimper and he heard, "HARRY!" followed by a stinging slap to his cheek. It brought his eyes open and they met Bessie's. He watched her lips move as the words poured out, "We've got to go… we got to go, NOW! Do you hear me? HARRY! They will be coming soon and then it will be our turn! PLEASE!"

She still had a hold on his arm and in a sudden moment of clarity, he jerked himself free. Giving her a venomous look as if she were an intrusive stranger, he turned and ran down the pier. Upon reaching the lean-to at the dock, he passed through, and dove into the harbor.

Bessie had given chase but stopped just inside the small structure and yelled, "Harry! I don't swim very well, you know that! What are you doing? Where are you going?"

Harry heard her words, but that didn't stop him. He figured she would do what she needed to, and going from a breaststroke to an enthusiastic butterfly, not even the weight of his bookbag filling with water impeded his progress toward the Fidelis.

When he arrived, he climbed inside, peeled off the bookbag, and fell to the bottom, wet and exhausted. He lay on coils of ropes and mildewed life jackets. When the reality of what had just happen took hold, he began to cry like a child. He felt the need to blame someone and he wanted that someone to be Bessie. It had been her plaintive cries that had pulled him from the fight, and now, he had to be alive to face the loss. However, a voice in his head that sounded a lot like his mother, told him that it was okay to be angry—but not at Bessie. His father had sacrificed himself for the both of them, and she was all he had left. The emotions, swirling chaotically in his mind, seemed to slow with the realization of the weight of his love for Bessie.

*You left her behind, you idiot!*

Through his sobs and jumbled thoughts, he heard, "Harry!" followed by coughing, and then, "Please, help me," followed by even more coughing. He heard splashing and felt the boat move like it was being tugged.

"Harry!"

*Snap out of it, Harry! How stupid would it be if you saved yourself only to let her drown?*

A terrible mixture of horror, guilt, and negligence, steamrolled its way in to crush the other emotions. Sitting up, he wiped his eyes and peeked over the gunwale to see Bessie clinging to the mooring rope just twenty feet away. Looking past her to the shore, he didn't see any activity and tried not to think about that one reason why the little fiends weren't out combing the beach right now.

Grabbing the rope, he pulled the boat closer to Bessie, allowing her to get a grip on the gunwale. Then taking a hold of the straps on her bookbag, he hauled her in.

They fell onto the deck together, and throwing his arms around her, he blubbered, "I'm sorry, Bessie, I'm sorry."

Bessie clung to him and said, "It's okay Harry, just stay down, I don't think they saw us. As long as they don't know we are out here, they'll probably pass us by. So, please, Harry, stay down."

After removing her bag, she tossed it forward and then reaching behind her, she pulled a dirty canvas tarp over the top of them and they snuggled beneath it. Harry's tears soon dwindled to just sniffles and an occasional stuttering sigh. He lay with his eyes closed, fighting to keep the ugly pictures of the Hystrix attacking his father out of his head. Bessie stroked his wet hair, her own tears trailing down her rain wet cheeks.

The clouds thinned and the rain slowed to a drizzle. A breeze pushed the gillnetter around and they felt an occasional jolt as the slack came out of the mooring rope. The storm soon blew out to sea, leaving a gray layer of overcast spreading back to the west. Even though there was relief that the storm hadn't been worse, it brought no relief from the heartache.

Harry pushed the tarp off of them, and peering over the gunwale, he saw there was still no movement back on shore. Bessie lifted her head and did her own bit of peeking, and then pushing some life jackets into a pile, she pillowed her head and lay down to watch him.

Bessie looked like she was going to say something, but she remained silent. After rubbing her eyes, she pulled a large square of cloth from a clear plastic package marked: 'Bag O Rags' that she had uncovered while rearranging lifejackets. After blowing her nose with it, she let it fall to the side and went to redoing her ponytail, acting as if Harry wasn't even there. That was okay, he was glad she didn't want to talk because, he surely didn't. Turning his attention to the Fidelis, Harry scanned the deck.

Billy must have removed the power roller, and the net reel with the intent of opening up the limited space for pole fishing. The folding chairs stacked in the corner, bolstered Harry's supposition. But the vast amount of things piled haphazardly around them, told Harry something else had been going on.

*Had Billy been planning a move before the Hystrix got him?*

Feeling fearful that the little beasts may use the lengthy mooring line to gain access to the gillnetter, Harry pulled in a useful amount of the rope before using a sword to cut the boat loose from the dock. Then crawling around on his belly, he poked his nose into boxes and bags trying to decide if there was anything that they could use.

The gillnetter rotated lazily now that it was free of its moorings. The breeze moved them further from land and closer to the seawall where the lighthouse stood at the harbor's entrance to the Atlantic. The thought occurred to Harry that even though there was at least a mile between them and that opening, if they didn't take control of the boat soon, they would be facing deep water within the hour. They still didn't know if the Fidelis's motor would start.

Pulling his face from a canvas bag full of large foam floats, Harry looked at Bessie with the intention of saying something about their situation. She now lay on her side with her eyes shut and was slowly rubbing a hand over her forehead like she had a headache. He felt reluctant to trouble her if that were the case, but time was a factor, so he needed to at least mention it. He never got the chance.

Out of the corner of his eye he detected motion on the beach and lowered his head. He let a few seconds pass before raising it again, pushing his eyes just above the gunwale.

A large group of Hystrix was moving up and down the sand as if searching. Occasionally a head would pop up and look around. They reminded him of meerkats he had seen on TV; just bigger and deadlier. Harry took some relief from the fact that the ID manual told him that they didn't have a sense of smell and being freshwater creatures, were unlikely to be found in or around salt water. Still, he was pleased with himself for having thought to cut the rope.

The bigger, darker Hystrix, which had relieved its scout at the windowsill in Billy's cottage, now stopped to look his way. It moved to the dock and leaning forward out over the water, it pushed its snout in the direction of the boat. Several more came to crouch beside it and do the same.

*They are going to swim out here and eat us*!

If they came, he and Bessie would not get away. They were trapped and would die right along with his father.

The creature's random squeaking cries were hardly discernible, but then came that same call the scout had used at the window. The little beasts all lined up along the docks edge about three rows deep, squirming and jostling each other. Harry experienced a most profound sense of dread, along with a serious dose of adrenaline. Turning his face to Bessie, he actually felt reluctant to disrupt her tranquil state, but it had to be done. The Fidelis would soon be under siege.

At the very moment Harry opened his mouth to speak, the sun broke through the clouds and lit up the mass of Hystrix. A frantic screeching filled the air and the creatures' broke ranks to become one big chaotic mob. The leader quit the group and raced back toward the cottage with the others in hot pursuit, seeking shelter from the burning rays of the sun.

"What are you looking at? Are they coming?" Bessie said with worry in her voice. Crawling up beside him, she shielded her eyes and peered toward shore.

"They were there… but they're gone now."

"And you weren't going to say anything?"

"Well, I was going to if they started coming out here. Uh… I didn't want to scare you unless… Bessie… forgive me… for everything."

Her face softened and she gave him a sympathetic smile. Kissing the tip of her index finger, she pressed it to his lips. He kissed it back, and holding hands, they lay together, studying the shoreline. The sun was well into the southwest and the breeze now had the boat at the half mile mark. Time was running out, they still had to get off the water and then use precious minutes searching for a place to hole up. At dusk, the harbor was going to get a bit lively, and they needed to be hidden away until the rising of the sun.

"Bessie, we got to get off the harbor, or… well, you know."

"I hear you, so… what should we do?"

Harry got up and moved into the wheelhouse. It was free of equipment, but it would only hold two people comfortably and only if standing. He found the switch marked 'Power' and flipped it on. The gauges on the white painted, plywood dashboard came alive and he saw there was little over half a tank of fuel. The battery's gauge showed low, but he figured there was just enough to start the motor. That would charge the battery and provide them with lights; if they needed them. He reminded himself that once they started the boat's engine, they would need to go full throttle to wherever they decided to head. The adult Thulu liked the deep ocean, but their young preferred the safety of harbors and bays.

"What do you think?" Bessie asked from the doorway, "Can you get it started?"

"I don't know, let's see," he said without looking back. Pushing the grimy, red starter button, the grind of the solenoid startled them both. The engine sputtered to life but quit. He pulled the choke and pushed the button again. This time it caught, black smoke rising up from the exhaust. Pushing off the choke, Harry turned and grinned at Bessie.

"Well, Captain Harry, where to?" Bessie said, moving to stand beside him.

"Wherever it is…we should go full speed to get there. Let's head for that point. That lighthouse, do you see it? It looks like there might be another dock over there, and I think I see buildings in those woods. There might be a store or something."

Harry pushed the transmission lever forward and engaged the propeller before bringing the throttle lever to the 'STANDARD' mark. The gillnetter began to pick up speed. It frightened him a little having not ever piloted a water borne vessel before.

"Ever drive a boat?"

"No, only my car. Oh! And a scooter, once."

"I've never done either. So, I guess we're going to have to learn as we go, huh?"

"I wouldn't mind trying?"

"Okay, take the wheel, you get to be the skipper now. I want to check out some things."

"Sounds like a plan," she said as she gently pushed him out of her way.

Taking the wheel, she brought them about, giggling as she overshot the line to the lighthouse. "Oops! Definitely not a car," she said, correcting her error. Exiting the wheelhouse, Harry heard the engine accelerate and the bow rose up, nearly putting him on his butt.

"Whoa, go easy, girl! We want to survive this trip, you know."

"You said full throttle, and besides, times a wastin'!" she said, flashing him a toothy smile. Harry shook his head in mock disbelief as he started his assessment of what was on board the Fidelis.

A huge flock of Kittiwake and a few other assorted gulls circled overhead, their strange calls filling the air. Harry figured they were probably hoping for a fish or two because of past experiences with other trawlers. "Sorry, birds, no food here," he said and started flinging items overboard that he, nor Bessie would ever use. The birds inspected each one to see if it were edible and then squawked their disappointment when they found it wasn't.

First went the nets, the bag of floats, several cardboard boxes full of smelly, old clothes, and a large metal container full of antique tools, which Harry was sure, went straight to the bottom. He kept some of the newer coils of rope but let the older hemp twists go away. Two of the life jackets and four of the floating seat cushions were allowed to remain, along with that Bag-O-Rags. A galvanized garbage can full of pots, pans, and plates, which sat at the transom, had to go as well.

Barely able to lift the heavy can, Harry rolled the steel container over the transom and sent it down to the silt. As soon as it cleared the side, the Fidelis bobbed up to sit higher in the water.

Pulling at a wet, brown tarp that draped something along the starboard side, Harry exposed two old whaling harpoons. Surprise filled his face and he shot a glance toward Bessie who was still preoccupied with her task.

The break-away hardware that secured them to the wood was still shiny new, and the edges of the barbed heads gleamed their sharpness. Pulling one from a clamp, he held it up, trying to get a feel for it.

"Hey, BB, look at this."

Glancing back, she said, "What the … What is that? A harpoon?"

"Well, yeah! What do you suppose Billy used these for?"

"Thulu, I imagine. I suspect he wasn't a whaler by any means. Hell, there haven't been any whale sightings for years. I think they are more for protection. Stick one of those through a Thulu and I can assure you, it's going down. What do you think?"

"Probably… should we keep them?"

"Sure! One more weapon in our favor. Just don't throw them like a spear. Use them more for stabbing."

"I'll throw it if I have to."

"Well, duh… that's what I meant."

Harry ignored her now, and taking it in both hands, he took a stance and jabbed the air several times, causing the gillnetter to rock. Bessie giggled and called out, "Ok, Ahab, enough horseplay, get back to work."

"Okay, dad," he hollered, and then regretted it. Their eyes met, and after making a sad face, Bessie turned her attention back to the windscreen without a word. Harry hung his head and his arms went slack, allowing the harpoon to just dangle. Remembering his meditative training, he worked to empty his mind and focus on the 'Now'. There would be time for grief later. He understood why people drank themselves to the point of passing out. With both parents' dead, he never felt more alone in the world, even with Bessie close by. Sticking the harpoon back in its clamps, he returned to his task.

Soon, everything they didn't need was either floating in the gillnetter's wake or fast sinking to the bottom. Sitting down on a now visible bench to the right of the cabin door, he leaned over the side and looked forward past the wheelhouse toward their destination. They were almost there, and he could see the short pier and dock more clearly now. There were old tires lashed to its side and spaced an equal distance apart to act as bumpers.

"We're almost there, Harry. Only one little problem, though… I'm afraid I don't know how to park this thing."

"I don't either, but when we get close, maybe shut down the throttle and turn the wheel to the right. After we 've straightened out, facing the opposite shore, bring the wheel back to center and slide in sideways. Try that and see if it works, but… I feel like we need to slow down a bit."

"Okay, whatever you say—Captain."

Harry grabbed what remained of the mooring line and waited to wrap it around a post. Bessie did as he suggested and with such ease that he wondered if maybe she was a natural born sailor. They hit with a soft bump, and using his rope, he secured the gillnetter to the dock. He waited for Bessie to join him before jumping down onto the wooden walkway, both bookbags hanging from her hands. Taking in the lighthouse where it rose above the tree tops, he listened to the waves breaking against the concrete wall, drowning out all the other sounds.

*Noisy place to live! You'd never hear the monsters if they tried to sneak up on you.*

Donning their bags, they walked the pier back into the wooded area. The jetty became a large open deck in front of a small store-like building.

It was much older than Grunt's, and it had a wooden ramp that ran down its east side to the graveled lane behind. The olive-colored paint was peeling in places on the clapboard siding, but the door and windows were still intact. A large, weather-beaten sign above the porch roof read: 'Snappy's General Store'. Underneath that, in smaller letters, it let them know there were: 'Fishing cottages for rent—Reasonable rates—Inquire within'.

They moved down the ramp to the lane and found it littered with limbs and other debris from the storm. It branched off a gravel road that ran down from the north, came into the trees, and made a complete circle, connecting a dozen one room cabins, all of them in a serious state of disrepair.

"Shall we inquire within?" Bessie said in a haughty voice and then giggled.

"Most certainly, my dear, but only at the ready."

Pulling their swords, they moved up the steps of the small stoop at the back. The door had been reinforced with a plank panel much like the ones they used back in Kilbury, and it had been secured with a heavy hasp and padlock.

Harry pivoted on the landing to look back toward the cabins. Not a pane of glass was intact, doors stood ajar, or, were missing altogether. Many of the roofs had caved in and vines had taken over everything. The dark, yawning openings, shrouded in vegetation, gave him the creeps.

Whoever had been there last appeared to have made use of the store for shelter. Close inspection of the huge padlock showed a spider had made her home behind it. From the size of the insect's web, Harry knew no one had gone through that door for a long time.

Picking up a stick, Bessie poked at the hasp until a huge, black widow spider, nearly three inches from claw to claw, scrambled out. She shrieked and jumped back. The huge arachnid fell through a crack between the stoop and the wall and could be heard scrambling across the dead leaves below.

"Ahhh… That was a big one. Scared the crap out of me. Kind of glad it didn't fall on the porch. I can just imagine it running up my leg."

"Just killed a Thulu not half a day ago and you're whining about a little ol' spider?"

"Little ol' spider? That thing was big enough to make me think we might have to do battle."

"Yeah, okay. It kind of made me jump too, and honestly… I hate spiders."

Harry made a face and pretended to be embarrassed. Sheathing his swords, he walked down the steps and coming back with a large landscaping block, he began to pound the hasp. It took a while for the two-inch-long screws to tear free from the door frame, nearly disintegrating his concrete hammer in the process. Dropping it over the rail, Harry turned, and remaining behind the plank shutter, he pulled on it to create a gap that allowed Bessie to open the inner door and peer inside.

"Looks clear," she assured him, and he opened the shutter the rest of the way to allow the sun's dying light inside.

There was a thin film of dust on the floor with no tracks apparent, reassuring them that there had been no recent guests. Harry pulled his flashlight from his pocket and Bessie did the same. They entered the doorway, and facing the first shelving unit, they split to take different sides of the room. The air inside was hot, stale, and filled with the odor of decay. Somewhere a large fly or wasp buzzed and ticked, trying to beat itself to death against a pane of glass.

"There's a lot of stuff in here," Bessie said.

"Yeah, mostly canned food and dry stuff—as usual. Hey, sardines! BB, there are sardines."

"Go to hell, Harry. I don't eat just sardines."

"Oh! Look, water bottles—cases of water bottles! Somebody was thinking ahead. A person could stay here through the winter if they needed to," he said.

"I think, just maybe, someone had."

"Could be…" Harry mumbled.

"No, look."

Coming around the shelving units, he met her at the front. She had been referring to a cozy nest someone had made in the large, open space just back from the big display windows. He caught a whiff of wood ash, and creosote, but there was no death, no rotten food, and nothing to show the monsters had been there. There was an old potbellied stove with a stack of wood next to it and the ashes were close to overflowing out its small metal door that now hung open. The pile of wood at its feet consisted mostly of chair pieces. Harry suspected that in years past people had gathered there to sit around that stove, smoke, and share stories. He had a fleeting sense of sadness for the loss of a Norman Rockwell way of life and he returned his attention back to the now.

A sleeping pallet lay on the floor to their right. It was made of wide strips of wall insulation that had been lain down and covered with a soft canvas drop cloth. At the head, was a tattered sleeping bag, rolled up to be used as a pillow. Next to that, a white enameled, but heavily stained, coffee cup sat on the floor. There were some fishing magazines, several Playboys, a well dog-eared copy of H.G. Wells' *War of the Worlds*, and a battery powered lantern. Pushing the on switch, the lantern failed to light. Harry wasn't surprised.

Bessie cleared her throat and said, "Suppose, we could stay here?"

"Well, I don't know… possibly. I always relied on my… ummm…" He didn't finish, realizing how much he depended on his father for those decisions. Guilt was creeping in now, adding weight to the heartache. The tears welled and he fought them.

*Think of something else, dammit!*

"Here, let me test the bed," Bessie said and after giving his butt a quick pat, she flopped down on the pallet.

"Hmmm… pretty comfy if you ask me." Rolling onto her side, she pushed herself up on one elbow. "What do you think? It's big enough for the both of us, and it doesn't stink." Leaning out over the edge, she looked past the shelving units toward the back.

"Looks like the backdoor has a good solid bar from what I can see."

"Well, okay, if you want. Good a place as any, I guess," Harry said, still feeling a little uneasy about it because a voice in his head kept saying, "No." In fact, it was screaming, "NO! Don't stay here!" It felt too perfect—like a trap.

The front door was boarded over, but the big windows showed little effort had been made to protect the glass. The huge panes had been whitewashed on the inside, and long, wide boards had been nailed randomly across them, leaving gaps as wide as the boards themselves. Why some huge creature hadn't bashed their way through, raised a question in Harry's mind. He just wanted to get their supplies and get out.

His eye detected the wasp as it bounced its way across the top of one of the large panes and he remained silent, trying to figure out a way to tell Bessie that he didn't want to stay.

The subtle approach seemed best and he said, "Should we gather our supplies? We are going to have to carry everything now. My… the molly pack is still back there where my… ummm… still at Billy's."

"Okay, but why are you avoiding my question?" Bessie said, and getting to her feet, she walked toward him across the pallet. She didn't quite make it.

Wood cracked and snapped, as one of her legs disappeared through the insulation. She plunged down to her crotch; her other leg stretched out in front. She shrieked and tried to push herself out.

Harry just stared in amazement as she hollered, "Awww…crap! What the … Harry, help me! Grab my hands." He took hold of her and back pedaled, pulling her free. They moved off the pallet and stood with their arms around each other. Looking back to where a portion of the soft canvas cover had disappeared down a hole. Harry said, "Kind of a shock, huh?"

"Ummm… YEAH! Surprised the crap out of me… almost literally."

Letting go of Bessie, he kicked the entire pallet, sending it flying to the wall. This exposed the transparent plastic sheeting underneath, part of it stuffed down inside the opening. After pulling it out, they peered into the crawl space beneath the store. The boards of the floor had been gnawed thin and the weight of Bessie's body had proven to be too much for them.

"Looks like something had been working at this for a while," Harry said.

Shining his light down inside, they could see a pile of woodchips and some deep claw marks in the clay. Leaning in, Harry shined his light back toward the foundation and saw a small cupboard like door lying on the dirt of the floor. Its hinges were twisted and broken like it had been forced from the outside. Beyond that, an opening about the same size as that small door, offered a view to the long, unmowed grass on the west side of the building.

"I really think we need to get some food for our dinner and get the hell out of here. We can come back in the daylight tomorrow to stock up, but we need to go before it gets much darker."

"What do you suppose made that? I mean, what can chew through wood? Maybe a beaver monster, or a… reptile rat?"

"I don't know, and I don't want to know. A lizard rat, beaver monster, whatever! Let's get our food and get out."

"Where are we going to sleep? We can't stay on the boat that would be just plain stupid, and those cabins back there, well, they kind of suck. So… where?"

"I don't know. Let's think about it while we look for our dinner, okay? But we got to get going."

There was a large, metal 'YELD' sign hanging on the wall that someone had stolen and brought inside to use as art work. Its yellow paint had faded, and rust streaks tattled its age. Taking it down, Harry laid it over the hole. Spying a heavy metal bench vice on a stand in a corner, he slid it over and let it topple onto the sign to weigh it down.

"Too heavy for me to pick up. So, heavy enough to keep the monsters out. At least for the moment, anyway," he said, grinning.

Bessie smiled at him and then strolled away to start her search. He did the same, starting with what canned foods remained on the shelf closest to him. After a short time, he had a sack full of items that included crackers, canned meat, canned fruit, canned vegetables, and a jar of mixed nuts with seal intact.

"Look for a can opener, will you?" he called out, and then doing the same, he lost hope until Bessie shouted from across the store, "Found one! It's the type with the sharp point. You know the kind… like to pry a bottle cap off with? It's kind of rusty, but it's hanging on a string over here behind the counter." He heard her jerk it loose, and then she added, "I haven't seen one of these in like, forever. It's a freaking antique."

"Whatever, just bring it and meet me out back."

He walked out onto the stoop and Bessie soon followed, her arms loaded down with potato chips, a can of corn, a can of fruit cocktail, soda crackers, and of course, numerous cans of sardines. She walked down the steps and around to the side of the stoop.

"No spider?" she muttered as she scanned the ground around her feet, then dumping her items on the waist high landing, she removed her bookbag and set it next to her pile. Using the platform as a work surface, she began to load her food inside.

A can rolled to Harry's feet and he pushed it back with a toe. She took it and dropped it in. Smiling up at him, she seemed satisfied with her ability to pack a bag.

"Pack mine too, will you? My bags kind of full. I promise I won't make you carry everything—all the time. We can take turns." She begrudgingly reached up to take his items, saying, "Of course you won't, you know I won't let you, and taking turns just sounds silly. It will all be gone soon enough, anyway. I can handle it."

Bessie put the food in her bookbag and strapping it shut, she hoisted it to her shoulders. Harry latched the inside door and then pushed the shutter closed. Moving together to the front of the building, they stood on the full-length gallery and studied the landscape. Harry felt frantic, but Bessie seemed calm as she backed off the porch onto the wooden deck that stretched to the dock. Gazing up toward the roof, she said, "Would you suppose this place has an attic?"

"Good chance, but I didn't see any access through the ceiling, or should I say, I didn't look."

"Me neither. Should we check? We can always go back inside?"

"Not so sure I want to," he said and looking out toward the ocean, the idea hit him like a Wing Chun straight kick to the gut.

"The lighthouse!"

"Hey! Yeah! The lighthouse!"

Bessie took off at a jog, eastward, across the vast expanse of deck and arriving at the edge, she jumped off into the weeds. The weight of her bookbag caused a loss of balance and she staggered when her feet hit the ground. Catching herself before falling on her face, she laughed and continued toward the trees. Harry chased after her and moving in under the canopy of leaves, he found her standing at the far edge of the grove, gazing at a field of waist high grass. The afterglow of sunset had just left the sky and a rising full moon now sat at the horizon. It was monster time.

"Suppose there's anything hiding out there?"

"Don't know, but… the hell with it," Harry said and took off at a run.

"Yeah!" Bessie said and raced after him. Catching up, he grinned at her and she began to giggle in a hell-bound kind of way as the long grass swished against their legs.

They soon came to that gravel road and saw it ended in a small parking lot just outside of their destination. They took an abrupt right turn and Harry followed Bessie as they sprinted to the base of the massive concrete pylon. Racing through the empty lot, they tried to stop before they collided with the metal, oval shaped door, their boots sliding on the marble sized stones. Panting, they bent at the waist, trying to catch their breath. Harry kept an eye on the grass, looking for movement in the shadows or any excessive rippling that would tell him something was coming. Seeing nothing, he felt the relief of knowing that they were safe.

His respite didn't last long, though, as a new worry formed in his head.

*What if we can't get in?*

Not wanting to waste time, Harry grabbed the long steel lever of the latch and tried to yank it down. Nothing moved. Bessie grabbed it too and together they pulled, but as much as they grunted and groaned, it only moved about an inch. She stopped, and pressing a finger to her lips, she looked around. Harry hung off the lever with both hands and grumbled, shaking his head in dismay.

"Step back, I got this," Bessie said, and moving out of her way, he saw she now had a soccer ball sized stone in her hands. Raising it above her head, she brought it down on the lever.

The old steel bar couldn't resist that kind of force, and screeching like a wounded animal, it gave up. The door squeaked open a crack, emitting a rush of air that brought an electrical smell. "Ha! See, I can do it, too!" Throwing her rock out into the grass she raised a flock of small birds who took their complaints to the sky as they sought a safer roost.

Harry looked at Bessie, cocked his head and said, "I didn't know it was a competition." She just shrugged and made a face. Turning back to the door, he peeked around the edge and shined his light inside before pulling it open all the way. The floor was circular and concrete. It had a set of iron stairs spiraling straight up at the center. Tall metal cabinets and shelving units lined the wall. A small desk sat on the far side, accompanied by a rolling chair and a stack of file boxes.

The windows were few, and the ones that did exist, were just eight-inch-wide slits that started about ten feet above their heads and made their way toward the top in a spiral pattern. Harry suspected they offered only a meager amount of light even on the sunniest of days.

Bessie pushed past Harry, disrupting his inspection. "Come on, slowpoke," she said, and walking slowly toward the stairs, she scanned the room.

"I think this will do," Harry said.

"Agreed," Bessie stated in a matter-of-fact manner. Turning to him, she added, "So… shut the door and lock it, will you?"

"Aye, Aye, Cap'n," he said, swinging the door closed with a resounding *clang!*

Harry examined the locking mechanisms and found the setup to be much like that of a ship. Four large clamps sat at equal intervals around the rim, operating independently of the outside latch. Harry rotated each lever to the center of the door, bringing the tang at the opposite end out over the surrounding steel frame. Unaffected by the weather, the levers still maintained a good amount of grease and rotated easily. Bessie followed along behind him, tightening the large, metal thumbscrews that locked the clamps in place.

"Nothing's going to get through that," she said.

"Yeah, it was designed to keep things out, like, water, snow, and… sea monsters?" No sooner had he finished his statement, then a loud, *Clang!* resonated from the lantern room far above their heads. The flashlight went out and swords hissed from their scabbards. Harry regretted having taken all that time to secure their exit without having first checked and cleared the interior. His eyes met Bessie's; their gleam barely visible in the ambient light. Turning together, they prepared to face whatever might be coming down that stairway.

# CHAPTER 7

## Shelter, Shade, Nor home Have I...

There was an overwhelming urge to rush upstairs to investigate. Moonlight now filled the top floor and trickled down to cast them in its glow. They waited, listening, their eyes straying back to each other on occasion. The sound came again. They both jumped and chuckled under their breath.

Leaning forward, Harry peered up toward the large glass surround as the noise came a third time. "The door leading out to that gallery is open. It keeps slamming shut in the breeze. I think we can put our swords away."

"Almost peed my pants—again. I was afraid we wouldn't get the clamps open in time if there was something up there."

"We'd still have to fight anyway; inside or out. Between the two of us, I'm sure we could have handled it. So, should we check it out? This room, I mean?"

"Good idea and then we'll go up and shut that damn door."

The acrid stench of an electrical fire coupled with the tell-tale odor of bearing grease and damp cement filled Harry's nose as they moved around the room.

As much as he tried look at the bright side of things, sorrow was dragging him down. The heavy weight of grief lay over his shoulders like a wet blanket. He wanted his old bed back so he could just curl up in it and grieve.

They were soon poking through the large metal cabinets and shelves, their flashlight beams making crazy arcs over the walls. They found assorted tools, rope, a small propane torch, a couple of strikers for that torch. Along with those, rolls of electrical wiring, and luckily for them, several railroad lanterns.

They also found a blue, plastic container of what smelled like kerosene, some large lensed, floatable camping lanterns, and several six-volt batteries to power them.

Bessie discovered a box of candles and matches that had been packed away together in waxed paper, and next to them, a small convection heater.

"We can use these," Harry said, pulling out the railroad lanterns and the blue plastic fuel can. Bessie showed him the candles and matches, saying, "These too! And, what about those floatables?"

"No. Look, the batteries are leaking. See the dried, rusty looking trails running out of the lenses? Bad news. That acid will eat right through your clothes and…"

"Right through, MY clothes? Then I'd be naked… wouldn't you love that?"

"Yeah, well… whatever."

"Oh! What? You don't want to see me…"

"Please, Bessie, it's been a really crappy day, okay? I mean, sure, I want… oh, forget it, let's just talk later. I want to get setup and eat something, my stomach's killing me."

"Sorry, just trying to cheer you up. So, we will actually talk later, right?"

Changing the subject, he looked around and mumbled, "It looks like we are going to have to sleep on this hard floor."

"Hey! Answer me," she said, slamming one of the cabinet doors shut in mock anger. She then made her 'Oops face' after realizing she'd overdone it.

"I just want to get some food in me and then sleep, and… DAMMIT BB! My dad is dead!"

Harry lowered his face and glared at the floor. The numbing disbelief that he wasn't ever going to hear his father's voice again was intense. The hollow feeling in his gut now felt more like heartache than hunger.

"Well, I am truly sorry, Harry," she said in a solemn manner. "That's just one more thing that we have in common. We are both parentless now. It won't hurt a thing to cry. It's just me here, you know, and…"

"No. I mean… sure, it's coming, no matter how much I fight it, but not right now. There's been too much of it already. I have to get strong—somehow."

"No problem."

Harry gazed at her face looking somewhat odd in the glow of her flashlight. She smiled sympathetically and cupped his cheek with her hand for a brief second before returning to her task. She shut the other door to the cabinet and then shined her light in the spaces between it and the next. Her hand disappeared inside and came out dragging a folding army cot.

"Oh, a cot, wonderful! These guys thought of everything." Picking it up, she hugged it like it was a favorite teddy bear. "So… where's yours?"

"Well, uh…"

"Just kidding," Bessie said, and setting her cot down, her hand disappeared a second time to drag another into view.

"I suppose they needed these on the bad nights when the lighthouse guy had to sleep over. Just in case the light went out or something. Maybe this second one was for his wife, or… lover?"

Harry managed a grin, shook his head, and walked away to light a lantern. He appreciated Bessie trying to humor him, and he was glad she was there, but he needed more time. His father had always taken care of everything, and now, Harry felt lost and directionless.

Returning to Bessie, she handed him his cot and then followed him to where he set it up in an open space along the west wall. Once he finished and had gone to light a second lantern to take up the stairs, Bessie unfolded and slid her cot up against his.

Sitting down on the edge, she said, "There, just like a double bed. Hey! Should we go up and take a look at the view? I've never been in a lighthouse before."

"That's what this lantern is for."

"Oh, good. You want to eat up there? That would be kind of romantic, right?"

Harry didn't answer, the prospect of moving to a higher elevation didn't appeal to him. Bessie got tired of waiting for a response. Leaving the cots, she grabbed her bookbag and ran up the staircase, giggling. He soon followed, trudging up after her, lantern in hand. The metal creaked, leaving him glad it was only two stories to the top. He never liked spiral stairs and the tighter, the worst. As he worked his way up, he wondered if he might have vertigo.

He soon passed by the watch room, a heavy, semicircular wooden platform projecting out from the east wall, butting up against the stairs. It was half the width of the tower and sat just below the lantern room supported by mammoth wooden brackets. Harry went back down a couple of steps and studied the interior through the entrance.

The space inside had been painted a bright white and the lantern room floor acted as the ceiling. It was occupied by what looked like a homemade couch constructed of rough wood with cushions taken from another piece of furniture; now long gone. There was a small folding table with two matching chairs and an ancient, metal coffeepot rested at its center. A tiny gas stove sat on a plank counter top under a bank of cupboards along the south wall. There was a set of long, wooden bookcases, which, like the couch, had been built on site with rough wood. They sat on each side of the opening, pushed up against the metal balustrade at the front. Harry suspected they had been placed there to keep the 'Wickie' from slipping between the two heavy metal rails and plunging to his death when drunk. They held assorted books, a wind-up clock, and a small TV sat upon its top keeping company with a shaded electric lamp.

Harry wondered if it might be a better place to sleep. But it was hot up there, and the air was stifling. It had one of those vertical slits of a window, but he suspected it hadn't been opened for years. They would just stay where they were.

Moving up into the lantern room, Harry set his light on the floor at the base of the huge beacon. He could see where the fire had been. The space inside the large, textured, glass surround that once held the light source, now contained a mass of blackened debris.

The temperature at the top was quite a few degrees higher than below, and Harry expected to break a sweat at any moment. He was grateful the sun was down and wouldn't be baking them to a crisp.

Bessie disappeared as she made her way around to the other side of the lantern room. There came the sound of startled seabirds, and Bessie muttered, "Fly away you seaborne devils, fly away," and then pulled the door shut.

Harry stood studying the sky where a waxing moon now hung surrounded by stars in a dark blue vault. A twinge of awe took the edge off his grief and turning to say something about it to Bessie; he changed his mind and just watched her stroll his way. She tapped on the textured glass of the beacon as she moved. For some reason, her actions made him realize how pointless the lighthouse was now—just like his father's death.

Bessie passed him without a word and moved to the seaside of the lantern room to flatten herself against the glass. She gazed out toward the eastern horizon and whispered, "Beautiful, just beautiful." Harry came up beside her and she turned like she was going to embrace him. But he didn't want intimacy; fearful where it might take him. So, he walked away to take his turn around the beacon.

She huffed, and he said, "Sorry," without looking back.

Arriving at the door, Harry opened it and stepped out onto the gallery deck. A sudden sense of panic gripped him as he looked down through the metal grate that formed the platform where he stood. He spun around to dash inside but couldn't because Bessie was coming out. This heightened his anxiety and he almost shrieked. Instead, a strange little noise escaped his lips as he forced his way past her to get inside.

"Hey, what's wrong?"

"I don't know… ummm… it scared the crap out of me, though."

"You're afraid of heights! Oh, Harry, I'm sorry, I didn't know."

"Neither did I—not really, anyway."

He stood staring out at her, and he must have looked shaken because she didn't argue. Hooking the door open on the outside, she stepped back in, "A little too warm up here, might be wiser to leave this open, after all."

Taking his hand, she led him back around to the other side and they sat cross legged on the plank flooring. She directed him to sit so he could face her. He knew it was because she wanted to see his eyes as they talked.

After he got situated, she removed the sardines and crackers from her bookbag, and they took to gorging themselves on stale soda squares and vacuum-packed fish. Harry was happy for any kind of food, but he longed for fruits and vegetables. The saltiness of the fish and crackers left him wanting for water.

"Uh… thirsty. I need some water," Bessie said, and rummaging around at the bottom of her bag she pulled out two water bottles that had come from Winnie's place. She handed one to Harry, and they drank.

"Should've grabbed some more of these over at the store," Harry said.

"We still have your two. That should last us through the night, right?"

"Yeah, I suppose we'll be okay."

"We also have these," she said, and reaching in, he heard the crackle of plastic packaging and she pulled out a large bag holding about a dozen smaller packages of crème filled sponge cakes.

"You actually took a bag? Wow, I don't know what to say. It's your life, I guess. Do what you want, but…"

"I couldn't resist," she said, grinning. "They are double wrapped, you know? I took the best one of the bunch."

"Those things will last forever—wrapped or not."

"Well, let's see," she said and popping open the bag, the escaping air brought a tantalizing odor to his nose, and his mouth began to water.

"Hmmm… great smell, huh?" Pulling one out, she ripped open the wrapping and sniffed the yellow cake. "A little stale, but I don't see any mold." Taking a small bite, she chewed and swallowed. She then grimaced and made a choking noise. Grabbing her throat with one hand, she began to jerk her head from side to side. Harry started to get up, but then he saw her grin.

"Just kidding," she said, and scarfed down the rest.

"Fine! Give me one."

She handed him a cake and Harry checked it out through the clear, plastic wrapper before opening it. His first bite triggered a craving for more. It took the salty taste from his mouth and sipping his water, he finished the rest of his dessert while staring out at the ocean. Bessie focused on having seconds.

Other than the occasional splash of a wave at the seawall, the surface appeared placid. The moon rose higher and the seascape around them grew brighter. Bessie soon slid over to Harry's side and taking his hand, she held it as she leaned her head against his upper arm.

Sitting in silence, they watched the moonlight reflected on the water. Harry tried hard to keep his thoughts in the present and enjoy the moment. A kind of calm came over him, and he thought it might be a good time to hit the sack. It would be easier to fall asleep in a more tranquil state of mind. Before he could say anything to Bessie about going to bed, motion caught his eye out where the short wall terminated at the harbors entrance. Something moving just below the surface had churned the water

*Maybe a school of fish in some kind of a feeding frenzy?*

"Do you see that?" Bessie asked.

"Yeah, I see it."

"What do you suppose it is?"

"Not something good—that's for sure."

A creature about the size of a killer whale suddenly burst from the water, and arching through the air, it dove back in. Then Harry heard the hooting sound as something climbed out to sit on the concrete wall.

"Thulu!" they both whispered, looking at each other, their eyes wide with fear. Harry blew out the lantern but could still see Bessie's fear filled face in the moonlight.

"Do you suppose it saw us?" Bessie said.

"I don't think so, but if that thing starts climbing this lighthouse, I guess we'll know for sure."

Soon there were four of them sitting out there perched on the top of the wave brake. They were all about the same size, and Harry assumed that from a biological perspective, one could refer to them as yearlings. They dove in and swam around, then leapt back onto the wall, interacting in a peculiar way. A fifth, smaller Thulu appeared and leapt up to sit beside the others. It hooted at them and made a strange cackling noise. Five more tentacle bewhiskered heads poked out of the water to study the others for all of a minute before climbing out to join them.

The first group appeared to be communicating with the leader of the smaller ones. Their long tails flicked about like cats and they made erratic gestures with their arms. Pretty soon their heads began to bob and dewlaps appeared. Their slimy bodies began to weave back and forth as tentacles climbed the air.

"What the hell are they doing?" Harry said. "It's almost like the smaller ones are trying to communicate something to the bigger ones."

"I don't know for sure, Harry, but… but I think they are getting ready to have some serious Thulu sex."

"Great, that's all we need, a pornographic Thulu show."

"Well, I'd like to say… hey, it's just nature, but there doesn't seem to be anything natural about those freaks."

The bigger ones soon fell lazily into the water on the ocean side, the smaller Thulu following. They coupled together and then bobbed around while attached to each other. This seemed to excite the odd one out, who began to run back and forth. Then jumping into the ocean, it disappeared from sight, only to reappear, and leap back onto the wall.

"Maybe we should just go down to our beds. I think I've had about all the Thulu porn I can stand," Harry said.

"Why? Are they making you horny?"

"What? No! If I had some explosive tipped arrows or maybe even one of those Barret fifty-caliber sniper rifles, I'd risk taking a few of them out."

Bessie gave him a look of disbelief and said, "What? And give away our location? All we need is for the ones you didn't kill to come banging on our door. Besides that, they could easily climb up the outside of this tower. So, the only thing that is keeping us safe is the fact that they don't know we're here."

"I can dream, can't I? Take it easy, huh? It's not like I have any of those things with me."

She started to say something and then her eyes strayed past him to the ocean. Harry watched the mounting terror in her eyes and turning back, he gazed out toward the deeper water. A large area of turbulence was forming and then something as tall as a ten-story building rose up above the surface. It looked like a moray eel complete with arms. Even though he couldn't see the portion that remained under water, he felt it safe to assume it had some pretty long legs.

The first thing that came to mind was, *Godzilla,* as it stood watching the Thulu, the tip of its tail whipping out of the water and then splashing back. Long scutes, much like the ones found on a crocodile's back, ran in a double ridge up its spine to a basilisk like crest, or comb, atop its head. Crystalline fangs as long as Harry was tall, gleamed in the moonlight as the beast scrutinized its prey.

The Thulu just froze in place. Bessie crawled over to kneel behind Harry and watch over his shoulder. Suddenly a chameleon like tongue shot out and impaled one of the bigger Thulu in the midst of copulation. It was yanked away as its smaller mate released its hold to splash into the sea. The mammoth beast grabbed the Thulu with its front paws and tore it in half before eating it.

The remaining Thulu dropped below the surface, the smaller ones diving over the wave brake into the harbor side to be shielded by the concrete wall.

Harry watched the leviathan search for more victims as it chewed. "Maybe we should lay down, huh?" he said and they both took up prone positions, side by side, their eyes just above the top of the steel kickplate that ran around the base of the windows.

"Did you see that?" Harry whispered.

"Of course, I saw it! Where'd you think I was, off having coffee and cake with the neighbors?"

"I think I peed myself a little."

"That makes two of us. If we keep this up it might be smart to start wearing diapers. What do you suppose that is? I never studied the ID manual like you did."

"It wasn't in there," Harry said, watching the creature submerge to where only it's eyes and crest remained out of the water. It reminded him of the alligators he saw at the zoo, floating with just their eyes above the surface, scanning for anything that might be on the menu. The creature soon submerged completely and the sea grew placid again.

Harry could just make out the shadows of seabirds as a flock formed over the area where the monster had been, their silhouettes fluttering across the face of the moon. He figured they were picking up what remained of the Thulu, and that left him to wonder if they were edible like a cow. The fact that they smelled like rotten fish turned him off the thought.

"Well, so much for tonight's show," Bessie said, and lay the side of her face on the floorboards, watching Harry, the moon reflected in her eyes.

"Yeah," was all he said, still thinking about the sheer size of that monster. Up until ten minutes ago, it had always been Thulu. Now, there was a new monster in town. Something else for him to worry about along with the terrible feeling that humanity was not going to make a comeback anytime soon. They lay there in silence. Harry watched his best friend watch him back, like she was waiting for his words.

All he could think about was watching movies as a little boy where a giant dinosaur invades the city, and how it had been the most awesome thing, ever. Now, he had just experienced it in real life, and it wasn't so great anymore. Harry had read somewhere that, because people were physically unaffected by the carnage portrayed in the films, the audience felt untouchable. It was this power that made the situation enjoyable. But that was then. There were no more Saturday afternoon matinees, buttered popcorn, or fountain drinks. Gone were the flashing cinema marquees and the brilliant movie posters that awed him as a kid. This was real—and it was death.

# CHAPTER 8

## A Fond Kiss and Then We Sever...

Their evening had lost its romantic allure. Feeling like he could doze off as he lay on that board floor, he sat up, and sliding over, he leaned back against the glass of the giant light bulb, trying to stay out of sight of the ocean. Bessie looked at him and said, "Shall we go down? I mean, might as well go to bed. I don't feel safe sitting up here, anymore. If that thing has any kind of night vision, it could spot us."

Not waiting for a response, she crawled past him to the staircase, dragging her bag with her. She moved down the steps backwards on her hands and knees, her face filled with concern. Harry did the same and when they arrived at the entrance to the watch room, they stood and stomped down to the bottom on anxious feet.

Harry sat on the end of his cot and removed his sword rig. After hanging it on a convenient rack of metal hooks attached to the wall, he stripped off his shirt and hung it there as well. Bessie fumbled with the lantern. He watched as she adjusted its wick down to a thumbnail sized flame. Since she was taking care of their lighting needs, he slipped off his boots and lay back.

Bessie soon appeared at the side of the cot and dropped her bag on top. Pulling something out, he heard the crackle of waxed paper. She tossed him a grin and moved away to a shelf-like cross member that tied two vertical I-beams together. A match was struck, candles were lit, and then three of those stood like sentinels on the heavy iron shelf. Harry closed his eyes and waited for her return.

It was not like he didn't want to make love—it was just bad timing. In the past, he always figured sex would come when his father had left them in private, and that's just what happened. Sadly, Harry hadn't anticipated that the old guy would not be returning.

When things were quiet for too long, Harry opened his eyes to see Bessie just standing there, looking down at him. Illuminated by candle light, her grin was assuming. She pushed her bookbag off the cot onto the dirty concrete floor, and unbuckling her sword belt, she laid them on top. Sitting down on the edge of the cot, she ran a fingertip over the stitches on her arm.

"How is it?"

"Good, but it itches like crazy. So, must be healing. Let me look at yours."

"Sure thing, Doctor Brown. Still kind of stings, but I don't think it's bleeding." Rolling onto his left side, he put his back to her, and she stripped off the bandage.

"Oh, looks… pretty much scabbed over. I'll leave the bandage off. I don't think you're going to leak anymore." Harry rolled all the way back onto his right side and raising himself up onto an elbow, he looked into her eyes and she sighed contentedly.

"Are you…" was all Harry got out when Bessie said, "Shush!" After putting a finger to her lips to confirm her wish for silence, she stood, and moving around to the foot of his cot, she grabbed the cuffs of his jeans and pulled.

"Let them go, Harry."

Not wanting to fight about the lack of consent, he popped the button at his fly. The zipper skittered down, and Bessie pulled them off in one quick motion. Rolling them up, she handed them to him, and he made a pillow. Stripping off her leggings, she tossed them onto her cot before crawling on top of him. Her lips found his, and then there were no more words for a while.

The lovemaking was awkward, much like their very first time. He still enjoyed it to a degree, and he knew by her vocalizations, that she had too. Now, he worried about her getting pregnant and how difficult that could be for travel. Condoms had been used in the beginning, but she didn't like them. So, she looted a drugstore for a whole supply of the latest in birth control pills; each one good for a month. He would just assume she was still using them, afraid if he asked, it would imply a lack of trust.

Soon she lay naked at his side, facing him, the top of her head pushed into his armpit. This was the part he liked best, just laying together, lost in thought. His eyes followed her finger as it moved through the hair that was sprouting from his chest. The whole getting pregnant thing wouldn't leave him alone. Pushing away his fear that she might get upset, he said, "Bessie?"

"Yes? You want more?"

"No... ummm... I mean, well yeah, maybe later. I just have a question about..."

"Yes, I do, and yes, I did, and... I'm sorry to say, I only have one left, then it's either pilfer more at some pharmacy somewhere, or start planning for a baby Harry."

"Or... a baby Bessie?"

"Either way, it will be best if we are somewhat settled by then—somewhere."

"Exactly, I can just imagine walking across the country with you in a motherly way. That would be a real problem," he said, and reaching over, he pushed the hair out of her face so he could see her eyes. They seemed to glow, and he wondered if it was the candlelight—or something internal.

"Don't worry, Harry, I have a plan, and... since we are on the subject, maybe we should decide what we are going to do now. I mean, it was your dad's dream to go to Canada, but..."

"Go ahead, say it. Now that he's gone, what should we do?"

"Okay, so... what do you think?" she said, and rising up on an elbow, she brought her face closer to his. This also brought her breasts into view, distracting him. Rolling over onto his back, he stared up into the lantern room at the top, watching weird little worms of light play over the glass as the moon reflected off the water.

"Well, to be honest, I don't want to go to Canada—or Maine, for that matter. Things are okay now with summer coming, and then we have all the fall months. But winter is going to suck. It was bad even when we were home. Having to burn just about everything we owned in some rigged up stove, and having to stay in one room all the time to keep the heat in. Even if there are fewer monsters around at that time, we could still freeze to death… among other things."

Bessie frowned and said, "Maybe, it would be better to go south, or… west to the desert. Tons of people have gone to the desert because there is less water. So, fewer monsters, and… no snow! Maybe we could…"

"Go back to Winnie?"

"Yes! We could go back to Winnie. She wasn't going anywhere for a while. I'm sure she'd be there and would definitely welcome us in."

"Okay, fine. That's the plan, then. We are going back to Winnie," Harry said with finality.

"Yes, we are going back to Winnie. But right now, I'm coming back to you," Bessie said, and crawled back on top of him. Harry didn't resist and even felt better now that they had a plan. But he wondered too, if it was more that he wouldn't have to feel like he had to be in charge when Winnie was around. He suspected it must be his upbringing by his father that made him feel that way. There had to be a 'man of the house'. If he remembered correctly, one of his teachers had referred to it as being 'patriarchal'. He knew Bessie could handle just about anything and that they were equals. But knowing, still didn't make the feeling go away. He was still plagued by his conditioning.

Harry tried to focus on the lovemaking and when Bessie finalized it with a kiss, he knew she'd had enough. After a minute of looking longingly into his eyes, she pulled on her panties and her tee shirt, and then promptly fell asleep. Harry lay for the longest time, thinking about all that had happened and about how he never got the chance to tell his father that he loved him. The sex had left him in a vulnerable place. The tears stung his eyes, and he quietly wept himself to sleep.

Waking a few hours later, he found the candles had completely melted away. The lantern still showed its smidgen of flame through the soot blackened glass of its chimney. At first, he wasn't sure why he had woken up. Maybe a noise, or Bessie moving around. Then the cramping of a full bladder pushed its way through his grogginess. Harry crawled off the end of his cot and after pulling on his boxer shorts, he found his flashlight and searched the room.

A plastic, five-gallon bucket sat next to the desk acting as a wastepaper basket. Dropping a grease rag inside to reduce the spray and deaden the noise, he let go with a stream of urine, sighing quietly with relief.

There came a noise from above, and tilting his head back, he looked up. They had left the door to the catwalk open, and now a gentle breeze caused it to rattle the hook that kept it from slamming shut. He realized that he was now peeing on the top of a metal box next to the bucket. Chuckling to himself, he readjusted the stream. Upon completion, he pushed the bucket up against the wall with his foot and walked over to the bottom of the stairs.

Bessie stirred, said a few words in her sleep, and went back to a light, purring snore. He snuck up the stairway, his bare feet making no sound. He soon found himself crawling along the boards of the floor and arriving at his destination, he unlatched the hook and pulled the door shut.

After locking it, he continued his crawl around to the stairs and stopped where he and Bessie had sat to have their dinner. Peeking over the kick plate, he studied the concrete seawall below.

The moon was just past its zenith and shone on what looked like two young Thulu crouched at the far end. They faced each other, and Harry could hear them hooting and squeaking over the other ocean sounds. The creatures moved like they were anxious, sometimes lunging at each other and then backing off. If anyone ever wanted to study Thulu, this would be the place. But nobody cared about that anymore. Now that the beasts had the upper hand, all any human being wanted to do was kill them.

The harbor roiled and a larger, darker looking Thulu shot up out of the water. It alighted on the very end of the wall, the once flightless wings, now, large and functional.

*It can fly!*

The creatures were evolving fast. Harry was sure it had something to do with being on the surface of the earth instead of under it. Their emergence had triggered a progression. Perhaps consuming some enzyme found in human flesh had bolstered the change. The comfort that Harry had once felt knowing that the monsters couldn't fly, dwindled to nothing. That thought he had that day on the beach, '*Having to keep your eye on the sky as well as the ground, would be a pain*', now came surging back. Sighing heavily, he resigned himself to change. He would just have to evolve, too.

The new arrival looked almost black in the moonlight and it sported a neck frill that lay like a shawl over its shoulders. It reminded him of that frilled-neck lizard he had seen on some animal show.

Crouching next to the others, its tentacles whipped about. Harry saw how it towered over them. He could clearly hear mewing and squalling noises, reminding him of a couple of alley cats going at it.

The new arrival raised its clawed hands up in a menacing fashion toward the other two, the wings going fully erect along with the neck frill. The display made it look even bigger, and the other Thulu backed away.

Emitting a sharp screech, the beast swiped the Thulu closest to it off the wall. The victim disappeared with a splash and didn't resurface. The other remained, not seeming to fear the larger creature. Instead, it turned left, then right, and after spinning one complete circle, it sat and bobbed its head.

Harry assumed it must be the female of the species. It ended its little dance by putting its backside to the bigger creature and bowing in the opposite direction. Raising its hips even higher, it flipped its tail over its back. Now—there was no doubt.

The larger one rose up to its full height and stretched its arms far above its head. It croaked toward the sky as its throat and chest glowed a phosphorescent green. A dewlap swelled at the Thulu's throat and after several jerky nods of its head, it emitted a loud hoot that ended in a cackle. The beast then pushed itself against the female and wrapping its arms around her from behind, they both fell sideways into the sea.

Harry remained on his stomach for a few more minutes just feeling dumbstruck. Gathering his senses, he crawled down the stairs and returned to his bed. Removing his swords from the hook, he lay down facing the wall, hugging the rig. When he finally got to sleep, he tossed and turned. At one point, he dreamed that the strange new Thulu was just outside, sniffing at the base of the door. It sounded like a dog, but mewed like a cat as it tried to catch their scent. He jerked awake, feeling the relief of knowing it had all been in his head.

Getting up, he moved through the dark to the door and ran his hand over all four clamps to reassure himself that they were secure. Satisfied with what he found; he tiptoed back to the cot.

Bessie now lay on her back, and he was certain she was watching him. But in a low, dreamy voice, she said, "Ice cream?"

Chuckling to himself, he knew she was talking in her sleep.

*I wish it was ice cream!*

He lay down on his back and watched through half closed lids as the space at the top of the stairs, slowly brightened. The next thing he knew, Bessie was shaking him awake.

"On your feet, sleepy head."

Standing alongside the cot in clean, navy-blue panties and a bandeau, she grinned and raised her eyebrows several times before pulling on her jeans and a pair of grey, knitted leg warmers. A red midi shirt followed and then the sword belt. She topped everything off with her blue and white plaid shirt, leaving it unbuttoned to expose her belly button jewelry.

Harry had woken up in a foul mood. Getting to his feet, he stood at the foot of the two cots, dressing slowly. Then snatching up the sword rig, he slipped it on and checked for the millionth time that the blades wouldn't bind upon being pulled.

"How'd you sleep?" she asked

"Like crap! Had all kinds of strange dreams."

"Yeah, I hear you," was all she said, and grabbing her bag, she finished with, "Meet you at the top for breakfast!" Running up the stairway in bare feet, she slipped once and exclaimed, "Crap!" as she grabbed the rail to keep from tumbling down. Regaining her footing, she jumped up two steps at a time until she reached the top. With a, "Whew!" escaping her lips, she moved out of sight.

Harry put on his socks and boots and grabbing his own bag, he moved slowly up the stairs to join her. Sitting in the same spot as the evening before, they finished off a couple cans of meat and the fruit cocktail. They could see the Fidelis was where they had left it. He thought of telling her about the new Thulu but decided to wait. If she knew, it would only bring more worry, and he preferred she remain calm and playful. They just sat, chewed, and grinned at each other. Occasionally, Bessie would lean over, kiss his cheek with her greasy lips, and then giggle. He suspected she was feeling good about the prospect of returning to Winnie. She seemed to have forgotten that his father had died the day before—but maybe that was best.

Finishing his share of the food, Harry got to his feet and moved around the walkway to where he could view the entrance side of the tower. Looking down through the heavy metal mesh of the catwalk, he could see that no monsters loitered there.

"We should go. I think now's a good time." Bessie didn't argue.

Returning to the ground floor, they brushed their teeth and took care of other things that involved personal hygiene. Harry waited for Bessie to put on her socks and boots. Then, after pulling down the leg warmers to envelop her boot tops, they left the safety of the lighthouse.

They moved back through the trees to the store and finding the door still secure, Harry opened it, and they went inside. The 'Yield' sign still covered the hole and the bench vice was unmoved. Harry's goal was to gather water bottles since they were minus the MOLLE pack and the canteens. The problem was—their bags were already full of food. He figured they might be able to stuff in a few bottles, but it looked like it was coming down to food, or water. Not both.

"Harry?"

"Yeah?" he said, poking his head around a rack of shelves.

"Since we are walking back to Winnie's, I was just thinking… if we took the boat across the harbor to the opposite shore at the other end of the bridge… it would save us a few miles."

"You want to take the risk of going across open water in a boat?"

"Well, we did yesterday?"

"Yeah, but I was a little out of my head, and besides, today we're not running from those freaking capuchipines."

"Yes, but it is daylight, and there isn't a cloud in the sky."

Harry remembered what he saw in the dark of the early morning and wondered if monsters, exhausted from breeding, would take the day off.

*Did the new Thulu have a daylight rule?*

He wasn't so sure he wanted to risk it, but what she said was true, using the old sternpicker would take a few miles off their journey on their way back to Winnie's embrace.

*Maybe we could race across at full speed? It would only take maybe ten minutes—fifteen at the most.*

"Well… okay, do you want to give it a shot?"

"Yeah, I do. It's only what? About twenty-five, thirty miles to Winnie's place? We could be there before dark. Just think, Harry, we wouldn't have to worry about a place to sleep tonight, and we can be with Winnie and Kappa for as long as we want."

"Okay, but you know we're taking a risk? You saw those Thulu out there, just like I did."

"But the boat can go faster than they can swim, right?"

"I don't know about that. Who's going to take the time to clock one? There was nothing in the book. It was more on how to kill one, where to shoot it, or cut it… not how to sanction a Thulu race."

"Oh, you're so funny, Harry T. Lumsdale. Grab your stuff and let's get on board that hunk of junk."

Bessie had found a stack of flour sacks with drawstrings and had loaded two of them full of water bottles. Harry walked over, looked at the sacks with disbelief and said, "What are you doing? That's a lot of weight. Do you think we'll need that much?"

"Well… yeah. I mean, we don't have your… what's it called? Oh yeah, molly pack. So, we can sling these flour sacks from the back of our bookbags. Easy-peasy!"

"That's a lot of weight… maybe just half that?"

"Come on Harry, I've already got them packed. If it's too much, we'll just toss them."

"Or—I'll just make you carry all four hundred ounces," he said and laughed.

"Whatever."

"It's a lot of weight."

"WHATEVER!"

Harry would let her find out for herself. He was confident his father would have cautioned her against it as well. Picking up one of the full sacks, he tied it to his bag and then hoisted it to his shoulders. Realizing it wasn't all that heavy, he kept that to himself. Bessie had solved the problem of food versus water and she had also done his share of the work. By the time they had finished their exchange, he hadn't loaded a single bottle.

Moving onto the back stoop, he waited. When Bessie came out, he studied her face. There was no hint of discontent, and she said nothing as if the matter was resolved. Shutting the door, she made sure the latch had seated before moving past him down the steps.

"Sorry," Harry said.

Bessie threw a neutral look over her shoulder and continued on without a word. When they arrived at the pier, she turned back and said, "It's not so bad. I can handle this."

Harry, wanting to perpetuate what he interpreted as clemency, just made a face at her, and then stuck out his tongue in an attempt at humor. She just giggled and stomped her way to the gillnetter.

"Do you have to walk like an elephant?" slipped from his mouth. It wasn't what he wanted to say, and he wondered if he was losing his self-control. He regretted the statement and wanted to correct it, but he was too late.

"You think I'm an elephant? You didn't seem to think so last night with your hands running all over my body like you didn't know what to grab next?"

"No! Wait! I said, do you have to walk like one, not that you are one."

"I'll remember that, Harry Lumsdale—elephants don't forget."

"Aw geez… BESSIE! I didn't call you one. Get over it."

Bessie made a loud elephant noise and removing a hand from the padded strap of her bag, she pretended her arm was an elephant's trunk and made the noise a second time as she whipped it up and down.

"All I'm saying is… maybe you could walk quieter now that we are out over the water."

She stopped with the loud footfalls. Looking back over her shoulder, she blew him a raspberry to finalize their exchange. Harry thought it best to shut up now.

Arriving at the Fidelis, she slipped off her bag and let it fall inside. Then climbing in behind it, she moved into the wheelhouse. He joined her there and prepared to start the launch. She was way ahead of him, though and he grabbed her hand as it moved toward the red starter button.

"Let me say this, first. Once we start it, we have to go like hell across the harbor. We don't want to give the monsters too much time to figure out where the noise is coming from. I want to be at least half way across before they even suspect there are humans around."

"Aye, aye, Cap'n," she said, and wresting her arm from his grip, she saluted him.

"Give it a break… huh, skipper?"

"Just toss those lines, swabby, and we're gone!"

With one hand on the wheel and a finger hovering over the button, she waited. Harry glared. Bessie's hair hung loose and fluffy, framing her face as she grinned back, her eyes imparting a mischievous glint.

Something about that expression triggered a warmth that seemed to encapsulate Harry's entire body. It was accompanied by a profound sense of fondness for this person who now stood before him. For a fleeting moment, he had a glimpse into the entirety of his love for Bessie and it seemed a whole galaxy's worth. The intensity of it made him want to weep. Harry turned away to keep her from seeing any tears that might escape, and he moved out of the wheelhouse, perplexed about his sudden insight.

Untying the mooring line from the post, he shouted, "Clear!"

The engine roared and he heard and felt the transmission lock into place. The bow of the boat rose up and being unprepared for the shift in plane, Harry lost his balance and fell backward.

Bessie must have pushed the throttle to the 'Full' mark. He wanted to bitch her out for that, but his previous epiphany wouldn't allow it. Besides that, she was doing just what he said they should do.

It was when she turned out into the harbor a little too sharply and caught the pier with an aft corner of the gillnetter that he almost blew his top. It peeled a short length of trim from the Fidelis and tore out two boards from the dock. He got to his feet just as she turned to him, and grinning. She made her 'Oops! Face' and said, "Sorry! But you know, we won't need this boat afterwards. So, we're good, right?"

"Let's just try not to sink it before we get back to shore, huh?" Rubbing a sore elbow, Harry moved back into the wheelhouse to read the gauges, saying nothing.

"Okay, again, I am sorry about all that. Still need practice, I guess," she said meekly, her face a bright shade of red.

Harry glanced at her and then turned his focus back to the dashboard. Pushing off the choke the sound of the engine evened out. The speedometer showed that the vessel was moving about 12 knots an hour. Too slow for what he wanted, but he knew that was all they were going to get. Even with the heavy reel and roller gone, they could only do about fifteen miles per hour. The fuel gauge still read half full and the battery's meter indicated 'Charging'. So, it was as good as it gets. He just hoped it would stay that way.

The gillnetter was cruising straight toward their destination. Harry was 'chomping the bit' as his mother used to say. He wanted to get off that harbor. "How's it going? Are you okay? Are you going to make it all the way across without a break?" he asked.

"Yeah! Why not? Unless I hit something else, like a… Thulu. Did you want to take a turn at the wheel?"

"No, you can handle it. It's not like I feel I could do any better."

"That's what I love about you, Harry Lumsdale."

She had never mentioned love before, even when joking. There had been times when he wanted to say he loved her, but he never did. With the way he was feeling about her at the moment, those words could easily find his lips, even with the confusion that whirled like a twister in his head. He wanted to find his stability again, blaming it all on the loss of his father and the unexpected intensity of his grief.

Harry thought about all he and Bessie had been through together. The onset of those thoughts brought a memory of a time when he was fourteen and had witnessed his parents first serious falling out. His mother had said to him in private, "*When you've been with a man like your father for as long as I have, you finally realize the reason you stay, is because of the love. Hard times will just bring you closer. Don't ever forget that, Harry.*"

Well, he hadn't. Now, it was just him and Bessie. It may be time for him to start sharing his feelings about her. He leaned over and when she turned to face him, he kissed her gently on the lips and then moved out of the wheelhouse before she could say anything. As he passed through the doorway, he heard her sigh, and he smiled to himself.

*Say it now, you idiot!*

Harry stopped and turned, "I love you, Bessie," he said with as much solemnity as he could muster.

She didn't look back, but sang out to the windscreen, "I love you too, Harry T. Lumsdale." Finally glancing over her shoulder, she gave him a big grin before turning her attention back to piloting the boat.

Moving out to the deck, Harry gazed back toward the dock. They were well out into the harbor now, almost to the halfway point. A few seagulls hovered overhead, their cries sounding eerie in the morning light. Studying the wake left by the Fidelis, he scanned for anything that might give him a clue that monsters were trailing them.

He glanced at the harpoons secure in their clamps. Deep down, he knew they didn't stand much of a chance if a Thulu came. It would probably capsize the boat and then attack them as they tried to swim and fight at the same time. His attention turned to the life jackets lying on the deck. They were Type 3; the kind that would keep you afloat, but not turn you face up if you happened to get knocked out. Least they would have a better chance of surviving if they were actually wearing them. Picking up two of the yellow ones, he moved into the wheelhouse and handed one to Bessie.

"Are you going to wear one, too?"

"Well, yeah, but I wanted to give you yours. Better for us in case we are attacked, least that way we can stay afloat if we go overboard, and are still able to fight."

"Just set it there," she said, pointing to an empty shelf at the side.

"Well... I was thinking maybe we could put them on, like... right now? You said you don't swim very well, so..."

She glared for a moment and then taking her hands off the wheel, she snatched it up and put it on, the plastic buckles snapping loudly. "There! Feel Better?"

"Uh-huh, I do, now that..." Harry didn't get to finish as the engine coughed, sputtered, and quit.

"What the...?" she said and ran the throttle lever up and down.

"I don't know... just leave it alone," Harry said.

Dropping his vest, he pushed the starter button. The engine caught but died again. He tapped the fuel gauge with a finger, and nothing changed. Rapping it harder with his knuckles, the needle suddenly plummeted to 'E'.

"Crap! We're out of fuel! Dammit!"

"What?" she said and leaned over to look. "Crap is right! What do we do now? We are almost half way across."

"We have to fuel up. Luckily, there's a full, five gallon can in the back. We'll just dump it in the tank and keep on going."

"Oh, good. Need any help?"

"Yeah... come on."

He led her out to the aft portion of the craft and pointed to the large, red plastic container strapped neatly under the rear bench seat. Pulling it out, he searched for the deck fill, and finding it at the top of a boxed-in area on the left, he attached the spout that came with the can and started pouring.

"Is it heavy?" she asked.

"Yeah... and awkward this close to the edge. Almost feels like I'm going to fall in the water at any minute."

"If I sit on the other corner, the boat will stop rocking so much." Moving over, she sat on the transom where it met the gunwale.

It was at the very moment Harry had shaken the last drop from the can that he caught movement just back of the Fidelis. The water had darkened for a moment, and there had been a brief shimmer as the sunlight played over something moving just below the surface. The alarm bells went off inside his head and turning he shouted, "Bessie! Get back inside, quick!" He was too late.

The Thulu came straight up out of the water. At the apex of its skyward lunge, its dragon like wings opened and flapped, pummeling them with turbulent gusts of air. The short tentacles at its mouth seemed to writhe in competition with each other. Torrents of water ran off the gleaming ebony skin displaying some meager greenish-yellow striping. Harry knew he was looking at the more evolved version of the species, very much like the one he had seen earlier in the morning.

Bessie cried, "Oh, crap!" and stood to run as the beast lowered its clawed feet down to the gunwale where she had been sitting. Its weight rocked the vessel, causing Harry to fall, and Bessie to tumble backwards into the beast's outstretched arms.

Harry stared in shock and disbelief as the Thulu wrapped Bessie in a bear hug, pinning her arms to her sides. Her right hand found the hilts of her swords, but the beast only squeezed her tighter to its simian-like body and he heard all of Bessie's air depart her lungs. Its whip of a tail jerked and snapped as the beast sent a loud hiss in Harry's direction, its large black eyes unblinking. The expression on Bessie's face was one of pure terror, a look he had never seen there before, but one he knew he would never forget.

His anger surged in, forcing out the fear. He tried to gain his feet, but the Thulu pushed off with such force that the boat rocked low enough to take on multiple gallons of water. The beast rose to hover, a hissing shriek filling the air. In its crushing grip, Bessie could only expel, "Harry," in a plaintive croak before the beast inverted and dove head first back into the harbor.

The splash soaked Harry from head to foot and he took it as a contemptuous gesture. Finding his feet, he lowered his center of gravity and drew his swords. His first impulse was to dive in after them. When he realized that wouldn't help, he bellowed his hatred in the direction the sea monster had gone. A sense of helplessness was eking in, but he fought to keep it at bay. Wavering wasn't an option; he had to do something. Anything.

He didn't move though, still standing dumbstruck, watching the water, his thoughts swirled as his brain sought a solution. Then the harbor boiled at the opening in the seawall. From the bubbling foam, he saw a flash of yellow life vest, and a human arm broke the surface, a shining sword in hand.

*Bessie's free and she's fighting!*

The feeling of impotence that had enveloped him dissolved away. Harry knew what he needed to do. Sheathing his blades, he scrambled into the wheelhouse. At the second press of the starter button, the engine came to life. Pushing the throttle forward to the 'FULL' mark, he whipped the gillnetter around and roared away to where Bessie's sword had broken the surface.

Slowing the vessel to a crawl, he scanned the water, his eyes frantically searching, as he muttered, "Where are you, Bessie? Dammit! Where are you?"

Catching movement out of the corner of his eye, he brought his face around to see the water roil again about a hundred feet to his right. There flashed a hint of yellow just below the surface and he sped the Fidelis toward it.

The sun, glinting off the rippling surface, made it difficult to zero in on the exact location. Harry brought the engine back to an idle and stepped to the window on the right side. Shielding his eyes with a hand against the glare and seeing nothing, he moved portside. A numbing shock ran up from his feet to the top of his head and his hair stood on end as the bile rose in his throat. A sleeve of Bessie's blue and white shirt, now stained red, swirled past, agitated by the wake of the boat.

Harry lost his mind.

A deep chill enveloped his body, and he shuddered as threats against every sea monster in existence resonated within that wheelhouse. When the Thulu showed itself about thirty yards just off the bow, Harry slammed the throttle lever forward with such force, it bent, cracking the plastic housing around its base. Hopping anxiously from one foot to the other, he kept a white knuckled grip on the wheel. Curses, more typical of a longshoreman than a well-brought-up eighteen-year-old, poured from his mouth.

He glowered at the creature as it swam ahead, sometimes just a 'V' cutting through the waves, other times, its folded wings and tail, breaking just above them. Long streams of bluish-green, trailed out behind the beast, telling Harry that Bessie had done some damage. He hoped the loss of blood would slow it down. The gillnetter was going top speed, and it seemed to be closing the gap, but that wasn't fast enough for Harry.

Stepping back from the wheel, he bent forward at the waist and clenching his fists, he cut loose with a growling scream at the windshield. When he had spent his breath, he drew another, and raising his face and fists to the ceiling, he bellowed his rage.

Taking the wheel again, he steered after the Thulu, who had changed its route to a more northerly direction. He went to stomping his right foot hard against the floor as if it would speed the process. Minutes passed, and his mumbled threats became punctuated with snarls of exasperation. The distance between him and the monster soon closed to about the length of two gillnetters, and within his madness, there came a transient rationality.

After tying the wheel in place with a short length of cord, he walked out. Yanking one of Billy B's homemade harpoons from its clamp, he scrambled around the outside of the wheelhouse to crouch on the prow deck. Finding the mooring line that snaked back from a cleat at the forward most point, Harry rose to his feet and pulled it taut with his left hand while holding the harpoon high at the ready with his right.

His russet hair whipped about his head and the spray doused him as he cried into the wind, "Come back here, you bastard! Come take me! I'm right here, you son of a…" His voice cracked as he struggled to see through wind and tear-filled eyes. He offered himself to the Thulu again and again, hoping it would turn back, but the tireless creature swam on, and Harry followed the beast far out into the Atlantic.

After a while he lost track of the creature and found he was only chasing waves. There were still spots and streaks of bluish-green in the water and Harry's head swiveled crazily from the left to the right and back again as his eyes scanned for anything that might be a sign of the Thulu. He jabbed at the air, continuing with his threats, each one coming slightly different and louder than the last. Like his mind, Harry soon lost his voice.

The engine began to smoke long before that point. At first, little wisps came filtering out of the compartment's cover, but they soon evolved into a heavy, black cloud that rose skyward to trail out far behind the vessel. Harry failed to notice as he raged. He stomped back and forth across the deck, twice nearly tumbling over the edge, saved only by the mooring rope still clutched in his left hand.

Ten minutes passed, fifteen, and then twenty, the lighthouse becoming just a mere speck in the distance. But time no longer mattered to Harry. The mind he'd lost—the one he possessed back in hometown Massachusetts—had actually been stolen. The theft had been a gradual process, starting with the loss of his mother, followed by his father, and now, Bessie. Climate change, the mutated H1N1 pandemic, and the monsters, were all culprits in the thievery.

Harry held no sway over the first two; however, he was quite capable of driving a sword or spear into the guts of some abhorrent sea monster. That's where he dominated, and like some kind of a twisted coping skill, it appealed to something deep down inside him. Something primitive. It was a caveman that now rode that boat like a mad surfer.

When the engine seized, and the craft became enslaved by the waves, Harry fell to his knees, sobs racking his body. Clinging to the harpoon like a child to its favorite teddy bear, he wailed up into the azure void. With Bessie dead, he now wished that he was too. His nose flowed freely, and saliva ran from the corners of his mouth as he rocked back and forth, rasping out, "Come take me… please… come take me."

The monster never came back. Nor did any other respond to Harry's invitation. So, moving to sit cross-legged, he cradled the shaft of the long, barbed weapon in his arms and bobbed along with the gillnetter, helplessly weeping. The breeze cooled him in his wet clothes as he struggled to push the picture of Bessie's fear filled face out of his mind. But it kept coming back. The look of terror in her eyes said, *"Only you can save me, now,"* and he had failed her.

It was hard to take. Harry just wanted to stop caring, to be devoid of emotion. He wanted to sleep a long, dreamless slumber from which there would be no waking. Exhausted, he lay down, pulled the harpoon close, and curled up into a fetal position. Closing his eyes, his incoherent babbling was perpetuated by the images cycling through his head.

Winnie's face soon appeared, bringing a halt to the endless reel of memories. From her lips came the words spoken at their parting, *"Take care of them, Harry"*. He promised her he would, and he had botched it. Muttering a mournful, "I'm sorry," he drifted off into a nightmare filled sleep.

***

So intent had Harry been on catching the murderous Thulu, not only did he miss the signs telling him the boats engine was about to become a thing of the past, but also, the sodden, bloodied figure climbing out of the harbor onto the wave break far behind him.

Bessie sat down on the top, coughing raucously, trying to expel what saltwater had made its way inside. Blood oozed from superficial cuts and scrapes on her bare right arm. A single rivulet, trickling from a small cut on her forehead, ran into her eyes. Moving to wipe it away, she stopped to study the sword she still held in her fist; a thin film of diluted Thulu blood coating the blade. It dripped onto the wall making light blue stars where the drops impacted the concrete. She still had her boots, but for some reason, most of her leg warmers were MIA, and her stretchy pants were torn in places. The yellow life vest still wrapped her torso, covered in deep lacerations along with some shallow punctures.

Bessie lay her remaining sword on the wall and after pulling off the vest, she examined herself for puncture wounds and signs of melting flesh. Fortunately for her, there were none. The yellow vest that she had spurned had saved her life in more ways than one. Dropping it into the water, she removed her shirt, and wiping the sword clean, she holstered it, and let the shirt follow the vest.

She watched small waves take them away, her eyes gradually rising toward the horizon to take in the large black cloud trailing up from a dark dot that could only have been the Fidelis.

"Harry," she whispered.

Getting to her feet, she began jumping up and down on top of the seawall, waving and shouting, "Harry! I'm here!" Her voice cracked on try number three, and she began to cough and hack in an alarming manner.

Returning to a seated position, Bessie's tears welled up, and she began to cry, her sobs disrupted by sporadic fits of coughing. The hot sun, almost at its zenith, baked her, drying her clothes and congealing the blood. The smoke in the distance soon dissipated and the little dot disappeared. She sat for nearly two hours in a daze before muttering to herself, "He's not coming back."

Getting to her feet, she winced. Running a hand over the small of her back, she fingered the rip in her red midi shirt and the long, but shallow, laceration running from hip to hip. "Nothing to worry about," she rasped, and walking along the top of the wall with her hiking boots squishing seawater, she sobbed her way back to shore.

Returning to Snappy's, she found another flour sack and filled it with food and bottles of water. Not bothering to shut the door, Bessie soon found herself on the beach staring through tear filled eyes in the direction of the Atlantic as if hoping to catch sight of a returning gillnetter.

Many minutes passed before she turned west and tilting her face to the sky as if to gauge the distance between the sun and the horizon, an exasperated, "Shit," escaped her lips. Breaking into a trot, she moved back toward the 1B, back toward the Seabrook Beach and, Winnie; the only friend she had left in the world.

# CHAPTER 9

## Deep In Heart Wrung Tears

It was dark when Harry woke himself, shouting, "Bessie, lookout!" With fire in his throat, he looked around in confusion. His sorrow and regret stampeded in like a herd of wild buffalo. He remembered where he was, and regrettably, that he was still alive.

There was a terrible pain in his gut and his chest felt heavy with heartache. The harpoon was no longer in his embrace and searching the deck, he presumed it had found its way to the ocean floor. So, he sat, leaning against the windscreen of the wheelhouse, scanning the sky, and listening to the ocean's night voice. The moon was up and reflecting off the surface like a silvery finger pointing at him—the guilty party.

Harry rocked with the waves, wondering what he should do next. It occurred to him to tie the anchor to his ankles and jump overboard. But that's not how he wanted to go. It had to be in battle—nothing else.

Bessie kept tiptoeing into his head like a specter from the shadows. Tired of crying, Harry let the images and the words she'd left behind whirl like a dust devil inside his skull. He still could not fathom that one minute they were just talking—and the next—she was gone.

*Bessie's gone.*

With a stuttering sigh, Harry moved back onto the main deck. He needed water and his head was splitting as if someone had cleaved it with one of his swords. Sitting down on the bench outside the wheelhouse door, he dragged Bessie's bookbag to him and opened the flap. Pulling out a plastic water bottle, he uncapped it and drank. Then setting it aside, he found the little flashlight he had given her, and turning it on, he held it in his lips while removing other items from the bag.

There were cans of food, another bottle of water, clothing, little personal things, a sharpening stone, a Swiss Army knife, and—her wallet. He wanted to look inside, but…

*Should I wait? No—better to get it over with.*

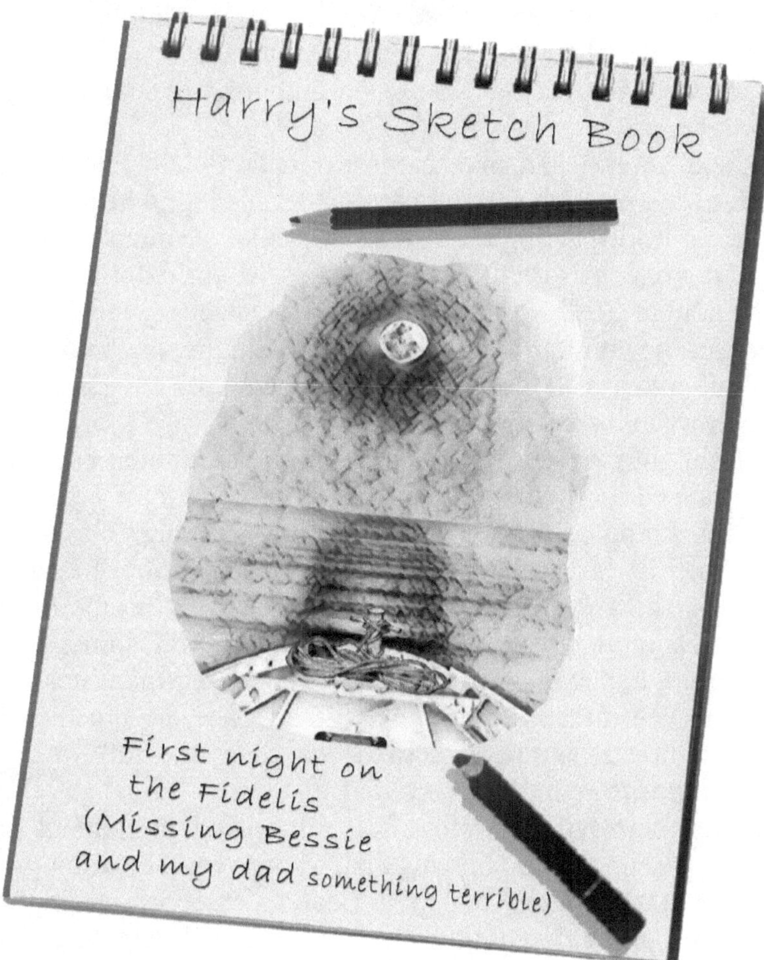


Flipping it open, a photo fell out. Picking it up, he saw it was a picture of him and her together after a tournament win at the 2029 Boston Martial Arts Expo.

In the photo, he was standing with Bessie seated on his outstretched arm, her feet dangling. There was a grimace on his face as he struggled to avoid dropping her. She had one arm around his neck and in her other hand she held a trophy high in the air, her head thrown back in glee. Strands of light brown hair covered her face, disclosing only part of her toothy smile. He remembered spinning her around afterwards, and losing his balance, they tumbled to the mat in laughter.

In the background, he could see Master Bik shaking hands with his mother and father. They had all been there on that joy filled day, and now—they were all gone. He was alone, and that was something he had rarely ever been.

He found he still had one teardrop left as it fell onto the photo. Wiping it away, he pushed the picture under his leg to keep the breeze from stealing it. Inspecting the rest of the wallet's contents and finding nothing but a bunch of defunct plastic cards, he stuffed it and the other things he couldn't use back inside the bag. Detaching the sack full of water bottles, he let it fall to the deck before flinging the bookbag aft to watch it fall onto a coil of rope. It bumped the empty gas can and sent it spinning away into a corner.

The flashlight perched in his lips soon offered nothing but a meager glow. He rapped it on the wall behind him and when the beam did not return to full strength, he grew annoyed. Flinging it high into the air, he smirked when he heard the splash. Then, in frustration, he stood and stomped across the deck to fling Bessie's bookbag after the flashlight, shouting, "Dammit, Bessie!" It twirled away with somewhat of a whistling noise and made an odd, *smack!* when it hit the water.

Gazing in the direction the bookbag had gone, he breathed in the ocean's salty breath, and listened to the waves lap the hull.

*Maybe that wasn't such a good idea…*

Harry felt screwed regardless, yet he needed to holdout until a monster showed up to grant him his final showdown. The drinking water would last a couple weeks, thanks to Bessie's stubbornness in packing more bottles than he thought they needed. She had persevered despite his crap. Now, he was glad for her foresight, and he so wished he could tell her. Then there was her share of the food, and even though he was unhappy about how it came to be his, he still felt thankful. If he was prudent, he might make it last as long as the water supply. Fishing could offer another source of nourishment, but he had no great love for fish.

However, he might change his mind if it became necessary. Time would be the deciding factor.

The thought of it being more acceptable for a sea creature to eat him than for him to eat a sea creature, brought a crazy little laugh to his lips. Shaking his head, he moved back toward the wheelhouse. Spying the photo he'd left behind, there came a hint of panic at realizing he could have easily lost it to the ocean. Snatching it up before the breeze could, Harry slipped it into his back pocket and went inside.

Moonlight gleamed off the large, red starter button and Harry gave it a quick push just to be sure. The relay sent out a staccato of clicks, but nothing turned. This was followed by the realization that he may not have only contributed to Bessie's demise, but he had also killed the boat.

A heavy sigh escaped his lips and he began to ransack his mind for solutions that would get him back to shore. There was no way to row or pole the boat. He could rig a sail, but he had no idea how to work such a thing. He would remain adrift on the Atlantic until the sea monsters came, he died from exposure or, found land.

The chance that some rescuer may just show up was a reoccurring thought—but a stupid one at that. There would be no one searching for him. It made him think about those old movies he watched as a kid where sailors had gotten lost at sea, floating for months on a little, rubber dinghy. He remembered the trepidation he felt for those fictitious characters. Yet always at the back of his mind, he knew he was safe sitting there in his living room. What someone acted out on the silver screen was hardly real life. He could only assume what would come in the days ahead, loneliness and boredom being the most certain.

He thought again about drowning himself, but with greater revulsion than the first time. The cowardice of it took him back to an episode in the third grade at Kilbury elementary. Jimmy Jamison, threatening to beat the crap out of him, had sent him fleeing to hide in the janitor's closet. The event had been the motivation behind signing up at Master Bik's. He vowed to himself that he would never run again.

"Better to go down fighting," he mumbled to himself as he stood leaning with both hands flat on the control panel. The loneliness was already creeping in and his sense of the isolation seemed to double. The only thing he could compare it to was being stuck in the house on a rainy day with no one else home and nothing to do.

*What are you going to do with yourself until the monsters come?*

In a burst of anger, he pounded on the panel with a fist, yelling, "Dammit! Dammit! Dammit!" Then stepping over to the searchlight, he switched it on and shined it around on the water, shouting as loud as he could, "Here I am, you bastards, time for supper!"

A burning sensation filled Harry's throat as his words dwindled to a gruff whisper. The searchlight used the last of the battery's energy, and its brilliance faded away to nothing. Stomping out, he pulled the one remaining harpoon from its stays and moved to the starboard side. Listlessly splashing the barbed tip in the water, he watched the lightning play among the thunderheads of a distant storm.

*The monsters aren't coming, you idiot! Why can't you get it through your thick head?*

A strange kind of lethargy overwhelmed him. Putting the harpoon back in its clamps, he picked up his bottle of water and sat down on the deck. After a long drink, he took off his sword rig and lay back, pillowing his head on his arms. Gazing up into the celestial sphere, he thought about eating something, but soon found himself waking to the dawn and, whatever had bumped against the bottom of the boat.

"What the..." he said with gravel in his voice.

Jumping to his feet, he strapped on his swords and seconds later, the harpoon was back in his hands and at the ready. It was time to meet his death, and the adrenalin flowed in as he stood patient, waiting for the beast to show itself. He felt strangely lucid. His mind was back—but it wasn't his old one. This was his new mind—and it was clear, focused, and ready to go.

*Time to face eternity.*

He wished for the monster to have a clear view of him, so he took up a position at the center of the deck, standing tall at arms, and prepared for battle.

The sun soon peeked over the ocean's surface, but only for a few seconds before a narrow band of clouds hid the brilliant orb from view, casting Harry's world back into shadow. Remembering his own flashlight, he pulled it from his pocket. Sticking the tarnished aluminum tube in his mouth, he sent a beam of light in every direction that he peered. He became a walking lighthouse, making damn sure the monster knew just where to find him. The tiny stream of light played over the surface and he watched as a huge, dark shape passed underneath after making an abrupt turn, rocking the gillnetter.

Waiting for it to return, his eyes remained glued to the surface. Soon, a dark hump speckled with large whitish spots cut through the water as it cruised toward him. His brain went into overdrive as he tried to figure out what type of creature had arrived to help put him out of his misery.

Harry couldn't recall anything with white spots like that, but new monsters had been showing up almost daily, beasts that had never made it into the ID manual. His instincts told him to throw the harpoon—but he hesitated. He wanted the satisfaction of having his hands on the shaft as he drove it home. Moving starboard, he waited to jump on the beast when it appeared. He would use all his weight to push the barbed lance clear to the wooden haft. Then he would take out his swords and go to work on whatever it was, least until it killed him, or he drowned. But the creature dove deeper just before reaching the vessel, and Harry lost sight of it.

*It'll come back. No way the bastard's going to let me escape.*

He braced himself for the jump, holding the harpoon high above his head with both hands, the tip angled down toward the water.

*This is it! The moment I become history!*

He was afraid, but also—excited. That was good. It was just what he wanted.

The sensation was much different from what he had experienced when confronting other monsters. But his father had always been there, or Bessie, standing by, ready to jump in. Harry wanted to impress them. Make them see he was good at this. He hadn't truly felt the finality of what his actions could bring. He never entered the fray thinking he might die, and now—it was his wish.

"Come back here, you son of a bitch. You're making me wait."

The creature breached the surface a short way out from the gillnetter, its full length breaking free of the water in a magnificent jump. Confusion rolled in and Harry relaxed his grip on the harpoon.

*A freaking whale!*

The young humpback splashed down and turned toward the boat. Harry had seen a live whale only once. It had been on a visit to the beach as a little boy. Everyone around him had grown excited as they watched through binoculars. He remembered his father supporting the large set

of field glasses with a hand, so Harry could get a glimpse. The common belief was that all whales had gone extinct, killed by humans, or sea monsters. But this one had obviously beaten the odds.

When it arrived at the vessel, it floated to a stop and turned parallel, rolling over onto its side. The beam of the flashlight rested on one large eye as it checked him out. Harry dropped the harpoon and stared back, wondering what was going on inside the humpback's head. He suspected it was just as amazed as he was. A mammal meeting mammal in a world of amphibious mutants.

It seemed something passed between them. A mammalian kind of telepathy. "Happy to see you've made it this far!" formed in large, white letters running panoramic across his mind's eye. Harry scowled in disbelief, but his skepticism didn't last because he wanted to believe he had made a connection. Taking the flashlight from his mouth, he dropped to his knees. Pressing his chest against the gunwale, he stretched out a hand and placed his palm flat against the strange, wet roughness of the whale's skin.

Nearly a minute passed before the whale fell away into the depths, leaving Harry to think it had gone. "Good luck, you're going to need it," he monotoned, the hoarseness of his voice sounding strange in the breezy morning air.

As Harry turned away, the whale breached the surface a hundred or so yards out. He turned to see it spiral toward the sky as if in a leap of joy at simply being alive. The sun broke through the clouds and the great creature glimmered in its light. A warm sensation blossomed within Harry's chest, and surprisingly, it felt a lot like hope.

# CHAPTER 10

## Lonely Wanderings, Mine...

The whale's presence had elevated his mental state toward the positive, however, Harry knew the river of rage was flowing just underneath. It wouldn't take much for him to slip and fall back into its fast-flowing current.

Hunger pangs stabbed his middle and he moved to the food pile. His hand strayed to the sardines, hesitated, but then picked up the can. Harry studied the silver tin with the tiny key soldered to the top. That gleeful moment when Bessie had pulled a can of sardines from the shelf at Winnie's place rolled into his head. They had kept their heckling to a minimum, and he remembered her embarrassed grin and the blush lingering on her face.

She had been this lovely human being, whose life had been reduced to monster food. His growling stomach did a slow flip flop and he felt a heaviness form under his breastbone. He slowly set the tin on the bench as if he feared disturbing the dead. His action brought no relief as his eyes fell on Bessie's black hoodie laying crumpled on the deck.

Harry had meant to stick it in the bookbag and send it out as well, but it had escaped his attention. He regretted having tossed the bag, so grabbing the hoodie, he wrapped the sardines inside and stuffed it under the bench.

*There! Safe for now!*

Twisting off the cap of the water bottle, he took another drink before opening a package of saltines. Crunching away on a handful, Harry reminded himself he needed to make the food last. Dying in battle was okay. Dying of starvation, was not. The former had to come before the latter, and he had to do everything in his power to make sure it happened just that way.

He kept catching the hoodie out of the corner of his eye. So, he pushed it farther back with his foot, and turned away.

Over the following days, Harry kept himself busy, napping whenever he felt tired. He cleaned and sharpened his swords time and time again. He did minor repairs on their rig, made a few slight changes, and reinforced highly stressed attach points.

Finding a tool box, he took stuff apart on the boat and put it back together. He checked out the engine, but it was beyond repair. Harry suspected the pistons had welded themselves to the cylinder walls and the two had become one. He checked the entire craft for leaks and finding it sound; he went to just general straightening and organizing.

The best thing he found, to keep himself busy, was swordplay. He created new moves and even added the one that Bessie had performed back on the beach. Then, sit ups, pull ups on the cabin doorway, push-ups on the prow deck, and running in place every chance he got. Anything that would push him toward exhaustion. He spent a lot of time watching sunsets, sunrises, and star gazing in between. Sketching was a pleasant diversion, and he soon went to sketching on the backs of the pages as well, fearful he may run out of paper.

The cloudy days and cloudy nights were almost unbearable. It wasn't unusual for Harry to find himself randomly weeping on those gray days. His situation made him think of convicts and the things they did while waiting for freedom. He too was a prisoner. The vessel had become his cell, and the ocean, his prison. He was fairly sure those detainees had only one thing on their minds—the day they would be set free. For them, it was the guard bringing the news that their time was served. For him, it would be the sight of land or the arrival of a monster. Harry would take either.

Days went by before his floating jail cell entered the North Atlantic Drift. He only noticed a slight change as the sun started rising on the starboard side and not at the prow. Checking the compass, he saw the needle pointed almost true north.

He went to keeping track of the days by using a black marker he had found in a small drawer in the wheelhouse. Marking a tiny 'X' on the door jamb every morning when he woke up, he would then have a light breakfast and start his routine. It was shortly after marking his eighteenth X that a small storm sprang up in the south. The rain came, and the Fidelis bounded. It never got as bad as it could have, leaving Harry glad he hadn't ended up in the middle of a serious squall.

It grew cold, so he ripped the soft canvas tarp from its tacks above the harpoon rack and wrapped up in it. Moving into the wheelhouse, he slid the door shut behind him. He thought about putting on the hoodie, but it needed cleaning. The tarp would do for now. He didn't need the memories the hoodie would bring, especially when he sat idle.

Gazing through the windows from his seat, Harry watched the lightning flash in the distance. The thunder boomed, and funnel clouds came down and pulled back up as if indecisive. Not even twenty minutes later, one, then two, and finally, three, touched the surface about a mile away. Officially waterspouts, they were almost invisible as they writhed, twisted, and squirmed. Had it not been for the turbulent vortices their tips made as they rode across the waves, he could have easily lost track of them. The wind picked up and Harry moved to sit on the wheelhouse floor. Backing into a corner, he tried hard to hold onto his lunch. Peeking up on occasion, he saw the waterspouts were tracking to the northeast and were soon completely out of sight.

A light shower fell most of the day, and at one point he disrobed and hung his clothing over the gunwale for a good rinse. Adding the hoodie to the lot, he left the sardines to rest upon the bench.

Standing out in the rain, Harry scrubbed his body with his hands. He decided to remain naked since no one was going to be around to see him. Turning over a large red plastic bucket, he allowed it to fill with rainwater because one never knew when that might come in handy.

Moving to the bench, he sat watching the turbulent clouds and listening to nature's orchestra. He wondered when he would start going crazy from the loneliness and if he would hallucinate other boats and people when he did.

*I feel sane… but crazy people don't know they're crazy.*

Harry thoughts turned to old Beatrice Butterfield who had lived on his street. His mother said she had dementia and couldn't remember anything. Marji had ended the discussion with a statement about how mother nature, in her infinite wisdom, wanted to make it easier for people who were afraid of dying, by blowing their minds just prior to their final years on earth. A tender mercy.

The sun soon broke through the clouds at the western horizon. Harry, still nude, ate from a can of peaches, and in no time, it was twilight. After tossing the empty can into the bottom of the boat, he went to working on a package of saltines.

Leaning back against the gunwale, Harry watched the afterglow dwindle to a cobalt blue. It wasn't long after the light left the sky that something flew past him about a yard from his nose.

He jumped up and turned to look in the direction from which it had come. He watched a second creature fly past, but it was the third one slapping him in the back of his head that really woke him up. It bounced high into the air and fluttered down to fall into the ocean. He ducked down and backed into the wheelhouse to watch from the doorway.

Whatever they were, there seemed to be a whole school of them. Instead of swimming around the gillnetter, they just jumped over it. He thought of flying fish and wished he could get a better look at them. They were much bigger than he had imagined. Too big, in fact. Grabbing his swords, he moved out in a crouch and waited.

A single one appeared, gliding overhead. He swiped at it but missed. Three of them came together and he swiped again, hitting one. Falling inside the boat, it flapped and fluttered back among the ropes.

Harry could hear it, but that was all. Pushing things aside, he found the beast in a small space between two coils of polypropylene rope. He could barely see it there in the twilight, looking up at him, its mouth open to expose a shark's maw of lethal looking teeth. It was about as long as his arm and looked more like a killer tadpole than a flying fish. It acted like it was going to vomit before letting out a croaking hiss that ended in a high shriek. It wasn't seriously injured and as Harry raised a sword to finish it off, the creature's long, fin-like wings buzzed, and it leapt into his face. He backpedaled and tripped, falling onto the deck. The thing flew over him and disappeared into the dark.

*Well, Harry, there goes your monster! Just not the one you wanted... Ha-ha!*

Getting to his feet, he grabbed the hoodie and moved into the wheelhouse. If one of those fiends had latched onto him, it would have done some serious damage and he didn't need to be nursing wounds right now. Laying the hooded sweatshirt over the dashboard to dry, he sat on a shelf just inside, watching for more of the creatures.

Harry was sure he had seen them in the section at the back of the ID manual marked, 'Least Seen Species'. The critters the government had rated as third-class monsters. It bugged him that he couldn't remember the name of the little fiends. He decided to sleep in the wheelhouse that night. The desire to do battle was strong, but he didn't want to wake up half eaten because a school of flying fish had gnawed him as he lay sleeping on the open deck. After opening the all windows about an inch, he dragged his bookbag in for some food.

Zipping it open, he removed most of what was in there and began to take inventory. A realization came to him in the form of fear rising up from the pit of his stomach. His old swords weren't in the bag. Harry couldn't remember picking them up from the table back at Winnie's place. His father must have set them aside when he packed the furniture away for the night. It was more his own fault than his dads, though. That he could lose his swords had always been a factor. The concern had grown over the years, though. There were no longer mail-order houses or martial arts outlets. They would have to be scrounged for, and it wasn't like there was a butterfly sword store in every town. It was one more thing he didn't want to think about.

He resigned himself to the loss of his first pair, reinforcing that with, should he ever lose Master Bik's, he could always fall back on a pair of fourteen-inch butcher knives, or a couple of good, sharp, machetes. He vowed to himself to see to it that, that never happened.

His supper consisted of a can of precooked pork, and he spent the rest of the evening cleaning and sharping his blades while nibbling, stale, mixed nuts. He tried to remember pop songs he had known as a boy, and then tried to sing them after they came to mind. When Harry got around to his favorite, '*On A Day*' by the Stomping Frijoles, his crescendo brought whale song in through the open windows. It was distant and subdued, but whale song none the less. He repeated the verse, and the whale sang again, only more melancholic the second time. The ocean borne vocalist made him feel lonelier than he already was. So, Harry stopped singing and heard the whale no more. Wrapping himself in the tarp, he drifted off with the smell of the Thulu tainted hoodie in his nose.

# CHAPTER 11

## On The Seas and Far Away

Harry awoke the next morning to the sound of a tin can hitting wood. In the throes of waking, he had knocked the empty meat container to the floor. Fog slithered in through the gaps of the open windows and he could see the grayish white cloud now enveloped the Fidelis. The waves lapped at the hull as the gillnetter slowly rocked, adding a smidgeon of spookiness to the mix. Sliding off the shelf, he rolled the tarp and tossed it forward to the windscreen. A slight chill in the air drove him to get dressed, and while removing his sword rig, a finger brushed the wound on his lower back.

He had felt the itch periodically throughout the night whenever he came close to consciousness. Now, pieces of the scab fell away, and he found some relief in knowing he had one less thing to worry about. Infection was an ever-lingering concern.

Pulling on his pants and shirt, he donned the sword rig. Sliding the blades from their sheaths, he looked them over. A few specks of rust told him the ocean air was taking its toll on the old steel. He would have to buff them somehow and give them a thin coat of oil, or maybe, petroleum jelly. Not having what he needed to make that happen right away, it added to his ever-escalating exasperation.

There were fourteen X's on the door jamb now. The marker had given up, so Harry used a stub of a pencil to scratch on number fifteen. Then, grabbing the stinking hoodie, he slid the door open and dropped it next to the bucket of rain water. Harry figured he would have his breakfast first and then get to scrubbing it over the side until it was reasonably stench free. He would use the rain water in the bucket as a final rinse.

Finishing off the bottle of water he had left outside on the bench, he tossed the empty plastic container aft. It bounced around, making a light knocking noise as it did. A single, almost indiscernible, metallic *Clank!* punctuated the end of its dance as the plastic bottle wedged itself inside the collar of a life jacket. That sound of steel striking steel had not resonated from within the boat, though. It had come out of the fog. Harry moved to stand in the center of the deck, and cocking his head, he slowly rotated 360 degrees, just listening, trying to determine the direction from which the noise had come.

The fog was the thickest he had ever seen. But Harry had never been lost at sea before. So, it could very well have been a common occurrence. He didn't think there was any chance he could crash into something, but the noise made him doubt. If another vessel was coming his way, he'd want them to know he was there.

Imitating a foghorn, he enunciated as loud as he could. However, he sounded more like a Thulu then a boat and it creeped him out. So, he gave up on that idea. His bladder told him his hydration plan was working, and moving to the portside gunwale, he unzipped his jeans and peed into the water.

He stood, looking hard into the fog. Something was out there and he felt the need to be vigilant. When his eyes grew fatigued from staring, he started to hallucinate giant boulders, trees, other watercraft, and even a rock-strewn shoreline. Then, whatever he thought he saw, changed, and became something else. This made him even more anxious. Closing his eyes, he just listened to the urine hitting the water, the waves beating against the boat, and that metal-on-metal noise in the distance.

Feeling a little lighter afterwards, Harry decided to work out before having breakfast, hoping it would take his mind off the weather. Breakfast could wait.

When his routine got to the part where he employed his swords, he got the gillnetter rocking so badly that he had to stop. He switched to calisthenics and remained at the center of the deck, trying to keep the motion to a minimum. When the sweat ran freely, he called it quits.

Harry felt he had waited long enough to eat. So, digging through the pile of food for his breakfast, he chose a package of Shemberg's cured turkey slices in a vacuumed sealed bag. Sitting on the bench outside the wheelhouse, he ripped it open, and sniffing at it, he inspected it for greening and any other signs of rot. Then taking a small bite, he was convinced it was safe for consumption. Folding pieces between crackers, he made small sandwiches and finished off the entire package.

Feeling satisfied that he'd had enough to eat, Harry wiped his greasy hands on his pants and delved into taking stock of his supplies. He counted everything twice, and then methodically returned them either to his bookbag or one of the two flour sacks. The words from *Hush little baby,* poured from his lips as he worked, and he wondered if, maybe, his mother had sung that lullaby to him as an infant.

He soon found his eye lids growing heavy and drowsiness overtook him. It struck him odd because he had slept soundly all night.

*You just ate a whole package of turkey, fool!*

The excessive amount of tryptophan had released a serious dose of melatonin into his blood stream, sedating him. Leaning back against the wheelhouse wall, Harry made himself comfortable and dozed off.

Twenty minutes later a terrific jolt knocked him from his seat, the pain of his butt bouncing off the deck bringing him fully awake. The Fidelis had run into a huge black wall shrouded by the fog. Harry shook his head and rubbed his eyes thinking he was still asleep and had just dreamed it. There was no ignoring the pain in his rump, though, or the fact that he was now sprawled upon the deck. The grinding noise of wood against something much harder, confirmed the reality, bringing Harry to his feet.

The impact, even though slight, had brought his stern around so the gillnetter now paralleled the obstruction. Running his hand over the surface of the huge black wall, Harry found it rough, cold, and, surprisingly—coated in thick paint. Rapping on it with a knuckle, it sounded hollow. He walked aft, knocking as he went. No change.

The fog continued to roll, lift, and then thicken, only to lift again as he tried in vain to see if this strange new thing had a top or end. The gillnetter bumped against it continuously, rising up and down, the squeaking grind becoming almost unbearable. Then the fog lifted to the point where Harry could see further up the side and the words, 'DESTINY'S ENCHANTED' appeared in large white letters. Below them in a smaller font, 'MIAMI'.

*It was a ship!*

Harry couldn't contain his excitement. "Hello! Hello! Is anyone there?" No answer. "Hello! Can someone hear me? Help! I need help! Someone… please!" Still no response.

It dawned on him that there was no engine noise and when a slight breeze blew, there came that familiar metal on metal clank. It was followed by a second, and then a third, and soon developed into a loud, odd sounding, wind chime.

Placing his palms flat against the Enchanted's hull, Harry tried to palm the gillnetter backwards along the side of the larger vessel. That didn't work, and it left his hands sore and covered in rust. Picking up the harpoon, he sat down with his back to the transom and placing the barbed point against the welded joints in the ship's side, he pushed. Even though it was a painstaking process, it started the Fidelis moving in the direction he wanted to go and closer to solving the mystery of the sound emanating from above.

The rhythmic clanking continued and soon a bowsing block appeared, swinging out of the mist. After passing over the wheelhouse roof, it reversed direction and took out the antennae array for the gillnetter's useless radio.

*Lifeboat hooks!*

Harry sat and watched as it swung back and forth in the vacillating fog, sometimes impacting the ocean liner's hull. He wasn't sure what to do next, his mind a jumble of thoughts.

It was one of those moments when his father would have said, *"Get your head out of your ass, kiddo, or suffer the consequences."* The bowsing block passed by again, making a slight whistling noise as if it was trying to attract his attention.

*What are you waiting for, dodo? Climb that rope and get on board!*

That brought him out of his stupor, and he realized his window of opportunity was fast shrinking. The Fidelis was moving back toward the Enchanted's prow where the two had first collided, and it seemed the gillnetter was trying to outrun the cruise ship.

Harry frantically strapped his bag closed and slipped it on. Then he wasted precious minutes pulling water bottles from the flour sacks and tossing them up and over the railing of the lowest deck. Missing the mark several times, he was grateful that they landed in the Fidelis upon their return trip. However, when one hit him on the shoulder, Harry howled his frustration and swinging the flour sack with the remaining bottles inside, he flung it with every ounce of strength, sending it right where he wanted it to go.

Grumbling to himself, he climbed onto the wheelhouse roof and waited for the bowsing block to come his way. When it did, he caught it, gasping and gritting his teeth when it slammed into his outstretched hands. Keeping a firm grip on the mechanism, its momentum carried him from the roof, his feet pedaling empty air as he climbed with just his hands. Once he was able to get his feet on top of the block, he rested, swinging slowly back and forth, sometimes gently bumping into the ship.

Summoning all his strength, Harry started skyward, hand over hand. It was harder than he imagined. The ropes were the twisted wire variety and there was the occasional patch of grease. He had to lock the rope with his feet and reach up past the greasy sections, sometimes slipping, sending his heart into his throat.

It was the fear of falling and being dashed upon the smaller craft that kept him moving upward. The feeling of vertigo lingered just on the edge of his consciousness and he fought to keep it there, steadfastly concentrating on his task. Upon reaching the davit, he pulled himself up onto its cranelike arm and crawled along its top to drop onto the Enchanted's deck.

Harry fell onto his rump for the second time, and howling with pain, he frantically grabbed the horizontal bars of a safety gate and pulled himself up. His vision swam and dizziness overcame him. The strain of the climb had been too much. He felt like he was going to pass out. Laying down to avoid banging his head against the steel of the walkway, he swirled away into unconsciousness.

When he came to, there was an all too familiar odor in his nose; the decaying corpse kind. It was the same one that permeated his neighborhood back in Kilbury. Scrambling to his feet, Harry frantically looked about and almost passed out again. Latching onto the railing with both hands, he forced himself to take slow, even breaths as he scanned the walkway from end to end. Seeing nothing, he figured the stench must be coming from an open door along the wall behind him and to his right. The sun soon appeared, enveloping Harry in its light, sending the fog fleeing along with the Fidelis, which now had put some distance between itself and the ship.

He had traded one boat for another, and he comforted himself with the fact that at least it was small to large and not the other way around.

Then sadness stabbed him like a hot knife; he'd forgotten Bessie's hoodie. He could see it, still lying beside the bucket, and then there was the silver tin of the sardines, still on the bench, gleaming.

It felt like the final scene of a movie that had been about his life before losing Bessie. The chipped and faded, red gillnetter floating away, the hoodie and sardine can, a symbol of the first love of his life lying in plain sight for all to see, and the boat slowly being enveloped by the remnants of the fog, smacked of finale. Harry wanted to think about it in a humorous way, but the tears that welled in his eyes changed that.

*Time to get on with it, Harry! No time for tears*

Moving away from the railing, he wiped his eyes and began to collect the water bottles. He filled a flour sack to overflowing and set the rest along the wall so they wouldn't roll overboard. He figured they'd be safe there until he could return to collect them, but for now, he wanted to get familiar with the ship and moved toward the Enchanted's bow.

Harry found he was on the main deck for sure with no idea how many decks were above him. All the life boats on his side had been deployed. So, he suspected the same for the ones on the portside. Stopping in front of that open door, he could see it was a corridor linking the two sides. The light coming in the far entrance illuminated several man-sized lumps lying on the floor. He decided not to enter, the smell inside almost unbearable. He turned away and continued, drawing his swords just in case.

The first body that he came across in the open, out in the sun's light, sat on an exterior set of maintenance stairs. An old man, or woman, he couldn't tell which, sat with its back to the railing in a faded green, running suit and straw gardening hat. Its bluish black face was contorted as if they had died in severe pain. He poked it with a toe and was startled when it collapsed in on itself. Slipping between the rails, a set of false teeth tumbled out of its gaping mouth as the body plummeted over the side to splash into the sea.

Harry was never sure how to feel about dead people to whom he wasn't acquainted. There had been just too many. But it wasn't like they would care, or that anyone would judge him for developing a tough, outer shell. Yet, there were exceptions, and more often than not, it was the little kids and teens that could easily pierce his armor.

Moving up to the next deck, he found more. They were everywhere—bloated, blue corpses still dressed in their best. The numbers included a few grotesquely displayed in bikinis, their bodies swollen to the point of exploding. Examining the corpse of a young woman in a single piece bathing suit who had only adopted a greenish pallor, he noticed the tell-tale signs of the Bug. The virus had taken its toll on board this ship. Escaping by lifeboat had probably just been a waste of time. Harry imagined little, yellow boats full of bloated corpses just floating randomly about on the ocean. The thought made him shiver.

Locating the kitchen, Harry found the supply pantry devoid of bodies, and felt the relief of being in a space free of casualties. Making a mental note, he set the room aside for future inspection and continued making his way upward.

He was able to determine that there were six levels above the main deck with the bridge at the very top. The large, spacious control room was also free of human remains, and because the wind could blow freely across it, he noticed the absence of the nagging stench he'd encountered on the decks below.

The massive bridge stretched from portside to starboard in a huge hexagon, the three sides at the front glazed with heavy, laminated glass for a windscreen. There were two entry doors just back from that, one on each side. The back wall supported two large control panels divided by an access door and bordered on their outside edges by two more of the same. The instrument panels, once showing an array of blinking diodes, small, backlit computer screens, and digital navigational monitors, now hung dark and as useless as all the silver toggle switches, little key pads, and short, black levers that, at one time, controlled the mix.

Turning back to the wheel, Harry found the power steering was in-opt, so he was unable to budge the rudder. Moving to the knobs that read: 'Generator', they did nothing when he pushed them. The ship was as dead as the passengers on it.

Harry decided to set up camp there. Opening the door in the center of the back wall, he found the room paneled in light brown wood and possessing a single desk. It was a mess as if someone had ransacked it. Two small, armless chairs lay on their sides in front of the desk, and the rolling chair behind, lay on its back. A small filing cabinet in the corner, hung open. Most of what littered the floor looked like the paper files that someone had pulled from the drawers and tossed. Stepping further in, Harry's foot kicked something buried in the paper. Picking it up, he found it was a semi-automatic Glock 45. Its slide was locked back showing that the last round had been fired. Popping out the magazine, he found it empty.

Dropping the pistol, Harry pulled his flashlight from his pocket and shined it around. There were bullet holes in the walls as well as the door. Blood had coagulated on the chair behind the desk and spent cartridges lay everywhere. There had been a gun fight and it looked like whoever sat behind the desk had lost.

He studied the single, framed portrait hanging on the wall. A suave looking older man, with graying hair, stood dressed in a starched white uniform, sporting a captain's hat. He stood beside a short, blonde woman and two teenagers, one of them a boy, the other, a girl. The Enchanted sat docked in the background with blue sky all around.

The nameplate affixed to a fake gold bar that sat upon the desktop, declared, 'Captain Richard 'Dick' Dekker'. Harry wondered if Captain Dick's body had been committed to the deep. Backing out, he shut the door and moving past the second control panel, he opened the last door on that side before arriving at the deck exit.

Harry found the space inside was only a little larger than the first. It was about ten-foot square, and a bunk bed sat secured to the floor at his right hand. A single, stainless-steel shelf had been affixed to the wall beside the headboard to act as a nightstand. Both bunks were neatly made, and the room held the slight odor of disinfectant. Pulling the blankets from both, he checked the sheets and the mattresses to find them spotless. A large, red leather chair sat across the room, its back to the wall, a reading lamp affixed just above it. Harry couldn't have been happier about his discovery and claimed the room for his own.

Returning to the control room, he moved to the remaining door on the far side and found it led into a housekeeper's closet and store room. It was full of sundries, cleaning implements, and plastic jugs of disinfectant. Harry figured he would find them beneficial in the days to come.

Happy with his accommodations, he left the bridge and used what remained of the daylight for exploration. He soon determined the amount of space the ship had to offer was almost overwhelming. The Fidelis had been a place to perch, but the Enchanted offered him room to move. Harry was going to take advantage of that.

There were many lounges on board, plus a vast atrium-like space positioned amidships. It had a large, cutaway model of the Enchanted proudly displayed on a pedestal in the center of its immense floor. He would have to come back and study that later.

The swimming pool was at the bow and a dead body floated in the now greenish-brown water. A white deck lounger accompanied the corpse as it drifted. Harry imagined the person had been lying in the chair, breathing their last snotty breaths, when a large rolling wave had tipped the ship and cast them into the heavily chlorinated pool.

Harry continued with his survey and soon found an expansive weight room with an open floor for aerobics fans. That's where he would practice. There was also a game room full of the latest video games, a small casino next to that, and a tiny bar to finish out the wall space.

He didn't go below. Standing at the top of the interior stairwell, he just stared down into the dark, the sign above his head indicating that's where the third-class cabins were. He wanted to go down and shut the massive fire door to isolate those rooms, but he would save that for another day.

Since all ventilation was fan driven, the air would be static and unbearable down in those corridors. Another sign said that the common shower rooms and toilets were down that stairway, as well. Harry decided he would just bathe on deck with buckets, and the ocean would be his toilet. He only needed a single, small space to sleep, and a clear path to the kitchen and pantry.

It was water that might be a problem. Access to a potable source was everywhere, but none of the faucets worked. His first goal: find the water tanks, make sure the water was good, and then, sort out a way to extract it.

Moving back to the bridge, Harry dumped his bag in his room, and remembering the photo of him and Bessie that he had stuck in his back pocket, he slipped it inside the pack to accompany his mother's. With the bookbag open, he couldn't ignore the food, and the urge to eat overrode everything else. Grabbing a tin of pork and a can of fruit cocktail with a pop top, he sat in the captain's chair next to one of the two steering pedestals and ate an early supper. He would invade the kitchen later in hopes to find something tastier. The map table sat just behind him, and pivoting around on the stool, he studied the Atlantic Ocean and the routes laid out for the Enchanted.

One particular map showed the currents in long light blue arrows and what caught his eye were the words 'North Atlantic Drift'. Its dark blue line was segmented by arrow heads pointing north as it ran between the Americas and the European continent.

Harry remembered that very moment when he felt something had changed while on board the Fidelis. Like a light bulb coming on inside his head, he knew that was when he had caught the current, and a good reason why he had bumped into the Enchanted. He wondered how many more vessels were floating aimlessly about out there, and if any had a stowaway like him on board. Harry's long-term goal was to get his feet back on solid ground.

He saw the dark blue line ran close to Ireland and he wondered if the ship would come within swimming distance of its shore. Maybe he could get off at Dingle or further north at Belmullet. Those were just hopes, though, driven by the fear that he would be stuck on board this drifting morgue until he too joined the dead.

Finishing his meal, he slid from the chair and searched through the many cabinets and cupboards. He really wanted a good, full-sized flashlight. He missed those Faradays that had been in his father's pack and wished that the captain had thought to utilize them for the Enchanted's last cruise.

All he found was the standard, long, black anodized aluminum type. Only two of them worked, and leaving one on the control panel, he took the other and returned to the captain's office.

Moving to the desk, he opened a small door on its side and a smile braced Harry's lips. A large lantern with 'FRANKLIN' stamped on the wide base, gleamed in the light; the captains own personal stash. Instead of shaking this one, you pulled out and pumped a rod to get the internal generator going. The starting unit sounded like one of those antique toys that you had to roll several times over the floor before you released it to let the thing buzz away under its own power.

Harry pumped the rod a total of ten times before he hit the switch. The bulb glowed, and he found it could light an area about the size of his room. Harry's smile grew wider at the prospect that he could now read at night if he wished.

*Thanks again, Captain Dick!*

Setting the lantern next to the flashlight, he left the wheelhouse. Finding a deckchair on the observation gallery just out front of the windscreen, Harry sat with his feet on the railing, watching the starlit sky. An intruding thought that he might not be alone, kept pushing in.

*What if there were others onboard hiding from me?*

The thought made him feel paranoid. There were a lot of sounds onboard a ship, ones that he wasn't familiar with. Harry got up and walked around. When he heard an odd sound that he didn't recognize, he searched it out. Solving the mystery would bring him piece of mind. But he soon got tired of that and returned to his chair. He would resume the task in the daylight and continue until he had mentally catalogued every sound that the Enchanted had to offer; as well as its source.

Harry could see the body floating in the moonlit pool five decks below, and the longer he sat out there, the more it bothered him. Deciding it was time for bed, he went inside. He vowed he would snag that body tomorrow, pull it out, and toss it overboard. Closing the doors on each side of the bridge, he locked the simple night latches. Taking his lantern into his room, he closed the door and locked it too. Until he knew the ship better, he felt the need to secure himself within. The door had a louvered panel at the bottom, so he would be able to hear anything that happened outside.

Removing all his clothing, Harry lay naked on the top bunk, the ceiling just a few feet from his nose. The lantern glowed from the simple metal shelf, and he realized how quiet it was. He couldn't even hear the ocean. That unnerved him. He figured it would take one or two nights to adapt. When he felt more comfortable with his floating prison, maybe he would slumber out on the deck.

Dozing off, he slept fitfully through the night. The room grew hot, and even though there was a vent with a fan in the wall, nothing flowed in or out of that box. Along with the heat, he also suffered nightmares. There came endless dreams about his mother and father and even a short one about Master Bik talking to him about philosophy and the need to take his art seriously. Then Doc Smith, laughing about the Capuchipines tearing his father apart across the room as Harry, staring in horror, stood next to the mirth filled doctor. And finally—there was Bessie. He sat with her underwater in what looked like a public pool. She talked to him in a bubbly language he couldn't understand. Then getting up, she walked across the bottom, sans bathing suit, to a large Thulu who sat like a king on a coral throne. Climbing into its lap, she leaned back against its chest. She sat naked, rubbing the creature's arm as a clawed hand massaged her belly. Throwing Harry an evil grin, Bessie opened her mouth and tentacles dropped out as her eyes turned a gleaming ebony.

Harry awoke with a start, his shout still echoing in the metal room. His face was wet, and he knew he had been weeping. The sheet, saturated with sweat, would have to be changed. Swinging his legs over the edge, he almost forgot he was on the top bunk and barely caught himself before tumbling off. Awkwardly lowering himself to the floor, he threw open the door and stepped out into the control room.

The air was cooler out there and he took some deep breaths as he watched the sun break the horizon. Unlocking the two outside doors, Harry left them open. The morning breeze cooled his skin even more, and he moved to the rail to watch the sunrise. He was seriously missing Bessie. His dreams had brought her many faces. One after the other. Happy Bessie, sad Bessie, seductive Bessie, and finally, the disturbing, 'Thulu Bessie'. Harry thought it odd that he missed her more than his mother or father. He wondered how long it would take before he would get over feeling this terrible longing. He needed to get busy to keep his mind off the past.

Returning inside, Harry dressed, donned and checked his swords, and then moved toward the kitchen. On the way, he wondered if it was a good idea to eat before starting his project. His first planned task of the day was to remove that body from the pool. He didn't want to puke, risking dehydration. Breakfast would wait. If he still felt like eating afterwards, then, so be it.

Changing directions, he went down to the bow deck and stepping out onto the patio, he walked to the side of the pool where the corpse lazily floated.

It was an old woman, her swollen body bound by a red, one-piece bathing suit with a long-flowered skirt now wrapping her rotting legs. One foot still held onto its lime-colored beach sandal, while the other floated free alongside as if it didn't want to leave its mate.

Even in the greenish-brown water, he could see where mucus and other body fluids had baked onto her skin. A pus-colored halo floated around her necrotic face. Her faded blue eyes were open, and she stared as if to say, 'Well, what are you waiting for? Get to work!' Harry tried not to look at them.

It was the kind of a face that could easily come back in dreams and he had enough of that going on. Finding the pool net, Harry brought it over, and then having second thoughts, he traded the net for a long-handled pool hook. Using it to pull her to him, she started to come apart almost at once. This gave rise to the doubt he would be able to finish the job.

The impulse to just grab the skirt and pull was strong. But if he did that, he would eventually have to grab a hold of the other end and he feared if he seized her hair, it might come off. She bobbed next to him, pushing dirty little waves up onto the deck as he tried to formulate a plan. Harry's fear of touching her only made it worse. Needing a breather, he stepped back to a nearby chair, and sitting down, he faced away to take deep breaths. He just wanted to be done and suspected this particular body would be the worst of them all.

Getting to his feet, Harry walked to the high metal wall surrounding the patio to gaze at cartoonish sailing ships that had been painted on it as a mural. They gave him an idea. He had watched a movie once where there had been a battle between a British Man of War and a French privateer, set sometime around 1700. The crew wrapped the dead in their canvas hammocks and after sewing them shut, commended them to the deep.

*Worth a try!*

Harry moved back to the pool to put his plan into action. He would use a tarp, two donut life preservers, some rope, and the pool hook.

Cutting two, yard-long pieces from the coil of rope, he tied each preserver to opposite corners of a longer side of the tarp, using the tarnished brass grommets. Then, tying a rather lengthy piece of rope to each corner on the opposite long edge closest to him, he left lengthy tails hanging and plenty of slack in between knots.

With his feet planted firmly on the concrete deck, he stood in the loop of the longer piece to keep it anchored. Using the pool hook, he pushed the life preservers under the body, so that they popped out on the other side. The buoyant donuts took the edge of the tarp with them and he was able to position the rig to get the dead woman in the center of the canvas. Pulling the preservers over the body to meet the opposite corners, Harry succeeded in trapping the corpse inside the fold.

With the life preservers within reach, he crouched and cut one loose; leaving enough rope so he could tie it to the free hanging tail just opposite. He then repeated the process on the other end. Tossing the plastic donuts aside, he stepped out of the loop and grabbing the long rope at its center, he pulled the woman's corpse up onto the deck.

Harry needed to take a breather after that. Walking around the pool several times, he took deep breaths and steeled himself to what he had to do next. At Bik's academy, Harry had to learn how to will away the pain of an injury. In all actuality, it only worked to lessen it to a bearable degree. He thought to do the same with the smell. He would will it away by narrowing his focus to just the task at hand, but still wished he had brought something to plug his nose.

Going back to the dead body, Harry utilized Master Bik's method and found, like with pain, he could reduce the stench to something more tolerable. Moving with some urgency, he cut the long rope at the center and bound the entire thing with the two loose ends to form what reminded him of a huge burrito that had gone bad. The thought brought a fleeting wave of nausea and he hurriedly tied off the rope before his stomach decided to give up whatever contents it contained.

*So much for self-discipline!*

Stumbling away, Harry gulped for air and swallowed bile. He leaned forward, his hands flat against the pool surround, his head hanging. Focusing his eyes on the deck drain at the base of that high steel wall, a light bulb came on in his head. The grill covering the drain could be slid left along a track, and in doing so, he found the opening was just big enough to push his two-hour long project through and into the ocean.

*Good! Now, just go over, grab her, and get this done!*

Forcing himself to act, he stomped over to the pool hook, picked it up and snagging a loop in the ropes at the head of the bundle, he dragged it to the drain. Keeping a grip on the pole, he moved around to the dead woman's feet and pushed, sending her tarp covered corpse, and the pool hook, through the opening. It went easily enough, and he waited for the splash. When it came, he fell back against the cool steel of the pool surround and sighed with relief.

*One down, one hundred and ninety-nine to go!*

The job had been harder and took longer than Harry had imagined. But he didn't need to remove every corpse on board the ship, just the ones that lay out in the open. He could keep himself busy while waiting for his freedom by being the sanitary engineer for the Enchanted. Least that way, he wouldn't have to look at them when he was out and about for a much-needed stroll.

Trudging up to the observation deck to stand outside of the mammoth windscreen, he watched as the body put some distance between it and the ship. "So long! Not so nice knowing you," he shouted.

Soon, large fins appeared, cruising toward the body. He watched it get pulled under a couple of times and bobbing back to the surface the last time, the fins abruptly moved away before disappearing altogether. Not even the sharks wanted to deal with it. Feeling satisfied with the work he had done; Harry made his way to the galley.

The food pantry was huge, but only about half of what was stored there was useful to him. Cracking the freezer door, he soon wished he hadn't. Even the dead didn't smell that bad. He gagged and almost vomited. After slamming the door, he dropped the locking pin in the latch as a reminder never to do that again.

The pool job and the freezer nearly put an end to any desire for food. So, Harry sat at a stainless-steel prep table snacking on prepackaged granola bars and a warm glass of powdered milk. The room was windowless with the open door offering the only source of light. It was gloomy and he decided he would take his meals on the bridge or outside from then on. Feeling he'd had enough to eat; he went out and gathered the water bottles he had tossed on board from the Fidelis. Taking them to his room, he found his sleeping area had cooled considerably. He made it a rule to leave the doors open all day unless there was a storm or, an invasion.

Harry grabbed one of the flashlights and went to the atrium where he had seen the ships model on display. There were at least twelve bodies in there.

Some sat propped up in chairs, staring at him with long dead eyes from mummified faces, others lay behind tables and sofas. A few had even crawled into the patches of flora made to look like residential flower beds. The plant life had grown wild with neglect, and then died from lack of water. The bodies lay among a multitude of leaves and long brown stems; some even wrapped in vines. He would have to cut those out before disposing of them. Then there were the children; they would be the worst.

He forced himself to keep his focus on the ship model, but it was difficult as his attention kept straying to the little blond girl lying on the floor to his right. The child lay on her side, her left arm hiding her face. She looked like she had just lay down for a nap. When he got around to removing bodies from the atrium, she would be the first to go. Looking back at her one last time as he walked away, he muttered, "Don't worry, sweetie, I'll be kind." Picking up his pace, Harry wiped away the tears that had welled up in his eyes as he moved back out onto the promenade deck.

Having determined the best path to the water tanks by studying the cut-away, he formulated a plan. They were somewhere at the bottom, close to the so-called bilge. It would be dark down there and he clicked the flashlight on and off a couple times to make sure it would work. Returning to the kitchen, he grabbed a clean, stainless steel ice bucket and finding the closest access to the stairs, he moved down into the bowels of the ship.

He had left the doors at the top open to offer a beacon of light back to fresh air. Only twice did he have to step over corpses. The first was dressed in the outfit of a cook, the second, an older man in the jumpsuit of a maintenance worker. One of the old guy's legs hung through a railing, now too swollen to pull back through. Harry would have to amputate in order to dispose of that body.

*Maybe... leave that one*

Descending further, he found himself in total darkness. The sunlight through the doorway far above him was now just a dim illumination painted across the white ceiling of the stairwell vestibule.

Harry moved into a corridor on his left, cautiously shining the light around. The beam soon found a door marked 'Water Tanks-Authorized Personnel Only'. Stepping inside, he found two mammoth, stainless steel tanks sitting in the silent gloom. At the base of each tank, a drain cock protruded out over a funneled conduit that Harry assumed ran down a pipe to a small hole in the hull.

Rotating the lever on one of the petcocks, he let the water run down into the funnel for a minute before placing his bucket underneath the stream. It beat staccato in the bottom, creating a sound that echoed weirdly in the gloom.

It made Harry self-conscious, and he imagined some crew member popping in and asking, 'Is there a problem here?' He impulsively glanced over his shoulder at the open door and then laughed at himself.

At three quarters full, he turned off the spout. The water appeared clear. So, he smelled it, and then gave it a taste. It set off no alarms, so unless there were bacteria, he was good to go.

Hauling the bucket back up the stairs, he put it in the kitchen. He would go back tomorrow with a second bucket. That way he would have one for bathing and one for drinking. Finding a clean plastic coffee cup that would float, he dropped it in the water to use as a dipper.

Grabbing two linen napkins from a pile, he wetted one and used it to make a 'robber's mask' to cover his nose and mouth. After making sure it would stay in place by twisting his head to the right and left, he pulled it down to cool the skin of his neck. Stuffing the dry one in a back pocket, he left the kitchen and went on to explore the rest of the ship.

Starting at the mid-deck pool, which was still clean enough for use, Harry worked his way forward toward the bridge. Arriving at the stairwell that led down to the corridors that allowed access to the staterooms, he pulled up his mask and reluctantly descended.

It was just as he had expected. The air was heavy with an unbearable stench and the dark hallway gave Harry that haunted house feeling. Many of the doors were locked, while others stood wide open. Most of the rooms were lit just enough with their small windows to show corpses lying in beds and on floors, while others were empty, pristine, and inviting. There were still chocolates mints on pillows, little welcoming notes, and wilted flowers in glass vases. Swaths of paper still lay draped across toilet seats telling the arriving party that it had been properly sanitized and was ready to accept their bottoms.

Harry forced himself to investigate every nook and cranny, trying every door that he came across that was signed as something other than a place to sleep. He walked through every dining area, rec room, and TV lounge that the Enchanted had to offer. Poking his head inside a door marked 'Staff Only', he found it to be a small office. There was a rack of white uniforms for the deck crew, a wall with floor to ceiling shelves full of manuals, and a small metal cabinet with a dozen floatable lanterns. They all had the same charging mechanism as the one he had found in the captain's office. Taking two of them, he would store them on the bridge with the other one.

His black metal flashlight quit just minutes before he completed his exploration. Leaving it behind, Harry cranked up one of the floatables and used it instead. It was a more trustworthy form of illumination. Besides that, they were more of a floodlight than a spotlight. They would be highly beneficial in large, dark spaces.

Harry had walked just about the entire ship with the exception of the bilge, engine room, and the stern at the backend of the ship where a gazebo-like building sat upon a large, round pylon. It was a good hundred yards from where the ships huge, black funnel stretched skyward. Luckily for him, they were both on the top of the ship. So, plenty of sunshine.

His legs and feet ached along with his head and he wondered if the perpetual stench would ever leave his nose. His next visit to the pantry would include a search for any herb, or seasoning, he could douse his robber mask with. The infirmary may have some mentholated salve that he could smear on his upper lip, but he really didn't want to go to that place. He suspected there were more bodies in there per square foot than anywhere else onboard the Enchanted.

Pushing past his aversion, Harry searched for, and soon found, the door marked 'Health Clinic'. He tried to open it, pushing as hard as he could, but something heavy lay against it. Ramming it with his shoulder, he got it to move about an inch or two each time. It was slow going. When it was open far enough for him to get his head inside, he could just make out the large obstacle that blocked his path.

Shining his light on it, Harry felt bad for having been mercilessly smashing the door into her corpse. She must have been a nurse, her body sitting with legs splayed out in front, the weight of her torso still on the door. She appeared to have sat down on the floor, leaned back against the heavy metal panel, and promptly expired.

Keeping pressure on the door to keep it from closing, Harry brought his lantern up to illuminate the rest of the room. He regretted it almost instantly and the adrenaline flowed in. A teenage girl sat propped up by pillows in a bed, her blue eyes in a fixed gaze. She looked as if to be waiting for someone. Her long blond hair had been brushed out to frame her face and lay over the chest of her hospital gown. She reminded him of Mindy Lindyberg from his junior year at Kilbury high. His flesh crawled and the hair rose on his arms.

The girl looked like a ghost because she had not turned bluish gray like most of the dead. She had just paled to the color of crème and her lips had gone bloodless. But it was her eyes, open and staring that bothered Harry the most. Quickly pulling out, he let the deceased nurse close the door for him as he hurried away.

Stopping in a mid-ship dining room, he was overcome by emotion and sitting on a nearby chair, he wept, his face in his hands. He wondered if all this death was slowly pushing him over the edge. Yet it was healthy to cry as Bessie was always saying. There was no one around to see or make fun of him. It was good to get it out, and Harry felt much better afterwards. Returning to his task, he hoped he wouldn't have to look at anymore dead kids for the rest of the day.

Harry filched aspirin from a gift shop along with antibiotic crème and some calcium carbonate tablets. It was a 'just in case' thing until he could put together a trauma bag. He hoped there might be one stashed away on the bridge. There would be plenty of time to look.

Hours had passed since breakfast, but Harry didn't have much of an appetite, considering what he had just gone through. Drinking from a water bottle that he had brought along, he mounted the main deck from a murky stairwell and moved out past the funnel toward the stern.

The gazebo like building was enclosed entirely in glass and parts of patio furniture were visible through a railing on its roof. A couple of seabirds, that had been roosting there, squawked and took flight.

He felt excited, and then hopeful. He never saw those birds hanging around unless he was on, or near land. Searching the horizon, his elation melted away when he failed to find any long, low shadows that indicated dry land was close. The birds had probably ridden the Enchanted out of port and would be with the cruise liner until it grounded. Shaking his head in dismay, he made his way to the foot of the pavilion's steps and dashed up through the open door.

The interior had the ambiance of your standard barroom. It was dressed in floor length light blocking curtains that now hung open, and sitting up on that pylon, allowed a view to the ocean except for on the funnel side. A narrow, spiral staircase granted access to the roof, offering sun worshippers, who wanted a full body tan, some privacy. There were stuffed chairs and sofas forming a large circle around a tiny bar at the center, and several glasses sat abandon on its top.

Harry noted that the only other exit was on the opposite side of the room from where he stood. There was a small platform just outside some sliding glass doors that now stood open. He shut the one behind him and walked across the room to step out onto that balcony.

Leaning forward on the railing, he saw below him, two more corpses. They lay along a chest high transom wall, both with barely a stitch of clothing. Blood, contrasted by the white paint, was spattered everywhere. None of it had gone rusty, telling Harry the splashes were only days old; a week at the most. He felt reluctant to view more dead bodies, but something about them sparked his curiosity. Climbing over the banister and hanging from the top rail, he dropped the remaining six feet.

It was a young couple, probably in their twenties. She had been a natural blonde, and her companion, a young, black man. They both had been thoroughly gnawed on, the internal organs being the focus of the predator. The woman had been torn open at the side to allow some beast access to her liver. The man's entire lower back was opened up, and other than his spine, there was nothing holding him together in the middle. There were no signs of illness, and Harry assumed they had survived the Bug, only to meet their demise by monster.

Harry forced himself to study the woman a little closer. Her thin face was turned up, her eyes were closed, but her mouth was twisted in agony. Her right arm and hand appeared to have melted to some degree and evidence of a Thulu sting showed at the palm of the decimated hand. A blood-stained pair of panties wrapped an ankle, and a single sneaker, minus its shoelace, remained on her left foot. Their clothing lay scattered around in blood-soaked pieces and the remaining three shoes were nowhere to be seen.

The man lay face down, his stylish haircut caked with blood. A black tee shirt still covered his shoulders, but the bottom portion was torn away. The faces of 'Rap Crew' the rap group, stood glaring at Harry, their silk-screened image tinged in crimson. Both of the man's hands and arms looked gelatinous. It appeared as if he too had tried to fend off a Thulu's stinger.

Stepping in between the bodies, Harry peered over the transom into the ocean far below. The first thing he saw was that he was positioned just above the rudders. The second thing caused him to gasp and duck back. Crouching down, he waited, listening. When nothing came, he peeked back to see the Thulu still staring up at him. Relief flooded in with the realization that the beast was dead.

Its body hung tangled in a makeshift ladder composed of three volleyball nets stitched end to end with what looked like shoestrings. Three light ropes had been twisted together to make a heavier cable, and then had been threaded through one side of all three nets. A heavy rope had been stitched through the other side for added strength and both were tied to the short railing that ran along the top of the transom. They were the tightest knots Harry had ever encountered. After several attempts to untie them, he became aggravated and, in his exhaustion, he gave up.

*You got all the time in the world, worry about it later*

Harry leaned forward against the transom and letting his arms dangle over the edge, he rubbed the stiffness out of his fingers and watched the ocean.

The ladder stretched all the way down to the surface and trailed out behind the Enchanted. Occasionally it would spin, twist, and roll over, allowing him to see that the Thulu was minus its bottom half. After it twisted so far in one direction, it would slowly roll back, lowering the remains of the monster to the point that it appeared to be waterskiing.

Out of the corner of his eye, Harry noticed a single, red nylon rope had been tied to the railing a few yards over to his right. Following it down to the water, he saw it towed a mass of yellow rubber. It took

Harry a few minutes to grasp that the yellow mass had once been an inflatable dinghy. He deduced that the young couple, after lowering the little watercraft to the ocean, had then prepared to make their way down the homemade ladder. They had been surprised by the Thulu and it must have slaughtered them on the spot. The beast had somehow gotten tangled in the net on the way down, and was then attacked by sharks, or other monsters, while trying to get loose. Probably the same group that went after the dead woman.

Bringing his eyes back to the victims, he wondered if they had been immune to the virus and were the only two alive at the time of their attempted escape. They were not the warrior type. There were no makeshift weapons lying around, and the lack of a supply pack told him they had been desperate to get away at whatever cost.

Pushing it out of his mind, he left them and returned to the bridge. After taking a couple of aspirin, he grabbed something to eat and moved out onto the observation deck to sit in his chair and watch the sunset.

Harry's thoughts eventually worked their way back to that young couple and a mild frustration came with the realization that they might have been alive and here to greet him had he shown up sooner. He tried to imagine what they had been like when alive. That just made him sad, and then the loneliness crept in.

Remaining in his chair until the moon appeared; Harry kept himself busy by identifying constellations. When his eyes got heavy, he returned inside, locked up the bridge, and went to his room. Leaving his door propped open, he crawled into the lower bunk.

He stayed cooler and slept better than the night before, yet it was sometime in the early morning that he awoke with a start. Gazing out through his open door, he could see the stars through the windscreen. In his dream, several Thulu had come up the ladder and were breaking the windows to the bridge.

*You should have cut that whole mess loose back there, you idiot!*

The Thulu would not be able to scale the side of the ship, not with the way the hull angled out at the top. There was no way for them to get a grip on the slick, steel side. The makeshift ladder was their only means. So, unless he ran into that Godzilla thing, or any of those flying Thulu, he'd be okay.

Harry got up, dressed, and left his room, strapping on his sword rig as he went. Grabbing a floatable lantern off the control panel, he made his way back toward the funnel, his sixth sense telling him to be extra cautious.

A full moon sat in the western sky with light so bright that its illumination was almost surreal. The shadows it cast seemed even more distinct than those seen at high noon on a cloudless day. Harry suspected he wouldn't need the lantern.

Arriving at the base of the funnel, he stopped and turned to watch a meteor shower in the northern sky. A noise drifted to his ears, one that brought goose bumps and raised the hair on his head. It was the low mewing of a Thulu.

*The nightmare hadn't been a nightmare at all… it was a premonition!*

Relieved he hadn't switched on the lantern, he set it down and pulled his swords. Tiptoeing around the funnel and over to the lounge stairs, he crept up and peeked over the top tread through the tempered glass of the door. There was movement inside, and when his eyes adjusted, he could just make out four Thulu standing in a group at the bar, their silhouettes contrasted by the moon lit sky. Harry froze in place and waited for the usual foghorn-like alarm, but the Thulu's attention lay elsewhere.

Harry had to think this thing through. One Thulu was too many; taking on four would be suicide.

*Why couldn't they have showed up back when I wanted them too?*

Even though the situation was rather dire, Harry still saw the humor in how they all stood around the bar as if there to drink and discuss the state of the nation. He could see that the door on the opposite side remained open, just as he had left it.

*They must have come in over the balcony*

The creatures were all man sized. So, Harry knew they were youngsters. A single, mature Thulu, wouldn't have fit inside the lounge. He thought about returning to his bed and coming back to cut the ladder loose in the daylight. The beasts were already onboard, but the odds of them locating him were not in their favor. They couldn't smell him, so they would have to see or hear him. Sunrise was only a couple hours away and they would vacate the Enchanted to avoid the sun. It was a simple, nonviolent solution.

Harry couldn't let it go. The Enchanted was his, and he wanted them off his ship. He thought about backing himself in an alcove where they could only come at him one at a time, but that would best be left as a last resort. Better to just distract them and somehow lure them off the ship so he could cut that ladder loose.

Putting together a simple plan of decoy and diversion, he slowly backed down the stairs and snuck around to stand underneath the balcony. He could just make out the dead back at the stern and they appeared to have been undisturbed. Their presence triggered a desire for vengeance, which intensified as Bessie's face materialized in his mind's eye. Harry wasn't afraid—he was angry. He knew he could kill at least one of the four, and that's what he wanted. But getting rid of the other three was the problem. Pushing back his yearning for retribution, he put all his mental energy into focusing on his plan to get the Thulu off the Enchanted.

Moving through the shadow, he felt along the wall of the silo-like pylon. He found a knob and giving it a turn, he cautiously pulled open a door. The smell of garbage rolled out and reaching inside, he could feel several large, plastic garbage cans.

*That'll do just nicely!*

Picking up one of the containers, he set it just under the lip of the balcony, and reaching inside, he pulled out an empty champagne bottle. Listening hard for a few minutes to get some idea where the Thulu might be, he flung the bottle into a corner where the transom met the gunwale. At the sound of the bottle smashing against steel, Harry picked up the garbage can with both hands and flung it, directing it so it would fall and roll down the makeshift ladder.

Chaos unfolded overhead.

The first Thulu, one with a weird, yellow birthmark on the back of its head, dropped from the balcony just as the can disappeared over the edge. Harry was already inside the garbage room with the door all but shut. The thrum of the ropes could be heard as the container rolled down the net ladder. He had hit his mark.

With the door open just a crack, he watched the other three Thulu drop from the balcony and begin hooting the alarm as they followed their leader to the transom. They fought each other to see who would go down first. Mr. Birthmark won out and scrambled over the railing. Two decided not to wait and dived from the boat. That left number four, who just stood and looked around in a suspicious manner.

It lingered by the bodies, scanning the area like a hawk searching for prey. Just when Harry thought he might have to spend the night in the trash hold, there came a hooting noise, followed by a cackle from below. The skeptical Thulu clambered out of sight.

With no time to waste, Harry moved out to where the ladder attached to the railing. Pulling one of his swords, he sawed at the homemade cable on the right-hand side. The monster was still climbing down, causing the ladder to sway. It made his work more difficult, but the heavy rope was the polypropylene type and cut easily. When it separated, the creature fell off. It hit the one below it that was coming back up, and they both splashed into the ocean. The dead Thulu Harry had seen the day before was gone and he figured it must have become a midnight snack for the others before they came up for drinks.

He went to work on the rope twist, hoping he could finish before the next Thulu got to the top. The bunch of ropes would not be as easy as the first. One of them was a thick, hemp mooring line. The two that wrapped it, were the dynamic type used for mountain climbing and designed to resist abrasion. Harry didn't want to think ill of the dead, but the ladder's designers could have accomplished their task by simply using the thicker rope without the other two.

*Cuss them out later, Harry, you've got a job to do!*

Mr. Birthmark was on his way back up but stopped for some reason to hang at the halfway point. Harry tried to hold the cord away from the ship with his free hand to make cutting easier, but he kept getting pinched, and a couple of times it was so bad he almost screamed. His throbbing fingers grew numb, diminishing his ability to keep a firm hold. Changing his grip on the sword to a double handed hold, he stuck the blade underneath the rope and sawed upward.

Suddenly, the Thulu was there. Another shot of adrenalin coursed into Harry's veins and '*The Waltz of the Flowers*' rolled into his head. Everything went into slow motion, and pulling his second sword, he held the beast off with one hand and sawed with the other.

The odoriferous ogre emitted hissing shrieks while it dangled from one set of claws and swiped at Harry with the other. An older, more experienced Thulu would have strong-armed him or sprang over his head to land on the deck. This novice was reluctant, and Harry assumed the beast had never come up against a human being who fought back.

The other Thulu were just below, waiting for their cousin to get out of the way. If this one got past him and he had to turn away from the rope to fight, the other three would most certainly get back on board and overwhelm him.

The Thulu brought its tail up between its legs and whipped its stinger at Harry's head. He saw it coming and moved out of its trajectory long before it arrived. Taking a micro second away from sawing, he brought the swords together well below the spaded tip and amputated it along with the stinger.

The creature gave a cackling shriek as the severed part of the tail fell at Harry's feet. He kicked it aside and returned one of his blades to the rope. His foe had gotten quite vocal by this point and soon its tentacles came into play. Harry had to bob and weave to avoid them as he fended off the free claw with one sword, still sawing with the other.

It was like rubbing your belly and patting your head at the same time, something he had been quite good at as a kid. One of the smaller ropes finally popped, but that left two. The Thulu grabbed the rail with both hands and the beast's head suddenly came up to look Harry square in the face, its rotten fish breath bringing him to gag. His anger increased, triggering the butcher's dissection chart. Harry knew just what he needed to do.

With the fiend's head well within arm's reach, he drove the points of both swords straight into its mouth. They went in pretty easily and the tentacles that tried to pull them loose were severed and dropped away.

Upon pulling his weapons free, a geyser of bluish-green blood hit his shirt and worked its way up to his face. That elevated his ire to rage, and raising both swords in one quick motion, he severed the Thulu's fingers from its hands using the railing as a chopping block. It screeched at the sky as it fell backwards and hitting the others like a bowling ball hits a set of pins, they all plummeted into the ocean.

The rope he had been working on separated when the falling beast crashed into the others. That left only the heavy line. Applying the same tactic he had used to separate the Thulu from the ships railing, Harry chopped at the rope's knot with both swords, each blade cycling through at a blur.

One of the uninjured beasts started up, putting enough tension on the rope to help Harry finish the job. The heavy line frayed more and more with every strike, and when it parted, the 300-pound beast carried the whole mess down to the ocean.

He watched it splash into the water and then took notice as to why the other two hadn't followed it up. The cannibalistic fiends were snacking on Mr. Birthmark and seemed to have lost interest in returning. The third creature, acting as if it was missing out on breakfast, quickly joined the others.

Harry swiped at the red rope towing the ruined yellow dinghy and it separated with a *Twang!* He watched it fall away, and what was left of the little yellow boat gradually sank from view. The distance soon increased between the Enchanted and the pack of Thulu still gorging on their dead companion.

"So long, you stupid idiots!" Harry yelled.

Large, black, lidless eyes turned his way and transformed into three pairs of bobbing red spots as they picked up the moonlight. Taking both swords in one hand, he flipped them the bird and walked away.

Trudging to where he left the lantern, Harry stopped and removed his sword rig before taking off his shirt. After wiping his face with a clean spot, he tossed it overboard. Now he was completely without anything lighter than his M.U. sweatshirt. He could just go bare-chested, but he didn't want to have to nurse sunburn. There would have to be a stop at one of the many gift shops to see if they had one or two shirts to his liking. Right now, he just wanted to wash off the stink and go back to bed. Everything hurt, and his breath came ragged as if he had just run a race. He needed a drink of water and maybe a little something to kill the muscle ache.

Snatching up his lantern and the swords, he went to the galley and grabbed a bottle of dish soap. Returning to the amidships pool, he stripped naked and doused himself in soap before moving to stand on the second tread of the steps leading down into the water. He scrubbed away as he walked down to the bottom of the shallow end and then submerged to wash his face and hair. Swimming out of the cloud of soap and Thulu blood, he played in the water to rinse himself.

Climbing out at the starboard edge, Harry moved to a poolside chaise. Staying long enough to dry off, he sat just watching the moon. Scenes of the event rolled through his head as the adrenaline dissipated.

Evaluating his performance, he concluded that this had been the oddest of all his battle experiences. He wondered if he should check to make sure there was no other way the monsters could climb back onboard. From what the cut-away model showed, there were none. But he wouldn't be comfortable until he was one hundred percent sure.

Now that they knew he was onboard the ship, the word would probably get around in whatever way monsters communicated. He should probably retract all of the lifeboat ropes just in case. But that job could wait until after his morning workout.

Getting to his feet, Harry decided not to put on his jeans. They had received their share of Thulu juice and would never really come clean. Pushing on his boots without tying them, he then kicked his jeans overboard, sending them the way of his shirt. He stayed long enough to watch them flutter down to the ocean before walking back to the bridge in his birthday suit.

Upon arriving, he sat in his chair on the observation deck. Realizing he had forgotten the lantern, he decided to let it stay. When the sun had cleared the horizon, he scanned it with the large binoculars he kept beside the chair. Still no land. Harry no longer felt the need for sleep, but there was still the desire to eliminate some of his muscle pain. Going to his room, he used a black marker to add another X below the others on the door jamb. Then pulling on his last pair of clean jeans, he swallowed a couple aspirin, strapped on his sword rig over his bare chest and went apparel shopping.

***

When Harry wasn't working out or doing swordplay, he was disposing of dead bodies. He had set up a removal system that included yellow rubber gloves from the kitchen, a cotton napkin robber's mask soaked in coffee, some ropes, and a large plastic tarp. He got rid of every corpse in the atrium, all the open decks, the starboard to portside passageways, and anywhere else he moved daily. Every one of them went over the side, and always to the appeasement of the school of sharks that began shadowing the Enchantment since the day Harry began his task.

The children were the hardest, and he often wept in the process. The thought that the sharks would have their way with them made it even more difficult. He had to remind himself constantly that they wouldn't

253

feel a thing. Luckily for him, children and teens were the minority. The girls always made him think of Bessie. He often found himself ranting and raving as he paced next to a newly found body, his rage triggered by the thought of the unfairness of a life lost so young.

The day came when no more corpses littered the decks. Harry spent the rest of that day and night in his bunk, consoling himself. He desperately needed to recreate his own life's illusion and crawl back inside that bubble to find solace. There was no doubt he would need a couple of days to 'feel right' again and wondered how any mortician could handle a job that kept one's own mortality constantly being shoved in their face.

Late afternoon of the following day found Harry sitting on the open metal steps of an outside stairway, eating his lunch. He watched the big fluffy clouds float across the sky and savored the fresh air as he rocked along with the ship. With no more cleanup to perform, he took to sunbathing, reading books and magazines from the shops, or searching through his binoculars for land. His practice session and workout always came first and usually lasted until the sun was at its zenith.

Harry started to include weights in his routine and visited the two weight rooms every other day. He kept track of his bulk in the many mirrors that lined the walls, his concern about 'overdoing it' bordering on the neurotic. His skin had turned a golden brown and his once auburn hair was fading to blonde.

Measuring himself, he discovered he was now a good six foot, two inches tall. He could no longer set the buckles of his sword rig in the usual holes, evidence that he was gaining muscle mass. The monster slayer lacked for nothing except for companionship and conversation. If it hadn't been for that, and wisps of the stench leaking up from the staterooms, it would have seemed almost a proper vacation cruise.

By day twenty-three, Harry was growing exasperated with such limited activity, and cabin fever took him in its grip. By the time he had placed X number thirty-one on the door jamb, he found the only thing that satiated his frustration and anxiety was reading, his exhausting workout, and sketching.

Using the charcoal pencils from his bag, he created likenesses of his father, Bessie, and himself. Sleep was the best, though. He napped whenever he could. Coming across a stash of erotic magazines in the captain's office, he added another activity to his daily routine, being ever vigilant not to overdo it.

It occurred to Harry to start a journal, but he wasn't the kind to do such a thing. It was too much like memorializing things he wanted to forget. There would come moments when he found himself mourning his dead and he would sob openly while aimlessly walking the decks or curled up in his bunk with his photos spread out on the sheet before him.

There was no way he would ever forget Bessie, his mother and father, or Winnie, for that matter. In time, only the best things about them would manifest without effort, acting as pleasant memories rather than something to trigger his tears. Harry hoped by that point he would have established some kind of a new life involving other people. He just had to figure out a way to get off the Enchanted.

Being out on the ocean had given birth to a preoccupation with the weather. There had been nothing serious in the way of thunderstorms or hurricanes, so far. Harry had experienced dark days with fog, some punctuated with rain showers, but the heavy weather had kept its distance. So, with regard to the law of averages, Destiny's Enchanted was about due for the big one.

Harry wasn't to be disappointed. On day thirty-three, the big storm arrived. The sun was up for barely an hour before the clouds rolled in and the sky turned black. The ship started to bound, and the waves rose high. They washed up over the head high pool surround, splashed onto the bow deck, and filled the swimming pool with seawater. The level within began to rise and Harry feared with all that weight at the front, the ship would nose dive and not recover. Slipping into an oversized raincoat, he went down to the pool, and sloshing through water up to his knees, he opened all the drain doors to keep the patio from filling to the brim. The action alone had been perilous, and several times he found himself clinging to some railing to keep from achieving, 'man overboard' status.

Once back inside, he vowed not to go out again until the storm had passed. Seasickness soon took hold, and all he wished was for the ship to stop rolling. The rain came heavy, and he sat inside the bridge with his puke bucket between his knees, watching the lightning rip the sky.

Each clap of thunder overlapped the next. Gusts of wind drove a fusillade of fat rain drops against the glass. During brief lulls in the storm, Harry could see waterspouts hanging like serpents from the ragged clouds as they slithered across the sky at the horizon.

They seemed to be in search of something, and in a state of delirious trepidation, Harry feared it was him. Calming himself with the reason and logic that waterspouts were not thinking, breathing creatures bent on revenge, he relaxed and hugged his bucket.

His physical state was worsened by the fear of the dreaded 'rogue wave', something he had learned about from watching videos on the

Internet. He grew afraid that every time he looked out the windscreen, he would catch a mounting ridge of water rushing his way.

When it got to be too much, Harry retired to his room. Shutting the door, he curled up on the bunk with his bucket close by. Laying in the dark with eyes shut, he tried to block out the sounds that meant the Enchanted was seeing its last day afloat.

He awoke to a loud grinding noise and a serious jolt. The ship tilted portside, and he was thrown from his bed. Flailing about in the dark, he tried to get his bearings. There came a heavy, rattling vibration that sent his body rolling back toward his bunk.

Fortunately for Harry, that particular piece of furniture was secured to the wall and floor. However, the big, overstuffed chair had no such anchorage and it charged him like an angry bull. He couldn't actually see it, but he heard it coming and scrambled back up onto his mattress just in time as the red behemoth slammed into the side rail. Then all motion came to an abrupt halt.

Visions of Dorothy's house from *The Wizard of Oz* played in his head as it spun inside the twister under a dark, foreboding sky. Any minute, the ship would slam down onto the land of OZ, and Harry doubted he would survive. But there was no spinning, twisting, or rolling, only the odd tilt of the room.

*Maybe the ship was sinking? Get out, now!*

Climbing over the big chair, he scrambled to the door and flung it open.

# CHAPTER 12

## Never See Him Back Again...

Stepping out onto the bridge, Harry fully expected to be looking out of the windows as if peering through the side of an aquarium, but with water jetting from its seams. Instead, the sun was peacefully breaking through the clouds over a mountain range on the starboard side.

*Land!*

His anxiety melted away and a delirious joy took its place. Not only because he had survived, but because there was land. Dashing out, Harry stood at the railing, grinning like a madman. The Enchanted, grounded by the storm, now sat unmoving, stuck in the sand of the ocean floor about half a mile out from a short stretch of beach.

*Land! Dammit… LAND!*

It had been a long time since he had shed tears of joy, and never at such a simple thing. Wiping his eyes, he studied the shoreline. The short swath of sandy beach ended at a stone outcropping rising up at the south end, and just out from that, standing sentinel in the water, a vertical tower of boulders projecting up like a finger.

*A sea stack! I know what that is… that's a sea stack!*

Harry calculated the distance to the beach and deduced he could easily swim the first half and wade the last. The sharks had vacated the Enchanted just days after Harry had completed his task of corpse removal. So, he highly doubted they would be out there, waiting to bite the hand that fed them.

He needed to prepare to get off that floating cemetery. Returning to his room, he grabbed up his bag and ran to the largest of the three gift shops on board—the one with the most clothing. Everything had

'Destiny's Enchanted' printed on it in one way or another, but that didn't matter at the moment. Grabbing a large, transparent plastic compression bag off a rack, he ripped open its box and pulled the bag free.

Walking around he picked through stacks of clothing and stuffed the things he needed inside. Two pairs of black sweat pants, a couple of polo shirts, several boxer shorts, a 3-pack of giant-sized paisley handkerchiefs, and a woman's blue, long sleeved tee shirt with a scoop neck. It was the closest thing he could find to what he had tossed overboard. Compressing the bag, he sealed it and folded it over.

His eyes fell on a medium sized, green polyester duffle bag, sitting on a nearby shelf. Stamped across its side was, 'I Sailed With The Enchanted!' Snatching it up, he unzipped it, dropped it to the floor, and let the compression bag full of clothes fall inside.

Looking around for anything else he might need, Harry grabbed a package of five plastic cigarette lighters, a sealed bag of tiny chocolate bars, and a waterproof bubble pack of three, small multicolored LED flashlights. A small orange sunburst printed on the packaging declared: 'Batteries Included!' He could only hope they were still good.

There were cheap, slip-on style canvas boat shoes that he could use while he swam, and that would save him from having to dry his boots. His choice of colors was light blue, pink, or white. Finding his size in white, he removed his hiking boots and slipped the boat shoes on. Sealing up his boots inside another compression bag, he dropped them into the duffle to accompany his clothing.

*Socks! You forgot socks!*

The only thing available was the white, knee-high, athletic variety. 'Enchanted!' in a rainbow of colors replaced the usual stripes running around the cuff at the top. He couldn't go without socks, not if he was walking any great distance. Stuffing four pairs in with his boots, Harry resealed the compression bag before zipping the duffle shut and attaching it to his bookbag with two karabiner hooks.

Tucking his black, gift shop tee shirt into green running shorts before pulling the now weighty bag on over his sword rig, Harry tightened the straps. He caught his reflection in a dressing mirror across the room and grinned.

*Summer camp nerd!*

"Ready to go, nerd?" he said and chuckled, giving himself an exaggerated wink.

His excitement was hard to control. Harry feared the ship might float away before he could disembark. He wanted to take off in a run and jump right over the railing into the ocean. The thought that he would have to do more time on board the Enchanted was overwhelming and fed his urgency. Taking some deep breaths, he only jogged to the lifeboat stations at the starboard side. Pushing one of the bowsing blocks from where he had laid it atop the davit, he watched it drop and swing.

*Life Preserver! Don't forget the life preserver!*

Turning back, Harry grabbed the closest plastic donut and hooking an arm through the hole, he worked his way out onto the small, crane like arm, seized the cable with both hands and rolled off. Going down was easier than climbing up as the cable was greasier than the other. He slid all the way down and after his feet impacted the block, the cable went to swinging. The fourth time he swung out, he checked to see that he was well clear of the Enchanted's hull and dropped in.

"So long, you floating turd," he bellowed as he fell and then took a deep breath just before hitting the surface with a splash. Opening his eyes, he saw the ocean floor was well within sight and he figured the ship was in about twenty-five feet of water.

The preserver brought him right back up and gripping it with both hands, he pushed it out toward shore and kicked his feet like crazy. He felt a great sense of satisfaction in having chosen to use the life preserver method. The weight of the food and water bottles in his bookbag, plus the clothing and sword rig, could have been problematic without it.

Harry stopped every so often and treaded water, figuring his feet had to touch bottom sooner or later. When they did, he abandoned the life preserver and began to wade toward the beach. Upon arriving, he fell onto his knees and kissed the sand. Then sitting back, he gazed at the mountains rising in the distance. After several minutes, he was overcome with emotion and began to weep.

When the feeling passed, he wiped the tears from his eyes and the grit from his lips. Then standing, he unstrapped the bookbag to toss it and the duffle inland to keep it out of reach of the surf. There came a weird sensation that the ground was pitching and rolling under his feet, but he knew that was the effect of a month on board a ship.

On impulse, Harry took off running in the direction he assumed was south. The freedom of it felt so good, he wanted to jump and shout. He stopped when he ran out of breath and stared out toward the sea stack.

He imagined the rock formation underneath the surface resembled a hand flipping off the Enchanted. Chuckling, he turned his gaze to the ship and gave it a sloppy salute before leisurely strolling back to his bags.

*Certainly not Canada, or Iceland. Could possibly be Ireland, but…
did Ireland have mountains like that?*

Picking up the bookbag and duffle, he walked to where the grass
started and then proceeded to plod up the slope. Reaching the top, he
saw—more grass—and what he believed to be heather stretching on for
miles. Harry wanted to spend the night on the beach, but the wind
wouldn't allow it. He had to assume there were monsters there as well.
So, he began his journey inland. Making his way down into a sandy
gully, he would come up the other side only to find, more sandy gullies.

When Harry came across one that resembled a large, golf course
bunker, he opened the duffle and changed into dry boxer shorts,
sweatpants, and the blue, long-sleeved tee. Pulling the M.U. sweatshirt
on over it, he found the heavier garment helped cut the wind. Opening
the duffle, and then the compression bag with the socks inside, he pulled
on a pair, followed by dry hiking boots. The wet tee shirt, shorts, and
cheap shoes remained where he dropped them. Feeling somewhat
exhausted by the whole process, he sat in the sand and downed an entire
bottle of water.

A moment of panic hit, when Harry realized he had left the sleeping
bag onboard the Enchanted. He had untied it from the bookbag and set
it in a corner of his bunkroom. Since he had sheets and blankets there,
he hadn't felt a need for it, and the tattered green 'Forester' had been
neglected the whole time he floated the Atlantic.

*I'll be damned if I'm going to swim back out there and get it!*

When Harry felt rested, he donned the bookbag and duffle, and then
finding what looked like a really old trail leading toward the southeast,
he moved away from the coast. The landscape stretched for miles
without a man-made structure in sight. He soon came across a small
sign, face down in the grass. Turning it over with a toe, it read:
'Welcome to Sandwood Bay! Respect Nature. Please dispose of your
rubbish properly' and in tiny letters down in a corner it stated: 'Thank
You, From The John Muir Trust-Lairg, Scotland.

"Scotland?" he shouted at the sign as if he expected it to reply.

*You actually got as far as Scotland!*

Sitting down on his bags, he scanned the horizon. He was still having
trouble fathoming that he was once again on dry land and only the grass

and clouds moved. Looking across the vast, now heather filled space, brought a kind of lethargy. Harry's eyes grew heavy and he knew what he needed most at that moment. Moving off the path, he trudged up onto a small, flat-topped hill and using the duffle as a pillow, he lay down in the deep grass to nap.

Harry awoke later to the cries of skua hovering overhead. When he threw his hand up to shield his eyes, the aggressive seabirds squawked and flew away. He needed to find shelter for the night. Anything away from water.

*Was that possible in Scotland?*

Trying to remember the orientation of the country from the map in his head, he gauged the sun. It was at its apex, so he would keep it to his front, and as the day progressed, always on his right. He took off at a fast walk.

Topping a small rise, he looked back to see what looked like a large loch in the distance. Not wishing for confrontation, he wanted to put a few miles between him, the ocean, and that large body of shining water. His position left him to wonder if Scottish monsters were any different from what he knew back in Massachusetts, and, if the British Armed Services had produced its own monster ID manual.

Harry walked for what seemed like hours without any sign of civilization. The wind constantly blew, and he had to stop several times to determine a path that would keep him clear of any water source.

There was plenty of normal wildlife around, mostly seabirds passing overhead. At one point he watched a flock of what looked like ravens rise from the grass. They were dark grey instead of black, unlike the ones he knew back in America. Their calls were different, as well. They swirled overhead with their raucous cawing and then left him, flapping eastward.

Moving to the spot from which they had risen, he found the skeleton of what he believed to be a sheep, its bones picked clean. There were no signs it had met death by monster, so probably old age, or disease.

Harry continued without returning to the path and wandered into a moor. He had to backtrack and find the trail before continuing. The position of the sun, now closer to the horizon, brought the fear that he was going to have to spend the night out in the open.

He started to jog even though his knees and ankles hurt. He found himself hoping for an outbuilding over the next rise. Scanning the moor for any sign of human activity, Harry found the countryside desolate.

The path curved left, then right, sloped down between two long, low hillocks before it rose up to a large worn circular area that was bordered on the left and right by a string of knee-high boulders and several wooden benches in differencing states of decay.

*An official rest area?*

Moving to sit on the sturdiest looking of the seats, his eye caught something that didn't go with the surroundings. It was the ridge of a roof contrasting the rolling hills beyond, and with it, an almost indiscernible stone chimney.

Harry ran, and then promptly fell when he misjudged the width of a narrow trench cutting across his path. Too excited to care about a scraped knee, he got to his feet and moved at a fast, limping jog. When he got closer, he saw it was a small stone shack with a slate roof covered with decades of lichen. A shepherd's cottage. It stood alone with no other out buildings or fences. Just a lonely stone abode out in the middle of nowhere. A small body of water, probably too small to qualify as a loch, sat a short distance off to the southwest. When he got close to the cottage, he drew his swords.

"Hello! Is anyone home? Is anyone in there?"

Harry tiptoed around the corner as the door slammed shut. It startled him, and he went into a defensive stance. Edging up to it, he watched it slowly open as a gust of wind came up. When the pressure lessened, its weight brought it back to slam again.

"Just the damn wind," he muttered, trying to still his racing heart. Moving to a tiny window, he peeked in. With what light filtered in through the dirty glass, he was able to see it held some rough furnishings. Walking up to the door, he saw a tiny metal sign tacked to the right side of the frame. The letters were hardly readable, but what he could make out, said, 'Welcome To The Strathan Bothy'. What was listed underneath that, could no longer be read. Harry supposed it must have been a list of rules for its use by backpackers.

The west side of the bothy had caved in, but a wall and a door still stood between what must have been a bedroom and the living area. Piles of stones lay on both ends of the building and Harry assumed they must have been walls or fences for enclosures where sheep were kept.

Pushing the door open with a toe, a family of mice scurried, jumped, and squeaked before zipping past him for the safety of the heather. Harry let them go and stepped inside. No one had been there for some time, but why anybody would want to remain for any great length of time was beyond him. He yearned for companionship, and at this point, he felt willing to chase down anyone he came across just to hear another human voice. But for the moment, he would settle for the relief of knowing he had accommodations for the night.

Now, his only concern was how to secure the doors. The bedroom door had opened into that space and a pile of stones kept it secure. The entrance, on the other hand, had only a heavy sliding bolt screwed on just above the ancient iron, rim latch. Harry knew it wouldn't hold if forced. Gazing around the room, his eye fell on the hearth. A beach ball sized stone sat there with an old rusty frying pan resting on its flat top. Harry figured he could just roll it to the bottom of the heavy plank panel, and nothing could gain access. The windows were too small for anything bigger than a Hystrix to crawl through, and there were also interior hinged shutters that could swing down and latch at the sill.

Letting his bags fall to the floor, Harry went to straightening things up. Collecting anything that could burn, he piled it next to the fireplace. Discovering the box for firewood back in a dark corner, he found the wood inside had grown punky. Only a few pieces were suitable for burning.

*You could always burn the box, and maybe… the furniture?*

Making a fire would be taking a risk. The smoke rising from the chimney would be a definite sign of occupation. Harry decided to wait until dark. He would be gone at first light, anyway, so no sense in doing a complete refurbishing of the place.

After cleaning things up to his liking, Harry slid the stone over to prop the door open and sat down on it to gaze outside. There was no noise except for the unceasing wind and the occasional passing seagull. Eating raisin laced granola bars, a can of pears in nectar, and a few of the stale, but tasty, chocolate bars, he decided to save the canned meat for the next day.

Harry sketched until the sun dropped below the horizon. There was still a great deal of ambient light in the sky and it didn't seem to matter how long he sat there afterwards; it never seemed to grow any darker.

He suspected the monsters of Scotland might live by a separate set of rules and the 'darkness required' factor wasn't one of them.

Growing tired of the wind whipping his hair, Harry closed, bolted, and blocked the door. After lighting a fire, he lay down on the hard-packed dirt floor a safe distance away, wondering who, or what, might smell the smoke as he drifted off to sleep.

The mice returned shortly after, and slipping in under the door, they moved to huddle in a pile of moldy straw across the room. It wasn't so much the cold or wind that drove them in, but the shadowy figures loping by a short distance out in the heather.

Waking in the night to a full bladder, Harry sleepily moved the rock and opening the door, he stepped out. There came the realization that he had broken rule number one, but it was too late. With his sword rig still by the fireplace, he was helpless should any beast be lingering outside.

The wind was blowing steadily against the front of the bothy, so he moved around the corner to pee. Harry could tell it was well past the midnight hour, but the sky still held a strange afterglow at the horizon. As he shook off the last remaining drops, a banshee like cry rolled out across the blowing heather. It sounded like some kind of a wildcat.

*Did Scotland have wildcats?*

He hurriedly pulled up his sweatpants and hastened inside. Securing the heavy plank panel, he peeked through several different cracks to see if any beast might be approaching. When nothing appeared after several minutes, Harry stretched to relieve a few kinks in his spine and returned to his spot.

Wriggling and squirming for a few minutes before settling in, he found himself missing his mattress back onboard the Enchanted. There came only a fitful state of sleep, the kind where one eye remained open. In his semi state of unconsciousness, Harry waited for the banshee that never came.

The sound of the mice plundering his bag of saltines brought him awake. Jumping to his feet, Harry snatched up his bookbag. The creatures poured out, some having to jump or fall a good three feet as the bag went airborne. Two of the smarter ones jumped on him and ran down his legs to the floor avoiding what would have been a painful belly flop. They scattered in all directions, vanishing into crevices and under the dilapidated furnishings.

Harry saw that the sun was now streaming through the cracks in the shutters, and he felt like it had only been minutes since he had gotten up to pee. Looking inside his bag, he saw his furry friends had failed at their mission. Feeling badly for them, he ripped open the package and tossed several crackers onto the floor. Anxious to head out, he finished off what remained of his water bottle, and departed, leaving the mice to their empathetic reward.

The day started sunny, but as the morning progressed, large fluffy clouds appeared, and the temperature climbed. The wind never ceased blowing. Harry soon grew accustomed to being back on land, but his progress across the Scottish countryside was slow, and it would take some serious acclimation.

Pushing through waist high heather, circumventing soggy ground, and trudging up hills, only to have to scramble down the other side, wore him out. He had to stop to rest more times than he wished, and all too often, in his weary state, he failed to pick up on the warning signs of a looming, unseen drop-off. It happened often enough to bring on a gnawing reluctance to move at any speed faster than a walk. He would then waste even more time working his way around the rocky outcropping just to get to the bottom. Harry wished for aspirin and the bulge of the bottle poking through the side of the bag teased him. Better to wait until bedtime. A painless sleep would ensure a productive day and he felt it best to use the pain reducer sparingly in the case he couldn't get any more.

Arriving at a roadway, he felt the relief of being on a flat surface, and it reinvigorated him. He turned right, hoping the strip of asphalt would curve south instead of running straight back to the ocean. After a mile or so, he came upon a sign that faced the direction he was going. Walking past it, he looked back to read:

**Gaulin House–5½**

It made him wish he had turned left instead, that way he'd be assured of a place to shelter for the night. Harry didn't think he had another five and a half kilometers left in him. So, he continued, hoping for something closer.

Progress was better on the asphalt, but Harry's hope didn't pan out and soon the Atlantic came back into view at a tiny town called Rhiconich. A small sign tacked below the village limits marker showed he traveled the A83A. Fearful of going any farther under a starlit sky, he hurried into a small, roadside maintenance shack. Barring the door, he slept cramped in the enclosed cab of a road grader, the cushioned seat and a couple aspirin making the event tolerable.

Out again at sunrise, Harry ate a quick breakfast and making better time, he passed through villages that were no more than seven to ten cottages as a whole, the A83A acting as their main street.

Harry never saw a human or a monster until arriving at a small village that sat less than a mile from the shores of Loch Shin. Knocking on the secured front door of the local grocer, he waited a reasonable amount of time before breaking the glass and going in. He helped himself to a dozen tins of sardines, several tubes of oatcakes, a box of shortbread (for the fun of it) and a couple of bottles of fruit juice with their seals still intact. They didn't have aspirin, but they did have ibuprofen. Harry took all five bottles.

Moving to the back of the store he discovered a small stack of plastic water kegs in the five-gallon range. Filling his smaller, more manageable containers, he spilled just about as much as he took. Once he had all he could carry, he moved back outside.

Standing on the sidewalk and studying the town, he tried to imagine what the main street had been like on a busy day. Gazing at the cottages and shops brought a sad nostalgia. Harry suspected that, like Kilbury, there were many decaying and mummified corpses behind those doors. Pushing it out of his mind, he walked away, trying to come up with something to be grateful for.

Stopping at the corner of the building, he smelled it before he saw it. A pungent odor that, at this point in his life, never failed to initiate his fight or flight reaction. Back peddling, Harry moved into the street, flinging the bags to the opposite curb. Pulling his swords, he took a stance, keeping his eyes on that corner.

The first thing he thought was: *skinny, hedgehog, platypus.* It walked upright on webbed feet, with the usual talons, wagging a short tadpole like tail. It had a long, curving spur at the back of each ankle and wore a coat of mini spikes. Its arms were chubby like a toad's, but it had five, sharp looking, amber colored talons finalizing its digits. A short war bonnet of feathery, salamander-like gills framed its head and vibrated when it hissed.

Harry waited for it to come after him, but it seemed uninterested. "Hey! Come on ugly duckling, what are you waiting for?" he shouted. Stomping a foot, he waved his swords and screamed, "Heeey!"

His efforts proved fruitless, as the beast turned its duck billed face left, then right, studying Harry with each eye. It honked like a goose several times and he saw it had no teeth to speak of. He backed up a few steps, and yelled, "Come on, daffy, come for me!" It just stared, kind of like an old cow chewing its cud.

*Maybe I can walk away from this one?*
If he did, it would be his first. Sheathing the sword from his left hand, Harry kept the other at the ready, and moving to the bags, he picked them up and walked backward about a hundred or so feet. The creature

did nothing. But Harry did something—something he never thought he would. Sheathing the single sword, he left the area.

Looking back once, he saw the ugly beast digging in a flower bed just across the street from the grocer. Harry wondered if all of Scotland's monsters were that passive. If they were—he was out of business. He wasn't so sure he wanted that; however, he believed the odds were in his favor and, for a very long time. Harry's next encounter supported his belief.

At Loch Shin, the highway ended at A836 and he walked straight across the T-intersection into the heather. Hiking in what he figured must have been an easterly direction, he stopped to rest with his feet dangling over the edge of a singular stone outcropping bordered by a rocky slope leading down to the loch. It faced into the afternoon sun as the bright orb played hide and seek among the clouds. He drank water and munched on stale shortbread. When the need for a nap overtook him, he found a grassy spot and curled up for a short snooze.

He woke to a whole different world. The clouds had thickened and blocked the sun. A light mist swirled and rolled around him making everything a mystery. It was such an abrupt change that it awed him. Unless it started to rain, he would stay and nap some more. Harry wished for a tarp, or at least, a blanket. Before falling back into sleep, he made a mental note to scrounge for one at the next town.

The dreams came and he was back in Kilbury. A woman stood on the street in front of their house screaming for no reason. He opened the front door and yelled for her to shut up because his mother was trying to sleep. The woman stopped her noise and throwing him a wicked grin, she shouted, "Sic'm." A pack of Cayhond materialized and raced for the open front door.

Popping awake, he sensed real danger. Somewhere, a woman was, in fact, screaming, and there were children crying. The adrenalin surge that came to Harry in his nightmare still coursed through his veins. Jumping to his feet, he tried to get his bearings. The mist had thinned enough for him to see at least a couple hundred feet, but there was no one in sight. Moving cautiously back to the outcropping, he looked over.

It was about thirty feet to the bottom of that bordering slope and huddled within a niche between two large boulders, a woman stood with two small children squeezed in behind her. She had a melon sized rock raised above her head, waiting for anyone of the four, sled dog sized creatures to come within smashing range. They were long legged, wild boar-like beasts with form fitting armadillo jackets. Their wide beaver-like tails were projecting up at an angle, quivering. It was a sure sign they were ready for a fight.

Harry remembered seeing the same behavior in the fish headed monsters back at Winnie's, their wide, flat, triangular shaped tails standing up and vibrating like timber rattler's.

Taking a cue from the woman, Harry attacked the beasts from above by dropping large rocks on two, crushing them like beetles. One of them ran away to the loch and dived in, leaving the biggest of the four behind. Hopping down from rock to rock, he skated the last ten feet in the shale to confront the remaining beast. It all went rather quickly.

The waltz played, and time slowed as the beast leapt for him. Even before the waltz's intro was complete, Harry had impaled the creature in midair, driving both swords, edge up, into the gill set just above where the hard jacket terminated. The impact caused him to slide back on the loose stone, but he was able to maintain his balance and with every ounce of strength, he held the creature off the ground.

It twisted and squirmed, bringing about its own demise as the razor-sharp steel sliced through its flesh up to the jaw line. The fiend's lifeblood spilled out over Harry's arms, its fetid odor filling his nose. Forcing the beast off his swords with a front kick, he watched it tumble down the slope and slam into a car sized boulder. Bringing his eyes around to the loch, he checked to make sure the creature who had retreated, wasn't coming back. Seeing they were now monster free; he turned his attention to the people.

The woman was seriously shaking, her cheeks wet with tears. Dropping her rock, her hands trembled as she pulled the two blubbering, dark haired children to her. One was a girl, and the other, most likely, her brother. Their clothing was old fashioned and ragged. They were barefoot and dirty. Harry thought it odd, since it would be so easy to loot a store to get proper footwear or slip into a shallow stream for a bath.

All he could think to say was, "Is everyone alright?" She didn't reply at first and watched his every move as if she feared they were next in line for a stabbing.

She finally managed a, "Who are ya?" Releasing her children, she bent and picked up a large basket by its handles. The children remained behind her and gawked from the folds of her dress, their big brown eyes wide with curiosity.

"I'm Harry… ummm… Harry Lumsdale... from America."

"Aye, I can tell. I've never seen swords like those before. They're a wee sort, aren't they? But yer pretty good with 'em."

"Yeah, I've been at it for a long time," he said, and then realized he wasn't being polite. Sheathing his weapons, he reached out to offer her a handshake, but she shirked back. Harry realized his hand still dripped with monster blood. He lowered it to his side and just grinned. Her dark eyes became slits of distrust, her tangled hair swirling in the light breeze.

"So… what's your name? Are these your kids?"

She didn't answer his questions. Taking the little girl's hand, she towed the child away, calling for the boy to follow.

They moved up around the end of the outcropping and disappeared, only to reappear at the top. Now at a safer distance, they poked their heads over the edge, and appeared to be studying him. The woman then threw him some semblance of a smile and said, "Excuse me, sorry… thank ya, kind sir, for rescuing me and my bairn, I won't forget it. Good day to ya… we're off." She stared a moment longer before disappearing from sight.

It surprised him when the boy reappeared, grinning. Pointing with his finger, he said, "Harry Lumsdale, ya say? Highland Harry, ya are! Aye… ya are. They sing about ya, ya know?"

"Charlie Boyle! Ya get yer wee arse over here, ya…" he heard the woman shout. The boy dashed away, laughing, and then was heard to exclaim, "But ma, its Highland Harry. Ya know? From the song?"

"Aye, laddie, and so?" was all she said. Then they were gone.

Harry wished they had stayed, or that he could have gone with them. But there was no trust, and he was a stranger even if he had saved their lives. He knew the song the boy had been talking about. He heard it performed once at a Celtic Music Festival sung by a group of Scottish singers down in Cambridge; a very long time ago. Turning to the dead creature, he thought how easy it had been to kill and how they had acted more like dogs than monsters.

It was definitely a kind of Cayhond. The shell was an odd thing he had never seen before. It made him think of the ballistics vests the police used to wear, or maybe even more like a flak jacket. The boar-like tusks were almost useless, seeming to impede its ability to bite.

Harry figured they had to work in packs in order to bring down their prey. The one that had run away had been quite speedy. So, if they chose to chase you down, there was no getting away. Harry gloated on how quickly he dealt with the situation, but still wished the woman hadn't been so anxious to leave.

Finding his way back to the road, Harry came upon a large puddle and cleaned his swords. The woman's statement, *"They are a wee sort, aren't they?"* came back to him. Scotland was known for the Claymore. He remembered picture book images of kilt wearing, long haired men wielding great broadswords. Then there was the basket hilted style that must have come later. Neither were suitable for him.

The butterfly swords were originally meant only to maim, removing parts like fingers, hands, or feet at lightning speed. Harry could accomplish with his two swords, what one could do with a Claymore. There were different methods and ways of thinking, thanks to visionaries like Bruce Lee and his art of Jeet Kune Do. Harry had progressed up through the levels of his fighting art quickly, and with such ease, he felt that it had to be 'the way'. If one wanted to survive battle, there could be no restrictions. He could see the benefit of other weapons like short spears or axes, but his swords were his obsession. Bruce Lee's philosophy, *'Be like water!"* came to mind. He grinned to himself.

"Be like water, Harry, and then use it to wash your stinking hands!"

After rinsing off the congealing monster slime, he walked away into the mist. Continuing south, Harry stuck to the motorway. The gnawing fear that a car might hit him as it exploded from the ground bound cloud, lingered at the edge of his consciousness. Then he heard the rattle of a car engine miles away to the south, coupled with, of all things, the rise and fall of a motorcycle engine as the rider ran through the gears. Somebody still risked plowing head first into a roadway pileup unseen in the mist. From that point on, when Harry walked the road, he stuck to the shoulder.

More often than not, he found shelter in abandon cottages, keeping his distance from those that reeked of the dead. Pilfering his shelter in the morning before his departure, he only took canned food. The opener, Bessie had found in that store back in Massachusetts, became indispensable. Without it, he would be stuck eating boxed foods and most of that stuff was beyond edible now. He couldn't afford food poisoning. Checking everything twice before he stuck it in his mouth, assured a diarrhea free night.

One cottage presented him with a walking stick upon entering the tiny foyer through an unsecured front door. The creator of the fine, varnished piece of hardwood had stamped '*Blackthorn*' in tiny letters just up from the tip. Harry presumed that's also what it was made of. Taking possession, he decided to notch it every morning to keep track of the days. He wasn't so far into his journey that he couldn't remember how many times the sun had rose and fell since he arrived, but there would come a time.

Harry woke one morning to discover his boots were too worn to repair and he would soon be walking barefoot like that woman and her kids. He was down to two pairs of socks, the sweatpants he wore, and one polo shirt. The duffle hadn't worn well and when the seams gave up, Harry abandoned it along with the plastic compression bags in a cottage kitchen already littered with trash. Loading everything into the bookbag, he pushed the limits of its capacity. The need to bathe was overwhelming and he found himself looking for any water source that would offer him a chance. Everything he wore was filthy and sniffing at himself, he wondered how he could smell so bad and not notice. He thought again of the woman and her kids and smiled to himself, now, with an empathetic understanding.

*Time to find a town and resupply... maybe jump in some shallow stream on the way!*

He scanned the horizon more often now, looking for tell-tale signs of any metropolis. When he wanted to rest, he left the road to find a comfortable patch of grass to curl up in. On one particular afternoon, after traveling a short distance through the heather, Harry stopped to peer over a high bluff unseen from the highway. Deciding to take a risk, he climbed down the craggy outcropping to straddle a finger-like protrusion and then sat gazing out across a massive glen.

Searching the horizon for city skylines, he picked up movement at the base of a distant slope. At first Harry thought just cattle or horses. Looking harder, he could just make out some people too. It looked like a small tribe herding livestock. He wondered if that woman and her children had been part of such a group.

*Maybe good you didn't follow her, Harry!*

The last thing he wanted was to get into a territorial dispute with some patriarchal tribe leader. Much safer to study them from afar with the option of presenting himself later; if he wished.

Finding and following the A9 south, it was late afternoon when Harry arrived at a bridge crossing a wide river that led into the sea.

Standing with no food and little water, he read the sign at the entrance to the concrete span that declared he had arrived at the Moray Firth.

On the other side sat that city he was looking for and an anxiousness overwhelmed him. He felt a reluctance to cross that river. There was a different kind of danger over there—the human kind. But Harry's need for food and water outweighed his aversion. Maybe he could find a safe place to bathe.

His thoughts traveled back in time to when the Morel Street Marauders had confronted a crazy man at a drugstore in Kilbury. An old guy so delirious with fear that he tried to warn them off with the jagged edge of a broken wine bottle. Harry was glad the old guy had run away, saving them from having to put him out of his misery. Their goal was monsters—not humans. But some people were not in their right mind enough to avoid confrontation, and that's what he feared—crazy people. That included aggressive tribes and warlords.

*Would there be warlords, now? Or... again?*

Harry thought of the tribe he saw miles back in that glen and imagined being held captive and forced to do slave labor after revealing his presence. There was a chance they may understand the value of a warrior type though. He believed he could prove to be beneficial to any clan that took him in. Books told him that Scottish folk had a tradition of taking in 'Broken Men'. So, that's how he would approach it; should he ever find himself in that situation. He could become part of something again. Harry smiled to himself and pushing past his fear, he set off across the bridge.

# CHAPTER 13

## Now Looking Over Firth...

At the halfway point, Harry stopped to gaze eastward as the seabirds swooped, dived, and floated overhead. He was no longer looking at the Atlantic Ocean, but now, the North Sea. If he remembered correctly, he was leaving the Western Highlands and moving into the Grampians. He could now smell the city from where he stood. It was an unpleasant mix of odors that assailed his nostrils and they all seemed to be riding the magic carpet of odoriferous decay. It suddenly came to him that some of it was coming from a nearby car that had crashed into the concrete railing.

Moving closer, he could see the skeletal remains of the driver. As he took it in, he thought again of his time onboard the Enchanted and the overwhelming body count in that space. Now, he was walking right back into it.

Harry wished for other options. Yet until he learned to prepare food, butcher meat, or raise crops, he would have to find his food on shelves and in cupboards. Then there was the need for clean drinking water. He needed to learn the process for making H2O potable. For him, ignorance (and a little fear) was motivation enough to drive him to want to learn. Then he could avoid urban areas with their particular displeasures.

Slowing his pace after clearing the bridge, Harry noticed the city wasn't like Boston or Springfield. There were no buildings over five stories high. Only church spires rising above all else. It was an old place—and a spooky one.

Coming to a roundabout, Harry took a right. It felt like he had walked more than an hour before he arrived at a place where the buildings were older, taller, and made of stone. Like Kilbury, most of the shop windows were broken out and the cars had piled up with more human skeletons manning driver's seats. Death and flies went together, and they were everywhere. He came across the occasional corpse lying on the sidewalk accompanied by white, squirming masses of maggots, filling, and spilling from every orifice.

Legs, arms, and torsos protruded from smashed windows and doorways. What looked like it had been a man, dangled by a foot from an electrical wire just below a broken fifth floor window. A single ray of sunlight illuminated the body, as if to highlight the failed suicide attempt. Even at that distance, Harry could see the cloud of flies attending their buffet.

*One window more to the right and you could have missed that wire, mister! How long did you hang there before the Bug had its way with you?*

Another city block brought him a little boy draped half out a large, broken, display window. His clothes were ragged, and he appeared severely malnourished. Harry imagined the kid had passed out and fell against the glass from the inside, causing it to shatter. The large, keenly sharp pieces had opened him up and he bled out, bringing an end to his misery.

Harry felt the emotion rise up and start to overpower him. Using his walking stick, he levered the body up to fall inside and out of his sight. Turning away, he hurried down the sidewalk trying to push that picture out of his head.

A feeling of self-consciousness overcame him, and he wondered how many of those upper floor windows concealed the curious eyes of those who still drew breath. Harry never experienced this level of anxiety when hiking the countryside. He needed to get back. Making a mental list of what he needed, he tried desperately to focus on his task.

*Get in and get out, Harry Lumsdale. This is no place to hang around.*

Stepping around the corner of a building, he scanned the next block. Movement caught his eye and he was positive someone had run by a narrow opening a block away. Just a second-long silhouette and—gone. Harry's hands automatically moved to pull his swords. They were halfway out before he stopped to reconsider. He felt afraid, but not monster afraid. More like fearful of what he might have to do. Sparring in tournament was one thing—fighting a human being to the death was another.

*You're hyping yourself up, Harry. Calm your ass down!*

Seating the swords in their scabbards, he slowed his pace; all five senses on high alert. Whoever that was, they had been a safe distance away. So, no need to react—or overreact. A long, brown curtain blew out through a broken window, giving him a start. He decided being jumpy was a good thing. It gave him the edge. With reflexes honed, he could respond in seconds.

On the other hand, he could always get off the street for a while and maybe rest in some store behind locked doors. That would give whoever was hanging around up the street time to move on.

Harry found himself standing next to a clothing store with all display windows still intact. There was no sign of forced entry and the interior looked like they had just closed for a Sunday. The large sign, stretching all the way across the front, just above the awning, read, 'Dunbar & Son's'. Below that had been printed, 'Scottish Gifts for your loved ones! Come in and browse!'

*Don't mind if I do, Mr. Dunbar*

Checking the door, he found it locked. Kicking it hard, the bolt broke through the wooden trim on the inside, making a hellish racket. Harry stopped, scanned the street, and waited. There came only the occasional gust of wind, shaking and rattling unknown things. A few minutes passed, and when nobody showed up to accost him, he stepped inside. There was a small barrel bolt higher up on the door for added security and it had not been locked. Harry took advantage of it and slid it into its stay, giving him added piece of mind that no one was going to follow him in.

The air was stale, and the smell of dead human was slight. Standing at the windows, looking out, he waited, listening. There had been the tiny bell that tinkled when he pushed the door open, and then, when it shut. Now, there was only silence without the wind. The shop was small, dark, and overloaded with clothing. Shoulder high racks covered the floor, and the shelves on the wall ran from floor to ceiling. There was also a second level in the style of a loft at the back. A short set of open stairs took you up where piles of tartan items lay piled on tables. A small sign hanging from the ceiling said, 'Kilts! Get Measured Today! (Two week waiting period for most items)'

*Not anymore! Besides, I prefer pants.*

Moving slowly through the store, Harry was glad for the large windows that allowed in just enough sun for him to see without a flashlight, which reminded him, he needed to open the package of the three he had taken from the ship and check the batteries.

Moving to one of many shelves marked 'Men's', he found a pile of souvenir boxer shorts of assorted clan tartans. Others had the Scottish flag imprinted on them, and a few had a pretend Sporran embossed over the crotch. He grabbed four of the reddish 'Lumsden' tartan and continued browsing.

There was a rack of off-white cotton shirts with laces to draw the neck closed at the collar. The sign perched on the top read, 'Kilt Shirts—For The True Jacobite Look!'

They appeared comfortable enough, and finding two in his size, he took them as well. Then after grabbing a wide, tan colored, leather kilt belt stamped a size bigger than what he usually wore, he helped himself to three pairs of green, knee high, wool socks before moving to a large round table signed: 'Discounted Items'.

Rummaging, he uncovered what looked like a pair of plaid pants. They appealed to him for some reason. Picking them up, he saw the tag read: Black Watch Tartan 'The Innovative Truis For Extreme Comfort—Comfy Clothing for the 21$^{st}$ Century!'/Unisex. They too, were a size bigger than what he normally wore. Slipping off the bookbag and the sword rig, he shed every stitch of clothing—starting with his worse for wear hiking boots. Standing naked on the display floor, he examined himself in a mirror. He was now quite tanned and a little wind burned on top of that.

*How much of that darker complexion is grime, Harry T. Lumsdale? Damn, man! Take a bath!*

Chuckling to himself, he held up the pants by the waistband and looked them over. They were a lot like skinny-jeans, something that had been popular back in the early part of the millennium. They had pockets just like most pants and were stretchy like his old pair of kickboxer jeans. He pulled them on and checked the mirror.

They were form-fitting and there was no way he could wear any kind of underwear.

*Going commando!*

They showed every dimple in his butt and enhanced the bulge at his crotch. Harry hoped the shirts were long enough to hide all that. Before he turned away, he examined the wound on his back. It was now just a long pinkish scar with broken pieces of dental floss-sutures sticking out. They needed to be removed and now was the time.

Pinching the end of each one, he yanked them free. No blood came trickling out, so it was safe to wear his new shirt. Picking one of the two, he pulled it on and checked the fit.

*The perfect Jacobite! Well, maybe not…*

After strapping the kilt belt on over the shirt, he donned his sword rig. Then glancing one more time at his backside, he decided to just let himself grow accustom to having his small, muscular behind on display.

Leaving his old clothes where they lay, Harry pushed his feet into his hiking boots without the socks. His food and water were all gone, so there was now room in the bookbag for his new shirt, socks, and boxers. Pushing his M.U. sweatshirt all the way to the bottom, he put everything else in on top of it. That left plenty of room for food and water. Now, all he had to do was find some.

Shopping his way over to the stairs, he slowly ascended the creaky treads, stopping briefly when his eyes broke the top. Studying the area, he decided it was safe and finished his climb.

The dead body smell had grown stronger. He had a clear view through the racks of kilts and dresses to an office in the back and suspected the body was in there. It was well lit, and Harry assumed there must be a skylight. Walking that way, he passed a rack of women's traditional highland dresses and promptly tripped over something. Catching himself, he looked down in the dim light to see a ghillie shoe— still on a foot.

Pushing the clothing aside, he presumed he had just made the acquaintance of Mr. Dunbar. He had been elderly, and was now, just a little mummy in plaid. His hands clutched the breast of his once white shirt and tie. His grey blazer was askew, and his kilt was hiked above his waist. He wore no underwear, but a purse like sporran made of white fur hid his private parts. His skin was a dry and powdery grey. His mouth was frozen in a grimace, and his open, colorless eyes seemed flat and dry.

*Heart attack—maybe?*

Per Harold Sr.'s logic, the ancient guy was one of the lucky ones. Harry's father believed that by the year 2035, a heart attack would be considered natural causes.

*But how does one become mummified?*

It was beyond him, and Harry didn't care enough to give it too much thought. Pulling the hangers with their dresses back across the thick, chrome plated rod, he gave Mr. Dunbar his privacy and moved into the office.

It was more spacious than Harry expected. A large table sat inside, just to the right of the doorway. A great square of tartan fabric had been spread out on top. Pinned to it, a postcard sized, yellow order form read:

Tartan: _Davidson_ Filleadh mhòr (Big Kilt-Belted Plaid)-_Yes_ Filleadh Baehg (Small Kilt)-_No_ Fabric: _Premium Heavy Wool_ Length When complete: _4 & 1 half meters_

For some reason, Harry wanted that square of fabric. Maybe it would make a good blanket for bedtime, or something to wrap up in while sitting in front of a fire on the chilly nights he knew were coming. There were plenty of coats and sleeping bags around the city just waiting to be looted, but he didn't want to have to carry anything except for the minimal. A good woolen wrap would work quite nicely and he could always double it and still cover his entire body for added warmth. Folding the swath several times until it was about two feet wide and about twelve feet long, he rolled it up to where it was perfect for strapping to the bottom of his bag.

Coming out of the office door, his eyes fell on a table covered with every kind of sporran imaginable. He wasn't sure how he would feel about having a purse-like object banging against his crotch for hours on end. He decided it would be good for quick access to all of those little things that he needed throughout the day. It would save him from having to dig inside his bag. It would also hide the bulge now enhanced by his choice of trousers.

*A lovely, dark brown one, with three little tassels at the front, will do nicely.*

Picking one that wasn't too fancy, he took off his new kilt belt and buckled the sporran around his waist, keeping its strap just short enough so the pouch wouldn't fling about in battle. Then strapping the wider belt on over the narrow sporran strap, he was able to lock the pouch in place just below his large silver belt buckle.

*There! Can't get no more Scottish than that!*

Not seeing anything else he wanted, he quietly left the shop, whispering, "Good day, Mr. Dunbar, nice doing business with you."

Instead of continuing up the block, he crossed over the street and backtracked two shops to one whose sign told him there were shoes inside. Not a pane of glass remained, including the door. Someone had pushed over the ceiling high shelving units and a sea of shoes covered the floor.

Glass crunched under foot as Harry stepped in over the windowsill, and stopping just inside, he studied the area at the back of the room where the checkout counter sat. It was dark back there. The entry door was on the right side of the shop at the front, so he moved left, all the way to the wall, scrutinizing shadows as he went.

There came a scrambling, scurrying kind of noise from the rear of the shop, and the adrenalin poured in. Something rocketed from the dark and the swords hissed to the ready as Harry prepared to take on the approaching beast. But the large, scrawny alley cat didn't give him a second look before veering left and leaping out a broken window to disappear down the street.

"Shit! Thanks a lot, cat. You almost got yourself skinned!"

Sheathing the swords, he took a couple of deep breaths and hoped there would be no more surprises.

He avoided looking outside to get his eyes to adjust to the dark and when they finally came around, he moved toward the back. A pink, stocking covered foot could just be discerned sticking out past the end of the sales counter. A single, black sneaker sat nearby; its laces still tied. Harry stepped into the massive pile of footwear and plowed his way in that direction. There was a set of windows high on the wall to his left, just adjacent to where he saw the foot. Pulling the curtain back, the light flooded in, and the bile rose in his throat.

She had been, perhaps, sixteen. Her round face with its unseeing brown eyes, rather than showing fear, just looked sad, almost like she had grown tired of constantly being on the losing end of everything. The large pool of congealed blood that she lay in bore no tracks and hadn't been smeared. Harry found that odd and wondered if she had been unconscious when whatever had brought the blood happened. *Maybe she had been strangled first?* He decided against checking to see if that had been the case.

The girl's long blonde hair fanned her head as if she had met the floor with great speed. A heavy, blue sweater lay piled on her chest like someone had dropped it there. Pinching the knitted fabric between two fingers, Harry pulled it away. Her red and black, checkered, flannel shirt lay open, and the handle of a large butcher knife protruded from between her exposed breasts.

Her jeans and panties had been pulled down to her knees. A tattoo of a tiny, red rose showed above her shaven pubic bone, and a few inches above that, a large bloody handprint minus the middle finger. Harry gagged and turned away. He could only imagine what had gone down here. She couldn't have been dead for more than a few days.

Bessie's face appeared in his mind's eye and he quickly pushed it away to be replaced with, of all things, that vast, serene, heather filled space that he had crossed to get to this sick place. Before this moment, his soothing picture had always been an immense field of yellow flowers waving in a warm, spring breeze. Harry figured he must be liking Scotland enough now that his subconscious mind had, without his consent, replaced the yellow flowers with purple heather.

He ploughed back through the shoes and stopped at the front of the shop to stare out into the empty street. Taking some deep breaths, he watched the trash swirl in the breeze and wondered if he should go back and cover her up.

Harry didn't want to look at her again, but it would be proper, to at least, cover her with something. If he did, maybe she would haunt him less in his quiet hours before he was granted the mercy of sleep.

Returning to the back, he found he couldn't look at her for more than a few seconds. His eyes welled with tears and he tried to blink them away. Pulling up her jeans would mean having to touch her. He didn't want to know what she felt like. He angrily ripped down the big curtain from the window and lay it over her. Then, with some urgency, he shambled back to the front, irritably wiping the water from his eyes.

He stood at the window taking in slow, deep breaths, trying to calm himself. The urge to just leave the shop was strong, but he still needed shoes. It wasn't like she was going to force him to stare at her. She was covered now. So, he was safe. Turning back, he studied the massive pile of merchandise.

A few minutes passed as he tried to determine the best course of action to deal with the sea of shoes. When no method presented itself, Harry became frustrated and began moving through them, sweeping them with a foot, sometimes kicking them, all the while hoping to catch sight of a pair that suited his needs. Peering under fallen shelves, he'd think he saw something that would work, only to be disappointed when he pulled them out. They were mostly fancy shoes, nothing suitable for walking any great distance. There were some work boots with the heavily lugged, white rubber soles and heels, but not one of them was big enough to fit him. By the time he had reached the opposite wall, he was exasperated.

He stood looking around, trying to talk himself into making another pass when his eye caught the small shelving unit in the corner back by the cash register. It was the only rack still standing. Making his way to it, he saw why; it had been affixed to the wall and would require a pry bar to break it loose. The sign attached to its top declared, 'Minnheetahkwa Shoe Co.-The World's Finest Moccasins!'

*Moccasins! How American can you get?*

To Harry's great relief, the shoeboxes were still in order. A divider split the shelves into two sections: men and boys on the left—women and girls on the right.

Finding a knee-high pair of mocs for men, he tried them on. No good, too small. Looking further, he found another box one size bigger. Taking them out, he looked them over. They were similar to the other pair, but with fringe. Harry didn't want fringe. He figured he could cut that off, and trying them on, he found they fit perfectly.

*But... fringe?*

He laced them up and then taking out his Buck knife, he cut off the finger long pieces of leather that ringed the top. When they were all gone, he dropped the knife in his sporran and then checked the boots out in a little mirror attached to the side of a short, carpet covered bench meant for trying on shoes.

The moccasins went well with the skinny jeans and were extremely comfortable. They had a double bottom and a thin, flat rubber sole sewn over that. It could prove to be a benefit when walking on rocks. Harry smiled.

The upside was: they would last a while. The downside: they wouldn't fit very well with socks. But Harry didn't need those right now and supposed by the time winter rolled around, the leather would be broken in and then be loose enough to accept thin, knee-high stockings. So, something to worry about when the time came.

He had his new shoes now, so—time to get the hell out of Dodge. Pushing his tattered hiking boots under the 'TRY THEM ON!' bench,

Harry chuckled to himself and muttered, "Moccasins in Scotland, got to love it."

He left the shop and stood outside gazing in one direction and then the other. The dead girl's face manifested in his mind's eye where she was very much alive. Whipping her hair back, she stared without blinking and whispered, "Nice moccasins, aye, lad?"

*Focus on something else, Harry!*

Shaking his head as if to clear the image, he walked to the next shop and stopped to admire his new look in an unbroken pane of glass. The girl materialized behind him in the reflection, her hips cocked, hands at her waist, head tilted to one side. She grinned and said, "You're going to love 'em, laddy." Harry closed his eyes and took some slow, deep breaths.

*You didn't know her! She could have been rude, mean, and obnoxious!*

Opening his eyes, Harry saw she had gone. He had to focus on his next task—on the, now.

*Just find your food and hit the road! The sun's going to set sometime today, and you don't want to be here when it does!*

Struggling to avoid the compulsion to start internalizing, he looked around for a grocery store. A block and a half down on his right, hung on a large bracket above a doorway, he saw a sign that read, 'Highland Market-since 1902'. Heading that way, he concentrated on concentrating. Stopping just short of the obliterated door to the grocer's, he peaked around the jamb.

"Hello?" he called, not wanting to surprise anyone. Like a watering hole to animals, it would be the most likely place he would run into other humans.

*Where there was food, there was...*

"Hello? Is anyone in there?" he called.

With hands resting on the pommels of his swords, Harry tiptoed just inside. He got no response to his presence but did get something else—the stench was incredible. It only took a second for him to realize it had been a real market, not just a name. There were big square tables placed in front of the long bank of windows. They had been full of produce, and what had not been taken, remained, rotting, infiltrated by insects.

The sweet, rotten fruit smell from fermentation, mixed with lesser smells. You couldn't tell oranges from apples, or eggplant from zucchini, and when he moved close, a cloud of gnats and flies rose up, forcing him back. As his eyes became accustomed to the dim light, he could make out scattered patches of little, white worms going about their task at a leisurely pace.

Sidling around the end of a table, he moved down the first isle on his right. It ran all the way to the back of the store and disappeared into the gloom. This was not the kind of job one could do without some sort of illumination. Harry pulled out the bubble pack holding the three tiny flashlights and tried them out, one at a time. The red one didn't work, so he tossed it. The pink and green both projected strong bluish light from a multitude of tiny bulbs. Dropping the pink one in his sporran, he used the green one to move closer to the back of the store.

The smell of rotten meat soon replaced that of the fruit. The buzzing grew louder as he approached the butchers counter and large bloated flies soon began landing on him, keeping their visit brief to avoid being swatted and crushed.

Harry figured, he too, was going to keep his visit brief. The place really got on his nerves. He feared that at any moment, his light beam would move across another human corpse, or worse yet, a monster snacking away on a honey glazed ham. Filling his bag from the surrounding shelves, he completed his task in less than twenty minutes before dashing back outside.

Kneeling down on the sidewalk, facing the building, Harry gulped fresh air while organizing his plunder.

*You forgot water, idiot!*

Harry hadn't caught sight of any in his search, but he hadn't really been looking.

His eyes moved up to the swarm of flies that covered the inside of the large, single pane of glass that hadn't been bashed in. He dreaded going back in there. Getting to his feet, his eyes went from the multitudes of insects layering the inside of the glass, to his own reflection, and instead of the shoe shop girl standing behind him; it was a man watching from across the street. He spun around, but the new arrival remained as still as a statue.

The man was maybe in his thirties; his hair, dark, as were his eyes. His brown, long sleeved, button-front shirt hung in tatters, and his grimy blue jeans were torn at the knees. He had on bright orange running shoes and Harry wondered if he had visited the shoe shop as well.

The man's face said possibly affable—but his body said, 'Let's dance!' The stranger centered his gravity and hunched forward as if to prepare for a fight. Then he confirmed it when he pulled his right hand from behind his back and Harry saw a large butcher knife, much like the one stuck in the chest of the shop girl. The man switched his grip and went from a chopping hold, to an underhanded stabbing one.

"Hey! How's it going?" was all Harry could think to say.

"My store, laddy," he said flatly.

"Oh, sorry. It's just… I needed a few things."

"My city, too. Get out."

"I can do that," Harry said, and throwing a strap of the bookbag over a shoulder, he walked away.

The man now started a slow walk across the street, bending his knees slightly as he came. Harry could see the guy was serious and if he wanted to avoid a fight, running like hell was in his immediate future.

"I'm going to stick this knife in ya a dozen times before ya can blink. So, get ready to meet yer maker."

"Hey! I said, no problem. I'm going."

"Leave the bag, laddy."

"Uh… like I said, I need the food. There's plenty more inside. Should be enough to last you a couple months."

The guy was closer now, gritting his rotten brown teeth, his body odor reaching Harry's nose. He was short, but a lot stockier. If this man got his hands on him, things could go badly.

"Drop the bag."

"Come on now, least let me have a little food, you've got a whole freaking store full!"

It had been a long time since he had fought another human being, but that had been in tournament with fake swords. This guy was going to try to carve him to ribbons with a kitchen knife made famous on TV by cutting aluminum cans. Harry didn't feel afraid, though. The guy surely didn't have the fighting skills, yet, he was serious—and crazy. Which meant, Harry would have to kill him. That was something he wasn't ready to do. So, came the running part of the equation.

"Come back here, ya!"

Looking over his shoulder, Harry saw the guy giving chase, and the space between them closed rapidly. It must have been the heavy bag, otherwise he knew he could have out distanced this guy, easily.

Harry stuck to the sidewalk to avoid the parked cars and the wrecks. After two blocks, he turned up a familiar road that he knew led back to the A9. The man wouldn't quit.

Harry thought to climb up on something, but there was no time. He felt the anger come and moving to a clear spot in the center of the street, he stopped, dropped the bag and moved into position to meet his foe.

Anyone watching would have equated his actions to those of some cinematic action hero, but for Harry, it all came naturally, bolstering his confidence. He went into a modified front stance, the adrenalin flowed in and he felt like he was vibrating, a sign he was ready to accept the coming battle.

His rival was less than half a block away and wasn't stopping. The guy had changed his grip back to chopping mode and carried the knife raised above his head.

He reached Harry without slowing and as the knife came down, Harry simply side stepped and straight kicked him in the thigh. It caused the odoriferous predator to stumble awkwardly and windmill sideways. Catching himself, the man turned and came back with underhanded jabs.

Time became like molasses, and the music was right on cue. He thought it strange how his dissection chart included human beings as it materialized in his mind's eye. There were more dissection points than any monster he had ever confronted. Humans were too easy.

"So, yer a blade man too, huh, laddy? This should be fun. I'm guessing now I won't feel so bad when I cut yer throat, aye?"

"Big difference between being a fighter and being a sushi master. Are you sure you wouldn't want to just go fix us some lunch?"

The words just kind of slipped from Harry's mouth, and through the tension, he felt a few seconds of insane glee. Like his mother, he was fond of people and would go out of his way to get along. But this guy was obviously a walking pile of crap.

"So… ya think yer the great warrior, do ya? We'll see soon enough."

With that, the butcher knife killer made a few false thrusts, trying to lure Harry in. When that didn't work, he started to circle. Harry turned with him, waiting for the guy to make his first serious move. The man started to flutter his left hand up and down as a distraction. It was an act that finalized Harry's decision to kill him. The distracting hand was minus its middle finger.

The shop girl had died at the hands of this predator. Murdered and raped in a stinking shoe store on the city's main street. It wasn't so much fear or anger that Harry felt, it was more like a feeling of deadly detachment.

Looking into the crazy eyes of his enemy, Harry watched the murderer stomp a foot in his direction several times to make him think that he was advancing. Then, issuing his version of a war cry, the psychopath rushed forward, the blade coming straight for Harry's gut.

*Stupid amateur*

Harry moved forward and then stepped left. Turning out, he parried the butcher knife, his right blade coming down on the man's wrist, the left blade coming up to meet it. The hand tumbled to the pavement, still clutching the knife, severed at the wrist. The blood spurted, and his antagonist screamed, clutching the wound. Harry continued spinning left and came in behind the man, his sword tips stopping an inch from his adversary's kidneys.

He could have ended it there, instead, he back peddled a couple yards and braced himself just in case the man wanted more. The blood pulsed out in streams as his foe bent forward still holding his arm. Then he did the unexpected.

Releasing his injured arm, he spun around and flew at Harry. Grabbing a sleeve of Harry's new shirt with his remaining hand, the man's other arm sent a stream of blood over it. The fabric tore loose at the shoulder and the killer fell onto his back, taking the bloody sleeve with him.

Harry backed away to remain clear of the crimson pool on the street and said, "Stay down and you might live. Come back for more, and I'll surely kill you for what you did to that girl in the shoe shop."

His opponent didn't speak, he just growled and cursed. Rolling to his feet, he let his injured arm just hang, blood dripping. Walking over, he peeled the knife from his dissected hand and then came at Harry in a lurching walk. The murderer pushed the knife's point out toward Harry and mumbled, "Bitch had it coming… just like you."

Harry could have just stayed a step away and waited for the guy to bleed out, but he wasn't feeling very sympathetic. When the tip of the butcher's knife was about a foot away, Harry caught it in his swords quillon and simultaneously thrust his other in between the man's ribs, severing his aorta.

The killer's eyes went wide in disbelief, and he fell back onto the roadway, his knife clattering to the asphalt as he pressed his remaining hand to his new wound. He coughed, spraying blood, and then his eyes bulged as he tried to draw a breath. His head rose from the pavement, only to slam back down, an audible gurgle escaping his bloody lips.

"Now you know how it feels," Harry muttered, and after wiping his swords on the man's pant leg, he picked up his bookbag and walked away.

He looked back only once to see the butcher knife killer still lying in the street, a cloud of dust and trash swirling around his body.

Harry wasn't feeling too good about what he had just done. Still, he felt it was one of those things that was going to happen eventually— whether he approved of it or not. The adrenaline waned and the tears welled. He fought to keep them from spilling out.

*Are you going to cry for some homicidal maniac?*

It took him a few minutes to realize it wasn't that. It was because he had killed another human being. His martial arts training had brought him skills, and along with those, a type of discipline. Master Bik taught: *"Avoid rather than check, check rather than hurt, hurt rather than maim, maim rather than kill. For all life is of value... and no one has the right to take it away"*

*Did you do that, Harry?*

Up until the very second before he took that guy's life—he had. He slew monsters with the intent of saving the lives of other human beings; or his own. Now, he had killed a human being for the same reason. That man had intended on slicing him to ribbons, and without a doubt, had raped and murdered the girl in the shoe shop.

Harry could safely assume this man had killed others. That made him a monster. Harry was a monster slayer. He felt justified—schooling or not. Besides that, there was no one there to judge him but himself. Deep down he felt he had avenged the girl, and any others that had come before her. No one else was going to die by that man's hands.

Heading out toward the motorway, the feeling of exhaustion was ever growing. Unpleasant images from the confrontation cycled through his head and he forced them to the back of his mind, pushing his focus toward finding water.

Harry kept his eyes peeled for the most likely source while singing a favorite song under his breath. The lyrics didn't come easily, and he had to start over each time he remembered new ones, but that kept his mind where he wanted it—off the city.

The sun was at its zenith when Harry reached the roundabout. Instead of returning to the bridge, he continued southward. He went a mile or so before coming across an old gas station style convenience store. The sign out front read: 'ALBA'S BEST'.

*Well, Alba best have water or I'm screwed!*

Plywood covered the windows, but that peeled off easily enough, and there was water, a lot more than Harry could ever carry.

There were at least thirteen full cases of sixteen-ounce bottles sitting with the juice and soda, all wrapped in shipping plastic. The top tray was already open. Eight of the twenty-four bottles remained in the cardboard container. It was almost as if they had been the last thing the clerk took before abandoning the building. Harry had room for seven, so he chugged the eighth until it was gone. Dehydration was beginning to take its toll, and he suspected he would be downing another very soon.

Knocking the empty tray to the floor, he ripped open the plastic wrap of the next and pulled another bottle from it. Exiting the back room, he scanned the shelves on the main floor. There was little food, mostly snacks, but he wasn't going to touch that stuff. Taking his bottle of water, he moved to a bench just outside the door.

Making himself comfortable, it wasn't long before scenes from his fight returned to fill his mind. Harry shouted to the sky, "Get out of there!" and shook his head as if to clear them. But they wouldn't leave. Leaning back against the wall and closing his eyes, he consciously tried to fill his mind with positive things, but as soon as he stopped, they came rushing back in. He couldn't figure out why it troubled him so. Something deep down was gnawing at him, and then there was the overwhelming foreboding. He realized the tears that he almost shed back on the path to this place were still on the mark and ready to go.

He used to turn his mind to Bessie when he felt bad, but he feared if he brought back those memories, there would be a small flood right where he sat. But maybe being 'the tough guy' was more harmful than good. A Harold Sr. thing.

*Don't need to be the hard ass all the time, Harry. You're not your father*

So, he let the memories come and the tears soon followed. The moment lasted, maybe, all of ten minutes. Finalizing it with a stuttering sigh, he rubbed his eyes dry, and taking a deep breath, he marveled at how much better he felt.

*Bessie to the rescue, once again*

Turning his focus to his shirt, Harry decided he couldn't walk around with only one sleeve. Grabbing the cuff of the remaining, he gave it a hard yank, tearing it loose at the shoulder.

*So much for quality*

Sliding it off, his new shirt was now a sleeveless jerkin. His forearm was still spattered with blood, another reminder of how his afternoon had gone. Rinsing it with the last of the water in the bottle, he wiped it and his swords clean before dropping the red stained rag onto the bench top.

A sputtering noise rose and fell in the distance, getting louder with time. It was coming his way.

*That motorcycle, again!*

It was the same one he had heard off in the distance, back before he walked the A9. The two-wheeler topped a hill to the north and soon rolled into the drive. The rider was a boy, maybe all of thirteen. The kid's hair was dirty blond and ragged, as if someone had trimmed it with a knife instead of scissors. He wore goggles, and his bike was an old Triumph Scrambler, blue and white in color. It was a model that Harry knew well. The Lumsdale's auto mechanic, Seth Setchfield, had owned a green and black one and had given Harry rides when he was a kid.

The boy coasted slowly onto the stations concrete apron, looking at the ground as he rolled. Harry presumed he was searching for the fill caps to the underground tanks. The coil of garden hose slung over his shoulder, and the hand cranked pump lashed to the bike's luggage rack, confirmed it.

Harry stood, and the movement caught the boy's eye. The bike swerved, nearly crashing into one of the pumps. Finding his balance, the rider gunned the throttle and sped back to the motorway.

A feeling of delight welled up inside him, but he wasn't sure why. Simply a kid out thieving gasoline. His need for nonthreatening contact was greater than he first realized. He just wanted someone to talk to.

Walking over to the side of the motorway, Harry watched the cycle shrink to just a glint in the distance and wished the little guy hadn't spooked so easily. The kid probably had knowledge of the area and could have shared it.

The position of the sun reminded him that it was time to get moving. He had to find a place to hole up for the night and hoped for an abandoned house with a bed.

*Crap! My stick!*

The Blackthorn was still back at the market. He knew he could always find another, but he really liked that particular one. Going back inside to grab another water bottle, he found no walking sticks—but they did have small pads of paper and black markers he could use to keep track of the days. After slipping one of each into his bag, he turned away in clumsy fashion and promptly bumped a circular floor rack of the wire variety. Grabbing it before it fell, he set it back in its upright position.

*Damn! Road maps!*

Taking one titled: *Scotland's Motorways, 2032,* he briefly looked it over before pushing it into a side pocket on his bag. Then hurrying into the back room before something else distracted him, he snatched two more bottles, dropping one through his open collar to fall to where his jerkin was secured by the belt. With that one trapped inside his shirt; he carried the other.

Stopping just short of the door, he turned back for one last look around. His eyes fell on a large, three ring binder secured with a small brass chain to something on the other side of the counter. That feeling of delight returned when the label taped to the front told him he had found the U.K. version of the monster I.D. manual. The chain kept him from picking it up high enough to read, so he left it flat on the counter and bent down.

He quickly thumbed through it, trying to decide if he should break the brass chain and take it. Sadly, it was larger than the US version and would be difficult to carry.

Turning pages, he committed information to memory, especially when he came across the monsters he had already confronted. His eye soon strayed to the clock that hung high on the wall above the checkout counter.

A small sign hung below it and he read, 'Our Atomic Clock! Be sure to set your time piece!' It read twelve minutes after four and showed the date as June 28th. The display indicated it was still receiving a signal and keeping time. If Harry remembered correctly, the nearest clock was in London and he wondered if someone was still attending it. If the digital readout of this smaller version was true, he had missed his birthday.

"I'm nineteen now!" he blurted, and there came a slight feeling of embarrassment because his reaction had been so juvenile. Birthdays didn't matter anymore, especially if you didn't have someone to share them with. Yet Harry wasn't going to let it go that easily and decided to make one last belated birthday wish before giving into adult apathy.

"I wish that someday, very soon, I'll find someone to talk with that won't run away… or try to kill me."

Holding the flashlights lens within an inch of his lips so that it shined on the ceiling, he blew at it, turning it off in the process as if it had been a candle. With daylight getting short, he ripped out a few dozen pages of the manual, rolled them up, and stuffed them into his bag before departing the gas station.

Harry left the bloody cotton sleeve on the bench as the only evidence that he'd been there, and crossing the roadway, he moved out into the waving grass. Even though the sun was nearly at the horizon, it still warmed him. He would use the map to help him avoid large urban areas. He didn't want another day like this one, and the more time he could put between city visits, the better.

Harry trudged south and ran out of steam at a place signed as the village of 'Daviot'. There was a small school just off the A9 and what Harry assumed was the headmaster's residence, stood just across the street from the tiny campus. Finding the door unlocked, he stepped inside and called out to anyone who might be there. He got no answer and on further inspection, it appeared the house had been abandoned for a long time.

The dining table was still set for dinner, all chairs pushed in. The rather fancy curtains had been drawn, and all the beds were made. So, other than a light coat of dust, the place was practically spotless. Double latching the front door, he checked and secured the back entrance and all the ground floor windows.

Making his way up the narrow stairs, he soon found himself in a rather tastefully decorated attic bedroom. Closing and locking its door, he pushed a heavy bureau against it before opening all of the windows to bring fresh air into the chamber.

After dropping his bag, sporran, and sword rig onto the floor, he stripped the dusty comforter off the bed and tossed it into a corner before sitting down and removing his mocs. The mattress was soft and alluring. Harry just wanted to lay back and let his exhaustion ferry him into sleep. But curiosity drew him to a closet and opening it, he found there was still clothing inside. Thumbing through the hangered items, he found three cotton nightshirts. Taking down a green plaid one, he sniffed it. The shirt still smelled of fabric softener and an idea struck him.

Harry soon lay on the blanket covered mattress, adorned in that shirt, all his clothes piled on the floor next to the bed. The garment was a couple sizes too big, but that was better than too small. Grinning up at the ceiling, he lay with hands behind his head on the pillow, listening to the house.

It was quiet with the exception of a night breeze that whistled a lullaby as it rolled up under the eaves, accompanied by whispering pines. He had gotten the bed he'd hoped for, and now, if only his birthday wish would come true.

Harry's eyes fluttered shut several times as he began to work through a mental checklist to assure that he had done everything in his power to secure the house. In the middle of the process, he remembered he had vowed to study his map. Yet, the only thing Harry got around to studying, was the morning sun breaking through the small window in an eastern gable.

# CHAPTER 14

## Stately Strode He On The Plain

It was a week later when noontime found Harry at Aviemore. After spending the night on a sofa in a tourist center and departing to the southeast the next morning, he ventured into the Cairngorm Mountains. He started to keep track of his days by writing a single word onto his pad of paper such as: 'Boring!' 'Colorful!' or, 'Exhausted!' to describe his experience, and then added the date after each one. The trauma of his city encounter had dwindled to just a few bad nightmares. The killer's face became a blank canvas for others, some of them loved ones. The worst had been Harold Sr., causing Harry to awake in a cold sweat, glad his father had been one of the good guys in reality.

Harry had rescued two more people since he left the city. Two separate incidents, one involving more of what he now knew were Dasyhond, and the other, a large iguana looking salamander that he didn't have a page for, that had latched onto a teen girl's ankle length dress when she bent to dip her bucket in a loch.

Harry had arrived running and was just in time to slice her hemline free and she ran away. The creature had no real legs to speak of and propelling itself along on webbed feet, it crawled out after him. He made short work of it by jumping astride and driving a sword through the base of its skull.

The girl returned after he finished, telling him that the creature was edible, and if he didn't want it, she would return later with others to butcher it. She had told him he was, 'Braw' and then attempted to seduce him. There was something about her manner that threw up a few red flags. So, he declined, thanked her, and bid her good day.

It was about three miles northeast of Loch Muick that a group of people tore past him as he broke out of a pine forest onto a narrow road.

"Turn back, lad, the bogey's coming!" shouted an older man toting a heavy hiking staff. "Turn back now if ya want to save yerself!"

There were two women carrying screaming toddlers, followed by a teen boy and a raven-haired girl of about the same age. A younger version of the first man took up the rear, also carrying a wooden staff.

Harry just stood in shocked surprise as he watched them go. He turned back just as the monster came into view from around a distant pile of boulders.

*Another critter moving about in broad daylight?*

It was the Creature from the Black Lagoon.

Harry's memory came into play, and for a few seconds, he was seven again, sitting on the couch with his parents, a popcorn bowl in his lap, watching the 1954 version of the film. They were all laughing because of the poor special effects of the time. No amount of cinematic tricks could hide the fact that it was a man in a monster suit. But Harry wasn't laughing now.

This version of the creature was a little different. It had a short crocodilian like tail that was just long enough to slap you around a bit if it had a mind to. The beast was greenish gold in color and its scales were over-lapping bands, not plates. They encircled everything. It was well armored in all the right places with no soft under belly. As it moved, it gave a long, low whistling noise that crescendoed up the scale, ending in a short bray. On top of that—it was fast.

Harry let the bookbag slip to the ground and he moved into the grass on the opposite side of the roadway to prepare for battle. The seconds ticked away as the creature moved up the hill. The music flowed in and the beast's actions slowed. The butcher's chart, when it manifested in Harry's head, brought no relief. It showed limited dissection points.

The beast came at him, clawing like a boxer throwing roundhouse punches. Harry moved backwards, danced left and then right, his blades parrying every move. There was no getting behind it as it turned, bobbed, and weaved. He felt it was the worst of any monster to date that he had to confront alone. It didn't seem to tire. As his energy dwindled, he realized he had made no progress. Despite the whistling blades making contact again and again, it just kept coming. The waltz played on, and it dawned on Harry that it had never gone this long before.

*So, what happens when it reaches its finale? Does it start over—or am I dead?*

Slow-motion mode kept Harry just out of reach of those ebony meat hooks, but he grew weary. For the first time in his monster slaying career, Harry felt he might have to run away in the middle of a battle just to catch his breath in order to return later for a second round.

"Do ya need some hep, lad?" floated out from the pine trees behind him. The voice distracted the creature so that it stopped just long enough to gaze beyond Harry to the road. One of his swords ricocheted off its arm and scraped up toward the monsters shoulder. The edge caught the lip of the next band and bent it back on itself. A second sword strike, broke it off, exposing smooth skin much like that of the Thulu.

*Gotcha, froggy!*

Harry's discovery gave him renewed energy. Ignoring the question of the man behind him in the distance, he changed his strategy and went to slicing and jabbing in an upward motion. The beast seemed to get angrier and angrier with the loss of every boney band. It took to snapping at him like a dog. Harry soon caught on to the beast's pattern of swiping and snapping. When the claws shot out, he jabbed the wrist, pushing the sword point underneath the smaller bands. Prying them off, he was able to expose the skin covered joint.

*Take the hand, Harry! Take the hand!*

He dodged right. The creature turned with him and swiped with its left. In that split second, before it could counter with its right, a fist sized rock flew in and hit the beast in the face. Harry took advantage of that moment and going airborne in an unconventional move, he put all his weight behind bringing his sword down to sever the hand at the wrist. The beast literally shrieked, bending the cilia in Harry's ears flat like long grass in a gust of wind.

The beast continued to snap and swipe at him with its right hand. So, Harry took it off as well, but he slipped on the wet grass as he spun away and found himself inside the creature's now clawless arms. It wrapped him in a bear hug under his arm pits. Harry found his face not a foot from the beast's wide-open mouth and those deadly teeth. Its black eyes, under a heavy brow, seemed to project a kind of furious intelligence as the stench of decay rolled out of its maw.

Tilting his head back as far as he could, Harry drove both swords into

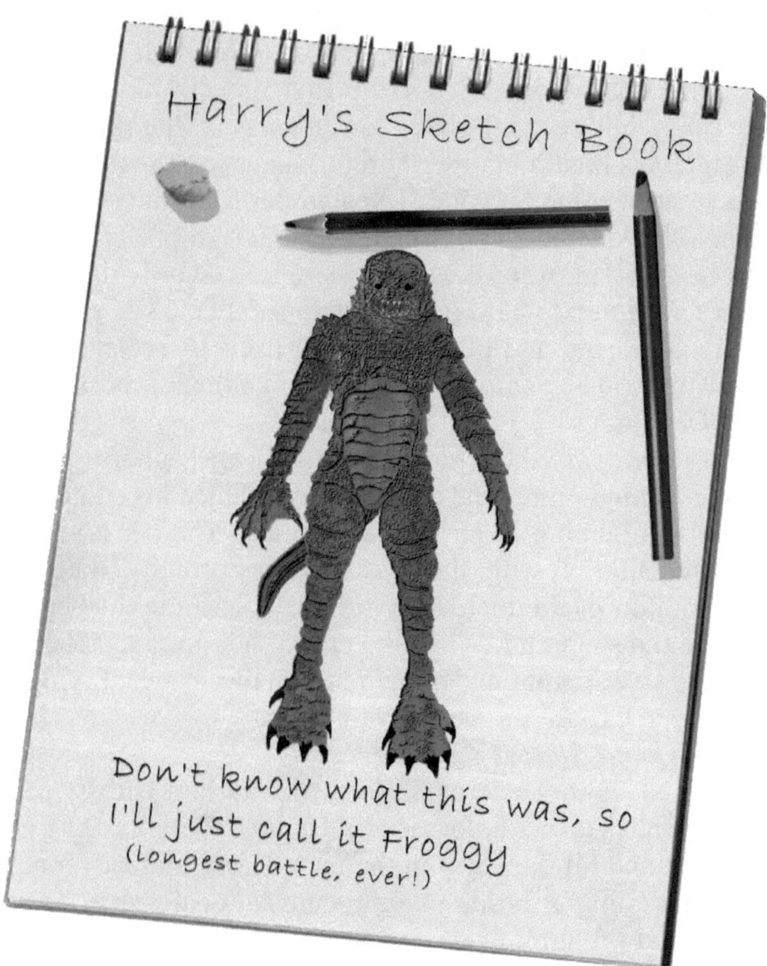


that gaping hole. The beast tried to vocalize, but only gurgled. Harry pushed even harder and the tips of his weapons blossomed out at the back of its neck, flipping the scales up like louvers. The quillons of the swords pushed into the creature's eyes, blinding it. Its teeth grated over the steel of the blades as its jaw twitched and spasmed.

Harry felt its body quiver as the remaining scales on its arms scraped at him through his shirt. He couldn't break its hold and all he could do was saw away with his swords and hope it would die before he lost more skin.

Heavy wooden staffs suddenly appeared from behind him, one on each side. Their tips were forced through the armpits of the beast at the front, and its limbs were levered back from Harry's body, allowing him to escape its crushing hold.

The creature tried to twist and fight, but it couldn't lift its arms above the sticks that had crossed at its spine. The Scotsmen continued moving forward, one on each side, until the heels of the creature's flipper-like feet began to drag through the muddy grass. They took it down onto its back and stood on their end of the wooden shafts, pinning the monster to the earth.

Stepping back, Harry drew deep breaths as he watched the beast's activity dwindle to nothing, its blood pooling in the grass behind its head.

When it stopped moving and its eyes glazed over, the younger of the two men stepped off his walking stick and moved forward to nudge the creature with his toe. Then turning to Harry, he said, "Well done, lad, well done! And who be ya?"

"Harry," he rasped out as he coughed, bending forward from the waist.

"Hairy? Like a hairy highland cou?" the old guy chuckled out.

"Father!" his younger companion chided. "Be kind… this man just saved our lives."

"Fine then. So… Harry? Like, Harold?"

"No, that was my father."

"Well, this auld fool would be… my father, Alistair, and I… be Kinney. That was a fine display of swordsmanship, laddy."

"A fine display, indeed," Alistair said, his light blue eyes flashing in his large, windburned face. His full beard, streaked with grey, waggled in the breeze as he bared his crooked teeth in a grin.

"Well… that was an excellent display of rock throwing, it… I… I appreciate your help."

"Aye, we're good at throwing stones, but that's about it. So, yer not a Scotsman, are ya, Harry?" Kinney asked, his eyebrows arching high above his own set of baby blues.

"Ummm…"

"Welsh? English? Ah! Canadian… eh?" Alistair said and laughed again.

"I'm…"

"Ah, it doesn't matter, there's not enough of our kind left anymore for it to be," Kinney lamented. Then turning to the pines behind him, he declared, "Ah, here ye are. Safe to come out now, safe to come out."

Harry turned and watched as the others moved toward him through the trees. They all fell in behind a tall slender female about Harry's age who was holding a blubbering baby girl. The troupe was being led by an older, grey-haired woman carrying a toddler-sized boy. The two men that Harry stood with, wore brownish tartan kilts with thick, knee-high socks and time worn, lace-up work boots made of dark leather. The women wore long dresses of the same material, and knee high 'wellies' as Harry had heard them called.

All wore thick, pullover sweaters and sweatshirts, except Alistair, who wore a dark blue wool coat belted over his kilt. Harry found it odd because the weather was so warm. But other than what appeared to be a burlap bag stuffed full of items hanging from the older woman's arm, they appeared to be wearing everything they owned. They looked like they hadn't bathed for some time as the children's bare legs and feet were streaked with mud.

Alistair and Kinney retrieved their wooden staffs and met the others halfway. Harry followed, and they gathered in a semi-circle far away from the monster's carcass. The grey-haired woman smiled at him and asked, "Who's this, then? Some kind of a highland hero sent to save us from the dreaded bogey?"

"This be, Harry," Alistair said and laughed, winking at their newfound champion. "If it wasn't for him, some of us might not be breathing right now."

"So, Harry…" the raven-haired teen girl said before being interrupted.

"Hush now, Evina! Is anyone asking ya a question," the grey-haired woman said.

"Ah no, but…"

Alistair hushed her with a, "wheesht-wheesht!"

Evina blushed and looked down, putting her hands behind her back. A few seconds passed before she squinted with her right eye and allowed her left to travel up to Harry's face. She smirked at him as if to defy her elder's. Harry smiled back. Alistair jumped in before the girl could be chastised a third time and pointing with his free hand to the older woman, he said, "This be my wife, Olivia, and that is Kinney's wee bairn, Angus, that she be holding. The spry young lad over there is Kamden—he's my dead brother's boy, and that noisy, wee imp standing next to ya, is Evina. She's of no relation. The lass fell in with us sometime back just outside of Eskadale. We kept her mostly 'cause we felt sorry for her. Last but not least, that is Rosalynn that be a holding our sweet, wee, Lorna."

"They be my wife and daughter," Kinney declared, beaming with the same crooked teeth as his father, his long dark hair blowing around his face.

Kamden left the group and walked over to the monster. "Messed with the wrong bunch of Scotsmen, dennae ya, frog face," he said, and grinning over at Harry, he winked and then kicked the monster.

Kamden didn't look like his kin folk. His skin was milky, his hair blonde. It was neatly trimmed and parted on the left. When he smiled, Harry could see his teeth were straight and bright. He wore blue jeans rather than a kilt and was much cleaner than the others. The boy appeared to have groomed himself for some reason. He looked like what Harry's mother had occasionally referred to as, 'Scandinavian'.

Whenever they met someone walking down the street that looked like Kamden, she'd say, "Scandinavian's are so pretty." Harry had taken that to mean, Swiss, Swedish, or Viking folk, like the Norsemen.

"So, Harry, yer some kind of warrior? Ya look it," Kamden said, as he came over to stand on Harry's left. The teen's finger snuck out and touched the quillon of one of the swords still in Harry's hand. Then making a face of disgust, he pulled it away and wiped monster goo on his jeans.

"Nice weapon… looks auld."

His polite manner said it all, he was probably city-born. Raised in a well-to-do family in some Scottish suburb before the Bug showed up.

"Being kind of bold there, aren't ya, Kamden? Dannae bother the man," Alistair spoke as he reached to grab a shoulder and pull him away.

"No, it's okay, I don't mind. I'd be curious too. Want to hold one?" Harry said, pushing the pommel of the sword toward the boy. Kamden looked at Olivia and then at Alistair as he reached for the weapon.

"Naw, lad. Dinnae take it. Leave the weapon be. Ya haven't a clue," Kinney said, and motioned for Kamden to come stand by him.

The boy mumbled, "Damn."

Grinning up at Harry, he moved away, kicking at a clump of grass. Olivia set Angus on the ground and helping him to stand, she took his hand and they moved away up the slope toward the trees. She crossed the road and sitting down on the low slope of the opposite side, she placed the toddler in her lap. Opening the burlap bag, she pulled out food items that were wrapped in what looked like brown butcher's paper.

"Come to me, all of ye… let's have a wee bite before we're off," she said. All but Alistair and Kinney moved toward her. The two men turned and walked back to the dead monster.

"Hep me here, Kinney. Let's put this rubbish in that thicket down the slope before we sit."

"I can help with that," Harry said.

"Ah, naw, lad, ya've done all the important work, we'll take it from here," Kinney said, grinning as he grabbed one of the flippered feet.

Olivia said, "Aye, Harry, come sit with us, ah've some lovely oatcakes to share."

"Okay, I can do that… I guess."

Moving over to the circle that was now forming, he brought his bag to lean against while he sat waiting for Olivia to complete her task.

Rosalynn lowered herself next to Olivia and sat with Lorna straddling her legs. She had not spoken once since Harry's arrival, but he figured since she was young and married, she was not supposed to speak to single men. She was trying to keep her distance. Any kind of an exchange between her and Harry might be misconstrued.

Angus soon moved over to Rosalynn's lap to slide in behind the little girl. Kamden sat on her other side, leaving Evina still on her feet. She remained that way until Harry sat down and began wiping his blades in the long grass to free them of monster blood.

He wasn't on his butt more than a few seconds before Evina moved over to sit next to him. Pulling up her knees and wrapping her arms around them, she laid the side of her face on top and studied him through hooded, green eyes. Her rock worn, knee high rubber boots, had been a shiny black at one time with a multitude of colorful little flowers scattered over the surface. They were too big for her. Harry wondered if she had the blisters to show for it.

"So, Harry, where do ya call home?" she said, smiling sweetly.

"Kilbury…"

"Evina," Olivia said in a harsh manner, but the young girl ignored her.

"Kilbury, in England? Ah'm from Eskadale, that's further north of here. My mum and da are dead."

Rosalynn finally spoke with the sternness of a big sister, "Evina, how ya go on! Dinnae trouble this man with yer nonsense."

Evina, having received an oatcake, took to nibbling on it and glaring at the grass, her face turning red out of frustration as she huffed between bites.

Olivia passed an oatcake Harry's way and Evina took it from her and laid it on his lap. "There ya go, Harry, eat up," she said, patting his thigh with her offering hand as she cocked her head and grinned mischievously. Olivia drew a breath to chastise her, and Evina quickly withdrew the hand and snickered. Harry didn't look at Olivia and pretended he hadn't noticed that Evina's hand had lingered too long on his thigh.

He wanted to rinse his swords before eating, fearful the monster's blood would dry and become difficult to remove, possibly damaging the steel. Besides that, it stunk. Pulling one of two unopened water bottles from his bag, he took a long drink. Then drizzling a few drops on each blade, he scrubbed them thoroughly with tufts of grass before sticking them back in their scabbards. Then, taking another drink of the water, he realized the others had stopped eating and were all watching him intently. Setting the water bottle down, all eyes followed it to the ground.

*They look thirsty*

Harry pulled the last bottle from his bag and offered it to Olivia.

"Oh! Thanks, laddy! Ya've read my mind. That's why we had a run-in with the bogey. We were down to the loch for water," she said, and twisting off the cap, she passed the bottle around and each took a drink. After the toddlers were given their share, the bottle was recapped and pushed into the burlap bag. Olivia gave him a wink with an affectionate smile and then went back to eating.

The two men arrived as he was finishing off his oatcake. They sat, completing the circle and Alistar said, "Evina, put yer knees down, lass, yer fannie's on display to the world."

She huffed at him, ignoring his command. Kamden's eyes drifted over to see what Alistair was going on about. He abruptly dropped his chin to his chest, casting his eyes down as if diverting his attention away from Evina's display. Harry waited and watched. Kamden's eyes soon drifted back up to slyly view the girl's display of anatomy.

Alistair startled everyone when he barked, "Go on, to it."

Kamden caught Harry staring at him and looked away as he pushed the last of his oatcake into his mouth.

Evina pushed her legs straight out in front and smoothing down her dress, she shrugged defiantly at anyone who glared.

Alistair pulled a small, silver flask from inside his coat, and twisting off the cap, he took a quick swig and then offered it to Harry. "Here ya go, lad. It's good whisky. helped myself to it at a wee cottage that appeared to lack a landlord. No sense in letting it go to waste, aye?"

The old man jerked the flask at him a second time, and Harry took the whisky in order not to offend his host. He knew the rules; don't dishonor the head of the house. His father had been that way. Harry took a quick sip and his throat caught fire. He gasped, puckered, and handed it back. He would never be a whisky drinker. Alcohol wasn't his thing, and intoxicated was the worse way to be when the beasts came calling.

"Tis good, aye?" the patriarch said, handing it to his son who took enough for the whole family. Kinney gasped as well, handed it back to his father and gave Harry a wink. His actions left Harry to believe that winking was a regular form of communication within the group.

"So, ya been at those swords for some time? Dinnae ya ever think about the Claymore? Ya could probably do some real damage with one of those?" Kinney said.

"Yes, I've been practicing the butterfly swords since I was about eight years old."

"So, how auld are ya, lad?"

"I think… I'm not sure, but I must be nineteen by now."

Out of the corner of his eye he saw Evina look his way, and turning, he took in her dreamy expression. Their eyes met, and it came to him why it was such a problem. She was smitten, and that created a tricky situation for her adopted family.

Harry studied her small, oval face, the upturned nose bridged with freckles, and the rosy red cheeks that contrasted the dirty tan of her skin. She wore a flowered bandana over her head that was tied underneath her long hair at the back. A tiny sprig of heather was stuck through the weave of her sweater just above her left breast, and it dawned on him how beautiful she was, in a rustic sort of way.

*Seventeen going on thirty.*

He quickly looked away when Kinney spoke, saying, "So, ya only think yer nineteen? Ya dennae ken?"

Harry took a risk in assuming he knew what Kinney had asked and said, "Just lost track of time." "My birthday is at the end of June."

"Aye, well, yer nineteen then, it's been July for some time now."

Evina blurted out, "So! Butterfly swords! Such a pretty name. Are they Japanese or something?"

"Um, no, actually, Southern Chinese. I was in…"

"Okay, well, we should be off… have a good distance to go," Olivia said, tossing a look at Alistair. Getting to her feet, she slung her bag over a shoulder and then picked up the sleeping Angus from Rosalynn's lap. Kinney's wife rose to her feet, and resituating the little girl in her arms, she followed obediently without a word as they moved toward the pines.

Kamden reluctantly rose and moved their way. The men got up as if to follow but stopped a short distance from Harry and put their backs to him. Their heads came together, and indiscernible words were passed. Harry felt their exchange pertained to him and he sat waiting for the outcome. Evina was the last to rise, using Harry's shoulder to pull herself up. She remained behind him for a minute, her hand on the back of his neck. She went to running her fingers through his hair, and when she drew a breath to speak, Olivia beat her to it.

"Come, Evina! Thank ya, Harry. Ah'm grateful for ya!" she called back, smiling.

Rosalynn turned and smiled at him too, giving him a kind of shallow curtsey while juggling Lorna. Evina started to follow and then turning to walk backwards, she threw him a kiss. Giggling, she jogged away. Catching up with Kamden, she took his hand and just before they disappeared into the pines, Kamden threw Harry a grin over his shoulder.

Getting to his feet, Harry watched until no one was left but the men. They came and stood beside him as if they had been waiting for the family to move out of earshot. The old man gave Harry's shoulder a light squeeze and grinned at him.

"Thanks, Harry, we're in yer debt."

The old man then glanced at Kinney and nodded in the direction of the others. The younger man strolled away, giving Harry a brief and indifferent wave of his hand.

"I could travel with you, Alistair. It would be no problem for me."

"It would for me, lad," he said flatly. "As ya have seen, that girl, Evina? She's fallen for ya. In her eyes yer some kind of a rockstar. So, that's not to be. She's to be with Kamden."

Alistair stepped over to face Harry, keeping his hand on the young monster slayer's shoulder. He looked him straight in the eyes and said, "Ah'm grateful for what ya done for us today, but ah will not let ya tag along. It's not too often we come across someone to champion us like ya did, even though we've met many a bogey slayer as yerself. That's what ya are, right lad? A hunter of monsters? Ah've seen that look in yer eyes, the same look in the eyes of others bearing weapons as ya do. Solitary warrior types that we've made the acquaintance of since the plague took hold here. It's not like there were many people here in Scotland to begin with. Now it seems the country lies barren and we've the responsibility to repopulate it with those immune to the sickness. Ah need to bring my clan back, and Evina is important to us in that way. Are ya hearing me, lad?"

Harry remained silent at first, and turning his head, he gazed out across the vast, lonely, heather filled space. He had underestimated Alistair, thinking he was just an out of work farmer or sheepherder. Yet the way he spoke now without the presence of his family, told Harry he was a thinking man who was on a mission. His eyes met Alistair's and the old man raised his eyebrows as a sign that he was growing impatient for an answer.

"I understand, no problem," Harry said.

"Ah hope ya find what yer looking for, lad, and maybe we'll meet again. Thanks a million for risking yer life the way ya did, and… for all those other Scots who ya risked it for, before us."

Harry gave him an inquisitive look and Alistair grinned and said, "Aye, lad, ah've heard of ya. Ah'm supposing ya'll be a legend someday here in my Scotland. A man all my wee'uns will talk about around the cook fires for years to come. Ya'll be our Highland Harry."

He didn't know what to say to that. Alistair took Harry's right hand and shook it hard. Then turning away, he hurried after his family, his heavy walking staff making divots in the ground as he moved.

The old man suddenly stopped and turning back, he looked up at the sky and said, "Ah'm supposing we won't be seeing the sun today." With that said, he touched a spot above his right eye with the side of his index finger, giving Harry some kind of a salute before pushing his way into the trees.

Watching the Scotsman walk away, Harry felt the loneliness start as a heaviness in his chest. There was no doubt what he longed for. It was the same as Alistair; he yearned for clan.

Picking up his bag, Harry continued in the direction he had been going. Coming to that set of tall boulders where he first saw the monster, he crawled up and sat on the one with the flattest top. Gazing toward the loch, he saw some buildings set among a large copse of trees. From the layout, it looked like some kind of a camp. A narrow road ran in from the north east but didn't exit on his side. So, probably a summer spot for people on vacation. At least he'd have a place to stay for the night.

Removing his sword rig and the wide brown belt from his waist, he pulled off what was left of his shirt and inspected the abrasions that ran from his armpits to his waist. The wounds were no worse than a lightly scraped knee, but he suspected he might have to break out the pain reliever at bedtime.

After pulling his jerkin back on, Harry lay out on the wind-swept granite with his head resting on his bag. He watched the small birds glide and dive in and out of the overcast as he pondered his situation. The desire to stay with Alistair and his family was strong. Harry figured he could handle being alone for a brief period of time, but he feared that a prolonged day-in and day-out situation would drive him insane. Those people were exactly what he was looking for and he had been rejected. Deep down he knew the odds of changing the old man's mind were slim. Like Alistair had said, Harry was too much of a threat.

The old guy was probably afraid that it might come down to weapons, and he, nor Kinney, would stand a chance against a warrior type. So, in his experiential wisdom, the patriarch didn't want to take the risk. He had counted on their, so called champion, to be reasonable.

Harry had to admit that Evina was quite alluring. He had never met a girl that looked like she did. Black hair over green eyes and light skin with freckles. The picture left him wondering if he could actually ignore her advances and keep his hands to himself.

Then there was Kamden.

*What did he think? Maybe he really didn't like Evina, or was feeling like he was being forced? Would he feel slighted if you hooked up with her? Or would he be relieved? You're never going to know sitting here, Harry T. Lumsdale.*

What he did know, was that there was a need to hear human voices and to have conversation. The compulsion to belong somewhere, and to be useful to someone, was strong. Harry thought of his father and shed silent tears.

He lay warming the cold stone surface as the wind blew around him, the nearby pines making a lonely noise in their swaying. Birdsong drifted across the plain, punctuated by a sound he had only heard at the zoo as a small boy—the bugling of caribou. Combined, they were the ever-present voice of nature in a life that no longer embraced technology. They were also the elements of an equation that equaled loneliness. The price he would have to pay for wanting to live a rural life, that is, unless he could hook up with someone.

The thought made Harry feel like he had surrendered to Alistair's wants a little too easily. If he wasn't careful, he may find himself wallowing in self-pity. Anger blossomed, forcing the feeling of isolation out.

*You found what you were looking for and you let it get away!*

Sitting up, Harry pounded the granite and turning his face to the sky, shouted, "Dammit!"

He had to try again and do it before Alistair's clan put too many miles between him and them. If anything, they may lead him to more people.

There might be a chance he could just stay close and shadow them. Perhaps Alistair would realize how badly he wanted to be a part of their lives. He could always promise not to interfere with Alistair's plans and endeavor to make Evina understand that his ultimate happiness, by sticking with Kamden, was in her hands. He could ask her to be kind enough to refrain from trifling with his life.

Begging was out of the question, though. That would be undignified. Something his father had told him, time and time again, never to do. But he had to act. Maybe they could come to some kind of an agreement and then shake on it. Alistair seemed to be the kind of man who took stock in a good handshake.

Harry wiped his eyes and put on his belt and sword rig. Then grabbing his bag, he climbed down. He hit the ground and took off at a jog. Speed was of the essence if he was going to catch up with the people that he hoped would find it in their hearts to accept him as more than just their champion.

# CHAPTER 15

## There Was A Bonnie Lass...

Harry entered an old growth forest at little less than a run and moved through the trees as fast as he could. It was just as difficult as all the other times. He was constantly pushing branches out of his way, a few of them pushing back. It made him growl and swear. Some of the moss-covered conifers were as old as Scotland itself and still held onto the thick, dead branches at their base. This forced Harry to constantly zig and zag, bringing an unsettling fear that it would put him off course.

He looked for signs of the group, but he wasn't a tracker. At one point he found a pile of human feces next to a large, fallen tree. A strip of cloth, used for toilet paper, lay across it. He was on the right track, but didn't have a clue which direction to go from there. He just stayed on the imagined path, wondering how they could move so fast through the forest.

When he broke out on the other side, he hoped to see them silhouetted against the sky or moving up some distant slope. But no such luck. It now grew dark, and he had to focus on finding shelter. That was something he assumed Alistair had to do as well or, had already. When it grew too dark to walk without a flashlight, he crawled into a sheep shed full of old musty straw.

Fashioning a nest and unrolling his woolen wrap, Harry spread it out over the straw before moving back to the door. Closing it, he found it didn't have a latch. Kicking off the top rail of a corner stall, he forced one end into the ground and then wedged the other under a cross member of the door. It wouldn't hold for long if forced, but it would give him time to act if something undesirable should attempt entry.

He closed the drop-down shutters that covered the two tiny windows at each end and secured them by pushing the steel prop arm affixed to their lower edge inside a rusty bracket at the sill. They couldn't be pulled open from the outside, and the wall would most likely collapse long before the shutter gave up.

Moving to his wrap, Harry lay down, stiff from his walk, and achy from his fight. He popped a couple of his precious aspirin and downed them with half a bottle of warm juice. His dinner consisted of sardines and the crackers from an MRE that had gone unnoticed in the bottom of his bag.

Afterwards, he lay on his stomach and used his flashlight to study the map. The wind was steady, causing the shed to creak and groan. But Harry was getting used to the wind, and it was now like an old friend that never seemed to leave.

With his flashlight clamped in his lips, Harry roughly calculated where the shed was located on the map and where Alistair's clan might be in proximity to it. Drawing a circle around that area with his marker, he would search it in the morning.

The air around him had cooled rather quickly and he wondered if another storm was on the way. Putting his flashlight and the map back in his bag, he rolled himself in his wrap and lay looking up at the rafters. The faces came to him one at a time, first his mother, then his father, and finally—Bessie. He thought about all the things they had done together before the monsters came. There were no tears this time, and he found he could reminisce without the devastating heartache. Not that the pain wasn't there—it was just more manageable, now. He was learning to carry it.

It surprised him when thoughts of Evina pushed their way in. He tried to push her out, but she pushed back. He started to imagine being with her in romantic situations. The two of them lying on their backs together in the sun with the long grass blowing around them, playing tag in a woodland free of obstacles, and finally, swimming together in the sea sans clothing. When he got to the part where they lay on the cooling sands of the beach with bodies entwined, he drifted off.

***

Harry searched for two days but never found a trace of Alistair's clan. They had simply vanished.

*Maybe they are actually trying to hide!*

There came a want to kick himself for changing his plans in order to catch up. The map told him if he continued south, he still had two thirds of the country to cross before he got to England. It was in the midst of his frustration that he experienced insight.

*What are you looking for down there that you can't find up here? You have the rest of your life to wander the world.*

Harry felt his exasperation dissipate. He decided to create a plan and set some reasonable goals. There came a brief foreboding at the thought of not having any purpose. He tried to force it out of his head. There must be somebody out there. The odds of him stumbling across other human beings was always in his favor.

*Just don't let them leave without first trying to make friends!*

Harry soon found himself back on the coast of the North Sea, just not as far north as Sandwood Bay and a great deal farther east. He came across a little, touristy kind of sign in an overlook that read, 'Welcome to Spey Bay-Please make use of Speyside Way…' The rest of it was unreadable.

Leaving the road where it turned west, he tramped straight out into the grass and headed into open country. Half an hour of walking brought him to where his route lay blocked by a patch of rough ground that was strewn with rocks and small boulders. A path no wider than his own two feet together, opened on his right and led down to a narrow beach that ran along the base of a cliff.

Not wanting to navigate through the rocks and risk a sprained ankle, he opted for the beach. There had been no encounters with monsters since he met Alistair's clan, but he knew the brutes were out there in that placid looking water. Harry wasn't to be lulled by its gentle waves breaking the shore.

*Probably watching you, right now, waiting for the foolish man-boy to screw up.*

If they were to make an appearance, the sea and cliff left him with only two directions to run, both easily blocked. Feeling the need to hurry, he sought for more open ground.

He checked his swords to make sure they were loose and ready to come out to play. He had sharpened them the night before, and he knew they could, *"...split a hair!"* as his father was fond of saying.

Harold Sr.'s smirking face materialized in his mind as the old guy forced his cap to the back of his head by pushing up on the bill with the point of the Ka-Bar knife.

"Okay, dad, I gotcha," he said out loud to no one, the memory bringing a smile to his face as he made his way down to the sandy beach.

Moving at a fast march, Harry hugged the cliff as he continued north. He grew fearful he may not find a way to escape the beach before sundown, but he soon found relief in the form of a grass covered slope cutting through the bluff on his left. It was well past the boulder filled rough spot and he hurried up it to level ground, hoping for a cottage or outbuilding. Breaking the top, he found he got more than that.

*A castle!*

The ruins sat at the far edge of a vast plain of grass where the cliff curved back on itself. Its location allowed an unobstructed view of the sea below. It was the first one he had come across since he arrived, which he thought odd because Scotland was supposed to be full of them. He had never seen a real one. The excitement was overwhelming and he broke into a run.

Upon arriving, he discovered piles of stones and numerous short foundation walls protruding just above the soil line. In the middle of it all, stood what he knew as a 'Keep'. It was the only part remaining that could be called a building.

He explored the inside and saw a large part of the roof was still intact, but the old wooden stairs were no longer usable. It had been a tourist site at one time, but the little metal sign tacked to a post was no longer readable except for a faded line at the bottom, reminding him to, 'Keep Scotland's Landmarks Clean, Toss Your Rubbish In The Bin'

Moving through a stone archway in the north wall, (which had once been the inside), he carefully picked his way over to the ruined stairs. They had been L-shaped with the very bottom step being a stack of stones formed into a square. The mortar had given up at some point and it had fallen apart. With no support at the bottom, gravity tore them in half at the first landing. The larger half now lay on its side at his feet, and the shorter portion still hung from the floor above.

*If a stairway falls in a castle and no one is around to hear it…?*

Harry chuckled to himself and tried to right the broken piece, thinking he could put it back. It was too heavy. His desire to explore the upper floor motivated him to keep trying. So, he leaned a long, loose plank against the bottom step of the remaining section and angled the lower end over to the open space on the floor at his feet. The idea was to make a run for it and gain the upper deck before the long board gave way. Moving back outside, Harry turned and raced up his makeshift bridge. He almost didn't make it.

There came a loud, *Crack!* and the sound of splitting wood. He felt the remaining steps break free, and at the last second, he leapt. His knees hit the floor and his pain filled yelp was drowned out by the deafening crash of the upper section meeting the lower. A cloud of dust rose up and he watched the plank bounce off the pile and fall out of reach. Harry rolled onto his back and bringing his knees up, he tried to rub the pain away, his body buzzing with adrenaline.

*Damn! That was close. Nothing like setting yourself up for a few broken bones, huh, Harry?*

Getting to his feet, he surveyed the room. The space was free of furniture and the floor had been replaced years before with modern, green treated lumber, leaving him to surmise it would take the rest of his life for it to rot away. Someone had designed it to support a large group of tourists. The main attraction being what they could see through the north and east set of windows. The Keep beheld a spectacular view of the sea and the western coast of Spey Bay, along with an unknown mountain range, miles away in the distance.

Walking around the large open room, he peaked through the other windows that were set at about hip height and spaced at even intervals within the walls. He was far enough above the ground that he felt safe and decided to stay for the night.

Moving over to the northwest corner, he made his bed against the wall, just back from the windows. The ruined part of the roof was mainly over the entry hall where he had almost broken his neck, as well as a corner of the south side. If it rained, he would be able to stay dry.

Harry sketched for a while and then decided to work out before having his dinner. Using the entire floor, he moved about its surface, his swords flashing. Happy for no roof support columns to impede his

movement, he worked through every one of his sword routines with enthusiasm. A short run of punching, parrying, and kicking brought him to calisthenics, and finally, stretching.

Walking twenty something miles or more a day, left him feeling there was no need to work his legs, and a complete stretching routine assured him the nights would be more bearable. Waking to cramps in his calves and thighs in the midnight hour, meant he had to be conscious during the loneliest part of any twenty-four-hour period. He'd rather pass it dreaming.

After a meal of yet more sardines, and some beef jerky (which he hadn't expected to ever find in Scotland), he just sat in the dark, drinking water, and listening to the North Sea breaking the beach. He wished for a book, wondering why, in all his pilfering, he never grabbed one. They were everywhere and usually coupled with some fairly decent old magazines. But those always brought a longing for things he didn't need, or worst yet; things he'd lost. Better a classic novel, or maybe, some erotica. There was no one here to judge him now and he could simply enjoy the sexual adventures of some fictional character in some other place that he wasn't.

*What would it hurt?*

There needed to be something between dinner and bedtime besides practicing. Now that his food supply was running low, he would have to find some place to resupply, hopefully, a shop with a book section. He could always look for a new sketchbook and was willing to accept any large pad of paper in the case he couldn't find one. It would also allow him the chance to see if they had any drawing charcoal.

*Why not visit the local library while you're at it? After a morning of pleasant looting, you could always swing on by and pick yourself up a copy of Frankenstein*

He recalled a sign affixed to a large, square brick column at the corner of a crossroads he had passed through. Its white paint had peeled, leaving only part of the upcoming towns name, '....PEMAN-7 km' was all it said. Harry figured he had already gone half that distance before taking to the beach. So, there was a chance to refill his bag in the morning from whatever he could find there. He still had his Robert Frost poems and that comic book, but he had read and reread them while on board the Enchanted and their covers were nearly obliterated by sweaty hands.

When his eyes grew heavy, he moved back to his sleeping spot and after removing his sword rig and setting it close, he wrapped up in his wool and was out cold before any troubling thoughts could rally. He awoke in the dark, still sitting up, his back pressed against the cold stones of the wall.

Nightmares had brought him from his sleep, mostly scenes from the early days of the pandemic and the chaos that followed. Pulling the tartan wrap tighter around his shoulders, Harry crossed his legs and snuggled into the corner. Tossing a glance at his butterfly swords to be sure they were close enough; he caught the gleam of their brass fittings reflecting the light of the full moon. Looking up, he studied the cold white orb through the broken roof and his thoughts turned to his mother. There had been nights where she had drug him away from the TV just so they could sit in the backyard and moon gaze.

*"A gibbous moon! Isn't that a wonderful name, Harry?"* she had practically crooned. Then she laughed her infectious laugh, and Harry couldn't help but giggle. Pulling him close, she'd put the side of her face to his and for the next sixty seconds it was just him and her out there in the silent twilight.

The room around him began to lighten, and the moon dropped from sight as he sat reminiscing. A sense that something wasn't right mushroomed and the more awake he became, the more he felt it. A feeling that he wasn't alone prowled the back of his mind like a tiger waiting to pounce. It was like when he got that feeling that someone— or something—was watching him.

His ears detected a slight noise that resonated just below the sound of the unceasing wind and the crashing of the waves. He strained his ears, trying to pick it up, but it was just out of reach. Short bursts of, "Hmmm… hmmm… hmmm…" reverberated from somewhere. Buckling on his sword rig, he left his wrap and moved to the middle of the floor to face the opening to the ruined stairs.

Dawn glowed in the eastern sky and the space inside the entry hall brightened just enough for him to see the texture of the igneous rock in the walls. He waited, listening—feeling. Soon the rays of the sun crept in the window behind him, and with them, a noise like claws scraping over the time worn stone. Crouching, he spun, pulling out his swords in one fluid motion. A plate-sized hand with long, webbed fingers sporting black talons, clutched at the windowsill, its catfish like skin, gleaming in the light.

*Thulu!*

The smell confirmed it, and going low, Harry darted its way. Using one swift downward stroke, he used the stones as a cutting board, and the ugly mitt separated cleanly from the forearm. A banshee-like scream followed, along with the scrabbling of claws as gravity did its share of the work. There came a sickening thump as the pony-sized brute hit the ground. Harry put his back to the wall just shy of the window to wait in case there were others.

Harry couldn't hate Thulu anymore than he already did. Bessie's loss had pushed him far over the edge. Before that moment, he had not been much on loathing anything. But now, he was more than willing to openly declare, "*I hate freaking Thulu with all my heart.*"

He had also thought about coming up with a proven method to eliminate Hystrix and had put them on the top of his list for extermination. His plan, so far, involved fire. Dumping a flammable liquid down any known Hystrix hole and striking a match would do the trick, and most probably, bring a great deal of satisfaction.

*Just show me where they are! Could really get off on listening to them shriek and burn.*

Believing no more beasts were coming up, he peeked over the sill. His head coming out of the open hole was timed perfectly with an elf-sized war cry that rose up to meet his ears. What he saw below caused his eyes to widen and his jaw to drop.

A small woman with curly blond hair was in the middle of a leap to drive a spear through the Thulu from behind. Bravely landing with her feet planted firmly on the beast's hips, she thrust the spear home, its tip exiting the Thulu's chest, the steel sparking against the stone of the wall.

She then speedily drew and pushed a large dirk to the hilt in its back where the heart would be. Without missing a beat, she unsheathed what looked like a roman short sword and with a defiant roar, she sliced off the creature's head with a two-handed grip. The head tumbled to the ground, its tentacle like whiskers still trying to secure a hold on something.

Her short build was athletic, the muscles in her arms and legs, well defined. Harry stared in disbelief as she turned her face up to him, and hollered, "Hallo, lad! Thought I'd hep ya!"

The beast had fallen forward and now lay propped against the wall, its hindquarters spasming. Pulling the large dirk free, she added, "I missed the sweet spot with my pike, so I figured with the dirk in his heart, there'd be no argument. Now it seems he's lost his head over the matter." Laughing, she wiped the blade clean on the creature's tail. Then doing the same with the sword, she sheathed them both.

Harry shouted, "Who are you?"

"Well, Susan Jean is what my parents named me, but ya can call me, Susie. I'm not sure what the monsters call me since I don't speak the language. Of course, I've never bothered to ask."

"Pretty good at killing Thulu."

"I didn't know it had a name."

"Stay there, I'm coming down."

"Don't have much of anywhere else to go, ya know, so aye, I'll be here," she said, giving him an inquisitive look.

Picking up his gear, Harry ran to the dilapidated stairs and dropped everything over the edge before carefully lowering himself to hang by his hands. Letting himself drop the last ten feet, he plummeted into a crouch, his legs acting like springs when his feet impacted the floor. After picking up his gear, he scrambled over debris and burst out the door closest to Susie. Stopping just outside, he dumped his personal effects into the long grass and just stared.

"Hallo again," she said and laughed, her green eyes flashing. Harry studied every inch of her. She was maybe all of five feet tall with a noticeable width to her hips. A bubble-butt would be how his dead friend, Bruce Toulouse, would have jokingly referred to it. She had the face of a cherub and a button nose with a heavy line of freckles across the bridge. There was a light smattering on her deeply dimpled cheeks and large, loose curls covered her head, falling to her shoulders.

She wore leather armor on her upper body, and the equivalent of a cowhide breechclout. A leather sporran, much like his, hung at her groin. On her wrists, she sported the thick, leather vambraces of a swordsman. However, that's where the old world stopped because she also wore black, canvas sneakers laced to the knee. On her hands, she wore fingerless, 'Cycleguy' brand leather gloves, and her midriff was bare, exposing the hard, flat abdomen of a bodybuilder. She had decorated her belly button with a jeweled piercing, and small Celtic shield knots had been tattooed in a line around each bicep. Another thing he noticed was that she didn't speak like Alistair and his clan. She used a lot more English and it made him wonder if it had something to do with being urban born versus country. He would have to ask her later.

"Who are ya, lad?"

"I'm Harry. Ummm…yeah, just Harry."

"Highland Harry? Ya are the monster slayer, Highland Harry?" she said, squinting. Stepping closer, she studied him.

"Uh… don't know about that. Nobody's ever called me that before," he lied.

"Well lad, that's what their calling ya. Least in most of the clans I've come across. Did ya hep somebody or rescue a damsel in distress? Word must be getting around, aye?"

He thought for a minute. "Well, there was this guy, Alistair, and his family, they…"

"Aye, I've come across that lot several times. Just yesterday, in fact. Tinkers probably, odd bunch if ya ask me, but who, or what, isn't these days?"

"Tinkers?"

"Aye, like… gypsies? That is probably how ya know 'em."

"Ummm… yeah… thought so, too. Kind of friendly, but—kind of not. The old man was afraid I was going to steal away with that black haired girl, Evina. She had a kind of crush on me, I guess and…"

"Aye, can see why…"

"What's that?"

"Nothing," she said, smiling shyly as he analyzed her expression.

An awkward silence came, and he was at a loss for words. Looking away from her to the sea, he drifted off in thought.

*So, even she knows me as Highland Harry. I rather like that. Highland Harry—monster slayer.*

That worked for him even though it was not something that he thought would ever come about. It was not like he went looking for notoriety. He just kind of fell into it.

"Where ya gone off to, lad? Earth to Harry! Come in, Harry!" she said and giggled. "Hep me with this stinking thing, will ya?"

Snapping out of his reflection, he asked, "What do you want to do with it? Just leave it for the buzzards."

"Naw! Let's drag it over to the cliff and push it off. I want to stay here for another night, and I don't want to attract anything that might want a taste of ol' squid face. Besides, we don't have buzzards here." Giggling again, she yanked the spear from its back, taking a few entrails with it.

"It was just a figure of speech. I wasn't serious about the buzzards."

"Ya are an American, aren't ya? I've met a few Americans, before."

"Uh…yeah… that a problem? I mean, don't you like Americans?"

"Oh! I don't care what ya are as long as ya can kill monsters, and besides, yer easy on the eyes. I can deal with that."

She winked at him, and then grabbed the Thulu by its tail below the spaded tip. Levering it back, she exposed the brownish, finger-long stinger. Breaking it off below the skin, she flung it away. "Can't have that poking me," she muttered.

Harry tried to focus on helping move the beast, but he was distracted. He felt captivated by this girl, and his eyes continually strayed from his task. The prospect that they might be hanging out together excited him. Now, it was he who was infatuated, and a strange kind of warmth filled his belly.

*Was this it? Has your moment arrived? That thing you've been searching for since Sandwood Bay? Your birthday wish, come true?*

Forcing himself to focus, he grabbed the small, flightless, bat like wings on the creatures back, and folding them together for a handle, he ogled her while he waited.

"On three. One! Two! Three!" she said, and they pulled it away from the wall, leaving a large, bluish-green stain.

"Oh! Forgot something, just a moment." Letting go, she jumped out of the way, so it wouldn't fall on her. Then pulling a small knife from a sheath stuck in the top of her sneaker, she grabbed its remaining paw and sawed off a claw at the joint. It was obvious that she kept her blades keenly sharp, as the knife made short work of the thick cartilage of the beast's appendage.

"Here, hold my sgian dubh, will ya?"

"Your what?

"My black knife, silly."

He took it from her and studied it while she stashed the claw in a small leather pouch that hung at the back of her belt. The blade was about four inches long and had a single sharp edge. The lower half held serrations for sawing, and smooth, dark wood formed the grip.

"Do ya like my black knife? It's got a German steel blade and a bog oak grip. I only use it for fighting when I'm in a fix, but mostly, for cooking and cutting off trophy parts."

"Okay. Great. Maybe I should get one, huh?"

"Most certainly, lad. If yer going to be Highland Harry, ya have to have yer own sgian dubh, ya know? We'll have to keep our eyes out for one, aye?"

"Sounds like a plan," he said, handing her back her knife.

She looked him up and down before grabbing the Thulu's tail, and smiling to herself, she sighed and said, "Americans."

He took hold of the wings again and they dragged and rolled its three-hundred-pound bulk over to the cliff's edge. It was an arduous task, and he wanted to stop and argue if the benefit was worth the exertion. But that would be too much like whining, and he wasn't one for that kind of thing.

When they got close to the edge, they sat down in the grass, side by side, and bracing their feet against its back, they pushed until it slid off. They watched it fall the seven hundred or so feet to the beach below, and breaking open on impact, its viscera spilled out onto the boulders.

"Technicolor," Harry said in a whimsical manner.

"Sorry?"

"Ah nothing… just something my dad used to say whenever he blew the guts out of some monster."

Susie studied his face for a moment, and without saying anything, she turned away and walked over to pick up the creature's beach ball-sized head. Harry followed, stopping a short distance away. She then did the unexpected. Holding the beast's cranium in front of her face, she directed its dead, black eyes toward him, the tentacle-like whiskers, swinging.

"Grrrr! I'm a… what did ya call it? Oh! Grrrr! Arrrgh! I'm a Thulu," she growled out, and then lowering it below her chin, she threw back her head and laughed.

She was trying to lighten the mood, and it was working. Harry liked this crazy girl. She was funny, and her fun-loving manner, despite the situation, appealed to him.

Susie grabbed one of the Thulu head's oral appendages with both hands and slung it around in a circle several times, spattering him with a little gore, before she let go. Harry watched it sail out into space and then disappear over the cliff. Squeegeeing monster juice from his pant leg with a finger, he flicked it into the grass while giving her a look of mock disappointment.

"Oops! Sorry, lad! Probably not the kind of shower ya had in mind, aye? Okay, come, I'm going down to the water's edge to wash this stink off me and my weapons."

Harry hesitated, lost in thought.

"Come lad, let's be off," she said and chuckled.

"Oh, sorry, okay, I'm coming."

Grabbing their belongings, they followed a path along the cliff's edge that eventually turned down to the rocky shoreline. Walking together in silence, the track gradually narrowed, and even though Harry was forced to tramp along behind her, it gave him a chance to study her some more without appearing rude.

The leather armor covered her entire upper torso, stopping about two or more inches shy of her hips. There he saw an elaborate, multi colored, thistle tattoo spread out across her lower back. A 'tramp stamp' his buddy Tommy, used to call them, but Harry felt there was something more respectable in Susie's body art. She was proud of her country and of who she was.

At one point, the breeze blew the breechclout up, exposing a partially bare and rather shapely behind. Harry saw she wore the primitive garment just like the indigenous people of North America he'd studied back in the fourth grade. The soft rawhide was pulled up between her legs with equal length, front and back. Then a slender belt wrapped around it and buckled, allowing the flaps to drape, giving added coverage, fore and aft. A wide brown belt, supporting both sword and dirk, along with her trophy pouch, was wrapped over the slender strap from which her sporran hung.

He looked up to see she was watching him over her shoulder. He blushed, and she grinned. "Don't worry, lad, yer not going to see anything I don't want ya to. I've got me skimpy knickers on underneath, so all the important parts are covered."

"Okay, fine, but I wasn't looking."

"Oh… right. So ya say."

Harry could never figure out why he could go forth and fight monsters all day and yet, all it took was one girl to immobilize him with embarrassment and make him feel like a fool.

She suddenly stopped and turned, causing him to almost run into her. He slid to a stop less than a foot away. Looking up into his face, she said, "Ya are embarrassed, aye? Yer face is redder than a tomato. So, yer what… about twenty years old?"

"Ummm... nineteen. Why do you ask?"

"Well, I'm twenty… just turned. So, we are both grownups, aye? So, don't worry about all the sex stuff. We'll sort it."

"Sex stuff? But I… ummm… oh forget it."

She smirked and turned back, continuing down the path. When the trail widened again, he fell in beside her.

"So… why the breechclout?" he said, pinching a bottom corner and giving it a slight jerk.

"Why, the what?" she said and feeling the tug, grinned and answered, "Oh! Is that what ya call it? Okay, fine. Sooo… why the Black Watch tartan tights?"

"They're not tights. They're like, skinny jeans. Remember skinny jeans?"

"Aye, I remember them, but what yer wearing is for a girl."

"What? No, they fit me just fine. I found them in the men's department."

"Aye, girly men! Naw! Just kidding, don't worry. They suit ya, and besides, nobody is going to care anymore that yer wearing a horseman's truis."

"What? Oh! Good thing 'cause I like 'em! They stretch well, and they're warm. So… answer my question! Why a breechclout?"

"Ya mean… my loincloth? Breechclout! Yer a silly one, Harry of the Highlands. I used to wear a philibeg, an uhhh… small kilt? But it was chaffing me all the time. This get-up I'm wearing… it gives me more freedom of movement, and I can be quicker in battle."

"And the leather, armor thingy? Where'd you get that?"

"Oh! Do ya like it? I found it in a shop for Roman re-enactors on the A6 close to Hadrian's Wall. Down around Hexam. Ya know? Down close to the border? The tag said it's a… ummm… lorica segmentata, whatever that is. I reworked it to fit me. Isn't it a grand piece, though? It saved me a couple of times, too," she said. Twisting toward him, she pointed to some short, deep scratches at the center over her sternum.

"Good protection. I have a chain maille shirt to wear under it. I just didn't have time to put it on before mister stinky arrived. Ya might want to consider armor for yerself, ya know?"

"Yeah, you're right, kind of hard to find that stuff, though."

"Aye, well, that's a nice cotton jerkin ya got there," she said, and giggled.

"Huh? Oh, right, well, it used to be a really nice shirt until some prick ripped off one of the sleeves and splattered blood all over me. But... I don't want to talk about that."

Susie just smiled and turned her attention back to the path. When they reached their destination, they dropped their accoutrements on the narrow strip of pebble-covered shoreline, and Harry followed her out into the water on a string of large stepping-stones. About twenty feet out from shore, they came to the end and stood together on a large, flat, oblong piece of pinkish granite that protruded only a few inches above the surface.

Harry had to think twice about her decision to go out there. But he saw the water was less than hip deep. Therefore, any large creature that came near them would have to show itself long before getting close enough to attack.

Susie knelt down and cleaned her weapons. He stepped away to the far end, and removing his one slimy sword, he dipped it in the water and then wiped it dry with his shirttail. He didn't want the seawater to make contact for too long. It made cleaning easy, but it was bad for the steel.

Standing there in the salty breeze, Harry studied his reflection while he waited for Susie. His hair was now past shoulder length and had turned golden from the sun. His skin was deeply tanned and there was a light growth of hair on his face. The Lumsdale family were not hairy people, though. It would take him almost a lifetime to grow a full beard, but that was not something he really wanted.

"All finished here," Susie called out. "Shall we go up and have our breakfast? I have some dried meat and fruit."

She suddenly went quiet as she scanned the sea, and then added in a rather grave tone, "I'm starting to feel like we've been out here a wee bit too long already. Do ya feel it?"

"Yeah, shall we go?"

Their intuitive moment had come too late as the water churned a short distance away on Harry's side of the rock. His swords were out before the creatures ever broke the surface. They were the same flying fish that had come during that night out on the gillnetter; only these were much bigger. The strange buzzing of their wings filled his ears as they flew, their jaws dangerously agape.

"Susie!" he yelled, but she was way ahead of him and already on guard.

Not having time to run, Harry leaned back out of their trajectory and cut down two as they rocketed past. He kept an eye on their plummeting bodies to be sure they weren't coming back.

Three more hurtled from the water behind him. He caught the movement out of the corner of his other eye and without turning, dropped to one knee. His butterfly swords, glittering in the morning air, moved in a circular pattern. Harry took out two more of the beasts as they passed overhead from behind. The third creature had better aim, but just a foot or so short of his neck, it found itself impaled on Susie's spear tip.

"Hah! Got the wee bugger."

Still on guard, Harry turned his head to face the little monster, its jaws snapping just inches from his nose as blood dripped from where the spear had pierced its body. He came to his feet and stepped back, panting hard, his adrenalin charged body vibrating. His face became a serious mask of menace as he glared at the fish-like brute and said, "What the…"

"Almost got ya, it did."

Harry looked to where the beasties had broken the surface. He was ready for more, but when they didn't come, he felt the relief of knowing it must not have been an entire school. If it had, things could have gotten out of hand. Turning back to Susie, he said, "I've seen them before, but I don't know what they're called."

"Dreda… look worse than they really are. They can only bite once. If they miss their mark or lose their grip, they have to swim out, and race back to get up enough speed to fly again. They were probably just starting their run, when ya stood up from cleaning yer blade."

Rotating on her heels, she pulled up a back corner of the loincloth and pointed out a circle of healed puncture wounds just below a well-formed buttock. It looked like so many sixteen penny nails had been driven in and then pulled out of her flesh. She ran a finger over the scar and said, "Luckily, they're not poisonous, so… they'll make a damn fine breakfast."

With the one still skewered on her pike; she stuck the sharp metal tip through the first two he had killed. Then tipping it up, she walked away, carrying all three like a banner as she made her way back to the pebbly beach.

"Fetch those others, will ya, Harry?"

Gathering the remaining Dreda by their slimy tails, he dragged them along behind as he hopped from rock to rock. "I've still got a lot to learn about this place," he mumbled to himself. Looking toward Susie, he saw her motion with an arm for him to hurry.

"Come on, Harry, time to eat."

Harry picked up his pace.

*I hope she's brought matches because I'll be damned if I'm going to eat these things raw!*

Meeting Susie on the shore, they moved in silence back to the Keep. She found a spot along the west wall and set about making a fire. She didn't have matches, but she knew how to use a 9-volt battery and some steel wool to get the tinder started.

"Get some wood, will ya? There are plenty of old sticks about, and maybe we should get some water from that wee lochan over yonder," she said, pointing toward a small pond.

"Oh! You mean that watering hole? Can't that wait? I'm starving."

"Very well," she said without looking up from her task.

Harry dropped his two Dreda next to hers, and moved to a thicket of small, dead trees. Gathering an arm load of sticks from the ground, he returned as flames licked up through a pile of dead grass Susie had pushed together. Taking the bundle of wood from him, she set it on the ground and began to feed sticks into the fire. When there was a considerable blaze going, she turned to dressing the Dreda, and the ease in which she did it, confirmed it wasn't her first time. Making spits, she soon had the meat sizzling. The edible part of the fish was small, limited to just the breast area and the muscles that controlled the wings. There was a little more than enough for the both of them, and she was right, Harry found them incredibly tasty.

"So, where were you when the Thulu came?" he asked, as they sat lounging in the grass after their meal.

"Just over there," she said, pointing to a thicket of blackthorn set down in a large depression. The growth was extremely dense. Harry could see where she must have hacked out a small entrance hole just big enough for her to wriggle in on her belly. It was a good place to hide for the night, not too many creatures would want to brave the multitude of inch-long thorns.

"I watched ya go into the Keep, last gloaming. I'm glad I chose the thorn bushes instead. If ya had come up while I was inside, there might have been a misunderstanding, and maybe… I'd be eating alone." She raised her eyebrows, and laughing, made a, 'What do you think about that?' face.

"How do you know it wouldn't have been me that was eating alone?" Harry asked, sneering.

"Just teasing ya, lad. Don't go off on me, now."

"Fine, but I think I'm just as good as you."

"Okay, maybe ya are, and… maybe we'll spar a little later, just for the fun of it, aye?"

"Sounds like a plan, so we'll see, huh?"

"Aye, we will," she said, and sneering back, she stuck out her tongue at him and crossed her eyes. Giggling, she got to her feet and went to gathering the items they had used to make breakfast.

There was silence as Susie packed away her kit. Then digging through her bundle, Harry watched her pull out a chain maille shirt and spread it out on the grass. It gave him a start when she quickly pulled the leather armor off over her head. He anticipated a bare chest and thought to turn away, but it was too late. Susie seemed indifferent, though, and then he saw why. The flesh-colored bandeau that wrapped her chest was worn and sweat stained. Harry stopped holding his breath, and followed its expulsion with a, "Whew!"

"Fooled ya, aye? Thought I was naked, didn't ya? Bet ya were expecting to see some boobies."

"Okay, yeah, I was…"

"Hoping?"

"What? No! What do you think I am?"

"Maybe a boy—who likes girls?"

Harry practically snarled at her, "What? Uh, of course I like girls. I was pretty sure you were…"

"Hoping?"

"Quit finishing my sentences!"

"Okay, sorry. So, aye, I won't lie to ya, I was hoping that ya did… like girls, I mean," she said, widening her eyes.

Memories of that last night with Bessie rolled into Harry's head. She had been so lively, yet, tender because of his father's death. She wanted him to feel better and expressed hope that it was in her power to bring him some joy. Bessie endeavored to lift him up. It was those moments that scrolled panoramic across his mind's eye, and it felt odd because he now sat with another. He feared he would fall into reflecting too much about Bessie and would offend Susie by seeming indifferent toward her.

"Sorry for being so bold, Harry, but… have ya ever had a girlfriend?"

He pushed the mental door shut on Bessie and put his full attention on his companion. Scowling, he said, "Yes, of course. But I don't want to talk about it."

The tone of his voice alarmed him. He didn't intend on sounding mean, but it came out that way. Susie drew back, giving him a hard look. She had taken him by surprise with her question and his machismo had pushed him to be offended.

*What guy my age wouldn't have already had a bunch of girlfriends?*

He didn't want to be that way, though, and forced himself to drop his defenses. He sighed heavily and said in a less threatening tone, "She was killed, okay? Her name was Bessie, and she's gone now, so…"

Harry turned his face away as he twisted a clump of grass, eventually pulling it from the soil. Tossing it for the wind to catch, he kept his eyes off his companion and softly said, "Please… don't ask me anymore."

"Sorry," Susie said, and giving him a sad look, she picked up her armor and slid it on over the maille. When her head reappeared, she cast her eyes to the grass and appeared to be reflecting as she toyed with a small stick. Abruptly rising to her feet, she gathered the leftover parts of the Dreda and carried them over to the cliff.

After throwing them off, she remained there for a time, just gazing out toward the sea, arms crossed. Harry watched her as he sat yanking out yet more tuffs of grass. He really wanted to be with Susie, and he hoped that the exchange hadn't changed her mind about him.

Susie began to pace back and forth and ten minutes passed before she returned to him, now wiping her eyes. She gave him a solemn look, then her face suddenly brightened and she smiled. Harry could tell she was trying to rise above whatever troubled her. This inspired him to want to say or do something to show her that there were no hard feelings. He decided to return to their earlier conversation about the Thulu.

"So, the Thulu came, and…?" he said with a forced cheerfulness.

"Oh, aye," Susie exclaimed, apparently eager to continue as well.

Grinning from ear to ear, she moved closer and planted her butt in the grass, excited about the prospect of telling a story. She now faced him, and he could see her eyes were red and moist. He reminded himself that it wasn't only he who was suffering loss. Leaning forward, Susie made eye contact and started in with her story.

"I was awake and thinking about making yer acquaintance up there in the Keep. I figured I'd just yell up to ya. That's about the time mister stinky came wandering up the path from the sea. I could even smell him from yonder. What I couldn't sort was, him being out of the water so close to sunrise and how he even knew ya were up there, because… as ya may know, they can't smell a thing. The dobber moved right over to the wall and looked like he was going to crawl up. His weird little wings were sticking up and fluttering, and those snaky whiskers were waving about all over the place like he was really excited about having a new friend for breakfast. I wanted to yell up a warning, but I also wanted to sneak up behind him. So, I stayed quiet, put on my armor real quick like, strapped on my belt with my weapons, and grabbed up my pike before I crawled out and ran over here. I came around the corner of the building just as the gobshite fell; minus a paw, of course. The rest is history, as ya know."

"Yeah, I had just woken up and put on my swords when it showed up. I heard it first and…"

Harry didn't get to finish because a faraway scream floated to them on the breeze. It was a very manlike cry; rough and deep. Jumping up, he ran to the corner of the Keep and peered toward the sea. Susie, already buckling on her sword belt, was soon there with him; spear in hand.

Looking down that grassy slope, they saw a man running along the sand, his knees rising high as he sprinted. He kept glancing back over his shoulder, but whatever was chasing him still wasn't in sight. When it did show, Harry knew the odds were not in the runners favor. The crab-like spider was about the size of a car and it was speedy. Its shiny black and orange mottled skin glistened in the sunlight as it scurried along on eight legs, its scorpion like claws stretched towards its prey.

Harry locked eyes with Susie for a second, and without a word, they broke into a run, picking up speed as they moved down the slope. There was a look of fierce determination in her face, and it gave wings to his feet. The little voice in his head told him they weren't going to make it in time, but the need to try remained strong.

Just shy of the beach, Susie let loose her war cry. It inspired Harry to do the same, even though he had never used one before. He cut loose with a roar and found it exhilarating. The downside—it brought the man's face around and he changed directions to come to meet them. That act gave the arachnid the advantage. The man lost his footing in the turn and the beast leapt.

It pinned him to the ground and drove it's woodpecker like beak through his body at the shoulder blades. Harry expected to hear the man scream, but the sharp bill must have penetrated the victim's trachea, cutting off the air flow. Only a loud, pain filled growl escaped the victim's bloody lips.

Harry and Susie circled the beast in opposite directions. Harry moved to the head and took up a stance, both swords at the ready. Susie moved to its backside and prepared to drive home her spear. However, the creature shot a slimy web like substance from its spinnerets, and she had to dodge out of the way. The bulk of the sticky mass flew by, but tiny tendrils still wrapped her spear hand. She tried to brush them away, but only succeeded in gluing her fingers together. She could still hold her weapon, just in an ungainly manner.

The monster didn't want to give up its prey. Harry took a step toward it, threatening the fiend with his swords. When it raised its crab like claws, he tried to cut one off. The lightly armored limb took two hits before the pincer fell away. That didn't seem to have much effect on the creature as it snake like pedipalps slithered and weaved. Then the other claw swung his way, and Harry had to dance around it, six, large, black eyes reflecting every movement.

Harry saw Susie raise her spear to plunge it into the beast, but one of its double clawed feet stepped on hers. Losing her balance, the spear tip tilted down and merely tapped the hairy abdomen.

Pulling its beak from the man's torso with a loud sucking sound, it spun to face her. She tried to retreat but fell on her bottom. Scooching backwards, she brought the spear point up to meet its head. The spider rose up on its back four legs in preparation to skewer her with its beak. She followed it skyward with the spear tip, but the spider grabbed the shaft with its mandibles and tried to wrest it away.

Up until this point, the music and chart hadn't come, causing Harry some alarm. There was no time to determine why. Seeing Susie on the ground like that triggered his rage. This narrowed his scope to just the creature, and then the music did come. He sliced off the spinnerets with one precise swing of a blade. A greenish liquid spilled from the wound, along with some of the sticky, web-like substance.

A whistle, much like that of a boiling tea kettle, issued from the beast's mouth, followed by a staccato of hissing sounds. It released its hold on the spear shaft and rose even higher on its rear legs, its head almost twelve feet above them. Its free limbs thrashed the sky as small, half-moon shaped fins projecting in a line on its metatarsus, rattled like a pit viper. Then it came down with enough force to flatten anything that lay underneath.

Susie must have anticipated just that. Getting up on one knee, she planted the pommel of her spear in the sand and moved a keen edged tip to meet the creatures head. The weapon entered at the mouth and then blossomed out of a gill set just back of its leftmost eye, piercing the brain. The weapon arrested the brute's downward motion and it swayed left and then right like an inverted pendulum; its front legs still flailing.

Its vertical attitude had put the point where the thorax met the abdomen, just level with Harry's eyes. With all of his strength, he brought both of his swords together, cleaving the thing in two, severing the aorta. The bulbous rear portion burst like a balloon, splattering them with a fatty, yellowish substance. The upper half then pivoted on the shaft and fell sideways toward the sea, its legs twitching as one last whistling hiss escaped its skewered maw.

Harry just stood there, dripping slime, trying to catch his breath. Susie, slime covered as well, jumped to her feet and whipping out her short sword, she stomped angrily toward the beast, bellowing another war cry.

Gripping the weapon in both hands with the pommel raised high, she plunged it through a crevice in the creatures armor where the legs attached.

Wiping the rancid muck from his face, Harry gasped out, "Is that kind of like your trade mark? You always do that? Yell at them after they're dead?"

"Ah, shut it," she growled, and pulling the sword free, she kicked the creature for good measure. Then lowering her face down to its quivering bulk, she yelled, "That's what ya get for causing such a fuss, ya fannybawbag."

Sticking the sword in the ground, she took out the sgian dubh and cut off a foot. She then stood, whittling away at it, trying to free one of the Y shaped, amber colored claws. Successfully completing her task, she slipped the claw into her trophy pouch. It was too big, though, and part of it stuck out.

*Going to need a bigger pouch, Susie*

After sheathing the black knife, Susie pulled her sword from the sand and turned toward Harry. She stood and stared for a minute, her eyes raccooned by the thin layer of slime on her face. It was almost as if she didn't recognize him, then snapping out of her rage induced trance, she grinned and said, "Sorry. Ya know, screaming at them does hep. It's all that stress that's built up from almost being wiped out. Does it bother ya that I do? Too bad, ya should try it sometime."

"Uh… no, it doesn't bother me. I was just curious."

"Good, because ya are just going to have to get used to it—Harry of the Highlands. It looks like we might be together for a spell and I'm going to be doing a good deal of it, so…"

She cocked her head and gave him the big eye stare, sticking out her tongue. Then spitting, and sputtering, she exclaimed, "Och! That tastes like… ah well, ya know. I guess spider monsters aren't as tasty as Dreda, aye?"

Harry nodded, chuckled, and walked to the spider's victim. The man's skin was now turning grayish-green in color. His mouth and chin were caked with blood and his eyes, nose, and ears were still seeping crimson. The hole in his back was big enough to insert a fist. He was, clearly, beyond help.

Susie was now wiping her face with a large rag that she had pulled from her sporran. Looking at Harry, she said, "I suspect he's dead, aye?"

"Yeah, should've just kept running straight ahead. We could have caught up. Oh well, now I feel bad for yelling."

"Naw, weren't our fault. He was a goner the minute that beastie set all six of its eyes on him. He should have had a weapon and learned to use it."

Pulling her spear free of the dead monster, she wiped it and the sword with the same rag she'd used on her face. "We'll just leave them for the tide. They'll be gone before the morning. I wonder where that man came from, though. Maybe a nearby tribe, aye?"

"Yeah, probably, or just a lone-wolf. Better if he was the latter, anyway. No one would have to suffer 'cause he was killed. Hey, got another rag?"

"Aye, just one more. Going to have to wash them when we're done."

Walking to Harry, she unrolled and handed him a handkerchief sized cotton scrap. As he wiped his swords, Susie peeled rubber cement-like spider web from her fingers. Then, as if talking to no one in particular, she said, "I think I may've pished myself." Turning away, she pulled up the front of her breechclout, and examined her crotch. After careful inspection, she dropped the flap, and turning back, said, "That moment when that bampot stepped on my foot? I thought it was the end of good ol' Susie."

"Bampot?" Harry asked, sheathing his swords.

"Oh, sorry. That big hairy idiot over there," she said, pointing across the victim to the spider. Something caught her attention and walking to the dead guy, she pulled an object from his boot. Coming back to Harry, she stretched out a hand. In her palm was another sgian dubh made of what appeared to be staghorn, or bone.

"He won't be needing this anymore, Harry. Ya might as well make some use of it, aye?"

"Thanks," he said, trading her the rag for the knife.

Harry looked it over, and separating the two halves, he saw the shiny blade was of stainless steel and had been honed razor sharp.

"Not German steel, but it's fitting," she said, and reaching over, she tapped it with a fingertip and grinned at Harry.

"I'm not going to complain as long as it holds an edge. I won't use it in a fight unless I'm in a fix, otherwise, just for cooking and cutting off trophy parts," he declared gleefully.

"Och! Ya are making fun o' me," she said. Giggling, she gave him a slight shove.

"Careful now, I might cut myself."

"Careful now or… I, might cut yerself."

Laughing together at her gruff manner, he sheathed the knife, and stuck it into his boot top. Susie tossed the soiled rags over her shoulder and rubbed her hands together.

"Time for new ones, I'm thinking."

"Yeah, those were done for. Probably never get that spider smell out of them, anyway."

Harry turned and trudged back up the slope. Susie laughed loudly and scampered after him. Halfway back to the ruins, she said, "Been a long day already and it's not even half twelve by the looks of the sun."

"Yeah, killing monsters is exhausting," he joked, thinking how absurd his life had become since leaving Kilbury. "Would be nice if we could have some peace and quiet for the rest of the day, ummm... and the next, and the next."

Susie moved in close, giggled, and leaned her head against his upper arm in an affectionate manner. It was a good sign, and kind of thrilled him. But he chose to ignore her, at least until she took that same arm and pulled it across her shoulders. They made brief eye contact, and smirking at each other, they quickly looked away.

"Aye, a little peace. That would be nice, but so would a bath. Ya know the wee lochan? Ummm… the one ya called a watering hole? That'd be a lovely place to bathe. Too shallow for anything to be hiding in there—like a Thulu, or a sea spider."

Harry looked down at the top of her head. Her dark blond curls now lay plastered together in a gooey mass. "Yeah, I suppose. I mean, I would like to wash this crap off of me before it crusts up."

"Well, ya know, if we bathe, we're going to have to get naked, aye?

Looking up, he scanned the clear blue sky and smiling to himself, he patted her shoulder and said, "Well, you know, Susie, there's always the first time… aye?"

# CHAPTER 16

## He Dearly Loved The Lasses...

They strolled to the pond, exchanging highlights from the battle, trying to 'one up' each other much like members of a sports team celebrating a win. Susie kept the tip of her spear pointed level as she walked beside him, her right hand holding his to keep that arm tight across her shoulders. Harry felt her occasionally caress the back of his hand with a finger as she chatted. He believed, she, like he, desired for a new friend. Simply, just for someone to be there.

When they reached the small body of water, they separated. Harry going left around the shoreline, Susie, going right. They inspected the surface, looking for signs that it might be unsafe. They found none. When they met on the opposite side, Susie backtracked to the point where they started their examination. Harry didn't follow, and just stood watching her. She poked her spear into the water with all but the last three inches of the shaft disappearing below the surface. Pulling it out, she shouted, "Not very deep, but looks safe to me. Good for a bath, I'm thinking. Going in!"

With that, she let the spear fall to the sand, and unbuckling her belt, it followed the spear. He watched in silence as she disrobed, her shoes taking the longest amount of time because of the laces. When she got back to her feet, she stood gazing at him, dressed only in a black thong.

*Skimpy knickers... don't get no skimpier than that!*

"To it, lad! Ya going to stare at me all day?"

*I'd like too!*

She was toned, the obvious results of time spent working out and definitely lifting weights. He could have ogled her all day, but time was of the essence right now, the sun was already in the western sky.

*"To it, lad," was right! Get moving! What, are you still in the seventh grade?*

Harry hurriedly removed his clothes as Susie stepped into the water and performed a shallow dive. Swimming a short distance just under the surface, she came up for air and called out, "Come on in here, Harry, it's just right."

He hesitated as he watched her drop out of sight and then resurface spinning her thong on an index finger before launching it to the shore. "Needed some scrubbing, ya know!" Diving back in, she continued toward the center.

Harry stood naked on the shore and just before taking the plunge, he looked around out of habit, half expecting someone to suddenly appear unannounced and make fun of him.

*It's not the locker room back at Kilbury Community, you know!*

He dove down deep and soon found Susie treading water, her head just below the surface as she scrubbed the slime out of her hair. He came up from below her and lightly pinched her toe. She swam away, grinning back over her shoulder to confirm that she was game for play. But Harry didn't pursue, instead he let his weight carry him to the bottom, to stand in the silt and watch her well rounded buttocks disappear into the murk.

Susie was a good swimmer, and it seemed like forever before she popped her head up to take a breath. Harry was above average in his swimming skills, but there was no way he could out do her. Susie circled back and made a beeline for him. Harry didn't wait, and instead, launched himself upward toward some much-needed air. They surfaced together to breathe and grin at each other, their faces dripping.

"Feels good, aye?" she said as she flipped her wet hair back and combed it with splayed fingers.

Coming to him, she grasped his upper arms and treaded water. Harry felt the strength in her grip and marveled at how such a small person could be so physically powerful. After some prolonged eye contact, she said, "Race ya!" and releasing him, she orbited his body one time before taking off in the direction of her clothing. Harry pursued her, his exertions seeming more like a struggle compared to her effortless movement through the water.

He was able to catch up before they reached the shallows and when they did, they rolled together onto their backs and then sat on the silted bottom near the shore, only their heads and shoulders above the water. Harry started to speak, but Susie beat him to it, shouting, "One more

lap!" then diving back in, she zoomed away toward the middle, remaining underwater as she swam.

Harry went into a butterfly stroke as he moved across the surface. He felt himself fizzling out and was unable to catch her this time. Stopping to just float, he tracked her as she zipped by, going the other direction.

*Show off!*

Changing from the butterfly to a front crawl, he went after her. When he arrived at the shore, he found her digging around inside her sporran. Pulling out a fist sized object, she unwrapped the brown paper and holding up the contents, she hollered, "Soap!"

"Soap? You keep soap in your sporran?"

"Well… the need to wash up could come at any time."

"I guess, I just never thought about it."

"Of course not. Such a typical lad." Giggling, she moved to stand hip deep in the pond and begin to scrub her body.

"I am not typical."

"Oh, come now, ya were stinking like most lads do," she said as the suds built around her.

"Well, it's not like you weren't smelling kind of like spider guts there for a moment, yourself. Hypocrite!"

"Oh, just take this and… to it!" she said, throwing the soap at him. He sidestepped and it fell onto the sand.

"By the way, I see yer getting a wee bit excited there. Might as well wash that too while yer at it," she said, and nodding toward his growing erection, she snickered.

Harry felt the flush come up his neck and he threw his free hand over his crotch. Picking up the soap, he splashed back into the pond, stopping when the water reached his waist. Susie turned and dived in, rinsing her body free of soap. She surfaced a short distance away, waved, and hollered, "Hallo, my sweet Harry. How's things over there with ya and yer little friend?"

"I thought, YOU were my little friend?" he said and laughed loud enough to be certain that she heard.

"Well… I was hoping to be more than that."

She didn't wait for a response and disappeared again, breaking the surface about ten feet away as she rocketed up out of the water in a naked spiral. She splashed back toward him and Harry dropped under to rinse off and watch her, a little concerned that she may try to prank him. But she had swum away and was just turning back when he caught sight of her. The way she streaked through the water made him think of the mythical Selkies he had read about. He liked to think of her that way. Susie—the Selkie Warrior.

*Are you falling in love, Harry Lumsdale?*

Susie moved to within half an arm's length of him and their heads popped out of the water at the same time, their chins just at the surface. They stared into each other's eyes with only the sounds of their breathing, the whisper of the reeds, and a distant raven.

Susie allowed her legs to drift slowly up behind her and she floated on her belly, face down in the water. Kicking her feet a couple of times brought her to him and she butted his chest with the top of her head. Then rising up, she surprised him with a quick kiss on his lips before submerging again. Kicking past him toward the shore, she crawled out across the narrow strip of sand to the grass. Laying on her back, she shouted, "Going to lay here and soak up some sun. Harry, come join me."

"Be there shortly," he said and walked the water's edge back to his clothes, wondering what he was getting himself into. Returning, he dropped his stuff next to hers and remembering he'd forgotten to wash his hair, he stepped back into the pond. Half heartily rubbing at his wet hair with the soap bar, he studied Susie.

She lay, pillowing her head with her hands, eyes closed, one knee up, one leg straight. A tune was being hummed, but it was unfamiliar to him. The scene reminded him of a painting he had seen once on loan to the Museum of Fine Arts in Boston. A piece titled 'Naiad' by Henner. Susie had become a muscular version of Jean-Jacques water nymph.

For a mere three seconds, her left eye opened just a crack. Harry could tell she was looking to see if he was checking her out. She arched her back in a stretch and pushed her breasts skyward, yawning. He found his level of arousal almost unbearable and feared he just might explode. Turning away, he got serious about his hair.

When finished, he rewrapped the soap and placed it next to her sporran. Susie opened her eyes and smiled. Rolling onto her side, she patted the grass next to her. He hesitated for all of five seconds and then gave in. Stretching out on his back, he felt a little self-conscious about being fully erect. Susie just held his hand, her eyes shut, still humming.

They lay that way for some time, with Harry keeping his eyes and thoughts off of Susie. Eventually he went flaccid, relieved that the tension in his groin had subsided. When she stopped humming, he thought she had fallen asleep, but then she softly said, "Such a lovely day, I'm so glad yer here with me. I was getting so lonely for a man."

"Yeah, me too."

"Getting lonely for a man?"

"Ah jeez, give me a break."

"Sorry, I'll stop for a wee bit—but expect more later."

"Whatever."

Harry turned his head and looked at her face. Even with her hair all messed up, he liked how she looked. Bessie had always had that Grecian Goddess thing going on, a refined lady kind of look. Susie was cute in a 'pixie' sort of way. Like a full-sized fairy warrior sent forth to regulate the monster horde.

He suddenly felt nervous. *Maybe she is a better fighter than you, Harry?*

Bessie, even though quite good at her art, seemed more submissive, than not. Susie, on the other hand, was more aggressive in her manner and radiated confidence. She actually frightened him a little, and he had to be careful not to let their new-found relationship turn into some kind of a competition. That would be problematic. He was going to find himself alone again if he didn't acclimate. That brought a different kind of fear.

*You're going to get an education, Harry T. Lumsdale… and another boner, if you keep looking at her!*

Harry brought his eyes back to the sky and threw an arm over them to block the sun. Minutes passed with no more words. The urge to converse overcame him and he said, "Still awake?"

"Aye, just dozing a wee bit, why?"

"Was just wondering how you got to be in such decent shape."

"Was into body building since I was all of… maybe twelve years old."

"Free weights and stuff like that?"

"Everything, laddy, everything. There wasn't much else to do other than school, whiskey, and drugs. Then the plague came and all that ended."

"So… your fighting skills? Where did you learn those? I mean… I was a martial artist in a school of the southern style of kung fu since I was eight."

"Aye, I can see that. I think it would be best for me to say that I'm self-taught. My da had a couple Claymores. Ya know, those big broadswords? 52 inchers! We used to play around with them. He was really good and taught me a few things. But I could never get used to them. Too heavy to suit me. It was the same with the basket hilted version. So… so much for Scottish swords. This Roman short sword suits me. I have to admit, I had a book with some really good pictures on some Roman sword fighting techniques. So, I adopted, and then modified them."

She smiled at him and stroked the nearby blade of her sword with a fingertip. "I suppose if I came across somebody who actually knew how to use one of these, I would probably appear a charlatan."

"I doubt that. You looked pretty… oh, what's the word, ummm… deft! That's it. You looked fairly deft, to me."

"Daft, ya say?"

"No… deft!"

What's that mean?"

"Ummm, skillful, proficient, you know…"

"Oh, okay, I got ya. At first, I only had my dirk and the pike. Uh, my spear? It's homemade, ya know. Made it in my da's workshop. I was going to get one of those, uh… Pilum, I think they are called. The Roman javelin? But I figured this was good enough and I didn't want to have to carry two of them. I just took the sword and its scabbard from the shop. I found the display case on the floor, buried under some other shite. So, I broke it open and took it. They must have had it displayed in a box behind the counter because it was old—and real. Not one of those replicas. Not that the modern ones wouldn't work. Ya just have to put an edge on them, is all."

"So… what shop is that?"

"Oh, sorry, 'Friend Of The Wren', it's down just below the Borders. I knew of it before this mess came about. I looked it up on the Internet. Was going to drive down, but… well, ya know. Ended up walking there almost a year later. It was a long way, but I didn't have much else to do.

That's where I picked up everything except my bits… ummm… my shoes. I had them long before everything went tatties over the side, ya know?"

"Yeah, I hear you. So, maybe I should carry a spear? It would come in handy. I learned to use the long staff at the academy. So, I have a little experience. Master Bik wanted us to be familiar with all weapons."

"Master Bik? That was his name? What happened to him?"

"He died… from the Bug."

"The Bug?"

"The plague, as you say. Just the American version. I…"

"Harry, I'm getting hungry, shall we go eat?"

"Okay… sure, no problem."

He could see she wanted to change the subject and he had to agree. If they got too far into the past, they would have to dig up dark things. Harry felt they hadn't known each other long enough, and that it might be best to save the woe for later.

Susie picked up her clothes and he sat watching as she stood and pulled her thong up her legs, adjusting the slender straps for comfort. Then, after wrapping her chest, she configured the breechclout to fit properly. Her eyes strayed to him on occasion and she'd throw him a half grin each time before returning to her task. She wasn't totally focused on getting dressed and seemed to be somewhere else in her head. Somewhere in the past.

Pulling his pants to him, he slid them on, all the while wondering what Susie's story was. *Where had it all started for her?* He was going to press her later when the dark of night drove them closer. This took him back to Bessie and how they would converse in hushed tones while cuddling after sundown. A time of day when there was nothing else to do but open your heart and let the contents spill out.

Like a sponge, Harry would soak up Susie's story and then reach out to her, hoping she would accept his consolation. There was no doubt in his mind where that came from. His mother had been that way. If anyone asked what Marji had brought to him, he would have to say, "Compassion." He understood compassion; his mom had made sure of that.

"Okay, Harry, ya going to finish putting on yer clothes now, or are ya going to carry everything back? Hallo, Harry?"

"Oh yeah, I was just thinking about things. You know, Susie, you have a great body."

She came to him and looking up into his face in a bold manner; she ran a fingertip down his bare chest, "Aye, I know." Then she grinned and walked away toward the Keep. Looking back, she said in a whimsical fashion, "Come along, Harry."

He put his shirt on as he walked, carrying everything else slung over his right arm. When he came abreast of Susie, she took his free hand in hers.

"Ya don't mind that I hold yer hand, do ya?"

"It's fine. My mom always said that 'good touch' is important. It brings comfort, and… well, it always worked for me." Harry smiled at her and she did the same, the smile lingering long after she faced forward.

"My mum would never have said no such a thing. My folks were strict. Sometimes my da would show a wee bit of affection. All that really did was make me want for more. I still miss him though. So… ya really don't mind?"

He squeezed her hand briefly but said nothing. That seemed to be enough for her. A minute passed before she turned to him and said matter of factly, "It was my friends that taught me to love. Alice, and then there was, Geordie… a lad I knew. We grew up together in Conval, just north of Cairngorms National Park. We were together every day until… well, ya know."

"So, Geordie was your boyfriend?"

"No, Geordie was gay. But we were the best of friends. He never came out even though he had his hush-hush lovers in other towns. He was funny and kind. I loved him. But not the way that most people love each other. I was his out. His excuse. Everybody thought we were an item. Only Alice knew otherwise. Oh… and of course, his secret partners."

"But… you had boyfriends?"

"Aye, I always had to make it look like I broke it off with Geordie in order to hook up with Andrew, or Angus, or… the one I'd rather not talk about. It was complicated. There were times I wished Geordie would just come out, but he never found the courage. Now, it doesn't matter." A tear slid from the corner of her eye and she didn't try to wipe it away. She just sniffled and walked, her eyes forward, her head held high. Harry squeezed her hand again, and for a few seconds, a sad, but grateful smile formed her lips.

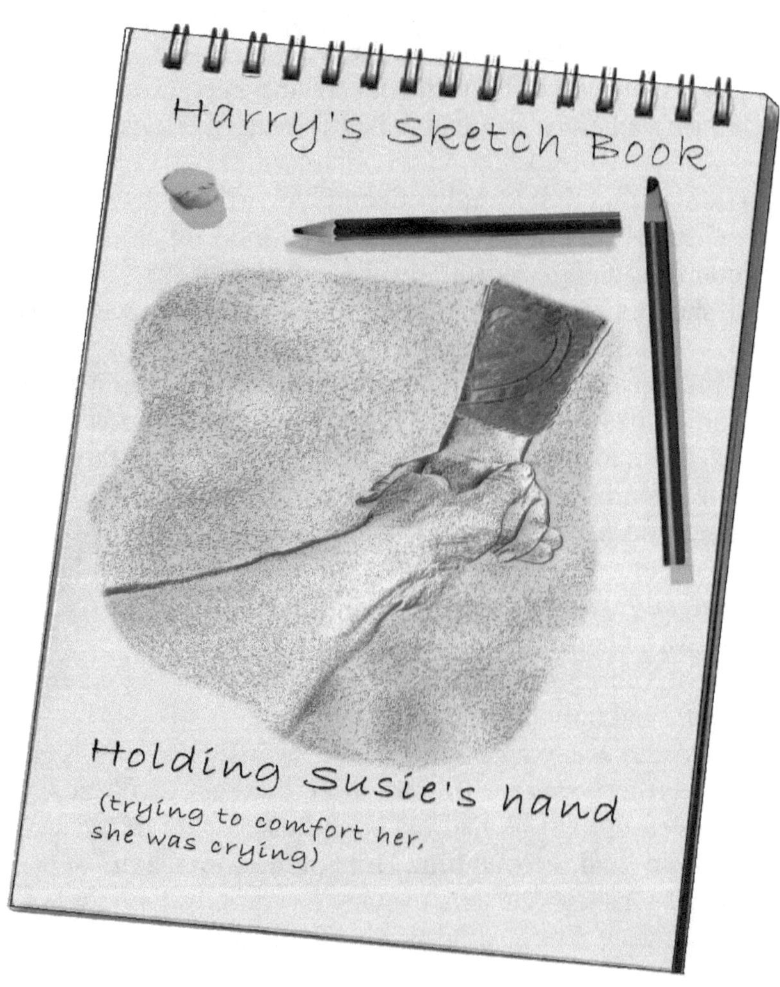

# CHAPTER 17

## Come, Let Me Take You To My Breast

Returning to the castle ruins, they sat down on the grass with their backs against the west wall of the Keep. Susie shared oatcakes and the remaining jerky. Harry shared the last of his juice. Nibbling on the remnants of roasted Dreda, he found it tasted just as good cold. They watched the sun work its way down toward the mountain peaks. It had been almost an hour since Susie had spoken, and Harry figured she just needed time to reenergize.

He couldn't have been more right about that. She suddenly turned to him and said, "We should spar! I mean… even though we had that fray this morning with that spider thing, I still want a wee work out. How's about it, lad?"

"Sure, I'm up for it. But did you want to use real weapons? That could go real bad, real quick."

"Okay, we'll use sticks."

Getting up, she unbuckled her belt and dropped it. Hurrying over to a lone, stunted oak that appeared to be on its last legs, she gathered up dead branches from the ground. Coming back with three that were about as long as she was tall, she brusquely yanked a sword from his rig.

"Hey! What the…"

"Relax, lad, I just need a measurement."

She held his sword next to a stick and marked it. Then replacing his weapon, she said, "Those are some sweet little blades ya got there, and sharp too!" She grinned, and he could see she was excited about the prospect of combat.

Cutting one stick at the mark, she then measured a second and cut it too, making it identical. Tossing them to him, she took the third, broke it down to the length of her Gladius and backed out into the open area at the top of the slope, stick in hand.

Faking the rough voice of a large man, she said, "Come lad, come get yer reward."

Going into an on-guard stance, she braced for his advance. Harry jumped to his feet and smiling, walked defiantly toward her. She stood her ground and he watched her face change. Something came into her eyes. Something dangerous.

They went to it, their sticks clacking and scraping. They soon found they had difficulty besting each other. They'd stop to catch their breath for all of five minutes and then she would want another go. One time she was able to tap the top of his head, and when she grew weary, he was able to get inside her defenses.

After an hour's worth of action, he called the match. Susie whined about having to quit, but her breath was coming in ragged gulps, a sure sign she needed to stop. He believed she would go until she dropped, and Harry found that unhealthy. She had become obsessed during the match, and there seemed to be a degree of 'crazy' involved.

When they had caught their breath, she stood with her hands on her hips, just looking at him. He stared back, and she finally smiled, saying, "My arms are terribly sore, it's good that I wear these leather cuffs or I think I'd have some bruises to show."

The waltz hadn't come, nor had things slowed down while he sparred. Harry suspected it was because, for him, it had all been for fun. He feared if the music and chart had come, she'd have more than just a few bruises. There was no need to tell her, though. Better to show remorse about having caused her pain, and then praise her prowess later.

"I'm sorry, I…"

"Oh no, lad! It's all good. I needed this. Yer really good, I mean… really, really good."

"Yeah, well, so are you, especially for not being trained. Uh… how can I say this? There's a method to your madness, so to speak. You get a little crazy, though, kind of like a berserker. You know what I mean?"

"Aye, I do. I think that's the Scot in me. A regular William Wallace, I am."

"Oh yeah, I saw that movie, too. It's an oldie."

"Aye, wasn't it just the worst? Anyway, ya want to do some stretches and maybe some push-ups and such? I always want too, after a good sparring."

"Sure, stretches are good, but nothing else, huh? I'm beat."

They spent a little time finishing up what Susie considered to be a good workout. Then moving back to their spots along the wall, they sat and drank water. She carried hers in a leather wine flask that she kept in a large cotton, flour sack. She had stuck a walnut sized stone in a lower corner and then knotted a piece of rope around the sack just above it. Then, wrapping the opening at the top of the sack with a bowline knot for easy release, Susie left enough slack so she could use it as a strap.

"I suppose I should get me one of those to put my stuff in. My bag is wearing thin at the bottom."

"Ya mean yer ruck? Aye, it's too small. My sack will hold a lot more. We should find ya a new one. I want to take ya down to the shop. I'd feel better if ya had armor. I saw that scar just above yer bum. If that sword rig had a good, thick flap that draped yer lower back, it could give ya some protection. I also want ya to have maille. Ya know, a solid link shirt? Just in the case something tries to stab ya. Do ya think ya could wear one of those and fight too?"

"Probably, if it's not too tight or bulky. We'll just have to see, won't we?"

"I have to say something. Hope ya don't mind. It's just… now that I found ya, I would be most grateful if ya didn't get rubbed out anytime soon."

Before Harry could say anything, she slid over and lay the side of her head against his upper arm. Placing a hand on his leg, she sighed loudly. There was no doubt in his mind that he wanted the same. In fact, he wanted it bad, but he wasn't as open about expressing it as she was.

"So, how far is it to this place you're talking about?"

"Why? Ya got some place else to be?"

"Uh, no, just curious."

"Okay, so the last time I went, which was also the first time, it was about two hundred kilometers, or so."

"What? That's a long way."

"Like I said, lad, ya got something better to do? Maybe ya have to study for an exam, or there's a theater play to try out for? Maybe a business meeting to get too? Maybe yer favorite show is on the telly?" She giggled and tickled him. He pretended to resist, realizing how long it had been since someone had done that.

"So, yeah, it will probably take two weeks or more, but I get to show ya Scotland!"

"And all the monsters that come with it?"

"Aye, but that'll be the unplanned part of the trip. I expect there will be a few surprises. This country is full of water, with all its lochs, and firths, and... watering holes." She giggled and continued, "Hard to go anywhere without coming across some beasty. So, what about it? Are ya afraid of a wee monster?"

"I'm afraid of nothing. I am Highland Harry," he boasted humorously to the sky.

"Hush lad! Time to get inside and settle down for the night. If ya haven't noticed, ya can't see a hand in front of yer face."

Making their way around to the door, they negotiated the broken stairway after tossing up the bags. Harry climbed as high as he could on the pile of debris and then with Susie on his shoulders, she climbed onto the upper floor. He found a good foothold and pushed himself up. She grabbed his hands and pulled while he climbed with his feet.

"Light as a feather," she said once he was secure on the platform.

"That's me, Harry The Feather. Just don't tell anyone, huh?"

They made their beds along the wall to the left of the doorway, the corner opposite from where he slept the night before. It was cozier and there were no windows over there. Harry spread the wool out to accommodate them both, and using their bags as pillows, they lay down on their backs to stare out through the hole in the ceiling on the far side of the room.

"So, tell me Harry, how did ya get to Scotland? I mean, I was born here, but America is a long ways away, so...?"

"Oh, I found the cheapest flight I could afford, and the next thing you know..."

"Ya what? Oh, now yer teasing."

"How else did you think I got here?"

"Well, I don't know, mister wise arse. Ya could have been here for the last five or six years. Maybe ya did catch the very last flight out. But ya know, I've seen many places where those big jets had slammed into the ground. Spent the night in an overhead luggage bin in the tail section of an Airbus, I think it was. Pretty snug, but lots of bones."

"Okay, stop there. Before you get into anything morbid, I'll answer your question. I came by boat. Destiny's Enchanted. You can still find her run aground up at Sandwood Bay."

Harry went on to tell her the story of his family and life in Kilbury after the Bug. He finally got to Bessie, the gillnetter, and the new strain of Thulu that had stolen her from him. He kept his talk of Destiny's Enchanted to a minimum, touching on how he had been adrift in the current for over a month. He also shared how the loneliness was the worst thing to bear after his grief had subsided, mentioning how he thought it could have easily driven him crazy out there on the ocean.

Harry soon tired of talking and Susie must have sensed it. Rolling onto her side to face him, she put an arm across his waist. He could just make out her sleepy eyes in the ambient light as they sought his. Rolling to face her, he rested a hand on her hip. He had always been respectful when it came to the opposite sex. His mother had given him 'The Talk' when he turned sixteen. It was more about understanding consent than anything else. His father was old fashioned but had a good grasp on being mannerly.

Up until this point, Susie had been the one to initiate anything sexual, but he could tell that she now waited for him. Just when he felt confident enough to make his move, she sat up quickly and he jerked his hand back in alarm, fearful he had misread her.

"Oops! Almost forgot," she said, and opening her flour sack, she pulled out what looked like a small, black vinyl shaving kit. "My medicines—aspirin and such. Bandages, suturing stuff, antibiotic salve and… birth control! Don't want no wee bairns at the moment."

Opening it up, a short stack of plastic bubble packs fell out into her hand. She didn't bother to remove the rubber band that bound them and bending back a corner of the bottom one, she popped out a pill that went straight into her mouth. Gulping it down without water, she said, "Pilfered these from the Conval apothecary. Took every last package. Each pill's good for two weeks. A wee bit early for my next dose, I reckon, but… won't hurt a thing to double up, aye?"

Harry said nothing and just smiled at her in the dim light. He thought back to when Bessie said, *'Don't worry, Harry, I got a plan…'* He supposed Susie did too. Any concern he had about taking care of a pregnant woman while on the move, evaporated away. Something he never shared with Bessie was the thought of having to deal with childbirth. It frightened him more than monsters. He believed when he came to terms with it, he'd be ready for that first child. He figured perhaps by the time he was twenty-five—if he was still alive. And, of course, still with Susie. Together, they could make some good babies.

Susie lay down in her original position. He tenderly brushed strands of hair from her eyes and ran a finger around the curve of a cheek on her cherubic face. She closed her eyes, sighed, and when she opened them, his lips found hers.

They made love for over an hour. She was aggressive. He found her to be much different than Bessie. More passionate, more experimental, and, much more curious. She wore him out. Afterwards, they lay unclothed, the light of the moon bringing a glimmer to the sheen of perspiration that coated their bodies. The evening breeze, coming through the windows, cooled them while bringing the smell of the sea. They lay quiet, and just when he thought she had drifted off, there came a, "Do ya want to get dressed, or should we sleep in our birthday suits?"

"What if monsters come, we wouldn't be dressed properly to greet them?"

"Well, ya know, the Picts fought naked. We could do the same, aye?"

"Aye," he said, and pulled his swords a little closer. Susie unsheathed her Gladius and laid it just back of her pillow. Then rolling over to face away, she pushed her back into his chest and pulled up her knees. Harry curled around her, laying his left arm across her waist. Susie gave a blissful sigh, and wrapping her arm in his, they fell into a monster free sleep.

They awoke to a cackling and fluttering. Before Harry even opened his eyes, his hands already gripped his swords. He heard Susie's blade being dragged across wood and they sat up together to scan the room.

Two gulls sat in a window, looking surprised. With unfolding wings, they fell away, squawking their discontent as they soared back toward the sea.

"Fookin' birds," Susie said and chuckled.

"Yeah, the problem is, they sound like some monsters I've known."

"But just fookin' birds, so we're good for now." Putting her sword back, she got up and began to dress.

"Um… good morning," he said as he swung his legs around so he could lean against the wall.

"Oh, sorry, good morning," she said, adjusting her breechclout. With her upper body still free from its restraints, she came to him. Straddling his thighs, she threw her arms around his neck and pressing her breasts to his chest, she kissed him.

Afterwards, she put her chin on his shoulder and held him for a moment. Then sitting back on her calves, she grinned, the sleep still in her eyes. Her hair was in wild disarray. Ignoring it, she reached out and straightened his.

"So, do you regret anything?" he asked

"What do ya mean?"

"About last night?"

"Oh, I regret not having bigger boobies."

Cupping both 'B' sized mounds of creamy flesh with her hands; she raised her eyebrows, laughed, and then got to her feet. Picking up her binder, she wrapped it around her chest. The chain maille followed, and she smoothed it out to lay flat against her skin.

Harry couldn't let it go. "What do you mean? What you got is fine. They're at least six, seven times bigger than mine. So, what's the problem?"

"Wouldn't ya rather they were bigger? Maybe like those melons ya see in the grocer's?"

"No, that doesn't matter. Not to me, anyway."

"Well, I've always been a little self-conscious, I guess, especially in school. I was the queen of the padded bra for a long time. They always made fun of me and I had to kick a wee bit of arse on occasion."

"Well, all that's in the past now, and besides, melons would just get in your way in battle. You're fine as you are."

"Yer the one who is fine, Harry of the Highlands," she said and picking up her lorica, she slid it on over the maille, still talking as her head disappeared inside.

"What was that? I can't hear you?

"Nothing, just happy yer here with me," she said as her head popped out, blonde locks bouncing. She pulled a small palm brush from her sporran and went to working on her curls. Harry stood up, dressed, and made a breakfast of stale biscuits, granola bars, and water. He wanted fruits and vegetables and had a craving for carrots.

Sitting on the edge of his woolen wrap, he crunched granola, and made plans to raid the next abandoned garden he came across.

Susie finished with her hair and came over to sit behind him. His eyes followed, questioning. She just wanted to brush his hair. He wasn't too fond of people messing with his hair, but he would allow Susie.

"Ya don't mind, do ya? I just like doing it. I'm a little excited about getting started this morning and this calms me."

"Have at it, but I could do it myself."

"Just let me, will ya?"

Harry figured he was going to have to accept her doing trivial things for him. Things to please him and seek his approval. Over time, he suspected she would abandon that as the newness of the relationship wore off. If not; so be it. He would probably do little things for her, too, making it a fair trade off. His mother had been prone to doing little things for his father and him. So, he had some idea as what to expect, as well as what he could do to express affection. His mind went back to the question he had asked himself earlier about being in love.

There existed a longing to be with Susie, but certain personal obstacles kept him from expressing what he wanted to share. That was the 'Harold Sr.' in him. Harry needed to get past that and knock down those obstacles; one by one. He would have to be proactive, as Master Bik had said. Otherwise, he would never grow as a person.

"There," she said standing up. "Now yer as pretty as me."

Patting the top of his head one time before moving over to get her food, she came and sat with her back against his side, facing the stairwell. After pulling out a bag of dried fruit, more oatcakes, and her beef jerky, she shared her food with him.

"Look, a T-Rex!" she said pointing out a window, and when he looked, she stole his last biscuit. He shook his head in mock dismay and said, "You could have just asked."

"What fun would that be?" she said, giggled, and bit into her prize.

"Want some water? Those things are hard going down."

"Ah, naw, I so badly want a cup of tea, though. We'll have to look for some next time we're scrounging. It's been so long since I've had a good cup of Oolong."

"A good cup of what?"

"Oolong. Well, it doesn't matter, anything black will do."

He just smiled, and they said no more. She seemed content just leaning up against him, gnawing away on the biscuit. He truly felt at peace for the first time in a long time. Yet he feared that it might take something away from his constant state of readiness. He worried it would soften him up in the same way Winnie had affected his father. Harold Sr. had been truly distracted, so much in fact that he had lost his edge—and then his life.

As they packed up to go, the worry stuck with Harry. Making their way south, he wondered if there was some way, he could love Susie, have a meaningful relationship, and still be a slayer of monsters. Back on the ship, there had been plenty of time to think about how he was going to spend the rest of his life. That is, if he didn't perish on board from lack of food and water—or lose his mind.

He still believed he would meet his end fighting monsters. He, his father, Winnie, and Susie, were all resolute by nature. It was something they had in common, and it seemed to drive their lives. Bessie—not so much. She believed that one day they would stop and settle down to some kind of a life similar to the American pioneers. A life where all that mattered was your children and grandchildren. Harry thought it was naïve and even told her so. But now, he was having second thoughts. Susie, and Scotland, being the reason.

The human race still bore and raised children in the Middle Ages— minus the monsters, of course. Life had been dangerous, but they didn't let that stop them. He had 250 miles in which to give it some thought and if he hadn't figured it out by the time they got to their destination, then, he just might be a hopeless case.

# CHAPTER 18

## We Wander There...

It was Susie's idea to stick to the countryside and avoid the motorway. She wouldn't elaborate as to why when Harry questioned her motive, something about other dangers besides monsters, and that was all she would say. She was a fast mover, and Harry soon learned why it was so easy for Alistair and his clan to be so elusive. There was a conditioning that Harry had yet to acquire about moving across open country. He ran better than Bessie, but he wasn't as good as Susie. Getting his second wind wasn't the problem; it was jogging on something that wasn't a track with a flat, composite surface and having to dodge obstacles in the process.

"It's all a state of mind. Ya get it in yer head to go forward, and after a few hundred miles, ya get the gist. Get my gist, lad?"

"Yeah, I get your gist. But it's freaking annoying always having to look so many yards ahead when I'm so used to looking at my feet."

"Don't be lazy, Harry! This is a good workout for ya. Once ya adapt, ya will be as good as I."

"Yeah, it's really more about you being a legend in your own mind," he said and chuckled. Susie didn't think it was funny.

"Och! Now lad, don't be that way."

"Well, I'm just saying."

"Aye, saying something that might piss me off," and picking up her pace, she moved a few yards ahead.

*Our first fight?*

He suspected there would be those. His mother and father had argued little while he was growing up. Marji had been a negotiator, and she was obviously smarter than Harold Sr. and they both knew it. They never let it be a factor between them. They had been quick to admit their errors, and trespasses were soon forgotten.

Harry felt the need to say he was sorry and hastened to catch up. But Susie had stopped and turning back to him, she faced him over the heather. When he got closer, he could see the fire in her eyes.

She drove the spear tip into the ground and leaving it, she stomped back toward him. Placing a hand flat on his chest while keeping her arm straight, she glared up into his face. Harry looked down at her, wondering what this was all about. They locked eyes and the fire that he saw there went out. It was replaced with a moist, sadness. She took her hand away and looking down at her feet, she said, "Harry… please… go with me on this. Ya'll adjust, take my word for it. Just, please…" Her eyes turned up to his upon finishing and regret roiled within him.

"Okay. I'm sorry about what I said, I was just being a…"

Susie didn't wait for the rest, and throwing her arms around him, she squeezed him tight. It was brief, and he was glad because she was making it hard to breathe. She was a force to be reckoned with, and Harry knew by this point in their relationship that Susie was no braggart. She meant what she said.

Sliding a hand up behind his neck, she forced him to lean forward and then kissed him softly on the lips. Holding her forehead against his for a few seconds with eyes closed, she sighed and then turned away without a word. Breaking into a jog, she plucked the spear from the ground as she jogged by, leaving Harry no time to stand and ponder her act.

When the ground leveled and the heather dwindled to be replaced with long grass, Susie looked back, presumably to check his progress. A grin braced her lips and she picked up her pace, forcing him to do the same. Harry knew she wanted to test him. His thoughts went back to his track & field days and his beloved 'mile'. He was going to show her what he was made of and soon pulled alongside. It didn't take long for it to become a race—the finish line—a broad line of conifers a quarter of a mile away with a vast glen beyond.

They were laughing by the time they reached the ancient fir trees. Their mirth made it difficult to catch their breath. When they stopped gasping, Susie walked away to the other side of the grove and flopped down onto the grass. "Come, Harry, sit with me." He moved to stand behind her, but before he could sit, his eyes picked up something white amongst the trees down in the valley.

"Do you see that? Looks like a building, maybe a castle."

"Aye, looks familiar as well, just can't remember who it belongs to."

"Let's go check it out. I've never been inside a castle, or at least, one that wasn't falling apart."

"Okay, if ya wish. We didn't make much progress and the day is already half over. Maybe we should just spend the night—if it's safe. Aye?"

"Aye."

They walked down the long slope and came out of the trees next to a large drum tower that punctuated a corner of the castle. They pushed through the knee-high grass that had once been a well-manicured lawn. Moving around the outside, they checked doors to see if any were unlocked. Not finding one, they turned their attention to the lowest of the windows.

There was a string of six up under the eaves of two single story wings projecting forward at right angles from the front corners of the main building. The lengthy additions formed a court yard at the front and were connected at the open-end by a wall with a high, wrought iron gate, centered, and housed within a massive stone archway.

They moved along the outside of the eastern most wing, Susie sitting on Harry's shoulders, checking windows as he walked. She finally found a sash that opened and climbing inside, called back, "I'll open a door for ya." Shutting the window, Harry heard the scraping of the locking lever and the metal sash seated tightly in its bed of rust coated steel.

He stood waiting, figuring it would take a while for her to find that door. He decided to make himself comfortable and started to remove his bookbag when she appeared around the corner at the front and waved.

"This way," she said, and led him through that big, iron gate.

"That was quick."

"Aye, well, to be completely honest, the reason it looks familiar is because I used to spend my summers here."

"So, you know these people, or… knew them?"

She just smiled over a shoulder, and not answering his question, said, "Shut and bolt the door, will ya, Harry?"

He didn't press her, figuring the mystery would be revealed soon enough. "Let's check the place out, aye?" she said after moving out of sight around a corner. Harry soon caught up as they strolled through the dim light of the rooms.

They spent the rest of the day searching the interior. There wasn't the usual stench of death and Harry figured no one had died there. The place had just been abandoned, with some rooms having been trashed as if the owners had made a hasty retreat. It was well-furnished, and the state of some of the rooms gave Harry the impression that it was still occupied.

Their search ended in the kitchen of the vaulted basement. He handed off one of his flashlights to Susie and they searched the room. She soon disappeared into what looked like a pantry. Harry strolled, slowly, just looking. Pots and pans hung from hooks, the big oblong table was still covered in a dusty table cloth, and the chairs had all been pushed in. It was almost like the owner had left on vacation, fully expecting to return.

Something crunched under foot and bringing his beam of light to the centuries old flooring, he saw it was a broken dinner plate. A small chip, surrounded by powder, was embedded in the well waxed wood, telling Harry that someone had dropped it. There was one large piece and two smaller ones lying nearby. Picking up the largest of the three, he studied it, front and back. It looked expensive.

*A family heirloom?*

A large part of a clan crest was centered on the back. Part of it was missing, but there was enough left to tell him whose it had been. The name 'GORDON' remained, painted in black on a gold banner above a blue shield with three boar's heads.

"What ya have there, Harry?"

"Part of a dinner plate. So, Susie, what did you say your last name was?"

"I didn't."

"Okay, so… I'm asking now."

"Not that it matters much. It's… Gordon. Why do ya ask?"

"Because the back of this plate says, 'Gordon'. So, you said something about spending your summers here?

"Very well, no reason to keep it a secret. This was my uncle's place. That weight room we went through coming out at the top of the stairs in the Dog Tower? That's mine."

"So, why act like you didn't know this castle?"

"Sorry, I don't have a good reason for ya. Perhaps I just wanted to leave behind who I was, or maybe… I didn't want ya to think I was some kind of a snob."

"Well, you're not that anymore. And if you were, I don't see it."

"Thanks a million for that," she said with sincerity. "I liked to think I was common folk, and then the plague came and made it easy. Sadly, at a cost. So, seems my uncle, aunt, and cousins abandon their home, locking up proper before they were off. Looks like we have the house all to ourselves for the night, and maybe for the rest of our lives. Honestly… after we get done with our business down south, I'd like to come back. There is enough canned food in that pantry to last a year and if ya don't mind, I'd like to stay a few days before we have to be off for the shop. I'm sure it's just another building in a world full of empty buildings for ya, but for me… it's home. So, I'm asking ya—please?"

Harry didn't want to shine his light in her face, but he needed to look. Raising the beam just high enough so the upper edge found her hair line, he saw the pleading look in her eyes. Walking across the room, he turned off the flashlight and embraced her, kissing her cheek. Susie pushed the side of her face to his chest, and they stood in silence, surrounded by the dark of the kitchen. Harry whispered, "No problem," and Susie punctuated it with a squeeze.

They slept in the bedroom at the top of the Drum Tower, bolting every door between them and the ground floor. Non-essential exterior doors had been barricaded on the ground floor and windows were shuttered and barred.

Harry helped Susie clean the room where they slept, freshening up the bed with clean sheets, blankets, and pillow cases found in a linen closet at the top of the stairs. For him, being in the castle was a lot like staying at a hotel whose power had gone out and had grown rather dusty.

They stayed for three nights, making love at the end of each day in a canopy bed before falling into an exhausted sleep. They worked out together, and Harry stood by, spotting Susie when she worked with the weights. She talked him into trying them, but he told her it was not something he wanted to make a habit. When Susie wanted to sit quiet, Harry left her alone and sketched, trying to improve his skill with charcoal.

"Your pretty good at drawing."

"It's just a past time. Takes my mind off things."

"You could have been one of the great artists, aye?"

"Hah! Such a funny girl."

"Well… great to me, anyway," she said, and getting up she kissed the top of his head and went out to sit in one of the two chairs they had dragged into the courtyard to watch the sunset.

The castle was just starting to feel like home to him when Susie announced on the morning of day four that it was time to go.

"You know, Susie, we could stay a couple more nights? It's just starting to get that, 'lived in' feeling."

"Naw, Harry, it's time. My mind is set on getting ya some armor. So, until that happens, I am not going to be able to get it out of my head."

"Okay, well, so much for the lap of luxury."

"Aye, but I'm itching to be off."

"So, when do we go?"

"Now's just as good a time as any."

Harry nodded in agreement and finding his bookbag, he set it on a large table in the entry hall. Susie left him for a minute and returned with two large flour sacks. "Here ya go. I'm going to replace mine with a new one. So, I brought ya one too."

Susie prepared her bag, retying the stone in the lower corner. Not having one for Harry's bag, she rummaged in drawers until she found a large, multi-colored shooter's marble and used it. With the bags properly rigged, she handed Harry his and he transferred only what he needed from his bookbag, leaving the rest.

He placed his stack of photographs on a small table next to an old hurricane lamp. The photo on the top was the one with everybody in it. His mother, father, Bessie, and Master Bik. They were all there with him doing the thing he loved best—with the people he loved the most.

That old familiar heaviness filled his chest, but the tears never welled. They may come later at a more vulnerable time, but at that particular moment, it was time to honor the dead by being the worthy person they had believed him to be. Each one of them had their own way of showing him that they thought him laudable and usually through actions rather than words. He had tried hard not to let them down.

Out of the corner of his eye he saw Susie put her inquisitive eyes on him after picking up her sack. He gave her a nervous smile.

"And so… who are they?"

"That's a story in itself. I'll tell you some chilly night when we are cozying around a roaring fire."

"Fair enough, but don't forget… or I'll have to remind ya," Susie said and chuckled.

Harry realized, leaving the photos behind, supported Susie's wish to return. He sensed that she knew, and nothing else needed to be said.

"Ready?" he asked.

"Aye," Susie said and grinned at him before unbarring the heavy front door and throwing it open.

He walked past her out into the courtyard and stopping, he turned to watch her pull a split ring with two keys on it from her sporran. A large skeleton type and a smaller, more modern, brass one. Locking the door with the larger key, she turned and shook it at him proudly.

"You have a key?"

"Aye, they kept an extra set in a dish on the table where ya put yer photos. It's mine now. The castle is mine—now."

She grinned and slapped the heavy wood of the door before walking away across the large flat pavers that made up the front garden. Stopping next to the heavy iron gate, she waited. Harry couldn't figure out why she didn't just continue out onto the cracked asphalt of the parking apron. When he passed, he threw her a questioning grin. Susie returned it, and then grabbing one of the heavy iron pickets, she slammed and locked the gate, using the smaller brass key.

"Yeah, I've got a second key. So… I'm also the gate keeper!" she sang out after finishing her task. Breaking into a jog, she slapped him on the butt before moving away across the car park to the narrow lane that wound its way through the trees.

"Ouch! You…" he said, and chasing after her, he caught up where the road made a sharp left turn. Instead of following it, they trotted straight out across the grass and leaving the castle grounds, they were soon loping together across the valley with the sun just hours short of its highest point in the sky.

***

For two nights straight, they slept out under the stars, either atop tall boulders that required some special maneuvering to gain their flat tops, or on the craggy side of some 'Ben' as Susie called it.

She hunted almost constantly, catching, and cooking some kind of a gamecock, or maybe, a partridge, that they found quite prolific in the heather. She'd silently crawl on her belly and swiftly skewer the bird with her spear before it could rise even three feet into the air.

Then there were assorted animals, like hares, and squirrels in the woodlands, but they were harder to catch. Harry didn't like them as much as he did the bird, but any kind of fresh meat was better than jerky; especially when cooked by Susie.

One time she had cornered several hedgehogs and was preparing to kill them, saying they tasted fairly good and could keep away the hunger pangs until they caught something bigger. Harry stopped her, saying he didn't have the heart to let her bring about their demise. She resisted, but then gave in for his sake, being sure to mention that he and she needed to eat and it had to be whatever they could find. They agreed to take hedgehogs off the menu—but only them.

Susie also had a knack for finding springs to drink from and carried a tiny bag of iodine tablets to purify any water they collected. She used them sparingly and only after filtering any suspect water through what looked like silk rags cut from pajamas. Occasionally she would gather small mushrooms and assorted plants such as wood sorrel, samphire, and something she called scurvy plant that tasted a lot like horseradish. Harry didn't like it much, but she insisted it was good for them and she would make it part of every meal.

Harry's new companion was a regular outdoors person and she never made a fuss. He realized he was just a scavenger and had a lot to learn. Deep down, he knew there would come a day when there would be no more looting, as the stock on the shelves dwindled in the abandoned shops they visited. Their food would have to come from the earth, and much to his delight, Susie took to raiding the overgrown gardens that usually came along with any cottage that looked good enough to pilfer. Harry finally got those carrots he'd been craving.

Susie insisted on remaining clear of large towns and cities, telling him that her proper place was on the plains and in the hills. Harry couldn't have agreed more. "I'm a highland lass, born and bred," she said, and reiterated on how it was the only place she felt at home. Once, she confessed she might go into the city if she needed to, but it would have to be a pressing matter.

That prompted Harry to tell her the story of the butcher knife killer and how it had affected him emotionally. It bolstered her concern of places like that, and she told him so. Susie too had no desire to kill humans, but she agreed that it might be necessary—someday. Soon after the discussion, in a moment of silence, she expressed right out of the blue that she sensed 'someday' wasn't too far off.

"No man dare put a hand on me. Least not without my okaying it afore."

That said, she whipped out her sword and went to cutting and chopping through the empty air in front of her. Then she adopted a whimsical stance and pointing to the ground, she said to an invisible foe, "Oh! Sorry mister, but would that be yer hand laying there in the dirt?" Sheathing her sword, she winked at Harry and they continued with their jog into the setting sun.

As they moved farther south, Harry noticed it grew blacker at night. Susie got noticeably more nervous at the prospect of sleeping outdoors since the dark was the bailiwick of the monster, and now there seemed to be more of it. They studied his map so that their daily jog would put them close to smaller villages at sundown, increasing their chances of finding a more fortified accommodation. However, four out of every five abodes revealed its hidden dead upon inspection. It was difficult to find a place that didn't reek of putrid decomposition. So, they searched for suitable outbuildings instead, spending only enough time in the main house to pillage the pantries of the deceased.

****

It was at a place signed 'Loch Glow' that they stopped to rest from a steady jog that had lasted all morning. Harry was getting good at it now. He had learned to dodge plants, rocks, and other such things on the run. He regained his, so called, 'second wind' that he had trained for in his track & field days. Susie and he now ran side by side, dodging obstacles in unison.

On one particular day, the noonday sun found them straddling the top of a smooth, concrete wall, facing each other. It matched another one across the wide stretch of sluiceway that served the loch. The wall was twice Harry's height at the 'high end' against the embankment, and it sloped for a great distance at a slight angle down into the water. The top was just wide enough to bring them to 'bow-leggedness' if they stayed too long, and Harry thought to turn and stretch out along its top. But that would mean putting his back to Susie to face down the sloping surface.

He wanted to talk and that meant being able to see her eyes. So, he would have to count on her to watch his back in the case some fiend should emerge from the loch as they chatted.

Two days before, they had been presented with a steady downfall of rain that finally sent them into shelter. Harry thought they'd never dry out. This was followed by a painstaking walk through a heavy mist. They finally gave up and took temporary residence in a small barn full of hay. They made love for the remainder of the day up under the roof and then burrowed into the dry fodder to sleep. They were happy upon waking to find that the sun shined again.

The wide concrete trough of the sluiceway had trapped about a knee-high amount of surprisingly clear water, and after careful scrutiny, Susie said, "That water looks clean enough to bathe in. Harry, I think I'm going to have me a bath."

They had placed themselves about two thirds of the way down the slope of the wall. So, Susie could easily drop in without hurting herself. But Harry would have to help her out when she wanted back up. It was either that or walk all the way down to where the wall dwindled away to nothing beneath the surface of the loch.

Removing her fingerless gloves, she went to work untying the double knots in her sneaker laces. She stopped mid process and said, "I sometimes wish I had a bow and arrow. It'd be so much easier for me to hunt. But I don't want the extra weight of it. I almost took a crossbow from the shop. But it was too heavy. I couldn't imagine lugging it around all day. Also, if I carried a bow and a quiver full of arrows, what would I do with my pike?"

"Right out of the blue, you want to talk about bows and arrows? What brought that on?"

"I don't know. Must be an easier way to kill gamecock than crawling around on my hands and knees."

"I met a woman, a monster hunter called Winnie. She carried one of those compound bows. She lived alone with her dog by a beach in Massachusetts. My dad and her had a one-night stand."

"Was she good? I mean… with the bow," she said and giggled.

"I don't know, never saw her use it. She just threatened us when we first showed up at her place. Never shot at us, though, or I suspect one of us would have been dead. She also carried a samurai sword. A Katana. I did see her use that. She was pretty slick."

"I'd be afraid I'd break it," Susie said and taking out her short sword, she fingered the blade, checking its sharpness. Laying it and the spear behind her, she added, "I want a good sharp, wide blade. I think the Romans knew what they were doing when they came up with this sword."

"I hear you on that. But I wouldn't give up my butterfly swords for nothing."

Taking one out, he looked it over like it was the first time. Susie reached out to take it, and he begrudgingly gave it to her with a mock scowl. She checked out the workmanship and then swiping at the air, she laughed and said, "Aye, that's certainly light and easy to use and its almost as long as mine. But I'd want more reach."

"They are for close in fighting; you have to whittle your way inside your opponent. Wing Chun is a scientific art, you know."

"Aye, I see, and if ya don't know it, these swords would be useless. I prefer the 'jump in and slash the shite out of em' kind of approach."

"Yes, I've seen that, and as muscle bound as you are, you could probably chop your way through steel."

Harry chuckled and raised his eyebrows at her, waiting for a response. She sat for a second as if unsure how to react. He broke out in laughter at her expression, and she let go with a guffaw that told him she accepted his teasing. Handing him back his sword, she said, "I'm not muscle bound, ya numpty boy, I'm just… toned!"

Leaning slightly left, she patted the heavy muscle of her thigh and grinned. The smile dissolved away as her eyes strayed past him to the loch and grew large. Drawing a deep breath, her hand scrabbled for her sword hilt.

"Harry," she said soberly, and getting to her feet, "Rise up, lad, we've got company."

Harry sprang up and with one sword already in hand, the second one hissed from its sheath even before he found his feet. Turning, he stared down the incline into the face of something that looked hungry.

He had once seen a picture of the American Horned Toad on a poster back in the biology room at Kilbury high. His schoolmates and him, standing around its likeness, had jokingly referred to it as, 'The Horny Toad'.

Now, what looked to be a mature pig sized version of that creature, studied them from the water. It opened its mouth and hissed, displaying a triple row of obsidian fangs, top and bottom. It then did a thing between a croak and a growl, its body quivering violently, sending ripples out over the water.

Almost immediately, nine just as ugly faces broke the surface, forming a 'V' behind their leader. A skunk-like odor filled the air, and

Harry saw yellow clouds forming in the water around where one would normally find the creature's tails.

"And wouldn't ya know it… they fart," Susie said cynically as she backed up the concrete cap.

"Just stay on the wall, Susie, their legs are too short to jump. They'll have to come up one at a time."

"And what are ya going to do with those wee swords, then? Fight them on yer knees?"

"If I have to…"

"No, lad, take my pike."

"I'd better stick to…"

"No! Take it! Ya said ya learned the long staff, so show me… and them, what ya know. I'll back ya with my sword."

Reluctantly, he sheathed his weapons, and snatching the spear from her hand, they retreated up the wall together. Suddenly the world swirled around, and Harry found himself facing a different kind of fear. It was the same feeling from the lighthouse back at Little Harbor. Harry tried to steady himself but nearly fell to the concrete floor of the sluice. Susie grabbed his belt from behind to steady him.

"Ya okay, Harry? Lower yer center, lad. They're almost here. Harry? Do ya hear me?"

He didn't answer, but he did as she said. Bending his knees, he gulped and tried to focus on the forthcoming onslaught, the fear of those black, shiny teeth piercing his flesh, overrode the dread of falling.

Harry drove the spear into the mouth of the first and out the back of its head. He couldn't pull it free, though, and struggled. His eyes were tearing up from the gas the beasts were emitting, and his nose started to run, making his vertigo worse. He heard Susie snort and sneeze.

"Oh, shite, Harry, my eyes are burning, I can hardly see 'em."

Using the edge of the wall, he scraped the first one free of the spear shaft and it fell with a splash into the sluice trough.

"I've gone as far as I can, Harry, I'm up against the backwall. Let's try to work our way down, one beastie at a time."

Harry barely heard her as he impaled the second monster that had made the same mistake as the first. Using the dead monster's body like a broom, he swept the third one off into the trough, the fourth one to follow. Number five moved up, but the sixth one in line boldly jumped on top of it and came straight up its back, an amber, gelatinous liquid spilling from its anus and coating its cousin from tail to nose.

The weight of the creature impaled on the spear, nearly pulled the shaft from Harry's hands and he struggled to remove the body. The tip of Susie's sword shot past him, spearing number six in its eye, forcing it off the back of the other.

Harry watched it fall off into the non-sluice side and wedge head first in a crevice between two large rocks. Its legs flailed weakly and more sickly yellow fluid seeped from under its tail.

Scraping number two loose, Harry skewered number five and then slung it away into the grass. The two slayers then moved down the cap and coming closer to solid ground, Harry felt his vertigo wane. They stopped their advance down the wall, surveying the rest of the creatures that now seemed reluctant to approach. The beasts just swam about, hissing, and shrieking. Finally, one moved around to join the two in the sluice trough.

They began to hop on their back legs, their front claws scraping up and down the algae covered wall. They snapped their jaws and shrieked like little demons, causing Harry to shudder. Two of the remaining beasts joined the other three. The last one, still in the loch, began its crawl up the cap toward them.

Harry and Susie soon found themselves perched above a mob of monsters; the air filled with their raucous noise. One of the larger ones in the sluice trough jumped high enough to hook an orange-colored talon through the toe of Harry's moccasin. Falling back, it pulled him with it.

"Harry!" Susie shouted, trying to grab him; the creature atop the wall, edging ever closer.

Slipping from her grip, Harry landed feet first on his aggressor's belly as it struggled to right itself beneath the surface of the now murky water. Driving the point of the spear through its throat, Harry felt the tip impact the concrete underneath. The other creatures in the sluice swam toward him as he struggled to pull his weapon free.

Susie battled the one left behind on the wall, the sound of her sword clacking on the creature's armor as she tried to cleave off its head. There came a loud croaking shriek, and through watery eyes, Harry saw Susie draw her blade back from what must have been a straight thrust into her adversary's mouth. The severely wounded beast rolled off the wall and landed on the closest toad in the sluice, submerging them both. Susie followed it down with a battle cry, and when the other monster had recovered from being walloped by its mate and was able to resurface, Susie challenged it.

That left three still coming for Harry. One of the monsters leapt from the water, spiraled through the air like a giant football, and attempted to clamp Harry's thigh in its jaws. He jumped off the other lizard and swinging the spear's shaft up underneath the attacker's belly, he flung it away, causing it to splash into the water far off to his right. It came back for more and Harry's spear point disappeared inside the beast's mouth, only to reappear out its odoriferous posterior. Putting a foot against its nose, he pushed it off and it floated away in a muddy, yellow cloud, its death throes sending ripples across water no longer fit for bathing.

Harry turned to find Susie had vanquished the one she had confronted and was now battling the next. The last of the ten came for him with a growling shriek. Rising up on its back legs, Harry pushed the spear through its soft underbelly and pulling it free, stabbed the beast one more time for good measure. When it collapsed, he turned to find Susie stood with a two-handed grip on the hilt of her sword; the pig sized creature dangling from the blade. He could see her arms quivered, reminding him of weightlifters he'd seen at the gym when they held the barbells a little too long. Then, as quick as lightning, she jerked the blade from its mouth, and the beast fell with a splash. Turning her face to him, she said flatly, "Let's be off, lad, before the relatives show up."

Harry stopped panting long enough to say, "Right behind you."

They moved to the wall, and leaning the spear against the concrete, he boosted Susie up so she could gain the top. She returned the favor by grabbing his wrists and lifting him up while he climbed using only his feet. Pulling up the spear and grabbing their sacks, they ran up the incline to the back wall, where they repeated their climbing method. They soon found themselves on the narrow dirt lane that served as an access road.

"Can ya believe it? Farting monsters! Never thought I'd see the day!"

"Yeah, but they weren't really farting, it was more like spraying… kind of like skunks do."

"Don't ruin it for me, Harry. Farting is funnier than spraying. I'd like to look at it in a humorous light, if ya don't mind. Helps me cope with the fact that they could have chewed my legs off with those fookin' teeth. Ya seen 'em, right?"

"Yeah, point made. Anyway, we're going to have to wash our clothes."

"Aye, agreed. I don't want to have to sleep in this stink."

They moved off the narrow lane and sat down in the grass. Bringing one of her feet as close as possible to her face, Susie gave it a sniff and said, "Going to have to wash my shoes. I think they farted all over 'em."

"Yeah, my flour sack as well, and look what they did to my moc." Harry fingered the small hole at the tip and added, "Missed my foot, but still hurt like hell. Felt like the little bastard pulled my toe out of whack."

Untying and pulling off the boot, he examined his foot. "Looks okay, though. No broken skin. Probably going to have a good-sized bruise."

"Well, I'm guessing we can be happy it wasn't worse. Och! I'm reeking!"

"Okay, but I hardly noticed," he said and laughed.

She rolled her eyes and lay back in the grass. "Going to have to get ya a pike, Harry. That's all there is to it. It'll do ya good when the wee ones come to chew off yer feet. Ya did a brilliant job, though. I could tell ya trained a good deal with a staff. We'll see if we can get ya one like mine, or… I could always grab that lovely Pilum I saw at the shop the last time I was there. Then, I'll let ya have this one, okay?"

"Sounds like a plan."

"Harry, bath time, let's get to it. Fookin', farting lizards… who'd a thought?"

After allowing the effects of the adrenaline to dissipate and their breathing returned to normal, they moved into a copse of trees. Finding a hip-deep stream, they bathed with clothes on, soaping everything with what remained of Susie's bar of soap.

Sitting with their backs against the trunks of the trees, they cleaned Susie's weapons. She kept looking at Harry like she had a question but didn't know how to ask. At one point she drew a breath as if to speak but expelled it and went back to working on the spear tip with her honing stone.

"What is it?"

"What?"

"What do you want to ask me?"

"I don't want to ask anything."

"Liar."

"Ah! Now lad, don't start…"

"Well, then stop with the hesitation and just ask it."

"OKAY, FINE! So… so what was that all about back there? Ya kind of froze up when we got higher on that wall?"

"Oh! Is that it? I don't know, maybe… maybe I'm afraid of heights. You know… what do they call it? Like, ummm… vertigo?"

"Acrophobia."

"What? How do you know that?"

"I read."

"Yeah, but I read, and I don't know that."

"Well, do ya remember the Internet?"

"Yeah, of course, but…"

"Did ya feel like ya were going to panic?"

"Yeah, my head started swimming, you know what I mean? I got dizzy and it was like I was more afraid of falling than of the monsters. Happened one time back in America, but never happened before. I don't know…"

"I have Coulrophobia."

"So, I suppose, the internet again? What is that? A fear of cauliflower?"

"Och! No silly! It's the fear of clowns."

"What? Are you kidding?"

"No, I'm just afeart of them. But I guess I won't have to worry about that anymore, aye? Unlike you, who still have to worry about falling, or being pushed off something high up… for calling me a liar."

Harry gave her a wide-eyed stare and she laughed. Dropping everything, she moved over to him and forced him to lay back in the grass. She kissed him hard and wrapped her arms around him. Then, in a meditative moment, they lay together in the shade of the pines.

"I'm shattered, I need a nap," Susie said.

"Okay, but first let's move out into the sun, so our clothes can dry. I hate wearing wet clothes."

"That's fine, but it was yer idea to wear them wet."

"Yeah, well, we don't know if we might have to make a run for it. I don't want to be naked if I do."

"Well, ya know… the Picts…"

"I know! I know! How many times are you going to tell me?"

Laughing, Susie grabbed her gear, and left the shade. Harry followed and they stretched out in the sun-drenched grass on their backs. She rolled to him and lay on her stomach to shade her eyes. Harry remained on his back and just threw an arm across his face. A few minutes passed before he said just loud enough for her to hear, "Clowns."

Susie giggled and whispered, "Picts." They both chuckled.

She then stretched an arm across Harry's chest, and he lay a hand on her arm, offering some assurance that he wasn't going anywhere. It didn't take them long to fall asleep, the unseen vapor rising from their clothes as the sun, at its zenith, worked its magic.

# CHAPTER 19

## You're Not But Senseless Asses...

It took Harry and Susie another week to reach their destination. At one point they stopped to rest and take in the lay of the land before making their way through. A motor noise rode the breeze from the southeast and they stared in bewilderment at each other.

"You hear it too, right?"

"Aye, I do."

"Saw a kid riding a motorcycle a while back. Wouldn't stop and talk. I guess I scared him. But what I'm hearing now sounds like a car, or maybe, a truck."

"Must be some kind of a fool," was all she said. The fleeting look of fear on her face hadn't gone unnoticed.

"What's wrong? You looked scared."

"Ah, naw," she said and putting a look of indifference on her face, she got to her feet and strolled away. "Come on, Harry, got to find a place to sleep." He didn't want to pressure her, so he just followed through the heather and let his thoughts turn to other things.

Evidence of monsters had dwindled to nearly nothing after they crossed the A27 south of Edinburgh, and their concern turned more to the weather. One evening they found shelter in a small cave just up the side of a craggy bluff that was the east wall of a shallow ravine.

A raging thunderstorm formed in the night and they woke to water rushing by just an arm's length below the lower lip of the cavern opening. They thought to flee, but their decision to wait it out had been the right one, even if the wind had blown so powerfully across the mouth of their rock shelter that it seemed to suck out all the air.

The noise had been deafening and Harry thought of freight trains. Moving back into a corner they sat behind a fat, head high stone, embedded in the floor. Bracing their feet against it, they pushed their backs against the wall and settled in.

The lightning flashed constantly and peeking out from behind their limestone barrier, they watched with fear and amazement as the lightning revealed the tail of a tornado jumping over the ravine and moving away across the plain. A portion of its debris cloud swirled in around them, forcing them to drape Harry's tartan wrap over their heads like a tent. The rain blew in, leaving not a dry spot within their grotto, except for the very place where they sat. Fortunately, their stone shield reflected most of it away and because the floor sloped toward the opening, the water drained out.

Hours later, the storm moved on, taking their fear with it. They slept sitting up, heads together inside their tartan tent. In the morning, the sun showed its dazzling face, but for the lack of dry kindling, breakfast was eaten cold.

Dropping from the cave into knee deep water they moved across and up the other side. Continuing on their way, they jogged south, the sun slowly dissolving the ground mist. It was when they stumbled upon a paved road marked B6318 that Harry started to feel like something had changed.

The countryside was gradually flattening, and more buildings dotted the landscape. The mountains and glens were behind them now. Susie trotted east down the middle of the road, and Harry followed a short distance behind.

"How far?" he yelled, as she slowed to trudge up a hill. Stopping at the top, she grinned back and said, "We've arrived."

Harry moved to stand beside her as she pointed down the slope. On the left side of the highway, there was a cluster of ancient stone buildings. Beyond them, on the right, a modern building of one-story design. A sign ran the full length of the roof's ridge, projecting vertically about three feet into the air. It was unreadable from where they stood.

"That's it there, the long one on the right. Let's go, lad, I'm too excited to be just standing here!"

She took off at her usual pace and he soon closed on her, saying, "You know, Susie, this doesn't feel like Scotland anymore."

"That's because it's England," she said. "Are ya missing the Highlands, Harry?"

"Well…"

"I am too. Let's be quick about this and get back to where we belong."

"It's getting late, we should be thinking about finding a place to hole up."

"That's such an amusing phrase yer always using, 'hole up'. Like we're animals or something."

"It's a cowboy thing, I guess. Got it from a movie. You know, like, *Let's head for our hole in the wall.*"

"Aye, I think I saw that one," she said, and slapping him playfully on the butt, she laughed and took the lead. They passed a roadside marker that told them the cluster of buildings on the left had once been an old Roman fort.

Arriving at the shop, Harry could now read the sign on the roof. It was made up of white painted plywood panels with a classic Romanesque border that read: Lawrence's FRIEND OF THE WREN, and underneath, in smaller letters, "For all your re-enactment needs!" In the upper corner, a gold eagle standard had been painted with its wings encircling, 'An MCO Sponsored Outlet'

Someone had taken the time to cover the windows. Yet, one old, graying sheet of particle board had a corner broken off, showing a man-sized hole minus glass. Harry and Susie stepped onto the long, narrow asphalt strip used for angle parking, and he stopped to study the building while she walked to the far end and peaked around the corner.

"So, this is the place, huh?"

"Aye," she yelled.

"Someone broke off the corner of that sheet of particle board."

"Aye, that was me. The last time. Be right back with ya," she hollered, and disappeared into the undergrowth.

Harry turned toward the old stone buildings behind him. Only a few were intact. One of them was two stories high and appeared to have been a garrison, or something of that nature. The others were just linear lines of stones forming geometric patterns projecting just inches above the knee-high grass. There was a large, Bastle style house up on a hill, surrounded by huge pines at the back of the property.

Harry could tell the fort had once been a tourist attraction and the house had probably served as an office/residence for the caretaker.

*Probably, Lawrence himself. A guy needs to make a buck, I guess.*

Harry suddenly got that creepy feeling like he was being watched. Squinting hard at the open holes that served as windows for the barracks, he checked for movement. There wasn't a trace of anything living other than some ravens, and a hare poking along the foundation, munching grass. Harry figured he must be getting paranoid and blew it off as something that came with his choice of lifestyles.

Susie broke from the shrubs where she had gone in, and it startled him. She cursed under her breath as she walked his way. Her thighs showed light scratches from the shrubbery, and she plucked leaves and small sticks from her hair as she came.

"Back doors sealed, so we'll have to use the window to get in. Don't much like not having a second exit, but I suppose we can kick the back door open from the inside if we have too. A well-placed kung fu kick should do the trick," she said, winking at him. "Oh! And just so ya know, there is an old stone cistern back there. So, if ya were thinking we could spend the night inside, think again. Maybe we should check out that big house up on the hill, aye?"

"Well, maybe we should just... get to it? As you are so fond of saying."

"Aye, can I have that flashlight back?"

"Sure," he said, and handing it to her, he added, "Just keep it. My gift to you."

"Oh, thank ya, kind sir, yer so..." she said and grinned, leaving him to finish her sentence however he wanted. She walked to the opening and he followed, shaking his head and muttering, "Whatever."

They both shined their lights on the big mess inside. Harry figured Lawrence must have had a big following of customers, considering the amount of goods in the store. He most likely had purchased four of everything used in Roman soldier reenacting and had found himself in a position of being overstocked about the time society fell apart. The place had obviously been ransacked numerous times. Only one rack of shelves stood upright at the center of the room, the rest had been pulled over, spilling their contents to create a massive pool of merchandise.

*Just like the shoe shop, but, hopefully, minus any dead girls.*

They tried to enter at the same time and found the opening too small to accommodate them both. They wrestled playfully to see who would be the first one in. Susie forced Harry aside and squeezed through the hole, squeaking out in falsetto, "My shop."

Harry leaned in and grabbed her sword belt to pull her back and said with a mock growl, "No, my shop!" Susie didn't relinquish and losing his balance, Harry somersaulted inside to fall onto a pile of brightly colored Roman battle shields made of foam.

"What the hell are these?"

"What's that, lad?" Susie's voice echoed as she ploughed through the pile of small boxes and blister packs on her way across the room.

"These things that look like shields… how does that work?"

"That foam made Scutum I believe yer referring to? The ones ya fell on? Oh, don't pay no attention to those. That's for a different kind of warrior."

"What do you mean?"

"I mean, the type that likes to play fight. Pretenders. Re-enactors, so to speak. Now, forget about them and come over here, I found the real article."

He did as she asked, shining his light around as he ploughed through plastic swords, helmets, and molded, plastic body armor made to look like metal.

*Halloween costumes!*

Harry found Susie at the south wall of the store, standing behind a glass fronted counter that ran the full length of the building. It was broken by two 'walk-through's' that granted access to a WC at their end, and a door labeled, 'Housekeeper' at the other. The lengthy, waist high cabinet then took an abrupt left turn about five feet short of the east wall and terminated by the front door. The early twentieth century cash register still remained, its drawer hanging open and '$26.55' still displayed on gold trimmed metal tabs in the 'Total' window.

At Susie's back, the wall was punctuated by racks that had once held shafted weapons like, Pilums, Halberds, and Tridents. The pile of goods where she stood was just as deep as the display floor. Most of the weapons had been pulled from the racks and the display shelves had been emptied. Susie bent down and rummaged around for a few minutes. When she stood up, she held a larger, lighter colored version of her lorica segmentata.

"Look what I found," she said, grinning like she had discovered treasure. She tossed it at him, but he failed to catch it. Picking it up, he looked it over. From the tag, he saw it just might fit.

"I think it's the right size. It's the only one though. The rest of these back here look like they were made for giants."

"It'll do, I like the color. British Tan, I think it is?"

"Aye, much lighter in color than my own, and it's shiny!"

Rummaging some more, she brought up brown leather wrist cuffs bound together with a white cotton string that sported a price tag. "What about these, uh… vambraces, want 'em?"

Shining his light on them, Harry said, "Ummm… no, they'd interfere with the flex of my wrists. Those are for long, heavy swords, anyway."

Susie dropped them, huffed in mock despair, and moved down toward the other end, her flashlight beam flitting about. She stopped and dropped out of sight. Harry heard her grunting, then a large chrome, display rack suddenly rose into view as she brought it upright from where it had fallen.

Different chain maille shirts still hung from the hooks and she sorted through them, her flashlight now clamped in her lips. Not finding what she was looking for, she leaned the rack against the wall and disappeared again. There came the skitter of metal links on other metal links, and Harry asked, "What are you doing? What are you looking for?"

"Chain maille," she said with aggravation, and straightening up, she displayed a metal shirt for him to see. With raised eyebrows showing in the beam of his light, she said, "This fell off its hook, but I think it will do ya."

"You know… I think this lorica will be enough. It will cover all of my front, back, and sides. It has a few more segments at the bottom than yours does. So, my stomach will be protected, unlike yours, where you'll need that chain maille. I'll just have to figure a way to attach my swords to it."

Susie scowled, and looking down, she made a show of examining the little white price tag. "It says it's a large. That would probably fit ya. But it's going to cost ya yer entire bank account. Let's see here… that would be 450 pounds, kind sir?"

She giggled, and holding it higher, she waved it back and forth to flag his attention.

"What? 450 pounds! That's a fortune! Okay, just joking. Bring it if you want. If it doesn't work, I'll just toss it. You're going to have to pay for it though, I'm all out of cash," he said, and laughed.

"Bring it? No, ya can take it, I've got something else I want a get a hold on."

Slinging it at him, it spun through the air and wrapped itself around the arm he'd thrown up to protect his face. One of the sleeves smacked him in the back of his head. He threw her a look of annoyance. Susie just chuckled and continued away, but then Harry heard a muffled, "Sorry," and when he looked at her, she beamed halfheartedly, shrugged, and then dropped her face as if ashamed. When she looked up, Harry shrugged back and gave her a forgiving smile. She sighed loudly and moved on, plowing merchandise as she went.

Eventually she stopped next to a shoulder high, cardboard display unit that someone had propped up against the back wall. Leaning toward it, she read the header aloud, "Latex and paints for creating realistic looking wounds!" She turned and gave Harry a look that said she thought it ridiculous. "What about it, Harry, want some fake blood? Howz about a big bag of rubber intestines?"

"No thanks, I get enough of the real stuff as it is."

Susie gave him a mischievous look and smiled too big for her not to be up to something. Harry, presuming she wanted to seek redemption for smacking him with the chain maille, prepared for some kind of humorous performance that would make him laugh. But all she did was push the display out of her way to expose a long, red, glass fronted box fixed to the wall. She shined her light inside, and he saw it was the Pilum she had been so hot for.

Harry moved to where she stood, and leaning over the counter, he shined his own light on it to get a better look. There was a small brass plate tacked to the lower edge of the case that read: 'Authentic Roman Pilum-600 AD'

Without warning, Susie smashed the glass with the pommel of her dirk, and Harry just about peed his pants. She laughed as she cleaned the shards of glass from the frame with the dirk's blade. Then reaching in, she lifted the Pilum off the hooks.

"Man, you scared the crap out of me!"

"Sorry. So, what do ya think?" she said, handing it to him.

Putting his flashlight in his lips to free his hands, Harry took the javelin and studied it. The weapon was tipped with a pyramidal point at the end of a short steel shank that passed through a long brass cap, a fist sized lead ball, another, shorter brass cap, and then into a heavy oaken shaft. The opposite end was capped with a sharp iron point. So, moving forward or backward, it was bound to cause damage.

In total, the weapon was as long as he was high. The metal was old and covered in a nice sheen of oil, but the wood was new. Harry could tell the weapon had been refurbished. He assumed that was why the shop owner had hung it out of reach. Unless you actually held it in your hands, you'd never be able to tell.

"It's not as authentic as the tag says. Well, the metal is, anyway. But the wooden handle is new oak."

"So, what? Isn't it a beauty! I love how it looks, and it's so well balanced. Can ya feel it?"

Harry stretched out an arm and centered the weapon across an upturned palm. Susie was right, it felt good. Supposedly the height of Roman technology at the time.

He handed it back and Susie traded her spear for it. "There ya go, lad, from Susie to Harry, with love."

"So, I think that's it? We can head out now, right?"

"Aye, kind of hungry, anyway. We can go back up into those trees across the way and sit in the shade. What say ya?"

"Sounds like a plan, let's get the hell out of here."

Susie vaulted across the counter and landed in the only bare spot on the floor. She planted the butt of the Pilum into the pile of merchandise, skewering a bag with a red, rayon cape inside. Gazing up toward the tip, a smile of satisfaction graced her lips.

"They say it was designed to pierce armor. I suppose it would skewer a Thulu quite nicely, aye?"

"I believe so. Should do the trick. It's a little heavier than your…uh… my spear. Are you sure you want to lug it around? That's about five pounds, you know?"

"I can get used to it," she said, and stroked the iron shaft in a loving manner.

Harry turned away laughing and made for the hole. Susie took a shortcut over the fallen racks, giggling as she hurriedly scrambled to beat him back to the window. "Ha! Got ya!" she said and slid out in one fluid motion.

He believed Susie had what his mother always referred to as, '*Short Man's Complex*'. A need to prove she was just as good as anyone twice her size. Shaking his head in silent mirth, he pushed a foot through the opening to step out.

Harry noticed Susie now stood frozen just outside in the parking area. His senses exploded, and he almost pulled back in, but it was too late, he had revealed himself. So, hopping out the rest of the way, his hands were already reaching for his swords. They stopped halfway when he heard the familiar racking of a pump shotgun.

There was a small, very dirty, gray Toyota pickup parked on the asphalt. In the back, two older teen boys stood with their shotguns trained on Susie.

Then came the sputtering idle of a motorcycle as it rolled over the hill. It was the same white and blue Triumph with the same small boy astride its saddle that he had seen back in that city. It coasted to a stop beside the truck and the kid grinned at Harry, giving him a short wave as if greeting an old friend.

The driver's door of the truck opened and a college aged boy with short, spiky, bleached hair stepped out. He leveled a British army issued carbine at them, grinned wickedly, and said with contempt, "Hallo, Susie."

Harry's Sketch Book
Habichie
(evil guy!)

# CHAPTER 20

## Were Some Villains Hangit High

Susie threw Harry a concerned look and shrugged apologetically. Spiky hair moved around to the back of the truck. He looked up at one of his cohorts and said, "Jackie!" while jerking his head toward Harry. The one with the short, black mohawk haircut, jumped out of the truck and walked over to stand behind him, blocking access to the shop. Harry turned his head and studied the boy's face. The kid's lips seemed to be set in a permanent snarl, and making eye contact, Harry could see that despite his frightful appearance, there was fear in the kid's eyes.

Harry grinned and nodded at Jackie, who raised the muzzle of his shotgun up to show Harry that he meant business. He recognized the shotgun as an 'over & under', the kind used for hunting birds. But that didn't matter. At that range, it could easily remove hunks of flesh from his body.

"Who's yer new friend, Susie?"

"Harry, meet Habichie. Bichie, meet Harry," she said with disdain, and even at that distance, he could see that she was seething. Bichie looked Harry up and down and said, "Some kind of a warrior, are ya? The kind that brings a knife to a gunfight, aye?"

Harry almost said the usual thing that people say, when in this situation, like, "We don't want no trouble," or, "Just let us be, we're not bothering you." But pleading was stupid. It only made people like Bichie want to hurt you all the more. He had the overwhelming urge to cut Jackie's head off and skewer the rest of them. However, that would be a mistake while two of their guns were still trained on Susie. There was no way she could get to them before they pulled the trigger.

"What's the story, lad?" Bichie said.

"It's certainly not about you," Harry said flatly.

"American?" he asked Susie. "He's American! Ya always wanted an American boyfriend, aye, lass?"

"Well, ya know, Bichie… he's a staircase full of steps up from what I had before."

"Oh now, Susie, ya are going to hurt my feelings. I thought we had something good."

"Ya can stop thinking that anytime, now."

"Kind of lost track of ya when ya disappeared into the hills. I think it was just after yer folks croaked from the plague and I put an end to yer nancy-boy mate… what was his name? Oh! Geordie… Geordie the Puff."

"A fitting reason to leave ya. Not that all the other reasons, before, weren't good enough, ya psycho."

"Still trying to hurt my feelings, Susie lass… be kind. Remember, we were lovers once." Turning back to Harry, he jerked a thumb over his shoulder at Susie and said matter of factly, "We were lovers, once." Throwing his head back, Bichie laughed wickedly at the sky.

"Aye, but that was before ya raped Alice as she lay dying from the sickness, and before ya stuck that big knife in Geordie's back, making jokes about him as he bled out on my dead mum's kitchen floor. Aye, we were lovers once, for all of a day. Enough time to get to know ya and regret it. Ya talk like it was a decade."

"Come now, darling, once yer mine—yer mine forever."

Walking over, he snatched the Pilum from her hand and gave it to the kid still in the truck and said, "Hang on to that, Willie."

Moving around behind Susie, he lifted the rear flap of her breechclout.

"Well, isn't this a sonsy thing. I see ya still have that lovely bubble bum on ya." Looking back at Harry, he added, "This lass always did have a brilliant arse on her."

She swiped at the hand that held up the flap, but Bichie had already dropped it and stepped out of reach.

"Oh, no ya don't. Slapping's not polite."

Coming back around to face her, he pulled a short length of cord from his pocket. "Watch that one, Jackie boy," he said, and slinging his carbine, he grabbed Susie's arms and bound them at the wrist. She didn't resist and just stood expressionless as they watched a lunatic's grin contort Bichie's lips.

"I was just wondering, how would ya feel about being somebody's sex slave, or better yet, a whole bunch of somebody's? I've got me a friend, Monk's his name. He runs a kind of trading post just south of here. I think he just might like to meet ya."

"So, how did ya find me?" Susie growled.

"We caught sight of yer friend up Inverness way. Mikey boy just so happened to see him sitting at the petrol stop. Then we got lucky enough to see ya together, crossing the A7 south of Selkirk. With the help of binoculars, of course, but not so lucky to be close enough to nab ya.

I knew where ya were heading, though. Ya were a true shopper back in the day. I know how much ya adore this Roman weapon stuff."

"Why don't you just let her go and we can talk—without the guns," Harry said.

"Ah, naw. Because I know who ya are. Yer Highland Harry, aren't ya? Don't think I don't know who ya are. I've heard the talk. Supposed to be some kind of a monster killer or… supposed to be damn good with those wee swords, anyway. Well, I'm not taking any chances with ya, and knowing Susie like I do…" he didn't finish his sentence and patted Susie on the top of her head before walking over to Harry.

"I have to confess, the lass is dangerous. Way too good with a blade for me to be comfortable, and it's quite problematic that we don't share the same sense of what is fair."

Turning to the boy still in the back of the truck, he said, "Watch her close, Willy."

"Aye," Willy said, and laying the pilum in the bed, he brought up what looked like a military issued shotgun and sighted along its barrel toward Susie.

"Don't shoot her, lad! Just give me a shout if she moves. We need her! I can trade her for more ammo, petrol, and better food, down at Monk's place and maybe even get you lads laid."

Directing the little boy on the motorcycle to come to him, the kid got off the bike, and taking the carbine from Bichie, he went back and sat down on the bumper of the truck. The way he held the short rifle told Harry that he didn't know guns.

Bichie now put his focus fully on Harry, and pulling a semi-automatic pistol from his belt, he moved right up into Harry's face. It was like in the sports shows on TV when they showed the two boxers facing off just before a match. They glared at each other, and Harry saw the insanity in those pale blue eyes.

"My mate, Monk, he's going to be really pleased with me. Maybe I'll even get a bonus. That lass is in real decent shape, and she really knows how to please a lad. I suspect there are going to be a lot of happy men down Carlisle way. Men who haven't seen a lass for a long time, especially one that looks like our Susie. As for our Harry of the Highlands, we don't need ya. But we can have a wee bit of fun with ya before we dump yer body out back in that old well. Maybe some target practice, first?"

Harry studied Bichie's handgun. It was an H&K45, another service weapon. So, they either had pilfered dead soldiers, or Monk's outpost was supplying young deviants with military issued hardware. He realized how easy it would be to take the both of them out since neither of them had their guns pointed his way. He could first kill Jackie and then use Bichie's body as a shield for gunfire from the truck. If he set things in motion, Susie could get to the other two before they decided to go against Bichie's wishes and shoot her anyway.

The Waltz of the Flowers came as if being played from far away, and the butcher's chart manifested in his mind. Bichie's eyes strayed back to Jackie for a second. Harry turned his head to look, only to feel the impact of the shotgun's butt on his forehead and nose. Susie shouted angrily as silvery stars filled Harry's vision, then all went black.

Harry found himself lying in his mother's bed. He was sick with the Bug and everyone was standing around him. His father was there, attired in his dress blues and his mother wore a brightly flowered dress, a crazy smile on her face. Bessie was there too, looking sexy in a scarlet matching bra and panties set with thigh high stockings and garters. A half-full glass of champagne hung in her fingers, and her lipstick was smeared in streaks over her chin and cheeks. She was giggling and winking at everyone. Bichie walked into the room with a topless Susie beside him, his arm over her shoulder, its hand planted firmly on her right breast. They were smirking at his discomfort.

"Looks like you're not going to make it, son," his father said, the words echoing. Then they all broke out laughing. Snot gushed from his nose, and his neck suddenly swelled like a balloon. He tried to talk, but only a gurgle came out and that made them laugh even harder.

He awoke with a start and found himself lying on a concrete floor in the dark. The smell of cleaning fluids were heavy in his nose, and readjusting himself, his knee bumped the ankle high, concrete wall of what smelled like a floor sink. When his eyes adjusted, he could just make out that he was in the housekeeper's closet. Scanning the space, he noticed a line of light on the floor and suspected it was coming in from under the door.

Harry's head throbbed and his nose stung. Running his hand over the latter, he was glad it wasn't broken. He was going to have one hell of a bruise, though. The swelling had partially closed his left eye, but he could still see well enough to function.

Reaching for his swords, he found them gone—along with everything else. He still felt the poke of the sgian dubh at his right calf and figured they must have overlooked it because it had slid down inside his moccasin.

*Well, least you have that!*

Getting to his feet, Harry's head swam. Lowering himself back to the floor, he waited for the dizziness to pass. When he felt right again, he slid on his butt over to the door. The latch had a lever instead of a doorknob and taking it in hand, he quietly rotated it down. It surprised him when the door opened a crack, but his hopes were dashed when he found its movement arrested by the same type of cord that bound Susie's wrists. It had been tied to the outside lever and then to the wall bracket of a fire extinguisher just to the right of the jamb. He could easily cut the cord and leave the room. These guys weren't too smart. Besides that, Bichie was probably blinded by the thought of the fortune he was going to make from Susie. The others were just too scared of their leader to do anything other than what they were told.

*Should've checked their work, Bichie!*

Closing the heavy wooden panel as quietly as he could, he turned his attention to the sgian dubh and the sharpness of its blade. Harry found its edge adequate enough to part the cord with one quick, silent swipe. Now, he just had to wait for the right moment to do that.

There came a commotion from outside the closet, and shadows passed, disrupting the incoming light. He recognized the hiss of a small gas camp stove, and soon the smell of cooking meat found its way to him.

"Push all that shite away from there, Willy," he heard Bichie say. "Clear a spot for us to sit on the floor, will ya? Check the rope on Susie's wrists, Jackie boy. Don't want her to get loose, ya know. She's our ticket to a better life. Monk said he'd give me all the ammo and petrol we'd ever want if I were to bring him some sonsy lasses. He even said he'd give me a place at his side and a room at the outpost, which means… all of ya amadans as well. I just have to keep bringing him lassies."

"Yer a maggot, Bichie. A real dobber. Why don't ya untie me and we can have a go at each other, no weapons. What do ya say?"

"Susie! What ya thinking? That I'm some kind of a fool? Aye, but if yer not careful, we're each going to take a turn at ya, and I don't mean fighting. I'd even give Mikey a turn at yer fanny. That way I can make a man out of him before we head down to Carlisle."

The small boy laughed nervously, and then the talking ceased. There was only the sound of fallen merchandise being pushed around and the hissing of the stove. A sizzling sound soon filled the air and the odor got stronger. *Chicken!* Moving over and peeking under the door, Harry could see them through the opening in the display counter.

A small camp stove sat in the center of a spot they had cleared by the unused front door. Harry could just make out Susie's sneakers on the left where she sat with her knees up. There was a chair on the opposite side of the stove and the toes of Bichie's slick boots tapped the floor in front of it. Harry watched as the shoes of the others moved back and forth, preparing the evening meal.

"Jackie, ya get first watch at that hole with Willy's twelve gauge. Ya have at least eight shots with that. Trade him that shite double gun, and he can keep an eye on our new girlfriend. Mikey, eat some food, lad, yer looking thin. All that riding around, looking for petrol for the truck has got ya working and not eating. To it, lad! That chicken we caught up at that house is going to taste lovely, and we'll have some of those rice cakes we found in Susie's ruck."

A subdued, "Aye, Bichie… will do," was all Harry heard.

"Shall we check the yank? It's been a wee bit since we knocked him out." That was either Willy or Jackie.

"Aye, to it!" Bichie said.

Harry heard footfalls move toward the closet and resuming his original position, he closed his eyes. The door opened and then shut after a few seconds.

"That one's still out cold."

"Ah, Jackie, ya hit him too hard. Probably killed him, ya brawny bastard."

Harry sat up and slid back to the door.

*They weren't going to block the hole at the window—bad move, boys.*

If they left it open, the guard was sure to fall asleep, and no telling what would come through that opening in the dark of night. Harry figured he would wait until they were all snoring away before he tried to rescue Susie. If they decided to have their fun with him after their meal, and then murder him before bedtime, he would have to act when they came through the closet door. Luckily for him, they hadn't bound his wrists.

*Third and biggest mistake of all, idiots!*

Hours passed, and Harry grew tired of listening to the talk of halfwits. Relief finally came when they got weary of harassing Susie. The stove stopped its hissing and the room went quiet. Laying his cheek flat on the floor, Harry peeked out with one eye. Mikey lay curled up, asleep on the floor. He had pushed himself up against someone who must have been Willie, who sat with his legs outstretched, his back against the counter. There was no sign of Jackie, so Harry figured he must have already taken up his post at the hole. Bichie's boots were still in sight but hadn't moved for a while.

Snores soon filled the air, coupled with the occasional rustle of bodies readjusting for comfort. Susie remained in the same spot, but now Harry could see the bottoms of her sneakers telling him she had turned toward the closet. It looked and sounded like they had settled in for the night. Bichie must have decided to let him live, at least until tomorrow, anyway.

Even if Jackie were still awake, he couldn't see the closet door from where he sat. So, pulling the sgian dubh from his moc, Harry got up on his knees and opened the door just enough to slip the blade through. Half expecting his actions to spark a flurry of activity, he prepared for a rush. But things remained quiet except for a slight gasp coming from Susie as he cut the cord.

After that, Harry didn't have much of a plan other than to crawl out and hide behind the counter until he could grab a weapon. He decided he would come out at the west end and jump on Jackie, take away his shotgun, and hold them all at bay while he and Susie escaped. They would want to find shelter as soon as possible in case there were monsters about. Harry figured the house up on the hill was their best bet.

Somebody was snoring extra loud and Susie muttered, "Willy, ya loud bastard." Harry chuckled to himself and after sheathing his knife, he moved into a crouch.

*Keep it up, Willy. The more noise you make, the better!*

Above all the snoring and snorting, Harry detected a different kind of noise. It came from outside the building, at the back, and it raised the hair on his neck. It was a scrambling, scurrying type of sound, punctuated with chirps and squeaks. The noise intensified, and Harry imagined a large herd of monkey sized creatures, their little claws working over the bottom of the outside wall as they searched for access.

"Bichie!" Jackie bellowed and then came the deafening report of the shotgun, followed by a few more. The room exploded into chaos, with Bichie commanding, "Get yer guns, lads! Get yer guns!"

The deafening sound of automatic gun fire ripped through the room. There came screams and pain-filled shrieks, clearly telling Harry that the humans were losing. He stood and threw open the door only to have Susie somersault through the opening. She rolled to the back and hollered, "Close it, Harry! Close it, now!"

He was way ahead of her. Hearing the latch seat, he got down on his knees and clamped the lever in both hands to keep it from rotating. No one needed to tell him that a closed and secured door was the only thing that could save them now.

Within minutes, the gunfire dwindled to the occasional shot and then stopped all together. There came the heartbreaking screams of a young boy, interspersed with the anguished cries of "Mummy! Mummy!"

Then they too ceased as thuds of small, but heavy bodies hit the outside of the door. Harry watched tiny paws come inside through the crack at the bottom, their familiar black, fishhook like talons, scraping and scratching at the wood in an attempt to pull it open.

The report of a .45 erupted and Harry's ears rang. The handgun reported nine more times, followed by Bichie shouting, "Ahhh, damn it." There came a scream and a door slammed.

*Take that, Bichie! Couldn't happen to a nicer guy!*

The squeaks and hissing growls continued. The creatures were still trying to figure out how to get inside the closet. The commotion went on for some time, coupled with human groans and the gurgling of someone trying to draw a breath. The worst was the ripping of flesh, along with the chewing of a thousand little mouths. Harry wished he could cover his ears as his mind filled with pictures of his captors being eaten alive.

"I don't want to hear this," Susie lamented in the dark of the closet.

Realizing that her hands were still tied, Harry wanted to cut her free, but he didn't dare risk taking his hands off that lever.

"Susie, my sgian dubh, it's still in my boot, can you slide over and get it?"

"Aye, I can," she said, her bare thighs squeaking as she slid across the sealed concrete floor. Her hands were bound in front, so wrapping a couple fingers around the bone handle of the knife, she pulled it from its sheath. Then rotating it backwards, she sawed through the cord that wrapped her wrists.

"I can help, if you want?" Harry said.

"Naw, I got it. Just hold that fookin' door. I'm not surprised they forgot to check ya for this knife. Stupid lads, they probably thought, 'American, so… no sgian dubh.' Ya had a pocketknife in yer sporran if I remember correctly? I suppose they reckoned that was all ya had. Now, they're all dead for their laziness… poor bastards."

Susie put the knife back after completing her task, and then knotting the pieces of cord together to make one long piece, she fashioned a loop at one end. Slipping it past his hands on the lever, she then ran the other end over to a metal mop rack on the wall to the left of the door. Pulling it taut, she tied it off. Her actions brought a short burst of activity as the creatures increased their attack on the door. The little beasts enthusiasm was short lived, though, and they were soon scrambling back to their victims as if they feared missing out on the buffet.

"Okay, take a break Harry, let's see if it holds."

Harry pulled his aching hands from the lever, opening and closing his fingers in a stiff manner as he sighed with relief. He stood up and they embraced. A sob slipped from Susie's lips and she whispered, "Not going to cry, not going to cry." He squeezed her a little tighter and kissed the top of her head. "I thought ya were dead," she said. "I thought they had bashed yer skull in. But when I saw the door open for that wee sec, I felt so relieved." She let out a stuttering sob and stepped back, putting a hand over her mouth. He reached out and cupped her cheek and her left hand came up to lay over his wrist.

"Give me just a sec," she said. "Ya'd think I was having my period, or something."

"No, it's okay. I've almost cut loose a few times, myself."

He could barely see her face, but he pictured a look of gratitude there. Moving to the back of the large closet, he towed her along. Sitting down with his back against the wall, he stretched his legs out along the front of a shallow, floor to ceiling shelving unit. Susie lay on her side between his knees, her head on his chest.

"Don't dare fall asleep. Keep thinking I'd wake up to those beasties chewing my feet off."

"You can sleep now if you feel you need too. I'll stay awake. They have to be gone by daylight. We just have to hold out until then. Go on, go to sleep, I'll keep watch."

"Maybe a quick doze," she said, and he felt her relax in his arms. "Those things, they're the… uhhh… what did ya call them… capoocha… what was it?"

"Capuchipines. Hystrix. I don't think they have the poisonous quills or you'd be lying here dead in my arms. There is no escaping those little… well, there's no getting away. Can't fight them, got to run and hole up until they're gone. I suspect these might have a poisonous bite, though. But I don't think I want to find out."

"Glad I made it inside… so glad," she murmured and a minute later, a light, purring snore reminiscent of Bessie Brown filled the room. The activity out in the store had dwindled to the occasional squeak with a rattle and scrape as the beasts moved over bubble packs and boxes. There came short squabbles with moments of shrieking that raised his hair. Harry assumed they were fighting over the last tidbits of human flesh. Susie stirred on occasion, mumbling something about the hounds escaping the Dog Tower. He figured she was dreaming of a time before the world had tilted further on its axis.

It seemed an eternity before Harry heard the creatures outside, behind the store. It grew quiet again and he figured they had returned to their lair. He and Susie would remain behind that door just a little longer. He didn't want to make the same mistake that Robbie and his faithful companion, Guy, had made.

Thinking back on America, he concluded that there was no need to ever go back. Then he chuckled to himself as he realized that there was no way to get back, even if he wanted to. His eyes grew heavy and Harry let sleep take him.

He awoke with a start, causing Susie to sit bolt upright. Her hair lashed his face as she whipped her head around to look into his eyes. Harry kissed her forehead and then looking past her, he noticed the crack under the door was now a well-defined line of light. The sun was up and some of its luminance had infiltrated the store. He watched Susie grin, her teeth gleaming as they picked up the light.

"It's morning now! We can get our bums out of this little space, aye?"

"Yeah, I think it's safe. I heard the Hystrix leave some time ago and as you can see, the sun is up."

Susie stood, moved to the door and began to untie the cord. Harry came up behind her, and with one quick swipe of his black knife, it parted.

"You need to wake up, girl."

"Okay, fine. Give me a minute, will ya?"

"Shall we?"

"Just a minute!"

She embraced him and said, "Just before we go out, can I have a kiss, please?"

Harry slipped the knife back into its sheath, and after a long kiss, they just stood, holding each other. When they felt they'd had enough, they separated, and he opened the door.

There were dead Hystrix everywhere. Some draped over counters, others lying on the floor, and several had been blown into two pieces, obvious victims of the automatic carbine. A putrid yellow substance that must have been Hystrix blood was splattered everywhere.

Jackie lay where Susie had been sitting, identifiable only by the Mohawk still stuck to the grinning skull. Stepping in sight of the opening at the window, they could see what was left of Willy, draped over the sill. His brown leather belt and strips of his tee shirt hung from a freshly gnawed skeleton. Bichie's and Mikey's bodies were nowhere to be seen.

Susie moved over to the cash register where their weapons, sporrans, and flour sack rucks had been piled. Harry started to follow but the door of the WC whipped opened, causing him to spin around. He watched as a bloodied Bichie emerged, his H&K45 pointed in their direction. His eyes were wide with craziness, and an evil grin braced his lips. Susie moved up beside Harry and they stared in disbelief as Bichie tilted his head slightly to his right and pulled the trigger.

# CHAPTER 21
## In The Prospect Of Death...

The explosive report never came, instead, just the hollow click of the firing pin. Bichie frantically recocked the weapon as he moved out of the opening in the counter. Harry and Susie were already on the move and they seemed to fly as they hopped lightly over the face of the fallen shelves to close on their foe.

Another pull of the trigger and again the firing pin found nothing but air. Harry returned Bichie's evil grin as he stepped into a spot free of clutter and took up a fighting stance. Bichie threw the gun at him and Harry bobbed right, the grip of the weapon barely catching the top of his shoulder before spinning away to bury itself in a pile of retail goods.

Harry waited, watching his opponent draw back a fist as he approached. Bichie's haymaker was only half way to its target when he became the unhappy recipient of three straight punches to his nose. He tried to hit back, but to no avail. Every move was thwarted with a Pak Sao parry and then rewarded simultaneously with a palm to the windpipe, a fist to the jaw, or a low straight kick to a knee.

Several times Bichie slipped and fell or was swept off his feet. He'd get back up only to suffer a multitude of bone snapping blows before falling again. Harry danced in and out in swift fashion, sometimes staying inside Bichie's arms just long enough to pummel his chest and throat. Then swiftly moving back out of reach, Harry re-assessed his progress while trying to stay clear of the mess on the floor. Susie circled, moving just out of range, so as to not interfere. But she soon grew tired of inaction, and Harry tracked her out of the corner of his eye as she moved behind the counter to come out at Bichie's back.

Appearing as if beaten, Harry's assailant went down on his knees and bent forward, resting his hands on the floor.

But it was a ruse, and Bichie came up holding a steel gladiator's trident. He charged Harry, who, in his haste to get away, slipped and fell backwards to tumble inside a fallen shelving unit. It was deep and made of steel, so Harry flattened himself out in hopes the trident would pass over or bounce off. The weapon struck and penetrated a sidewall of the metal shelf at Harry's right side, one of the points scratching his bicep.

Bichie fought to remove it, but the barbed tip wouldn't allow it. Releasing his hold on the weapon, he spun away in search of something else. Harry was on his feet in no time only to find Bichie facing off with Susie. She had a metal ballclub in her hand and swung it at his head. He parried her blow, yelping when the weapon bounced off his forearm. Susie drew back for a second strike but slipped on a pile of magazines and fell backwards, her legs splaying out in front. Bichie charged, and dropping to his knees as he did, he slid between her feet and grabbed her by the throat.

"I'm going to give ya what ya got coming, ya ungrateful hoor."

Susie tried to hit him with a back swing of the club, but he kept throwing up his right elbow to block the blows, wasting her every effort. She dropped the weapon, and grabbing his wrists, she attempted to pull his hands loose. She was able to break Bichie's grip several times, but he kept coming back. Susie's hands slipped constantly on Bichie's sweat slick arms, and readjusting his position, he tightened his grip. Her face became a mottled red in color as she gasped for air.

When Harry arrived, he thought to straight kick Bichie in the back of his head, but he couldn't get solid footing. Lowering himself to one knee, he let go with some rapid-fire punches, moving up Bichie's spine to the base of his skull. They seemed to have no effect, and Susie's attacker hollered, "Give it up, yank! Ye're next when I'm finished with her."

Bichie, hyped up on adrenalin and rage, seemed to have acquired super human strength. Harry knew what he needed to do to stop the attack, but found he was reluctant to plunge a sword in his foes back or cut his throat. So, wrapping his left arm around Bichie's neck, he locked it with his right, and squeezed with all his might. This decision only brought the realization that it was now a race to see which one of them suffocated first. When Susie's eyes rolled back in her head, Harry felt the panic take hold and another shot of adrenaline surged in.

*I'll be dammed if I'm going to lose another…*

He tried to drag Bichie backwards, but only succeeded in pulling Susie with him.

*The black knife, you fool! Use it!*

He reached for the sgian dubh but found Susie had beat him to it. A scream erupted from Bichie's mouth as he slammed backward into Harry's chest from the force of Susie's thrust.

She didn't stop there. Twice more Bichie slammed into him, his body growing slacker with every stab. His hands finally fell away from her neck in order to fight off the incoming blade. Harry wanted to move out of the way, but Susie, now able to fill her lungs with life giving air, had gone into full berserker mode. She rose up on her knees, her eyes wild with rage. Holding the knife with two hands, she thrust it home, growling, "This one's for Alice."

The short blade found its mark, snickering off a rib. Bichie coughed blood and once again flew backward, this time bumping Harry's nose with the back of his head. The sting of the blow enraged Harry even more, and he pushed back, forcing Susie's aggressor to meet the incoming blade with twice as much energy. The impact lifted Bichie up, causing him to fall on top of Harry. Together, they tumbled backwards into the clutter as Susie bellowed, "And that was for Geordie."

Dark blood fountained from Bichie's chest, and Harry knew Susie had found the aorta. He squirmed out from underneath the body, trying to direct the gush in the opposite direction. Getting to his feet, he stumbled backward toward the counter, trying to remain clear of the spray. Susie, on the other hand, wasn't so lucky.

She stood unmoving, her mouth set in a grimace, a stripe of blood running up her armor and across her cheek. She only had eyes for her opponent, though, as if she half-expected him to jump up and renew his attack. A fierceness glowed in her eyes, and for a few seconds, Harry feared her.

Their eyes met, and her face melted into a kind of terrified sadness. Letting the knife drop from her grip, she turned and walked a few paces before her knees buckled. Falling into a sitting position on a foam made shield, she didn't try to get up and remained where she landed, braced on her arms, her eyes cast to the floor.

Harry went to her, picking up the sgian dubh on the way. He found a tee shirt with 'Lawrence's Friend Of The Wren' silk screened on the front and wiped the knife clean before sheathing it. Then kneeling behind Susie, he embraced her.

Minutes passed and finally tipping her head back, she looked up into his face, and rasped out, "Fookin' Bichie… bastard… sorry Harry, it's just, I've never killed anyone before."

"It's okay, I know how it is. A lot different than killing monsters, that's for sure."

"Aye, yer spot on about that." She sniveled and wiped at her nose.

"Don't talk right now, it's probably not good for your larynx, or… whatever."

"Oh, so this is how ya get me to stop gabbing?" she croaked out. "I think I need to blow my nose."

Harry gently wiped the blood from her face with the tee shirt. When he finished, he moved down and scrubbed what had splattered her chest. She grabbed the shirt from his hands and said, "Stop, I'll do it. Yer rubbing my boobies and I'm not in the mood." Unfolding the tee shirt, she let it hang from her hands and said, "There's blood on this thing?"

"Yeah, silly, it was all over your face."

"I must look a sight, aye?"

"Don't worry about it, it will be okay."

"I hope yer right," she said, and finding a clean spot on the blood spotted garment, she wrapped it over her nose and blew several times before handing it back.

"Oh, great, thanks," Harry said and chuckled. "Now I've got to watch out for snot as well as blood. Life is so hard."

Susie croaked out a laugh and then started to cough. "Och! Ya bastard, Harry, making me laugh. Och! That hurts."

"Sorry… sorry… just wanted to cheer you up. And oh, by the way… I had a father, so…"

"Stop!" she said, breaking out in a strangled giggle. "Let's get to it, can't sit here all day, ya know."

"Just a second, let me wipe off this little bit," he said, and dabbing away more blood from her lorica, he saw it had soaked into the leather. He wanted to make a joke about how she would always carry Bichie with her wherever she went, but then thought better of it.

"Okay, lad, I told ya once, don't rub there."

She slapped him lightly on his arm and snatching the shirt from his hand, she tossed it across the room.

"Well, at least, let me help you up."

Susie offered a hand and he lifted her to her feet. She threw her arms around him and pushed her face into his chest. Harry thought she might cry, but she remained still and after a few minutes, she broke away and went to their gear. He followed and they were soon strapping everything on, their eyes sometimes wandering to Bichie, who now lay on his side in a pool of blood, his pale blue eyes wide open, his face frozen in a look of disbelief.

Susie was first to leave the building and she did so without a word. Grabbing the spear and his new lorica, Harry trailed behind her. Once outside, he saw her stop to look at Mikey, whose body hung out of the open door of the Toyota. He had run for it and tried to climb inside, but they had caught him. His body was severely gnawed, and his clothing hung in tatters. The sun had caught the Hystrix in the act and they hadn't been able to finish the job. Harry suspected they'd be back come nightfall.

*Not going to be around for that!*

Harry heard Susie sniff a couple of times and then she did break into tears. Hanging her head, she put a hand over her mouth and sobbed into it. He kept his distance, wanting to allow her the moment before he intruded. She didn't give him the chance. Moving around to the rear bumper, she opened the tailgate, and after pulling out her pilum, she turned and jogged away up the highway toward the fort.

He thought to run after her, but she turned into the drive leading to the house. So, he figured she wasn't going far. Taking his time, he made his way up the slope, figuring when he caught up with her, she would feel a whole lot better and want to talk.

Trudging into the lane, he noticed the tire tracks in the mud from where the pickup had been driven behind the stone garrison. Bichie and his bunch had been lying in wait. Harry thought it weirdly ironic how it was monsters that had turned the tables in his and Susie's favor. Not that it mattered to the Hystrix—they'd eat anybody. Monsters will be monsters, and not all of them sprang from a well.

# CHAPTER 22

## My Heart Is In The Highlands...

Harry soon came upon Susie sitting cross-legged under an oak tree at the side of the house where the lawn sloped away toward the north. Only the upper half of her body was visible above the knee-high grass as it waved in the breeze. Her pilum projected up in front of her; its sharp brass butt-sleeve stuck in the soil. The flour sack ruck lay hidden in the grass. When he got close, she looked his way and gave him a sorrow filled smile, her cheeks glistening with tears. Then her eyes shied away to the grass at her feet and she plucked at it; one stem at a time.

"Can't say I care too much about being this far from home," she said, gazing toward the north.

"My place is up there."

Nodding toward the mountain peaks barely visible at the horizon, she briefly pointed before turning her attention back to the grass.

"You okay? You sound a little sad."

"I'm fine, lad. Just sit, will ya?"

"Are you sure?"

"Harry, please…"

He pierced the ground next to the pilum with his spear, leaving them to stand together. Then dropping his sack by Susie's, he took his lorica and sat facing her with just a couple yards between them. She went to twisting long blades of grass together and then tied them in knots. Harry could tell she still wasn't ready to talk, so he turned sideways to her in order to take in the calming view across the open land instead of the side of the house.

The shadows of the clouds ran over the patchwork of overgrown fields where crops had once been cultivated. From a distance, it appeared as if nothing had ever changed.

There was still bird song in the air, the staccato chirp of crickets, and the smell of earth, grass, and their own bodies. The only thing missing— all the people.

They sat quiet for a long time, Harry waiting for Susie to break the silence. When she finally did, he felt relieved.

"Never thought my life would become so bizarre. Just a wee bit over six years ago, I was thinking university, a career in education, and then marriage. Wee-uns would soon follow, and I would grow old with the man of my dreams.”

Rotating back to his original position, Harry splayed out his legs and said, “Well, you can still have the last part, right?”

“Reckon so. It’s just… my way of thinking at the time was, all that talk about superbugs and the coming of… what’d they call it? Oh, aye, the Holocene, the sixth mass extinction. I thought that was all shite.”

“Yeah, I remember hearing about that too. But what could we do?”

“I just never counted on monsters or that exterminating them would become a career.”

“Same here, girl. It was my father who got me started and…” Harry realized that Susie wasn’t finished and blurted, “Oh! Sorry… go on.”

She reached out and giving his foot a squeeze, she smiled forgivingly. “The final chapter of my old life closed when I drove yer sgian dubh into Bichie. How ironic is it that I used yer knife to finish him off? I always thought it would feel good to do him in, ya know? To avenge Geordie and Alice. Now, even though the fear is gone, it’s been replaced with this sadness, and maybe—regret? Revenge sucks, Harry, it truly does. I didn’t want this. Why did he have to show up? Why couldn’t he just leave us alone? And why do people have to be so stupid?”

“You got me,” Harry said, thinking back on his life and all the foolish things he had done.

“So, the people in that photo… ya said ya’d tell me later. Maybe now’s a good time?”

“But there’s no cozy fire?”

“Harry, please, just tell me, and keep it simple.”

“Okay, my mother, my father, Master Bik, and… Bessie. All gone.”

“How?”

“My mother and Master Bik by the Bug, my father and Bessie, by the monsters.”

“And Bessie was…?”

“The love of my life. Dragged from a boat and carried out to sea by a Thulu back in New Hampshire. Went a little crazy after that. I chased after the bastard, but I was too late. Then the motor gave up and I floated around on the ocean for a while before I literally bumped into that ship in the fog. I drifted all the way here to find… the new love of my life?"

Susie got up on all fours and crawled over between his legs. She remained on her hands and knees and they shared a long, slow kiss. When they finished, she said just inches from his face, "I know I can't replace Bessie, but I'll do my best to be good for ya, Harry."

"Just be yourself, Susie. You didn't become the new love of my life because you weren't."

Harry saw something in her eyes that looked a lot like thankfulness. She sat back on her calves and said, "Okay, enough of this. Ya can show me how much ya love me later. Now, let's see if that thing will fit ya."

"Fine," was all he said, and removing the sword rig, he dropped it on the grass and pulled the new armor to him. He ripped off the price tag and slipped the lorica on over his head. It fit well except where the bottom rubbed against his hip bones. He got to his feet and the armor settled on his shoulders, the lower edge not quite touching the top of his kilt belt.

*I can get used to this.*

"Looks good. How's it feel?"

"Okay, now that I'm standing."

"Aye, well, I don't think yer going to be doing much battle sitting down." She rasped out a giggle and added, "Now take it off, I want to make a slight change."

"Like what?"

"Just take it off, will ya! No questions. I want to do something for ya."

"Whatever."

He slipped it off and bent to pick up his swords but she gave his hand a light slap and pulled them and the lorica to her. Harry huffed, conveying mock annoyance. Susie just stuck out her tongue and crossed her eyes at him.

"You're going to leave me defenseless!" he said. Falling to the grass, he now lay on his back in the spot where he had been sitting. Pillowing his head with an arm, he chewed on a grass stem and watched her work.

"Don't worry, luv. I'm here to protect ya. I'm yer knight in shineless armor," she said.

"Were there girl knights? I don't recall reading anything about them in my history books."

"Oh, Harry, of course there were. It's just that history was written by men for other men. So, let's just keep that straight, aye?"

Chuckling, Susie winked and scooted over to her flour sack where she pulled out a small leather pouch, and from it, she removed several small implements along with a ball of leather thong. Soon she was poking tiny holes in the armor and measuring with just her eyes as she looked back and forth between the lorica and his sword rig lying in the grass. He scowled when she removed his swords from it and gently set them aside. Then he watched in horror as she cut the bindings that held the scabbards to the rig. Something he had made with his own hands that had been produced with so much pride; now ruined. He almost protested, but she displayed such confidence that he forced himself to keep his mouth shut. Besides, the work seemed to lift her mood and he was all for that.

Susie skillfully secured the scabbards in a crossed pattern at the back of the lorica. When she finished, she tugged at them to be sure they would stay, and then handing the finished product to Harry, she said, "There ya go, laddy, try that, will ya? I made a few extra holes just in the case we need to raise or lower them a wee bit. Try it on. To it, lad!"

"You wrecked my rig."

"Good things come, and good things go, and sometimes they are replaced with better things. So, shut it, and give it a go."

"So demanding! Now I'm wondering... are you one of those better things?" He raised his eyebrows at her as he took her creation in hand and got to his feet.

He slipped the leather armor on over his head. She handed him his swords and he felt surprise at how easily it was to sheath them. Susie was a pro, there was no doubt. He tested the height of the grips to be sure and said, "Hmmm... I guess, you, are one of those better things."

"I could have told ya that if ya had just given me the chance."

"Don't need to, I answered my own question."

Susie packed up her kit and then rolled up what remained of his old rig and stuffed it into his flour sack. Grabbing hers, she carried both to him. Harry reached for his, but she dropped them on the ground at his feet before taking a hold of the bottom of his armor at the front. Grinning up into his face, she yanked it down.

"Hey!"

"Just wanted to be sure it's a good fit," she said, and gave it another jerk, this time keeping the pressure on so she could pull his face down to hers. Their lips met again, and they kissed as if it would be their last.

That was followed by a long hug in the wavering breeze, the sun dappling their bodies through the fluttering leaves of the oak.

Susie pulled back and they smiled lovingly into each other's faces for a few seconds before she ruined the mood by touching Harry's sore nose.

"Ouch! Why'd you do that?"

"Just checking to see if it was broken. So, no… but it's going to be sore for a long while, and that's quite a shiner you got going there," referring to the black eye he was now sporting.

"I know! I know! Just don't touch it."

"Terribly sorry," she said and shrugged.

Taking his hand, she planted an apologetic kiss on his knuckles before stepping over to pull the long weapons from the soil. Turning back, she handed him the spear and then gazed at his face the whole time they were slinging their bags and shouldering weapons. Her expression sparked a thought and he asked, "So, I'm wondering, am I… your better thing?"

Susie pretended like she didn't know what he was talking about and bringing a finger to her lips, her eyes searched the canopy of leaves as if the branches above their heads held the answer to his question. Then giving him a mock scowl, she said, "After what we just went through, is there any doubt, Harry?"

Sighing loudly in mock dismay, she pushed past him as if to leave him behind. Then grabbing his free hand at the last second before he was out of reach, she towed him from underneath the tree and into the sunshine. Looking back over her shoulder, she smiled affectionately, and said, "Come along, Mr. Highland Harry, let's go home, we've got a castle to clean.

Harry's Sketch Book
The road into
the Highlands

# R.C. Davis

R.C. Davis is the author of My Summer Of Kathy, Love & Death In The Miskatonic Valley, Within The Haunt Of The Unseelie Court, and a collection of short, coming of age stories titled: The Clarksburg Tales. He has a bevy of short stories published in many venerated anthologies and a cookie jar full of poems available in collections throughout the United States and India. R.C.'s ancestry lies in the Grampian Mountains of Scotland even though he presently resides and writes in the Midwest of the USA along with his wife and their two dogs.